VISAGE

By Denise M. Baran-Unland

Illustrated by Matt Coundiff

Illustrated by Matt Coundiff

Author photo on page 454 by Stephen James Tuplin

ISBN 978-0-9852748-5-6

www.bryonyseries.com

This book is lovingly dedicated to the reader, whoever you might be.

"There are a sort of men whose visages
Do cream and mantle like a standing pond,
And do a willful stillness entertain,
With purpose to be dress'd in an opinion
Of wisdom, gravity, profound conceit,
As who should say 'I am Sir Oracle,
And when I open my lips no dog bark!'"

William Shakespeare, *Merchant of Venice*

FORWARD

Boyfriends and romance fill the daydreams that frequently dominate the minds and hearts of teenage girls and young women. When romantic fantasies turn obsessive, young women find themselves not only in danger of compromising their convictions, but, at times, even their safety. Even without the vampires of Ms. Unland's BryonySeries, there are plenty of bad boys and older men to capture the attention of teenage girls while striking fear in the hearts of the girls' parents. We don't need to look far to find evidence of dangers of these relationships; headlines are filled with the stories and their consequences.

Visage is a cautionary tale for teens and their parents alike. The dashing, much-older college professor with a questionable reputation and the impressionable, naïve young student enter into a relationship that accelerates at a break-neck speed, leaving the heroine and reader alike wondering just how far and where her obsession will take her. Like other young women who find themselves in similar unequal relationships, Melissa believes herself to be obtaining the object of her obsession and willingly relinquishes control over her future into this man's hands without regard to where he will take her. In her youthfulness and inexperience, she sees only her fantasy and deliberately dismisses the warning bells that go off inside her head.

Visage takes this danger a step further as people aren't always as they seem, and relationships can be much more complicated than they seem on the surface. Who really is Johnny Simotes? And are Melissa's dreams of vampires really a thing of the past? And what happens when the truth that is kept in the dark comes crashing to the light? What cost will Melissa have to pay to live the life she thinks she wants?

Parents can take note of the numerous warning signs either missed by the adults in Melissa's life or set aside because of a common parental fear of pushing their child away.

Just like Melissa, teens in these types of relationships will often distance themselves from friends while spending more and more time with their boyfriend. They may center all their decisions on the reactions of the other person and blame themselves when his reactions are negative. They may even relinquish their personal control, allowing the other to make decisions in much the same way that Melissa allowed decisions to be made for her.

Steve's advice to Darlene was wise. They attempted to maintain a relationship that allowed for open communication without passing judgment on the relationship or the boyfriend. This makes it comfortable for teens to speak honestly without pushing them away. While taking a heavy direct approach may be tempting to parents, it is important to remember that telling a teen to leave the relationship will not work and may only make the relationship stronger. When a parent makes herself available and open, expressing her concerns without judgment, she stands the best chance of reaching her daughter. One wonders how Melissa's path might have changed had her parents been closer or other adults in her life had taken notice of the signs.

Vicki Thompson, counselor, certified parent coach, and mother www.fulllifeparenting.com

TABLE OF CONTENTS

THE PROLOGUE

The rain that shrouded the gray listless skies all afternoon now pattered onto the classroom roof with monotonous steadiness. The last appointment had left for home. Only he alone remained.

The day had passed in a steady stream of dull staff meetings, repetitive lessons with less-than motivated students, and telephone conferences with anxious parents regarding last-minute schedule changes for their little Messiahs, but he felt thankful for the semi-distracting activity. Night had descended that evening with unusual blackness, and it echoed the equally dark thoughts he had shoved to his mind's recesses, thoughts now clamoring for unveiling.

With methodical precision, he shelved textbooks, collected sheet music, straightened benches, folded chairs, retrieved stray gum wrappers, and tossed away the half-drunk soda cans devious students had smuggled past his oblivious colleagues. *He* did not permit food and drink beyond the double wood doors. The last can missed its mark and rolled under a chair.

"Damn it!"

He stooped for the offending can, crushed the tin between his fingers, and again tossed it. The can hit the wastebasket with a satisfying clank, but his annoyance persisted. He had misdirected his outburst, and he knew it.

Suppressing a heavy sigh, he abandoned pretense and strolled to the window. He gazed upward, contemplated the starless sky, and released his phantoms. Instead of dissipating into the mist, the specters encircled him and pressed closer. A half-sigh, half-groan escaped before he could squelch it. He stiffened at this weakness, stood taller, and, one by one, enumerated his successes.

He had slept well last night, drunk liberal amounts of coffee and water all day, eaten a hearty dinner several hours ago, and as for the sophomore who had come begging for her grade....

Crash!

He started and turned. The wood blinds at the west window had clattered to the floor. Well, he could do nothing about it tonight. Maintenance would need a ladder. He switched off lights and considered his habits. He paused at every bathroom mirror to comb a full head of hair and note clear eyes, an obvious lack of pallor, and perfect teeth.

And yet, he thought, as he walked down the stairs, subtle signs unsettled him. Nighttime restlessness. Occasional mid-morning sleepiness. Squinting in the brightest sunlight. A bite of raw hamburger when cooking dinner. An annoying discernment of the thoughts and motives of others.

If his misgivings came true, he would have to dismantle the life he had built, unravel the dreams he had woven, and implement the contingency plan he had fabricated long ago. He fully realized only one remedy existed, and he even more fully understood its slim hope for success, but chance it he must for survival's sake.

How fortunate he knew precisely where to find it.

CHAPTER 1: COLLEGE BOUND

"Snap!"

Melissa blinked against the flash.

"Snap! Snap! Snap!"

With an instant, self-developing camera in hand, Steve, tall and lanky, clicked picture after picture. He shot Melissa by herself and Melissa posing with her mother Darlene, who, with her petite frame and light corn silk hair, appeared only slightly older than Melissa. Steve even captured Melissa pretending to be excited while Jason, his feathered black hair gleaming nearly blue against the collar of his silver tuxedo, pinned a corsage near her left shoulder. She'd bet anything Jason's mother had selected the flowers at the supermarket while Jason thumbed through *Chevy Craze* magazine at the checkout line.

Steve pointed to her brother. "Brian, stand next to your sister."

Melissa expected Brian to object, but he slid next to her with an angelic smile. That's when she remembered her little brother was attending a junior high dance next weekend.

"Are you feeling okay?" Melissa whispered.

"Practicing," Brian whispered back, but his hazel eyes inside his thin face were sparkling. That's when Melissa noticed he had neatly combed his brown hair.

Steve beamed. "Great!" Snap! "One more!" Snap! Snap!

He brushed back the shock of blond hair that always insisted on falling onto his forehead and laid out the pictures on the coffee table for everyone to see. Not one photo had rabbit ears, a first for Brian, Melissa thought.

Darlene, beaming, planted a light kiss on Melissa's cheek as Jason held open the front door. Steve, mindful of the dress, gingerly hugged her. Depending how the light hit the fabric, Melissa's gown looked either pink or lavender, both colors she, in the past, would have shunned. Today, pastels appealed to her.

Pink reminded Melissa of the bryony flowers that filled Simons Estate in Munsonville, the fishing village where she had lived last fall after her father had suddenly died. John Simons, the nineteenth century pianist and composer who had married Bryony Marseilles, the minister's daughter, had worn gray and lavender to his wedding. The frock's modest style met with her mother's approval, but it possessed enough old-fashioned charm to please Melissa. The straps crisscrossed down Melissa's back; a tiny jacket covered any bare skin, the dress's saving grace, as far as Darlene was concerned. Melissa, however, worried that her long, dark, straight hair looked less attractive against pink than Bryony's mass of wavy chestnut locks. If only she had a frame as tiny as Bryony's, Melissa inwardly sighed. Try as she might, she never could lose that extra five pounds.

"Have a good time," Brian said, "but not too good...."

"Brian!" Melissa heard Steve say to him as he shut the door. She suppressed a smile as she turned to Jason. "Sorry."

But Jason was halfway to the driver's side of his family's station wagon. He stopped short, then headed back to open Melissa's door. He and the radio remained thankfully quiet during the entire ride to Leon's Great Steak House. Usually, Jason jammed on an air guitar to the heavy metal blaring from the radio, rattled about his favorite football team, or bragged about the new car he would buy, now that he had become an assistant manager at Pizza Express. Still, Melissa wished she had stayed home, despite her "forget vampires and forge ahead" campaign. How could a banquet room compare in elegance and splendor to the Rutherfords' all-white ballroom? Did she really expect Jason to dance with John's deftness?

John.

Ironically, it had been Steve who had endorsed Melissa's college plans. She really had thought her mother, a freelance writer, would have supported Melissa's choice, even though Melissa had suddenly made that decision.

Several weeks ago, Melissa had received a letter from Julie Drake telling her about the great English program at Jenson College of Liberal Arts, where Julie would be studying psychology. Folded inside the envelope was a recent clipping from *The Munsonville Times* outlining the new, last-minute, essay-driven scholarship program reserved for students who planned to use their skills in Munsonville following graduation. Melissa had less than a week to submit her entry.

"I know you've already enrolled in Grover's Park Community College," Julie had written, "but nothing's the same since you left. Think of the fun we'd have if you won."

That night she had read Julie's letter over dinner. Darlene was shaking her head before Melissa had finished. "Hon, everything's settled for the fall."

"It's a contest. What's the harm in applying?"

"Didn't you read the rules? You'll have to work in Munsonville."

"That's the idea."

Jason's voice broke into her thoughts. "We're here."

The banquet room hummed with boys in gray or powder blue rented tuxedos and bow ties and girls in cheap formals, an abundance of make-up, over-styled hair, and costume jewelry sparkling in the tables' candlelight. A banner hung over the refreshment table: *Making Magic Memories.* Near the back, Laura Jones rose halfway out of her chair and vigorously waved. Jason absently grasped Melissa's wrist and led her to the round table. Shelly Gallagher looked away from Melissa and whispered to her boyfriend Chuck Mitchell, an accounting student at Illinois State University.

"Iced tea, right?" Jason asked.

"Sure."

She glanced at Jason's class ring, sized to her finger with purple angora. *John was gone.* Henry's cultural heritage, however, could be very much alive, if Melissa worked hard. Of course, if anything existed of John, Melissa knew she'd find it on the estate grounds, once she made her way to Munsonville.

Laura interrupted Melissa's reverie. "Melissa, do you like my hair?"

Except for a few soft dangling tendrils, Laura had tied her auburn hair high up on her heard with fuchsia ribbon. The hot pink polish on her fake long nails perfectly matched her strapless dress. In vain, Laura tried smoothing down the false eyelash peeling up over her left eye, but she kept jabbing herself with the nails.

Laura handed her compact to Bob Wright, who worked for a local mechanic. "Here. Hold this," she said and patted the ball of her index finger over her eyelid.

Bob's smile above the oversized teal bow tie looked as bland as his perfectly blow-dried straw hair. By contrast, Shelly's blonde hair flowed over her baby green and blue print gown. Between the bushy perm framing Chuck's round head and the large ruffles on his white shirt, Melissa half-

14

expected to hear him say, "Baa." Jason returned with Melissa's iced tea just as the first strained notes of *Stairway to Heaven* began.

"The band stinks," Jason said, pulling up a chair.

"Got it!" Laura cried. She retrieved the case from Bob and eyed her work. Bob's insipid smile did not change.

Shelly jumped up and held out her hand. "Chuck, it's our song! Please!"

Grinning at no one in particular, Chuck allowed Shelly to pull him toward the dance floor. Laura hummed and swayed to the music while she reapplied lipstick. Bob leaned back and draped his arm over Laura's chair.

"The bassist is Mr. Barnett's nephew," Bob said.

"Really?" Laura cocked her head and studied the band. "He doesn't look like the principal."

Jason glanced at Melissa. "Do you want to?"

Melissa studied her dress. The white rose and baby's breath corsage had already wilted around its edges.

"If you do," Melissa said.

Once, Melissa would have considered dancing this close to Jason *her* entrance to heaven. He didn't trip over her feet too much, and he even stroked her hair a few times, but he remained strangely quiet. Obviously, Jason felt bored, too...or sick. Well, good. That should make for an early evening. Melissa nearly laughed aloud remembering the first the night, when Jason fumbled for her hand in the movie theater and clumsily kissed her goodnight, and then some, in her driveway. Laura was now dancing with Bob, but she was staring at Jason from over Bob's shoulder. So much for Laura "getting past" Jason.

After they ate miniature hot dogs wrapped in crescent rolls, chips dipped in sour cream mixed with dried onion soup, and gelatin salad, and the boys' conversation had moved to Chuck's prowess on the field, Shelly turned to Melissa.

"I wish you'd reconsider." The hurt showed plainly in Shelly's voice. "We've been best friends since kindergarten. I thought for sure you'd join me in a couple of years."

"I still might," Melissa said. Laura was inching her chair closer to Jason's, while pretending to be fascinated with Chuck's overinflated story. "The scholarship is only good for one year."

"But it might be renewed."

"Depending on my grades."

"What does Jenson College offer that you can't get at Illinois State?"

The possibility of finding John, Melissa silently answered.

"Oh, for God's sake, Shelly. It's a one-year free ride. Besides, nothing lasts forever. You should be happy for Melissa. It's the chance of a lifetime." Laura had saved all of her money from working at Pizza Express just to pay for one semester at art school.

Jason leaned close to Melissa. "I'm opening tomorrow. Are you ready to go?"

"Sure," Melissa said, eager to put the lackluster night and the remaining slivers of her childhood behind her. All at once, Melissa realized why Jason had been awkward around her all evening. He, too, felt upset about Melissa's leaving, but unlike Shelly, he couldn't express it.

With an unusual burst of compassion for Jason, Melissa tuned the car radio to his favorite station, sat in the middle seat for the drive home, and amused herself by mentally counting the days until she left for Jenson College, thankful Steve had taken her side and seen the merit of the contest.

"It's a creative way of bringing fresh blood into the village," Steve had said. "I give the officials credit. They don't give up."

"I can't believe you're siding with her. Teaching at Munsonville School means low pay and no advancement." Darlene turned to Melissa. "Why are you aiming so low?"

"But, Mom, that's exactly why I should go back. Those kids need inspiring literature if they're ever going to strive for something beyond a fishing village, like Julie is."

Steve looked hard at Darlene. "I completely disagree with you. Losing Harold Masters was a huge blow for the school. Melissa's enthusiasm could only be an asset." He laid a hand on Melissa's shoulder. "I'm proud you want to go back and help."

Melissa felt a twinge of guilt at her deception, but it was only a twinge. "Thanks, Steve."

Immediately after dinner, Melissa composed a five hundred word piece on the merits of Harold Masters' theatrical teaching style and how she hoped to continue his legacy in Munsonville. Two weeks later, Melissa received the official notice. She had won a full scholarship for her first year at Jenson College. If she earned high marks, it could be renewed for the remaining three years.

"Congratulations!" Steve crushed her in a jubilant hug. "I knew you could do it."

"Yes, congratulations," her mother had echoed, but she didn't look happy about it.

Brian had simply stared at her and then slunk out of the room without saying a word. Melissa had dashed away to write Julie the good news.

Jason slowed down to turn onto Melissa's street, which brought Melissa back into the present. He pulled up next to Steve's work van, shifted into park, and lowered the volume; he did not turn off the ignition. For a few minutes they just sat, Jason absently tapping his hand on his thigh.

"You know, Melissa," Jason said, still looking straight ahead. "We've gone together all spring. That's a long time."

Melissa nodded and said, "I know," but inwardly, she groaned at Jason's growing attachment to her. Where was he going with this? Surely, he didn't expect to continue their flaccid romance long distance.

Jason cleared his throat and loosened his collar. "Well, with you going away to school, and all, I think we should see other people."

"Okay."

"I don't want you thinking I'm breaking up with you, because I'm not. It's just that...hey! What do you mean 'okay?' You're not upset?"

Upset? It took all of Melissa's self-control not to cheer, but instead she said, "Of course I'm upset. It's just that I don't want to make you feel guilty by crying in front of you."

As Jason considered that comment, Melissa quickly kissed his cheek. "I'll always treasure the good times we had."

She slammed the car door, hoping that act would compensate for her insufficient disappointment. She then trotted up the front steps as a perplexed Jason screeched out of the driveway. Too late, Melissa remembered Jason's ring still occupied her finger. Inside, Melissa snapped off the light her mother had considerately left on for her and slowly climbed the stairs. Her first boyfriend had just jilted her, but she couldn't muster any sadness, not about Jason, anyway. Once she crossed the threshold of her bedroom, Melissa carefully unpinned the remaining rose petal from her corsage and tossed it into her wastebasket. Even more carefully, pretending for a moment she was fondling one of Bryony's ball gowns, Melissa removed the prom dress, smoothed its satiny folds, and hung it in the back of her closet. She twisted off the ring, stuffed it into the pocket of her best wool coat, and then fumbled in the opposite pocket for the key to the steamer trunk underneath her window.

One by one, Melissa removed her Munsonville treasures: the rose-scented manila envelope, two items she had "forgotten" to return to the Munsonville Public Library (a record bearing the title *The Best-Loved Compositions of John Simons* and her textbook on vampirism, *Creatures of the Night: Witches, Werewolves, and Vampires*), the book on her bed the first night in the servant's cottage *(Nocturnal Lore: The Collected Tales of Henry Matthews)* and Bryony's broken music box. She set the box on her lap, lifted the lid of the painted cherry-wood box, and imagined the now silent notes. Oh, how she longed for the days when the magical music would transport her back to eighteen-ninety-four so she could play-act Bryony once again.

What *really* had happened to John? Had he burned inside the fire at Simons Mansion, the home he had built for Bryony as a wedding present, so she could live in Munsonville forever? Had he somehow escaped? Did he still exist as a vampire, or had he obtained enough blood from Melissa to become human once again? If so, why hadn't he returned for her as she had fantasized he would? Would John the man retain the memories of both his former life and his vampire state, or had he received a fresh chance, a new opportunity, with no remembrances of the past? Would John even know Melissa if he saw her? Would she know him?

Her eyes fell on the envelope, and she remembered Henry's admonition to forget vampires, including him—her undead chaperone--and especially John, who brought only death to Bryony. She could resist no longer. Carefully sliding her hand past the dried purple rose petals, Melissa retrieved the sheet of paper whose words she had long since memorized. Nevertheless, she unfolded it and read the final message Henry, posing as her literature teacher Harold Masters, had sent her.

"Twenty years from now, you will be more disappointed by the things you didn't do than by the ones you did do. So throw off the bowlines. Sail away from the safe harbor. Catch the trade winds in your sails. Explore. Dream Discover."Mark Twain.

Helplessly, Melissa clutched the music box to her chest. The anguish Melissa should have felt an hour ago rushed into her throat and burned her eyes.

"Oh, John!" she cried, and the familiar hot tears fell hard and fast.

The summer blurred past. In rapid succession, Melissa graduated from Grover's Park High School, kept the books for Steve so Darlene could catch up on writing, sold most of her worldly possessions at the family's garage sale, and checked off each item for college as she and Darlene purchased them. Whenever Shelly or Laura called, Melissa told them she was "busy." Darlene overheard her one day and sat Melissa down for a talk.

"It's not good to isolate yourself," Darlene said. "You'll meet other boys at school."

"Huh? Mom, this isn't about Jason."

"Then what?"

"I *do* talk to Shelly and Laura, but...."

"But what?"

Melissa took a deep breath. "They might as well get used to it because that's the way it's going to be for a long time, maybe forever. Besides, I'd rather help you and Steve."

Darlene sighed in resignation. "You're so young."

"No, I'm not."

Finally, the day arrived when Steve and Brian loaded Melissa's few remaining belongings into the back of Steve's cleaning van. She had learned her lesson about traveling lightly last year, when they had moved to Munsonville. As the miles put Melissa's hometown behind for what she hoped to be the final time, an army of impressions besieged her: the storm in John's eyes the first time he kissed her, Henry's exhortations to "be herself," Fr. Alexis' reassurance vampire dreams were normal, and an envelope of dried purple rose petals, proving her dreams were real. *Forget the past*, Henry had warned, but Bryony's life held Melissa's most precious memories. Besides, Harold Masters had raised her reading standards long before Melissa had caught John in her bedroom. Be strong, Melissa told herself.

"Bring it on!" she said aloud.

Brian peered at her over his comic book.

"Did you say something, Melissa?" Steve called back.

"Just excited about starting school."

Brian stared at her. "If you say so," he said in a voice too low for Steve to hear.

"You're just jealous because I have a higher purpose in life."

"Yeah, that's why you spent last semester mooning in your bedroom."

"I was studying. It paid off, too."

Brian raised the book higher and slid far down into his seat. "What kind of a school gives away full, last-minute scholarships based on a corny paragraph?"

Darlene closed her book and turned around. "Who's hungry?"

Melissa hated to stop, but Jenson *was* a seven-hour drive. After a quick fast-food lunch, Melissa pretended to nap since it passed the time, but adrenaline surged through her limbs the closer Steve's van carried her to John's territory. Finally,

Steve exited onto Black Spruce Road. She closed her eyes, ordered her thudding heart to calm down, and rested her head on the hard vinyl. One more hour to go. Melissa imagined herself climbing the familiar hill leading to Simons Mansion. How desolate would the estate seem without the old gray stone building? Did bryony still grow on the property? Was the servant's cottage, where she had lived last fall, still standing? She felt the cool breeze on her cheeks while John led her through the estate's many gardens. She floated on ethereal giddiness as John waltzed them around the ballroom at the Brumfeldt ball. She felt John's warm breath, the night he offered the bargain in her bedroom, as he whispered, "Open your eyes, Melissa."

She opened her eyes. Tall, gothic, tower-like structures framed the street on both sides of Jenson's college strip; the main building of the six-story school towered above them all. The complete campus spanned the entire street. Years ago, the townspeople had nicknamed this street *His Majesty's Row* because the great castle-like structures once housed the area's notable merchants, entrepreneurs, attorneys, and physicians. Most of those homes had long since been converted into businesses or apartments for upperclassmen and staff. Whenever the college needed more space, it simply bought another house.

Steve pointed to a lovely sepia Queen Anne trimmed in brick red adjacent to the large parking lot. "That's the library."

Darlene shielded her eyes against the sun for a clearer look. "It's perfectly gorgeous. When was it built?"

"It's about a decade older than Simons Mansion."

Steve then pointed out a laundromat, a doctor's office, a restaurant, a small grocery store, and a bowling alley. "There's even a pawn shop at the far end of the street, across from the nursing home."

Sudden memory of that nursing home flashed.

Grandma Marchellis' nose turned crimson. She panted and drove her nails into the chair arms. She tried to speak and choked. Steve rang for the nurse. Grandma locked eyes on Melissa. Grandma's eyes bulged; her face turned blue; and her mouth foamed.

"Danger...blood!" Grandma gasped. "Blood! Blood! Blood! Blood! Blood!"

Melissa shivered and blinked twice to clear the image.

"See, Mom. I *told* you I'd be fine."

Darlene looked worried. "You're still stranded in one area. If only you could've stayed in Grover's Park until we were done with Steve's van payment...."

"Mom, Julie has a car. I will be okay."

Melissa stepped out of the car and surveyed her new home. The entire second floor served as the freshman dormitory; the last two floors contained only classrooms. With everyone grabbing a suitcase and knapsack, only one trip to Melissa's room was required. Even Brian couldn't help appreciating the high ceilings and scuffed wood floors. They passed the afternoon by touring the college's buildings and grounds. For dinner, they drove downtown to Jenson Family Restaurant, the place where Melissa, her mother, and Brian had stopped for hot chocolate during last year's mournful Christmas shopping expedition. Had only nine months passed since that lonely day?

To Melissa's dismay, her mother insisted Melissa spend the night with them at a nearby bed and breakfast. Melissa started to object, then saw Steve's sad eyes. She now understood some of her mother's resistance. The change had been too sudden. They weren't ready to let her go.

"It's not the official end," Melissa reminded her. "We're still going out to breakfast tomorrow, aren't we?"

"Of course." Darlene reached inside her purse for a tissue. "Okay, then...."

" You're not spending the night in a half-empty building."

The next day's goodbyes happened easier than Melissa had anticipated, for they said them from the parking lot of the bed and breakfast, at Melissa's insistence. After Steve's van disappeared from sight, Melissa fairly ran to her dorm room. Vague, shadowy dreams of her future beckoned to her. She could feel them. She couldn't wait to meet them.

Orientation weekend was great fun. The upperclassmen had planned a slew of activities for the freshmen. One was a scavenger hunt to acquaint the students with their new town. The freshmen and their mentors divided into teams and distributed a list of places to find. At each location, they snapped a picture with an instamatic camera, but the buildings blurred before Melissa's eyes, and she only saw Main Street.

On Saturday night, the school hosted a keg party in the gym. Melissa's roommate, Jill Eaton, had a good-looking brother, Bradley. He came to the dance that night with a few friends who were just as gorgeous as he, even though Bradley was twenty-three and too old for a college event.

"The lead singer is even hotter," Jill said with a giggle. "He's also a good friend of Brad's. That's why they're playing tonight for free."

"Cool," Melissa said, hoping she sounded enthusiastic.

The band *did* sound good. Melissa sipped her first beer, repulsed by its bitter taste. How did people drink the nasty stuff?

Melissa ditched her cup beneath a folding chair and remembered the punch glass she had hidden below a table, the night she had met Henry Matthews. Ignoring the sudden heaviness in her heart, she moved close to the stage area for a better look at the lead singer. Jill was right; he was much better looking than Brad. Then Melissa saw the keyboard player, and her gut hit the floor.

It was John Simons.

Or, at least, it was someone who closely resembled John. She tried to sneak a decent look at him, but he kept his head bent over the keys. He did not contribute to any of the vocals. How odd to think of John Simons wearing jeans and a T-shirt! *Impossible!* He had died in the fire...*hadn't he?* Melissa needed to know for sure.

At intermission, Jill talked nonstop about the lead singer. "I told you he was hot."

Melissa tried to act nonchalant. "I like the keyboard player better. Who is he?"

"I don't know," Jill said. "Hey, Brad!" She stood on

tiptoes and waved across several groups of people to catch his attention. "Brad!"

Brad gave her thumbs up and walked over to the girls. "What's up?" he said.

"Melissa likes the keyboard player," Jill said. "Can she meet him?"

"No problem," Brad said. "I'll get him."

After he walked away, Melissa turned on Jill. "I can't believe you did that!"

"Well, you wanted to meet him, didn't you?"

"Not that way!"

Brad soon returned. The keyboard player, tall and broad, wore his blond hair very long. He had striking, almond-shaped blue eyes and wore his beard and mustache thinly trimmed, hardly noticeable at all.

"The ladies wanted to meet you," Brad said. "Jill, Melissa, this is Johnny."

A broad smile broke out on the keyboardist's face, as he extended his hand to Melissa. "How's it going?" he said. "Melissa, right?"

She couldn't speak, not with his eyes boring straight into her soul, so she instead nodded. Jill noticed her plight and jumped into the conversation. "You guys sure sounded good tonight. Been playing with the band long?"

"Off and on for the last year," Johnny said, with a slow up and down look at Melissa which nearly made her heart stop. "I prefer classical piano to contemporary. Even do some composing."

It can't be, Melissa thought. It just can't be. But if it wasn't, John Simons had a double walking around twentieth century Jenson.

She lifted her chin and at last found her voice. "How interesting. I don't know much about classical music, but I knew someone who played piano, and I really enjoyed it."

Johnny fixed amused eyes on her. The barest hint of a smile passed over his lips and vanished. "Really? Well then, we shall get along fine."

A bearded man in a half-unbuttoned satin shirt clapped him on the shoulder. "Hey, Johnny! We're back onstage."

An enthralled Melissa watched him walk away. Her roommate had a connection to this John Simons look-alike, and Melissa intended to use it. She had to find out if this Johnny was John Simons, brought back to life.

To Jill she merely said, "It's all right. I forgive you."

Jill grinned through her plastic cup.

How Melissa could accomplish a second meeting was another matter, but she resolved that, no matter what, she would make it happen.

Soon.

CHAPTER 2: VAMPIRE OR REVAMPED?

"What do you think, Melissa?" Jill said, as she lit a cigarette, leaned against the closet door, and scratched one bare foot against the other.

Melissa scarcely noticed. Her roommate was a girl of contrasts. Despite her petite hour-glass figure and wispy hair, Jill had easily carried four suitcases, in one trip, up two flights of stairs. Now looking fresh and innocent in a melon-hued, scooped neck shirt and floral print skirt, Jill no longer resembled the staggering drunk who had awakened Melissa before dawn by vomiting sour rum all over the floor. After a shower and caffeinated pop, Jill had gotten busy. She pushed her dresser into a corner and her desk directly in front of the window. She then turned her bed sideways, splitting the room, but allowing access to her drawers. A small cabinet that sat flush with her desk held her stereo. With this arrangement, Melissa owned three-fourths of the total space, but Jill controlled the window. The lone closet door, wall phone, and exit resided on Melissa's half of the room. A small refrigerator, plugged into the outlet near Jill's bed, became the official spacer. The top outlet accommodated Melissa's desk lamp.

Melissa set down *The Prosecutor Rests and Other Short Stories* and nodded her approval. "Works for me."

Jill crushed her cigarette. She then hung smiling panda bear print curtains on her window and tacked up three posters with captions: a basset hound ("I need a hug"), a kitten clinging to a chandelier by a paw ("Is it Friday yet?"), and a flock of butterflies fluttering into the sunset ("If you love someone, set him free...."). Next Jill proceeded to remove carton after carton of records and stack them on her cabinet shelves.

In less than an hour, Melissa had unpacked her clothes and fastidiously arranged her school supplies. She folded her knapsacks into suitcases and hid them under her bed. She left her walls bare. She was attending college to become an English teacher like Harold Masters; she was not setting up housekeeping. Fate, however, had intervened and offered a reward for her lofty aspirations, although today, Melissa was wondering if she hadn't superimposed John Simons' likeness on Johnny's in the gym's faint light simply because she had wanted to see it. Well, only one way to find out.

"Oh, I'll never get it all done," Jill moaned. "How'd you finish so quickly?"

"I learned the hard way not to bring so much," Melissa said, closing the book and running her fingers over the words, *Harold Masters*.

Melissa had silently debated the merits of either leaving the steamer trunk in her old bedroom, which she did, or hauling it to Jenson. She now realized she had rightly chosen. Earlier that morning, when Melissa had returned from breakfast, she had caught Jill snooping under her mattress under the pretense of looking for a quarter for the vending machine.

Jill tossed an empty box into the center of the room. "I guess I have a lot of stuff that's important to me. Where will I put it all?"

"I don't need much closet space. Why don't you stack the extra boxes there? Your parents can take them away when they come to visit."

Jill flopped onto her bed and reached for her cigarettes. "I give up," she said.

"Then let's get dinner. I'm hungry."

The food line swelled the cafeteria long before Melissa and Jill reached it. Melissa had just selected a tray when someone tapped her on the shoulder. "Guess who?"

Melissa whirled around and smiled broadly. Julie had replaced the hated braids with a blunt, sleek page boy cut, but Julie's pretty, friendly face remained the same.

Julie grinned and returned the hug. "Long time, huh?"

"I guess! Jill, this is my friend Julie. We went to high school together for part of last year. Jill's my roommate."

"Hi, Jill. You'll have to meet my roommate later. Her parents took her out to dinner. Tracy's entire family went to this school, but she's the last one, so it's a weird, emotional thing for them."

Melissa picked through three glasses before she found one without dried food stuck to it, so she inspected the silverware before she placed any on her tray and repeated the process with the plates. As she moved through the line, Melissa surveyed the food with a critical eye. Brian could have done a better job preparing a meal even before Steve had taught him how to cook. She opted for baked chicken, instant mashed potatoes, and canned sweet potatoes. As an afterthought, she added a roll. Thank heavens the salad bar looked halfway appealing.

Jill was diving through some gloppy macaroni and cheese, and Melissa was buttering her roll when Julie reached their table, her plate piled as high as Henry Matthews' plate at the garden party at Simons Mansion. It amazed Melissa how some people could eat all they wished and never gain a pound. She did not have that problem.

"So catch me up," Melissa said, scooping some fake mashed potatoes on a spoon that bent slightly under their weight.

Julie twirled spaghetti around her fork. "Katie's going to cosmetology school here in Jenson, but she's commuting by bus. I told her she should join us here for lunch. We could sneak extra food on our trays so she wouldn't have to pay."

"What about Ann?"

"That's the most intriguing news. She and Jack Cooper are engaged. They're supposed to get married next year."

Melissa dropped her spoon. "No way!"

"Yes, way. They started dating right after Christmas. He proposed to her at senior prom. I think they're stupid to get married so young."

Melissa pulled the skin off her chicken and set it on the side of her plate.

"Anyway, Ann's parents are throwing them an engagement party the last weekend of September. She told me to tell you you're invited. You could stay at my house."

Munsonville! Melissa had absolutely intended to sneak away to the fishing village when she came to Jenson, but she had not expected an opportunity would surface quite so soon. Now that it had presented itself, waiting an entire month to walk on those beloved grounds seemed far too long. She wouldn't even mind seeing the terrifying mist that had chased her in the woods, if it somehow brought her closer to John.

"Of course, I'll go with you," Melissa said. "It'll be fun to see everybody."

By the end of Melissa's second full week at Jenson College, her life had assumed its new routine. Three days a week, Melissa attended Introduction to Literature, College Algebra I, and Western Civilization. On Tuesdays and Thursdays, Melissa sat through composition and general science classes. Among those classes, she studied, completed homework, and worked, for Melissa now had a job at the library's circulation desk under the supervision of its manager, Mr. Lowell Schmidt, human insect.

Tall and thin, Mr. Schmidt's arms, legs, neck, and head appeared too long for his body. He had large meaty hands, perfect for swinging a hammer, but clumsy for pasting envelopes into books. His wide eyes reminded Melissa of a katydid; his nose seemed too small to inhale sufficient oxygen to sustain life; and his small, bow-shaped mouth belonged on a Valentine card's cupid. He clipped his graying, blond hair crew-cut style, and if his shrill voice ascended an octave higher, only dogs would hear it.

Melissa's main duties were simply checking books in and out for students and staff, helping them locate pertinent material, shelving those they had returned. Not only did the job provide some extra spending money, it introduced her to a wider variety of classical reading than her literature course offered. Melissa looked forward to the days Mr. Schmidt sent her away with an armful of books, for she used those occasions to peruse titles and sneak into a corner with a good one, especially if it concerned Victorian history or literature. The library, a maze of rooms richly decorated in dark woods, oriental rugs, and lace curtains spanned three floors; it provided the perfect setting to fan her obsession. The second floor housed all non-fiction topics, and the third, at the top of the house, with its overstuffed couches and chairs under the slanted roofs for lazy weekend reading, lodged the finest literature. Not to be outdone, floor number two contained a coffee station featuring home-baked treats and small parlors in the turrets for browsing or studying.

Although Melissa spent most of her time on the main floor, which contained the card catalogues, reference materials, and offices, she looked forward to climbing the winding staircase to one of the upper levels. One afternoon, while shelving materials, a small, dusky blue paperback caught her attention: *The Cenci,* by Percy Bysshe Shelley. As Melissa flipped through the verses, she instantly became caught up in the story of Beatrice Cenci, executed in fifteen hundred ninety-nine for murdering her father, the count, to protect herself from incest. Someone had marked a page by creasing a corner, so Melissa, curious, turned to it. As the count hosted a banquet in honor of his sons' gruesome deaths, he pretended to drink their blood. Someone had underlined the count's words in red pen: *I have drunken deep of joy. And I will taste no other wine tonight.*

"Melissa?"

She hastily slammed the book as a tall girl appeared.

"Mr. Schmidt's looking for you."

Melissa spent most of her weekend days studying at the library, away from the distraction of Jill's retching, a regular Saturday and Sunday event, whether or not Jill happened to slip yet another young man past security the previous evening. After Melissa had spent the first couple of weekend nights sleeping on the lounge's couch, Julie and her roommate, Tracy Turner, offered a spot on their floor for Melissa's pillow and blanket.

"Even if it's not more comfortable, it's safer," Tracy had said, blowing her layered brown hair away from her face as she pushed a heavy glass coffee table across the room. Tracy was taller than Melissa and larger boned, too, but with a natural coolness that even made moving tables seem graceful.

"One of these afternoons," Julie said at lunch one day, as she dipped her roast beef sandwich into lukewarm au jus, "you should run up to the fourth floor."

"Why?" Melissa lifted her hamburger to take a bite.

"To see my piano teacher. He's John Simons."

Melissa's tomato slid out of the bun and landed onto her lap. "What!"

Julie giggled. "I thought that would get you. Well, he's not really John Simons, of course. But he sure as hell looks like him. Even his name is similar."

With shaking hands, Melissa picked the tomato off her jeans. She dipped the corner of a napkin into her water and dabbed at the ketchup stain.

"Who's John Simons?" Tracy said.

"He was a famous pianist and composer back in the nineteenth century. Melissa wrote a report about him last year when we lived in Munsonville. Well, actually, she wrote about his wife. She got a decent grade on it, too. Anyway, Melissa lived near his mansion, before it burned down."

"Oh, you must mean Professor Simotes," Tracy said. "When my sister was studying music, she thought he was really hot. One look at those blue eyes, and she melted. Girls sign up for his classes as electives just to have him for a teacher, but he's pretty talented, too. He's composed pieces for school bands and even made a record of his music for a fundraiser a couple of years ago. I heard it earned good money for our college."

Melissa found her voice at last. "I think I met him." Did she sound calm enough? "Did his rock band play at orientation weekend?"

"I can't believe he's in a rock band," Julie said.

"He played keyboards."

"That's not his band." Tracy took a swig of pop. "He just plays with them sometimes. I think he's friends with one or two of the members."

Excitement surged through Melissa and nearly overflowed into a whoop. Johnny Simotes taught at Jenson College. She wouldn't have to search far to unearth him, and Julie had unwittingly bestowed a reason to visit the music department. Heart racing, Melissa internally sprinted through her packed schedule. How might she accommodate piano lessons?

"I didn't know about the band," Julie said. "I just know he's an awesome teacher. I've been taking lessons from him forever."

Wham! Reality shattered Melissa's fantasy into a thousand pieces, but she managed to choke out, "Forever?"

Julie laughed, shook her head, and again dipped her bread. "Okay, so that's an exaggeration. I've really only been taking lessons for a year. I made a deal with my parents. They pay for college on the condition I keep up my piano lessons. At the beginning of senior year, when I told them I wanted to attend Jenson College, they dropped my old teacher and switched to Professor Simotes."

"So why don't you like the lessons if he's so good?"

"I just despise the piano. Hey Tracy, I forgot to tell you. Some Lyle guy called for you this afternoon."

Since last year? Tears pricked her eyes, but Melissa rapidly winked them away and summoned her sensible side to the surface. John Simons was a Victorian musician that died in nineteen fifty-five. So what if Professor Simotes resembled him? Wasn't everyone supposed to have a double? Anyway, even if John Simons had survived as a vampire, he had only returned to human life a few months ago, so he couldn't have taught Julie piano lessons last year. He wouldn't have been able to produce a record two years ago. They were not the same man. Anyway, Melissa had no ear for music. If she had been stupid enough to sign up for lessons, Professor Simotes would have laughed her out of the music department.

For the next few days, Melissa dutifully fixated her mind on two things: her current obligations and future goal of teaching English in Munsonville. When John Simons entered her mind, she whisked him away and focused harder on the current task. She avoided all mention of Professor Johnny Simotes, and felt proud of her tight control. *Henry* would be proud. Then Julie spoiled it.

"I'm tired of cafeteria food." Julie made a face at her breakfast tray. "How about meeting me in the music department? I'll be done with piano by four o'clock."

Despite her honorable intentions, Melissa's pulse shifted into overdrive, but she managed to serenely say, "I have to work at six."

"So we'll leave right away and just walk to Berkleys so you won't be late. How does that sound?"

"Okay, I guess," Melissa tried to sound indifferent. Do not, she told herself, count the minutes until the end of the day. Professor Johnny Simotes is not John Simons. For once, Melissa appreciated her full schedule. She desperately needed the occupation to pass the time.

"Super." Julie rose to leave. "See you this afternoon."

Although no one ever taught English as Mr. Masters had, today Melissa found Brenda Garboldi's Introduction to Literature class especially tiresome. The teacher seemed too syrupy perfect, in size, shape, and evenness of emotion; her soft voice lacked any dramatic traits to enliven their selections. Melissa missed Harold Masters' darkened classrooms and expressive recitations. Miss Garboldi merely imparted significant information to her students. They could enjoy it or not, their choice.

That day, as Miss Garboldi wrote her notes on the blackboard, Melissa noticed the tiny diamond on her left hand that caught and held the September morning sunshine. No wonder, Melissa thought, she doesn't put much effort into making her class interesting. She probably just wants to get married, quit work, and have a ton of babies. She doesn't have a vision and a lofty purpose for her life, like me.

College Algebra I moved fairly quickly, but Western Civilization dragged worse than Introduction to Literature did, thanks to the ancient Horace Phelps, who taught it in a metered monotone voice. He's so old and boring, Melissa thought, he probably witnessed everything firsthand. At lunch, she sneaked a tray up to her dorm room. Jill's classes that day extended into the afternoon, so Melissa counted on using this time for her homework. She didn't mind studying at the library, but it felt nice to relax in her own space for a change.

The afternoon limped away. One by one, Melissa completed her assignments and returned textbooks and notebooks to her bottom desk drawers. An hour before she met Julie, Melissa allowed herself the luxury of stretching flat on her bed with her literature textbook. At least she could pretend she was lying on Henry's settee and entertaining herself with a book from his extensive collection while he steadily typed a manuscript. In that mindset, those last minutes flew past. She finished reading at five minutes to four. Sudden panic caught in Melissa's throat. What if she arrived too late? She imagined Julie leaving the music room and heading for the staircase.

Melissa ran a comb through her hair, grabbed her purse, and sped out of the room, slamming the door behind her. She fled down the hall and flew up the steps, two at a time. At the top of the sixth floor, Melissa's legs turned to jelly. She wobbled down the hall toward the sounds of piano music and paused at the entrance. Peeping through the doorway, Melissa saw Julie laboring over a lesson while Johnny Simotes, in a gray three-piece suit, leaned over to correct several notes. As he stood erect, the professor shook back his hair, fully revealing his face, the face of John Simons. Melissa's hand flew to her mouth to stifle the gasp that escaped before she could stop it. Julie continued playing, but after a few minutes, Professor Simotes said something Melissa didn't catch. He sat beside her, and the music began again, but Melissa knew from its distinct quality the professor was playing it. She leaned on the door frame, mesmerized, watching him. It had been a long time since she had seen him play. She was no judge of piano music, but Johnny Simotes certainly sounded like John Simons. Why, even Julie saw the resemblance between her piano teacher and the old oil painting hanging in Munsonville Public Library.

Thoughts raced through Melissa's brain and chased away her doubts. Had Melissa's blood worked for him? Was he now human? Of course he had to be human. Otherwise, how could he teach all day at Jenson College? *This was John Simons!* Now, the big question: Had Johnny Simotes retained any memory of his life as John Simons or did his transformation erase it? Unbearable yearning tore her heart at witnessing him once again in action. Melissa had saved John. She had to have him. She *deserved* to have him. Instantly, she recalled Henry's admonition, *Don't squander it on the dead,* but the man teaching Julie looked anything but dead. Anyway, she and John belonged together. Melissa knew it within the deepest recesses of her heart.

Julie played a few lines and then looked up at him for his approval. Johnny provided it with an unsmiling nod, and she stood up, gathering her sheet music. That's when Julie saw Melissa standing in the doorway. She grabbed her books off a nearby table, and Melissa ducked into the hall. She wasn't quite ready to let Professor Simotes see her. After all, John hadn't come looking for her, but, then, he hadn't known she was living in Grover's Park.

"Sorry you had to wait," Julie said as they clattered down the stairs.

"That's all right. You sounded good. I didn't know you could play Mozart."

"Beethoven, and I do okay. I can't wait until graduation when I can finally quit. Anyway, what did you think of Professor Simotes? He really looks like John Simons, doesn't he?"

Melissa took a deep breath and willed her voice to stay casual as she said, "Oh, I guess, a little."

They had reached the bottom of the stairs. Julie stopped and gazed incredulously at Melissa. "A little! Are you blind? They could pass for twins!"

Longing, desire, and hope grabbed Melissa's throat, and she could not speak. So Melissa quickly asked Julie what piece she was learning and only half-listened to the answer as they crossed the street to Berkley's. The classic look of the tall, narrow brown brick building with arched doorways and windows complemented the inside walls, which the Berkleys had plastered with testimonials and photographs of satisfied patrons through the years. Customers filled the counter stools, which stretched from one end of the spacious dining room to the other and almost all the square oak tables and chairs. Julie found an empty spot in the back near the bathrooms. The menus rested between the salt and pepper shakers. Melissa smelled French fries and sauteeing onions.

"Did you ever come here to Berkleys, back when you lived in Munsonville?"

Melissa shook her head, marveling at the air of confidence and maturity Julie had assumed, all through a simple haircut.

Julie passed her a menu and said, "They cater to college students. Their hamburgers and homemade chips are only a dollar if you attend or teach at Jenson. Mr. Berkley grills everything out back, even in the winter."

"Sounds good to me."

"They have other specials, too, depending what night it is."

Melissa opened the menu. On Monday, the Berkleys served chili, but they prepared chicken and dumplings on Tuesday. For Euchre night on Wednesday, the Berkleys offered a steak and potato dinner. Thursday featured a "mystery meal" and Fridays, a fish fry. On Saturday, the

Berkleys cooked an assortment of homemade soups and sandwiches. Sunday afternoons always meant pot roast. Melissa smiled at the note at the bottom: *We are closed Sunday evenings so Mrs. Berkley can rest.*

After the waitress left with their orders, Julie turned happy eyes on Melissa. "Now we can *really* talk. So what was it like, going back home?"

"Different from what I thought. I guess Munsonville changed me too much."

"Yeah, that's our curse. Why do you think I had to get away?"

"I even tried dating someone I once liked, but that wasn't what I expected, either."

Julie leaned forward on her elbows. "Do tell."

So Melissa told Julie how everyone in her group, especially Laura, had crushed on Jason Frye all through high school. Although Melissa knew she should consider herself blessed he had chosen her, she couldn't appreciate her enviable prize once she'd attained it.

"Well, that can't be any worse than what Katie did," Julie said. "She actually went out with Joey Brown."

"You're kidding!"

"I'm not. She said she's rather have him for a boyfriend than have no boyfriend. She'd have dated Dan rather than stay home."

"Oh, well, I guess I'm no better. I didn't have the heart to break up with Jason. I let him do it for me."

"You guys are both nuts. I'd rather wait for the right person. I've got better things to do with my time."

"I'm realizing it now. Boy, am I glad you wrote to me and suggested trying for that scholarship."

Julie sprinkled salt over her chips. "What are you talking about?"

"You know, the letter you sent me last spring, telling me you were attending Jenson College and asking me to come, too."

Julie paused, still holding the salt shaker, and slowly raised her head. "Melissa, I didn't write you any letter."

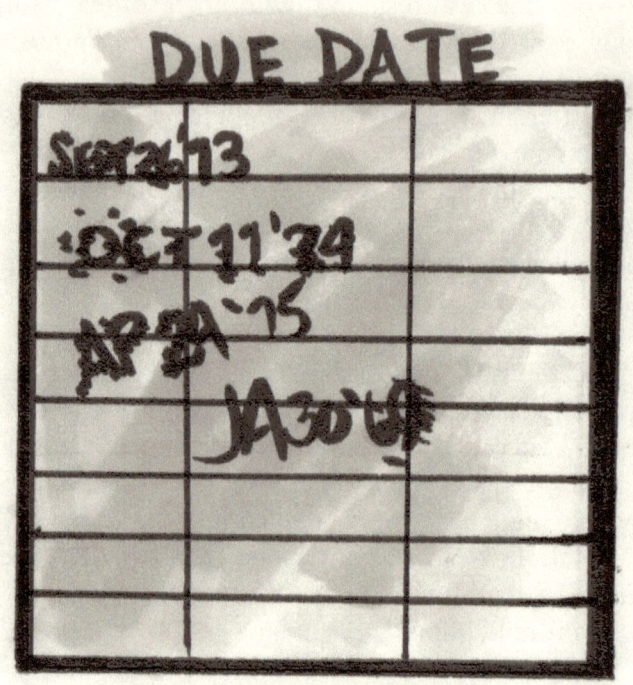

"Julie, that's ridiculous. I have the letter."

"Where? I'd sure like to see what I didn't write."

"It's in Grover's Park."

Julie set the shaker down and picked up a chip. "Sure, Melissa."

"No, really, it's with the information on the essay contest. That's how I won the full scholarship."

Julie's mouth dropped.

"A full scholarship? How'd you manage that? Hardly anyone gets a full scholarship to this place. Tracy's sister made high A's all through high school and so did her best friend, who, by the way, is a distant cousin to the head of the public relations department, and neither of them received a full scholarship."

"It's strictly for students planning to work in Munsonville following graduation."

"Who the hell wants to work in Munsonville? Remember? There's no jobs, no industry. Anyone with brains wants out of Munsonville, not in."

Melissa fell silent and looked at her plate. If Julie hadn't sent that letter, and she quite clearly did not, then who did? Who else would want Melissa at Jenson College? John? But...why go through the trouble of sending a deceptive letter? Why not contact Melissa directly?

"Hey, Melissa, before I forget, I added your name to my bowling team."

"Your what?"

"My bowling team. For the 'Bowling for the Arts' fundraiser. Tracy said it's a tradition here at the college. The whole community turns out for it. Students and staff solicit pledges for a bowling night and donate the proceeds to Jenson High. That way, the school can offer art, music, and drama to the kids. Anyway, it's a requirement for those participating in art programs at Jenson. Stupid piano lessons."

"I can't bowl."

"Everyone can bowl."

"Well, I can't."

"You've never bowled?"

Melissa cut her hamburger in half. "Well, sure, for fun, with friends, but not regularly on a team where you need good scores."

"You don't have to be good. Your handicap will make it up."

"How am I supposed to collect pledges? I don't know anyone here."

"Don't worry, we'll go door to door together. You'll help me out on this, won't you?"

"Of course, but I'm warning you. I'm really bad."

"It'll be fine."

As Melissa lay in bed that night, pillow folded over her head to block Jill's raucous voice as she cackled into the phone, she replayed her conversation with Julie. What possible reason might John Simons have for steering Melissa to Jenson? She thought of only one. John, now human, craved a permanent relationship with Melissa. Now that she lived here, he wanted to seize it. She wondered why he delayed it, but, then, John *had* waited two weeks before courting Bryony. Perhaps John, way deep inside, felt shy around women who mattered to him. Just daring the speculation that she, Melissa, could mean something to John sent Melissa's heart pounding. *Was* he too bashful to approach her? The Victorian era had passed. Times had changed. What if John expect Melissa to....

Oh, Melissa thought in anguish, I just can't.

Yet, to come this far, to be so close to John and remain separate forever was unthinkable, unimaginable, and unbearable. How had Bryony attracted this older man to her? Why had he found her so irresistible? Was it her appearance? Her mannerisms? The way she looked at him? Maybe her casual interest in art, spurred by Reverend Marseilles, had captured his attention.

Even if Melissa discerned Bryony's secret, could she duplicate it? Moreover, would she want to do replicate it? The time for playing Bryony had ended. Melissa wanted John's love her for herself, not second hand, and she simply had no idea how to attain it. A cavernous gap stood between them, of years, interests, abilities, cultures, and eras. Melissa fell asleep wondering if she should grow her hair as long as Bryony's or buy salmon-colored dresses.

Nevertheless, a full night's slumber settled something for Melissa. She awakened the next morning full of resolve for the future, hers and John's. While washing her face, Melissa confronted her reflection and vowed that if Johnny Simotes did not ask her out soon, she would do it for him.

The opportunity presented itself the very next day. Science had just ended. Melissa was heading toward the staircase that would take her from the third floor classroom to her dorm room when Johnny Simotes passed her on the way down.

"Good afternoon," he said, without stopping or looking at her.

It's now or never, Melissa thought. Aloud she said, "Excuse me."

The professor paused and turned toward her with a polite expression. His suit today was royal blue, and the cut was definitely not Victorian, but...oh God! John Simons was alive, standing *this* close, and looking directly at her.

Melissa paused and took a deep breath. "Would you have dinner with me one night?"

"I beg your pardon?"

"I said, 'Would you have...?'"

"I heard you just fine." Johnny peered closer. "Are you a music student?"

"No. I met you orientation weekend."

"I'm sorry, I don't...."

"Brad Eaton introduced us. You played in the band."

"Oh. Well, thank you for the invitation, but I'm not interested. I'm engaged."

He trotted down the stairs. Melissa closed her eyes and stood there, wishing the staircase would vanish and take her with it. What had gone wrong? Had she missed something in her reasoning? She could just hear Henry's mocking tone, *Is the truth of the little arrangement greater than your heart can bear,* ringing in her ears. Even worse, the incident spread through the Jenson College faster than brushfire.

"You asked out Professor Simotes? I don't believe it!" Tracy said at dinner that night.

"Shut up," Julie hissed at her. "There's no reason to broadcast it."

Tracy threw her head back and laughed. "There isn't anyone here who hasn't heard it."

"All the same, use some discretion."

In misery, Melissa scraped slimy gravy off her meatloaf. She had been so sure Johnny Simotes was John Simons! Such an awful blunder! She would never, never live down the shame.

Although some of the students nudged each other and pointed at Melissa when she passed them in the halls, in the days following her embarrassing conversation with Professor Simotes, Melissa learned that, beneath their smirking exterior, some of her peers held a grudging respect for what she had done.

Jill, of all people, had shared that tidbit with her. "You did know he's got a reputation for sleeping with his students, but he's always the one who calls the shots. No one has ever asked him out first, not that I've heard, anyway." She set one foot on her bed, opened a bottle of nail polish, and proceeded to paint her toenails blue.

Melissa sat at her desk while she pretended to proofread her essay, due tomorrow, on the beasts Dante encountered in his Inferno. She wondered how Mr. Masters might have enacted that epic poem, but Jill's words troubled her. Melissa hadn't known that about Professor Simotes.

"Well, not all of the students," Jill continued. "Only if he considers them pretty enough to be worthy of his affections. Not only do they get to, you know, be with him, he'll boost their grade if he's happy enough. I'm surprised Miss Garboldi puts up with him. She has to know what he's doing behind her back. It is a small school."

"Miss Garboldi?"

Jill sighed as she switched feet. "Melissa, you really need to get your head out of your books and rejoin life. The two of them are getting married this summer."

Married?

Melissa's entire existence collapsed. Married? She closed her notebook, glad that she had completed her homework for the night because her concentration for it instantly dissolved. She pushed her chair away from her desk and collected her shower supplies, but unbidden thoughts of John clamored for release the entire time she readied for bed. *Married?* How could John have done this to her? How could she have been so mistaken? If he was still in love with Bryony, then why was he engaged to Miss Garboldi?

Enough!

She plodded down the hall to her room. John Simons is not Professor Simotes. The nineteenth century composer had died decades ago. The vampire dreams are illusions. You'll go mad if you keep up the delusion. She ignored Jill and turned off her light. A final thought popped into her head before she fell asleep, and Melissa grasped at its lifeline. If John Simons hadn't orchestrated Melissa's coming to Jenson, who had?

The next day, Melissa fixed her eyes on Miss Garboldi's engagement ring as the teacher lectured on *The Divine Comedy*. a fitting, ironic theme to Melissa's life at this moment, she told herself. Did Brenda Garboldi, with her petite frame, light voice, and sweet demeanor, resemble Bryony Marseilles? Brenda's full, shoulder-length, brown hair contrasted to Bryony's long, wavy, chestnut-colored mane, but both apparently attracted John Simons. Did Brenda enjoy classical music? Did she play piano?

As she jotted notes about The Spheres of Heaven, Melissa imagined the different tragedies that might befall her teacher and cause immediate death. A rare disease. A horrific automobile accident. A psychotic ex-student who failed her class and attained revenge. Of course, as luck and her daydream would have it, Melissa would be waiting outside the music room for Julie to finish her lesson when the horrible news reached the ears of Johnny Simotes. He'd flinch, dismiss Julie from class, and ask Melissa to stay, breaking down in a torrent of tears in her presence and seeking comfort only from her.

Yeah, right.

It was bad enough she'd made a fool of herself with Professor Simotes, but Introduction to Literature felt hotter than Dante's Inferno, knowing her teacher must possess full awareness that one of her students had hit on her fiancée. Nevertheless, an evil gratification simmered inside her that Brenda Garboldi did not have an exclusive relationship with John, but Melissa once had. Her blood, and only *her* blood, had restored him to human life. Then Melissa remembered her resolution to forget John and slumped at her failure. By the end of class, Melissa had made up her mind, but she waited until after dinner to make the phone call.

"Honey, what brought this on?" Darlene sounded both surprised and a little suspicious.

"I'm homesick," Melissa said. "You were right. I should have stayed in Grover's Park."

"But you made a commitment when you accepted the scholarship. You should, at least, stick out the semester."

"But...." Melissa began and then quickly gave it up, afraid her mother might ask questions Melissa was unprepared to answer. "You're right, Mom. I probably just have freshman jitters."

Just twice since that incident had Melissa seen Johnny Simotes, and twice she avoided him. Once, she ducked into the women's restroom. The second time, she took an abrupt turn into a classroom not her own, waited until he passed by the door's window, and then hurried onto her next class, longing for John anyway.

To kill time until the commotion surrounding Professor Simotes died its natural death, Melissa agreed to join Julie and Tracy on Saturday morning scavenging the adjacent neighborhoods soliciting pledges. The broad leaves on the thick, gnarled branches of the old trees framing the beautiful architecture of Jenson's bungalows, Queen Annes, and four squares boasted summer green, but the still, chilly air hinted at autumn's imminence. Did she really have to knock on those heavy doors and ask the strangers inside to sponsor her for bowling? Could a person judge the competency of one's bowling by the strength of her sales pitch?

"Come on," Julie tugged Melissa's sleeve. "You can go with me."

Tracy crossed the street toward the even-numbered houses. Two hours later and one pledge later, Tracy moaned, a signal she wanted to give up. "I'll bet every bowler's walked through this neighborhood already."

"I should have guessed everything near the college would be picked over," Julie said with a glum expression on her face. "Let's get some lunch and go back for my car. We'll drive into Shelby. I'll bet no one's gone over there."

"Sounds like a plan," Tracy agreed. "Melissa?"

"Sure." Melissa hoped she sounded enthusiastic. It was better than hanging around her dorm room, moping about

John and wishing she could go back into time once again and play Bryony.

Fortified by Berkley's hamburgers and chips, the three girls rode into Shelby, half an hour away. Shelby was as quaint as Jenson was historic. Framed buildings of all sizes, many of them white with blue, green, or red accents and peaked roofs, lined each side of the cobblestone streets. Whereas Jenson's downtown seemed more utilitarian, Shelby sported numerous specialty shops and many cafes. A wrought iron sign hanging from a small one-story building advertised homemade soaps, while the wood sign posted on the two-story home next door promoted its hand-dipped candles, which reminded Melissa of the candelabra on John's desk inside Simons Mansion's library. The surrounding neighborhoods resembled Jenson in building style, but the streets were laid in narrow checkerboard fashion and densely populated with trees. As Julie predicted, the girls fared much better this time, collecting enough promised monies to divide over one hundred dollars in donations apiece.

"That's more like it," Tracy said from the back seat as she recounted the pledge sheets on their way back to school. "We did so well that I don't think we'll have to go out again."

"I'm not planning on it." Julie steered onto the road leading into Jenson.

"Me, neither." Melissa stared out the window and wished Julie's car might turn into a carriage.

"Hey, Melissa, what gives with you?" Tracy said. "You've been quiet all day."

"She's fine." Julie glanced out the rear view mirror. "She just gets into these moods. Used to drive us nuts when she lived in Munsonville."

On Sunday, Melissa accompanied a girl from her composition class to Jenson Mall. Short, with a chunky build, Jenny Mistakovich hated to go shopping by herself. Jenny favored peasant clothes, which, along with her large, round dark eyes, heavily accented with shadow and mascara, and long, shaggy dark hair, gave her the appearance of a cuddly rag doll. Turquoise rings and bitten-down nails adorned her fingers, and Melissa had not yet seen Jenny without a choker necklace. The one clasped around her neck today alternated aquamarine and white beads.

"I need some new shirts," Jenny said on the way there, "but I can never tell what looks good on me. You always look nice."

"Thanks," Melissa said, flattered at the unexpected compliment.

As they roamed the mall, Melissa learned she'd become quite the celebrity. Jenny, too, knew Melissa had asked out Professor Simotes, but she admired Melissa all the more for it.

"You are so brave," Jenny marveled. "I could never have done it."

I wish I hadn't, Melissa thought. Aloud, she said, "It was no big deal. I met him during orientation weekend, and he seemed nice, so I asked, that's all. He didn't even remember me."

"Still…" Jenny held up a red print shirt. "What do you think about this?"

"It's okay, but I think this green one will look better on you."

In the dressing room, Jenny twisted her frame to glimpse the green shirt from its side. "I like the scooped neck, but I still think the red one looks better."

"Yeah, maybe you're right."

Was Professor Simotes working on a composition this afternoon, or had he taken Miss Garboldi out to lunch?

"But the white one with the daisies and carnations is really pretty. Can you get it for me, Melissa?"

"Sure."

Within a few minutes, Melissa had returned to the dressing room with the shirt and remembered the excitement of trying on prom dresses, just to pretend she was attending a grand ball. Jenny was sitting on the bench, twisting a ring, waiting for Melissa. She pulled the shirt over her head and cast a critical eye at her reflection.

"I think it makes me look fat." Jenny sighed, took off the shirt, and slipped it onto its hanger. "So are you going to ask him out again?"

"Who?"

Did Jenny know about Jason Fry, too?

"Professor Simotes, you nut," Jenny said.

"No way!"

"Well, I wouldn't give up, not if I really liked him."

"I thought you wouldn't be brave enough to do it."

As Jenny paid for all three shirts at the counter, Melissa asked in surprise, "Didn't you say the white shirt made you look fat?"

"It does. But my boyfriend thinks my fat looks cute."

She and Jenny stopped at Berkley's, where Jenny's boyfriend Ronnie Powers had saved a table for them. He was taller than Jenny and thin almost to emaciated, with long, tousled, reddish-brown hair. The sleeves of Ronnie's red-collared shirt flapped around his arms, and the seat of his pants sagged in the back. After dinner, Melissa returned to her room, intending to grab her books and head for the library, but Jill was already sleeping. So, instead, Melissa buried herself in studies until she couldn't hold her eyes open anymore.

All day Monday, Melissa harnessed her will power and focused unwaveringly on her schoolwork. That night at closing time, as Melissa checked out a stack of books, Johnny Simotes walked through the front door. Melissa immediately dropped to the floor and pretended to search for something on the bottom shelf.

She counted to ten, stood up, and breathed a sigh of relief. The professor was gone. The student at the counter looked aghast at her queer behavior, grabbed his books, and nearly sprinted out the door.

Pat something, a tall, friendly girl with short brown layered hair, arranged books on a nearby cart for shelving. As she slid a stack off the counter to give to Pat, Melissa caught sight of Johnny walking to the desk with two books in his hand. Melissa spun around and quickly joined Pat.

"Um, I'll handle these," Melissa said in a low voice. "Why don't you wait on him? You've been stuck doing this all night."

Pat shrugged. "It doesn't matter to me." But she approached the professor just the same.

Melissa turned her back to counter and very slowly added her books to the cart. Johnny said something in tones so muted, Melissa only heard the sound of his voice.

"She's busy at the moment," Pat said.

"I'll wait."

Pat returned to the cart. "He's asking for you."

Melissa's face burned. She glanced up. Mr. Schmidt was observing the exchange and frowning. He preached, and monitored for, sterling customer service, especially when the customer was a teacher. Melissa felt stuck. She had no option but to face the professor. Great.

She returned to the front desk, gave Johnny a polite, "Good evening," and rapidly stamped his cards. Melissa noticed both books pertained to advanced music theory.

As Melissa slid a due date slip into the front pocket of the second book, Johnny placed his hand on hers. A flushing warmth flowed through her at his touch. All thought froze; every heartbeat hammered out a single syllable, *John*. Melissa forgot about Mr. Schmidt, Pat, the cartful of books, and her promises to forsake the Bryony fantasies. Nothing else mattered. John had made contact with her.

"So I turn you down for dinner, and you give me the cold shoulder," he said in a low voice.

The question only partly jolted Melissa into reality. She looked back at Mr. Schmidt, but he was ruffling through papers. Despite the cantering in her chest and trembling lips, she coldly met Johnny's keen eyes and asked, "Will that be all, sir?"

He smothered a smile. "Yes," he said, "for now." Johnny picked up his book and sauntered to the door.

CHAPTER 4: OUTDATED

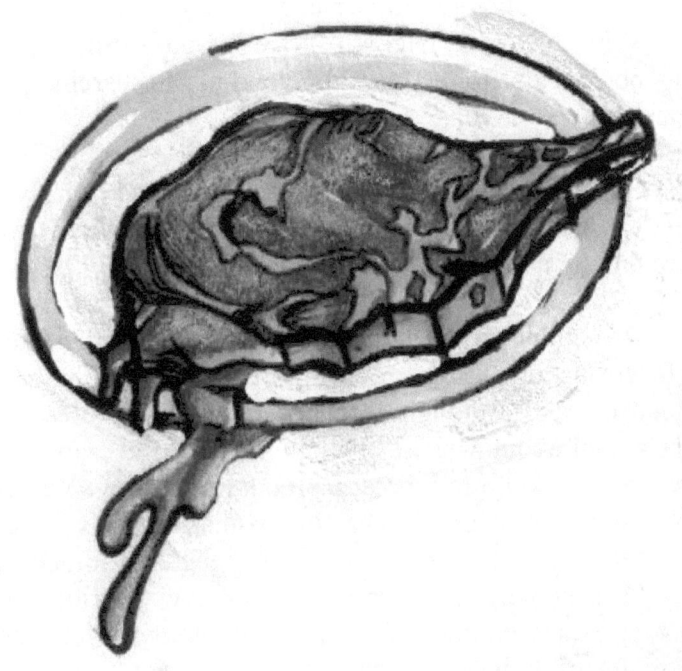

Melissa stewed about Johnny Simotes for the next two days. What had he meant by "For now?" And why should he care if Melissa had given him the cold shoulder? He's the one who didn't remember her from orientation weekend.

Yet, even as the unanswered questions bounced around her head, rapture that Johnny Simotes had approached her kept Melissa swooning. It was going to happen, Melissa happily thought. John Simons had finally moved in Melissa's direction. When, oh when, might she see him again? By day and between classes, Melissa anxiously scanned the halls for a glimpse of long blond hair or a three-piece suit. At night, Melissa worked the circulation desk as much as possible, since her post kept the door in view.

On Wednesday evening, Johnny returned to the library. Melissa, suddenly shy, started flipping through the card file. Johnny set his books on the counter and leaned close. The intense way he stared at her forced Melissa to look back.

"Do me a favor," he said in a low voice.

With difficulty, Melissa broke his gaze. She then moved his books close to the metal box and began searching for their cards. "What favor?"

"Stop embarrassing me."

She wiped sweaty hands on her jeans and quickly slipped the cards into one book after another. "I don't know what you are talking about."

"Your obvious avoidance of me."

Something in the tone of his voice compelled Melissa to glance up, but his expression was emotionless. She shifted uneasily, and a thought struck her. Had the professor spread the rumor about Melissa asking him out? But...why?

She took a jittery breath. "It's a free county. You can date whom you please, and I can shun you as much as I like."

"It doesn't bother you that I'm engaged to someone else?"

"It's dinner," Melissa said crisply, wondering how long she could maintain the facade. She could never let Johnny see how intensely he affected her.

Johnny eased back from the counter and walked toward the stairs. Melissa organized the returns on the cart, which Pat rolled away. Two students and three more teachers interrupted her task. Fifteen minutes later, just as Mr. Schmidt headed for the men's room, Johnny returned with his selection, another music theory book.

"Don't you know this stuff by now?" Melissa said in a sharp voice. She removed the card from inside the book and handed it to the professor to sign.

Johnny picked up a pen. "I have a particularly dense student who requires much remedial work." He slid the signed card and the pen back to Melissa while meeting her eyes. "Must be the fashion."

Before she could open her mouth to retort, Johnny added, "Friday night, seven o'clock. Meet me in the staff parking lot, by security. I'm taking you to Rudy's in Shelby. Wear something suitable."

Book in hand, Johnny turned on his heel and strolled out of the library.

That night, still too keyed up for sleep, Melissa lay in bed, trying to block out Jill's snoring while replaying over and over in her mind the glorious exchange. In two nights, she would be having dinner with Johnny Simotes. Henry was so wrong! The beginning of John's and hers relationship had arrived, and Melissa's pulse sped up at the thought. Calm down, Melissa, she told herself. You still have two more days to go, but...*She was in!*

After Thursday's composition class, Melissa accosted Jenny at the door and asked her to cut class Friday afternoon in order to drive her to Jenson Mall to buy a dress.

"A dress? For what?"

Melissa looked around and whispered into Jenny's ear. Jenny backed away from Melissa and brushed her long bangs away from her face. Her round eyes opened even rounder in amazement and disbelief, as she exclaimed, "You're kidding!"

"Shhh."

Jenny dropped her voice. "Oh, Melissa, how'd you do it?"

"I didn't. *He* asked me."

Jenny's face fell. "I can't take you."

"What?"

"I've got a calculus quiz."

"Oh, Jenny, please! We're going to Rudy's, and I need a really nice dress."

"Rudy's? In Shelby?"

Melissa nodded.

"I hear it's gorgeous. The owners restored some old Victorian building and turned it into a restaurant and hotel. I'll bet its over a hundred years old." Jenny paused and then added, "Miss Garboldi lives in Shelby."

Melissa's heart dropped like a lead ball, but she said nothing. Seeing her downcast face, Jenny added, "I'll talk to my professor. Maybe if I tell her I have a doctor's appointment or something, she'll let me take the quiz early. But I'm not promising anything."

"Okay, thanks, Jenny! You're the only one I can trust."

Melissa recalled Julie's cool reaction after Melissa had asked Johnny out. She was certain Julie would be less than pleased with Melissa's news. If Jenny couldn't take her, Melissa doubted Julie would do it.

She next approached Mr. Schmidt, but to Melissa's astonishment, Mr. Schmidt excused her from working Friday night. Not only had Melissa broken employee rules by not requesting the night off one week in advance, she would be absent next Friday night as well, due to Ann and Jack's graduation party. In fact, Mr. Schmidt had smothered a smile when Melissa asked for the schedule alteration. It's almost like he expected it, Melissa thought. I wonder if he'd overheard any of my conversations with Johnny.

Jenny waved at Melissa from the back of Friday morning's breakfast line, and, with a knowing, euphoric smile and a wink, held up two ring-bedecked, chubby thumbs. Melissa acknowledged her friend with a casual nod and placed two slices of French toast on her plate.

Julie, standing behind Melissa while reviewing notes to that morning's psychology quiz, looked from her to Jenny and back again. "What's that all about?"

"Oh nothing." Melissa drizzled syrup over the bread. "Nothing important anyhow."

The vague answer did not satisfy Julie. "Hmmph," she said.

Few teens packed Jenson Mall on Friday afternoon, an apparent haven for all young mothers. They chattered liked robins while clutching the bitty hands of whiny toddlers and pushing their fussy babies in strollers, oblivious to the commotion.

"My kids will never behave that way," Jenny said, biting into a soft pretzel.

"Mine neither."

After patiently scanning racks of blousy, lace-trimmed, print frocks in three different stores to placate Jenny, Melissa selected a classic, A-line red dress with a shiny, black, vinyl belt. Another store produced a black patent leather purse and pair of matching shoes.

By now, Jenny had caught some of Melissa's excitement. With rosy cheeks and shining eyes, Jenny twirled her long beaded necklace and asked, "Want help getting ready?"

"Sure!"

Jill sat at her desk, scribbling out homework as fast as her hand allowed. She lived for weekend fun, but since Jill fully understood college parties co-existed with her classes, she would not jeopardize her standing in them. Jill had once told Melissa if any grades dipped below a "B," her parents would pull her tuition.

Melissa dumped her packages onto her bed, peeled off her clothes, and grabbed her robe and shower supplies. Jenny fished in Melissa's top dresser drawer for a blow drier and curling iron. Jill leaned back in her chair and watched, with interest, the unusual burst of animation on the other end of the room.

"Back in fifteen minutes," Melissa mumbled breathlessly, fumbling for the robe's sash as she hurried out the door.

"I'll be here," Jenny called back, unplugging Melissa's refrigerator and replacing it with the hair appliances.

Melissa zipped down the hall to the showers, thankful it was dinnertime since that all but guaranteed a free stall. She returned in eleven minutes flat and flew into her clothes. Jenny lay on Melissa's bed and skimmed through a magazine. Jill closed her notebook and observed with a bemused expression on her face.

"You're getting awfully dressed up, Melissa. Got a hot date?"

"Yep," Jenny said.

"With who?"

Melissa buckled her belt and did not answer. She slid her feet into the new shoes while reaching for the blow drier. Jenny tossed the magazine to one side and rolled off the bed.

"I'll do that for you," she said.

Jenny carefully dried and curled Melissa's hair and then retrieved the magazine. She leafed through the pages until she found the picture she wanted Melissa to see. The model's eyes were well-defined with liquid liner; the shimmery copper eye shadow lent a dreamy appearance.

"Want to look like that?" Jenny asked.

Melissa nodded, obediently closed her eyes, and sailed away to Bryony's room, but, when she reopened them, Jenny, not Bryga, was carefully tracing Melissa's lips with pencil. Besides, why pretend anymore? Melissa had John here, in the present time. Move over, Bryony, Melissa thought, and rest in peace. It's my turn.

"Top secret?"

Melissa started at Jill's voice, but she did not reply.

Jenny cocked her head to one side and ran her tongue over her lips as she scrutinized Melissa's face. "That gives you a nice night look. What do you think, Melissa?"

Melissa opened her closet, pulled the chain to the bare bulb, and studied herself in the cloudy mirror on the back of the door. Please make him think I'm pretty, she silently prayed. At least as pretty as Bryony and much prettier than Brenda Garboldi.

"Well," Jenny gave Melissa a careful hug, "Have fun! I have to go. Ronnie and the pizza will be here shortly."

"Thanks, Jenny!"

Head held high, Melissa strutted out the door and toward the stairs. However, as she drew close to the security entrance, Melissa's legs began shaking so hard, she curled her toes to keep from buckling. She stumbled to the door with as much dignity as she could muster and willed her chattering teeth to be still. The security guard, an upperclassman with several textbooks spread out before him, didn't notice Melissa's distress. Melissa glanced at her watch. Ten minutes to go. She leaned against the wall and ordered her racing heart to behave. Tonight, Melissa would have no rehearsed Bryony script to guide her. What would she say? How should she act? She checked her watch again. Nine minutes to go! She half-expected to see Henry in a three-piece midnight blue suit stroll through the door, apologize for the professor's tardiness, and then announce he was the substitute date for the night. Oh, what was taking Johnny so long?

The big hand on Melissa's watch had just covered the twelve when a dark blue car drove up and stopped. Melissa flew outside just as Johnny leaned across the seat to open her door, scanning the parking lot as he did so. This last act of the professor's unsettled Melissa a bit, but not enough to change her mind. He's just being cautious, Melissa told herself. Besides, if the professor felt that worried, why take me to Shelby? His fiancee lives there. Surely people must know him.

As Johnny pulled out of the parking lot, Melissa shyly peeped at him under the street lights and then caught her breath. Johnny was wearing a pewter pin-striped suit, which reminded her of the gray one he had worn to his and Bryony's wedding, where she had the privilege of repeating marriage vows to him, even as he said them to the minister's daughter. She was alone with Johnny Simotes, for real this time. Melissa couldn't believe her greatest hopes were being realized tonight!

They were nearing the outskirts of Jenson when Melissa realized Johnny had not yet spoken. Another clue the professor was John Simons. The nineteenth century pianist had also been short on words, which always left Melissa feeling uncertain and timid. This evening was different. If Johnny had not wanted to be with her, he would not have invited her to dinner.

Remembering Jason's narrow conversation frame, Melissa turned to Johnny and asked, "What kind of car is this?"

"Blue."

"I...I'm sorry?"

"If you could appreciate the make and model, you wouldn't have asked."

He turned to her with a slight smile, and Melissa relaxed.

"Johnny, you're right. All I need to know is how many wheels it has and whether or not it runs."

"Call me 'John.'"

"What?"

"I prefer John."

"I didn't know. That's how Brad introduced you."

"That's Hollywood for you."

John said nothing more, but Melissa scarcely noticed. The way he handled the car mesmerized her. He drove under the posted speed limit, kept a five-second distance between cars, and used turn signals with religious precision. He did not flick off the moron that abruptly pulled in front of him near Rudy's parking lot.

"Okay, now I'm amazed," Melissa said.

"By what?"

"My ex-boyfriend always tried to impress me with how fast he could drive."

He shrugged. "I value my life."

"Oh," she said, silently adding, I'll bet he does. Look what it cost him to regain it.

One step inside Rudy's, a large Queen Anne of reddish-brown stone, and Melissa knew Jenny had understated its elegance. To one side of the main lobby sat a concert grand piano, although not, Melissa thought smugly, a Schwechten. A wide, z-shaped staircase led to the upper levels; to the left opened the entrance to the restaurant. Dark wood walls contrasted with the bleached linens and sparkling chandeliers. The waiter, in a starched white shirt, red vest, and black bow tie, seated them at a back table. Melissa picked up the menu and paused to admire the real china cups and authentic silverware.

John removed the folder from her hands and returned it to the waiter. He then ordered prime rib for Melissa and him.

"Well done," John instructed.

As he waiter turned to leave, Melissa interjected. "Oh, rare for me, please."

The waiter nodded with a half-bow and departed. Well done? That either meant John was completely cured of his vampirism or the professor was not really....

Melissa immediately halted that dangerous line of thinking. Of course, Professor Simotes was John Simons. How could he not be? Even Julie said they could pass for twins.

John eased back into his chair and regarded Melissa with amusement, much as John Simons had observed Melissa that first night in her bedroom, almost an entire year ago. Looking back, Melissa recalled her fear of John as a vampire, yet John had spoken truthfully in his reassurances. He had not hurt her at all.

"So, Melissa, have you a habit of dating older, attached men?"

She blushed at the laconic question. Was he mocking her?

"No, this is the first time."

"Why me?"

Melissa hesitated. "You remind me of someone."

"Really? Who?"

"Someone...not alive anymore."

"Hardly flattering."

"Well, actually it is. He was a famous nineteenth century classical pianist by the name of John Simons. I'm surprised you've never heard of him, being a musician and all. I wrote a report on him when I lived in Munsonville. He married a local girl and built a mansion in the woods for them. She died in childbirth, and he...."

Here, Melissa stopped. She had almost said, "became a vampire." Had John noticed? Either he did not remember his previous existence, or he wasn't ready to admit it to Melissa. John's expression did not change as Melissa fumbled for the words.

"Um...he left town and no one ever heard of him again."

"Your family moved to Munsonville?"

"Yes, after my father died."

"Why would anyone move to Munsonville?"

"Have you been there?"

"It's a fishing village."

"Well, somehow my father wound up with a mansion belonging to this pianist. My mother didn't find out until after he died. The village wanted it for a tourist attraction, so she sold it to the village to pay for his medical bills. Then the board offered her a job, writing press releases and brochures and giving tours. After a few months, we moved back to Grover's Park."

"She didn't like the position?"

"No, the mansion burned down before the village restored it."

The waiter set their plates before them. John peered at her plate and feigned disgust. "How can you eat that?"

"What?"

"That."

She smiled. How unlike the John Simons she once knew. Obviously, Professor Simotes wouldn't be taking her blood tonight.

"So, I suppose, cooking it to the consistency of shoe leather improves its flavor?" Melissa teasingly asked, amazed at her brashness.

John winked over his wine glass.

The evening passed far too quickly. Before long, they were back at Jenson College. Melissa paused after John stopped the car near the cafeteria door. The memory of John's lips on hers, warm and insistent, when she was replicating Bryony, drowned all thoughts except one: *It's really going to happen.*

However, John merely smiled politely at her. Suppressing a sigh, Melissa reached for the door handle, but John, with a quick dart of his eyes, leaned his hand across the back of her seat and locked the door. Melissa held her breath, but the pounding in her ears was deafening. Melissa closed her eyes, and time stopped.

She heard a click, then a creak, and her eyes flew open. John had unlocked Melissa's door and was now offering his hand. John grew blurry against tears of disappointment. Do *not* cry, Melissa told herself.

"Thanks," she mumbled, forcing a cheerful smile while taking his hand, reveling in the warmth of his fingers and trying to act unruffled by the contact. She failed.

"Say 'hello' when you pass me."

"Will do."

Melissa paused. Again, nothing happened. As she started toward the cafeteria door, John gently caught her wrist. She stopped. Heart racing, she turned to look at him. He slowly moved his eyes along her face and farther down, then back up again. It was how John had looked at her the night of orientation; it was the way he had gazed at Bryony when he lifted her veil. Melissa could not breathe.

John leaned forward, and his lips barely met her cheek.

"Later," he said and abruptly drove away.

Who could sleep when every heartbeat banged out John's name? By two o'clock, the magical hour when John most commonly appeared in Melissa's bedroom, she had stopped checking the time. Although the date had not concluded the way Melissa had wanted, she considered the whole affair a good beginning, and Melissa decided to accept that. She no longer had to live on Bryony's memories. She and John could now make their own.

The next day, Jill slept late into the afternoon, so Melissa completed her homework and settled into bed with a novel and a nap that Melissa hoped would include a dream about John. She wanted to be rested for that evening's fundraiser. She yawned and turned a page, wondering who else would be bowling on their team. Melissa received her answer as Julie drove to Starlight Bowl.

"A couple of guys in Psych One," Julie said. "I heard them talking about bowling scores one day and found out they had bowled on a league together this past summer. They had no problem helping out a good cause."

Tracy draped her arms over the front seats and laughed. "The fact David has a crush on you helps, too."

Julie turned into the bowling alley parking lot. "It certainly didn't hurt."

The words *Starlight Bowl* sat atop a bright yellow half-dome on the building's roof. An asterisk replaced the "a" in "starlight," and the entire sign flashed blue. Connected to the alley was Crossroad's Tap, a favorite weekend hang-out for Julie and Tracy. Inside the bowling alley, gray stucco walls and brown paneling clashed with the plastic green seats and orange celestial patterns on the bright blue carpet. The girls pushed through the crowds.

Julie tugged Melissa's arm. "See that man?"

Melissa followed Julie's gaze to a tall, balding man polishing a turquoise bowling ball. His red and black polyester shirt tightly stretched over his stomach, also shaped like a bowling ball.

"What about him?"

"That's the mayor of Jenson. Even he's bowling." Julie walked toward the counter, and Melissa and Tracy trailed after her.

"Seven," Julie told the skinny, pimply-faced, slightly cross-eyed youth near the cash register.

He handed her a pair of white and navy saddles shoes and popped his gum.

"What lane are we on?" Julie asked.

"Name?" the boy's voice cracked, and he coughed twice.

"Julie Drake."

The boy scanned the spread sheets. "Twenty-four."

Melissa trudged after Julie and then settled down to remove her shoes. Students bowled at the west end of the alley, the teachers and staff met at the east end, and community participants stayed in the middle. Two boys shouldering matching blue-gray vinyl bags soon joined them. The taller boy had neatly combed sandy hair, gold-wire glasses, bow-shaped lips, and a serious face. His much thinner companion, with wispy brown hair and a scrawny mustache, winked at Tracy, and she blushed, the first time Melissa had seen her even slightly flustered. The boys unzipped their bags and removed shoes, several balls of different styles and weights, wrist braces, and monogrammed hand towels.

"I think I'm in the wrong place," Melissa said.

Julie set her own ball on the return and grinned. "You'll do fine. Let's go find you a ball."

They perused the racks of scuffed and chipped bowling balls, but that didn't help Melissa, despite Julie's patient suggestions. Even when Melissa's fingers fit into the holes, the ball weighed more than she could lift without breaking her wrist.

"Here, try this one," Julie held up a bright orange ball with black scuffs and *Terri* stamped in gold on its back.

Just then, John Simotes and Brenda Garboldi entered the alley. Both wore jeans, and they held hands. John's striped, collared shirt was slightly unbuttoned; Brenda's hair was pulled back with a thick, tortoise-shelled barrette, making her look as young as the college girls. Melissa scowled before she realized she was doing it. Why were they here?

Of course, Melissa remembered. As a music professor, John supported the fundraiser. Naturally, he would bring his fiancé. She ducked her head before he could see her, grabbed the ball from Julie, and then scurried back to her seat. By experimenting with her standing position and craning her neck, Melissa obtained a clear view of them.

Julie snapped her fingers before Melissa's eyes. "Quit daydreaming. Practice bowling has begun."

"I can bomb without practicing."

"Don't be so negative, sheesh."

That stung, but Melissa still managed only a listless roll. The ball veered straight to the gutter. Discouraged, Melissa plopped on a chair and watched the others knock down pin after pin. They made it look so easy.

She did no better the rest of the game. Between turns, Melissa watched lane eleven with growing resentment. Every time her teacher knocked over a single pin, John high fived her, or even worse, kissed her. Miss Garboldi looked thinner than Melissa, too.

"Hey, Melissa, you got a hundred," Julie cried, beaming. "That's not bad for the first game."

Julie could afford to be generous. She had scored one hundred and fifty three. Then Melissa noticed Julie's excitement at Melissa's score, so Melissa resolved to concentrate much harder on game two, for Julie's sake. However, between rolls, Melissa's eyes strayed back to Professor Simotes and Miss Garboldi. Why did they have to handle each other so much? By turns, John cradled Miss Garboldi's waist, draped an arm over her shoulder, or perched her on his lap. Melissa's stomach began to hurt.

"They're acting like a bunch of kids," Melissa said, then caught herself. She hadn't intended to say it aloud.

"Who is?" Julie picked up a rag and wiped her ball.

"Professor Simotes and Miss Garboldi."

Julie peered down the alley. "So what? They're in love. I've seen more action in the TV lounge on Friday nights. Come on, Melissa you're up. Tenth frame."

Smoldering with jealousy, Melissa picked up her ball. She approached the lane and stopped. Ten pins were waiting for her to knock them all down, but Melissa only saw Miss Garboldi's face. She heaved the ball with all her might and then stalked away. Julie squealed.

"Oh gosh, Melissa! You got a strike!"

Melissa turned around. Every pin lay flat, with four still spinning around.

"Come on, Melissa, do it again!"

She did not strike a second time, but Melissa did pick up the spare, for a total score of one hundred and thirty one.

Julie squealed with glee. "See? I knew you could do it!"

Tracy raised her plastic cup in the air. "Let's celebrate!"

She and Julie headed straight for Crossroad's Tap. Melissa wavered with indecision and then followed, silently protesting. Her feet felt as heavy as her heart. Her date with Professor Simotes was a sham. He obviously loved Miss Garboldi. Celebrate, really? Melissa longed to crawl under the blanket on Julie's floor and stay there.

"Can't we just bring something back to the room?"

Tracy quickly looked at Julie and then at Melissa, incredulity spreading over her face. "Why do that?"

"I hate crowds." Melissa did, too, unless she was attending a Victorian ball with John Simons.

"One beer and we'll leave," Julie promised. "It's festive this way."

Half the bowling alley poured into the tavern, or so it seemed to Melissa. She slowly eased onto a stool, and a frosted glass magically appeared. She reluctantly sipped the clear amber liquid and sullenly watched the silly behavior of the already intoxicated.

"Having fun?" Tracy shouted to her over the din.

Melissa shook her head and pushed away her drink. "I'm walking back to the dorm."

Tracy hadn't heard. She bent down her head, and the brown-haired boy who had bowled with them said something near her ear. The tavern door opened, and Brenda Garboldi and John Simotes entered, again holding hands. A teacher hailed them from the far corner of the room. Without looking either left or right, the pair soon joined them and disappeared amongst the masses.

"Can't they walk into a room without touching each other?" Melissa muttered, the resentment she brewed all evening flaring into open hostility.

"You sure you won't have one more?" Tracy said. "Come on, Melissa, relax for a change."

The view eluded Melissa, yet how could she leave now?

"Okay, Tracy, you win."

How fast Melissa drank that beer or the next one or the one that followed, she wasn't quite sure. Every movement at the other end of the tavern preoccupied her. Gradually, the crowd thinned out, revealing Professor Simotes and Miss Garboldi sitting at the back of a corner table, talking and smiling. The scene blurred. Melissa winked and jerked her head back to the bar. Her ears whirred; her head whooshed. She tried shaking away the cotton, but the room lurched, and Melissa instinctively grabbed the counter ledge. Sweat beaded on her forehead and trickled down her cheeks. Loud, chattering voices pressed against her. The walls crept close. Professor Simotes and Miss Garboldi had disappeared. Tracy's laugh floated away.

Air, Melissa thought. I need fresh air.

Melissa had just stumbled to the door when a hand grasped the back of her neck and pushed her outside and around the corner the precise moment she began vomiting. When her gagging became sputtering, the hand passed her a paper napkin.

"Here," said a voice Melissa knew all too well.

Melissa wiped her face. She began to shake. Closing her eyes, she leaned against the cool bricks. Night closed around her. Melissa wished it would swallow her whole.

"Thanks," Melissa stammered, crumpling the napkin, too mortified to look at him.

"Next time," John said, "don't drink so much."

That night, she and John hosted a garden party, but instead of setting up croquet on the rear grounds, John had ordered Jackson to prepare the lanes for bowling. Melissa stood poised, ball in hand, when Henry Matthews, light and cool in his cream-colored suit, black bow tie, and straw hat, walked up to her, ready to bowl.

"You!" Melissa exclaimed, exasperated that Henry, even in death, would remain the ever-present chaperone. "I thought you had died!"

"As Melissa, you would know that."

"I'm not Melissa. I'm Bryony."

"Not when you're with me."

With perfect form, Henry rolled the ball down the lanes. The ball bounced over the pins and hit the backboard. A thousand bells pealed.

"I won! I won! I won!" cried Kimberly.

Kimberly stood before the balloon game, clutching a walleye-shaped dart. Her head flopped at an odd angle. Lifeless eyes stared at the target.

"Let Shelly win," Melissa said.

"Don't you mean Shelby?" Kimberly retorted.

Melissa started, but Kimberly's lips hadn't moved. The bells clanged wildly. Melissa covered her ears. Oh, why wouldn't Kimberly claim her prize so they would stop?

"Give it to her already!" Melissa screeched at the barker.

Fr. Alexis turned around. "Answer the phone, Melissa."

"Let Jill get it," Melissa said aloud, pulling the blanket over her ears.

The ringing continued. Melissa threw back the covers. With half-closed eyes, she struggled to her knees and yanked the receiver off the wall. No wonder Jill wanted the side with the window.

Julie sounded stern. "Don't tell me you're still sleeping! I'm ready to go."

"Go... where?" Melissa stammered into the phone.

"The mall, remember? We're buying an engagement present for Ann and Jack."

"Later."

"No, not later. The party's next Saturday, and you're working all week. You *did* ask Mr. Schmidt for Friday night off, didn't you?"

Melissa tried to think past the jack hammer in her head. "Dunno."

"Well, get it together. I'll be at your door in twenty minutes."

"What time is it?"

"Almost noon."

Almost noon! Melissa eyes flew open and then automatically closed against the room's staggering light. She squinted past the knifing pain in her temples. Through clouded vision, she saw Jill lying on her back, mouth slightly ajar and one arm flung above her head.

"Okay."

It took three tries, but Melissa managed to connect the receiver with the base. She lay back again, head throbbing, and recalled another time she had felt this way, when the Bryony dreams began, and Dr. Anderson diagnosed her with anemia.

Well, no iron pill would erase last night's stupidity, a glaring admonition to halt her unhealthy obsession now, before something worse happened. Professor Simotes was not John Simons. He was engaged to her literature teacher. Feeding a vampire delusion was psychotic. Melissa had no idea why Professor Simotes had taken her to dinner, but he certainly had no romantic interest in her. Besides, Julie did not seem in the mood for any nonsense today, and they *did* have to find a present. Melissa could get through this, somehow.

She groped around the room for her clothes and toothbrush. Eventually, she stumbled to the bathroom and back. Julie knocked on the door as Melissa clumsily tied her last shoe.

"Sorry," Melissa said, speaking with effort. She still felt queasy.

Julie grinned. "It's college. Everybody does it once. You should've seen Tracy and me during orientation. Even better, you should talk to some of Katie's brothers. They're in their thirties, and they still go through this every weekend."

Melissa shuddered. "No thank you."

"Drink plenty of water, and I'll buy you a coffee. That helped me."

Jenson Mall on this Sunday afternoon was packed full with people of all ages, so different from the mommy crowd ruling the space on Friday. Could that only have been two days ago? With the meekness of a punished child, Melissa docilely plodded behind Julie, sipping lukewarm gas station coffee, and hoping Julie was right, that drinking it would ease the agony inside her skull. To her surprise, the pain, little by little, alleviated.

Although Julie forgave Melissa's hangover, her generosity did not extend to the reason for it. Melissa's preoccupation toward her literature teacher and Julie's piano professor irritated her.

"So he likes her," Julie said. "Forget it. There are plenty of fish in the sea. If you felt so desperate for a boyfriend, you shouldn't have broken up with Jason."

"I didn't break up with him," Melissa said defensively. "He broke up with me, remember?"

Julie sniffed. "Maybe. But you didn't try too hard to get him back, either."

Melissa changed the subject before the terse debate turned into a full-fledged argument. "What did you have in mind for a present?"

"Not sure. She's registered at Kylies. Let's see what's on her wish list."

They pooled their money and bought Ann her first set of dishes, embellished with blue forget-me-knots in the center and edged in a thin stripe of pale blue. Had Miss Garboldi gone through these motions, wandering through stores, selecting colors and patterns while dreaming of future years ahead with John? The vision pricked Melissa's eyes.

"I hope Ann likes it," Melissa said.

"She'd better. It cost enough."

Melissa had just entered her bedroom when Mr. Schmidt telephoned and asked if she could work for a few hours because someone had canceled at the last minute. Fresh hope sprang up in her heart before Melissa could squelch it. The throbbing between her ears had diminished; her stomach only slightly churned. She had a better chance of seeing John at the library than pining away in her room.

"I'll be right over," Melissa promised.

She had never worked a slower shift. Melissa saw only one student all evening, and she had come inside only to return a book. To pass the time, Melissa tackled three shelves of books waiting for both envelopes and cards. While she typed out cards and pasted folders into the books, Melissa monitored the front door.

At eight o'clock, Mr. Schmidt stepped behind the circulation desk.

"There's no point in staying any longer," he said. "I'll take over until closing time."

Melissa smoothed down the corners of a pocket as she looked up. "I don't mind finishing these."

"I'm not worried. They'll be here tomorrow."

She couldn't argue with her boss, so Melissa put away her supplies and clocked out.

She did not see John Simotes for the rest of the week. To fill the time, Melissa collected advance homework assignments from her professors. She fully intended to leave all traces of college in Jenson for two days so she could focus on memories of John, not Professor Simotes, while she visited Munsonville.

Jill seemed miffed when Melissa told her she'd be gone all weekend. "Well, haven't we turned into the social butterfly?"

"Oh come on, Jill," Melissa tossed a towel onto her overflowing laundry basket and checked her pocket for change. "You prefer I'm not in the room on weekends, anyhow."

On Tuesday, Melissa celebrated a mournful nineteenth birthday with Julie and Tracy by sharing the care package of homemade chocolate chip cookies from her mother. As she prepared to blow out nineteen candles, Melissa pledged this to herself: *No more Professor John Simotes.*

Tracy's face fell. "Now your wish won't come true," she said, glancing at the lone, flickering flame.

With a brief glance at Melissa, Julie pulled out the candles. "Maybe that's good."

Birthday wish or no birthday wish, five minutes before closing time on Thursday night, John Simotes walked into the library, directly where Melissa stood restocking the magazine rack, and said, "I'm going out for a sandwich."

John's voice sounded so low, Melissa had to lean slightly forward to catch it.

"Hungry?" John asked softly, close to her ear.

"Starving!"

Melissa quickly positioned the last of the periodicals and rushed the cart back to the circulation desk. Mr. Schmidt glanced up as she flew past him, and Melissa slowed, praying he wasn't that discerning. She turned to leave. Professor Simotes had already left.

"Have a good time this weekend," was all Mr. Schmidt said.

Keeping a furtive eye on her employer, Melissa casually sauntered to the door, but the second the librarian bent over his work, she dashed outside. John was waiting inside the car across the street.

"Thank you for the invitation," Melissa said, speaking carefully as she shut the door, hoping John couldn't hear the excitement in her voice.

Without a word, John pulled away from the curb and toward the middle of town. He remained silent throughout the short trip, and Melissa wondered why he had invited her in the first place. He seemed too preoccupied to want company. Was he upset with her again? Maybe, Melissa hoped with crossed fingers, he and Miss Garboldi were fighting.

John's avoidance of her continued even after they had reached Jenson Family Restaurant, and he had placed orders for two club sandwiches. The bus boy arrived with glasses of ice water, and the waitress soon returned with iced tea and hot coffee. Was John waiting for her to initiate conversation? After all, Melissa *had* been the one to avoid him at school.

She toyed with the outrageous idea of inviting John to Ann and Jack's engagement party and then decided to risk it.

With a deep breath, Melissa said, "Have you made plans for this weekend?"

John looked away from the window. "Yes."

So much for that, Melissa thought, as her heart plunged with fresh disappointment. "Business or pleasure?"

"Both."

The waitress arrived with their food. "More tea?"

Melissa shook her head. "No, this is fine, thank you."

The waitress ripped their bill from her pad and moved to the next table.

"I'm seeing friends Saturday night," John continued, as if no breach had occurred, "and I'm a presenter at a seminar in Thornton on Sunday."

"Where's Thornton?"

"Half-hour west of Shelby."

"Oh."

John stayed just as quiet on the return trip. Tonight, however, he did not pull into the back of the cafeteria. Instead, he swung the car into the staff parking lot and stopped at the far end, in front of the tall hedges bordering the empty road.

"I'll walk you to the building," John said. "The car's staying here overnight."

"How will you get home?" Melissa asked in surprise.

"I live across the street."

"Then why do you…?"

"Drive to work? I don't always go straight home."

Melissa's face grew hot. She knew that. He went to Shelby, of course. She blindly groped for the door handle. She had to leave, now, even if only to hide the bitter disappointment and frustration filling her eyes. *She had misjudged John's intentions again!* Why did she keep torturing herself?

"Melissa, stop."

He leaned near, cupped her face with one hand, and gently turned her. Melissa quickly blinked away tears and melted into John's warm fingers. Her mind whirled. It's a dream, she told herself, expecting to awaken in the next moment. This is just a twisted Bryony dream. The hazy light from the distant lamp pole illuminated the frenzy in John's eyes as they searched hers. Melissa sat rigid, scarcely breathing, anticipating the impending jangling of her alarm clock.

"It's strange," John said, "but I feel we've met in another place, or....

John paused and inched closer. "....another time."

Melissa throat tightened. The stillness of the night roared in her ears. John's breath grazed her mouth.

"Does that make sense to you?"

She nodded, too astounded for words, petrified she'd pierce the elusive magic. Sleep, sleep, stay asleep, she silently begged, as John closed his eyes and swept a feathery stroke across her lips. This can't be happening, Melissa thought. *Oh, God, this is real!*

Taking her head in his hands, John kissed her in earnest this time, gently, then harder and faster until Melissa released her pent up desire for John and met those kisses with a fervor that astonished her.

She touched his face and ran her fingers through that glorious hair, then to his shirt and down, farther than she had ever touched him, not even in Munsonville, not even when she was playing Bryony. By the time John opened his eyes and smiled at her, Melissa knew what she wanted to know.

If John Simotes had ever been a vampire, he wasn't one now.

CHAPTER 5: UNDER THE STARS

The sudden brightness of headlights startled Melissa as a car slowly drove past them, but it was the glint of the ballpoint pen in John's shirt pocket that smacked her into nineteen seventy-five. *She was kissing the college's music professor!* She pulled back, but John slid closer and gently kissed the tip of her nose.

"Relax. It's only security. They patrol all night."

"It's getting late," Melissa hedged. "I've got an early class."

"I'll walk you back."

John did not touch Melissa nor talk to her as they crossed the dark parking lot to the main building. The abrupt, unsettling turnaround in his attitude forced Melissa to question her actions, what she was doing and to whom. Why hadn't she recalled Jill's words until now?

"You did know he's got a reputation for sleeping with his students, but he's always the one who calls the shots."

Me and my vampire fantasies, Melissa glumly thought, wishing John would just ditch her and go home. What a fool I've made of myself, playing into the moves of a cad. She remembered how quickly asking John to dinner spread around the campus and wondered just how soon her friends would hear of the events in the parking lot. Why couldn't she let last year's dreams, obviously the product of grief and some transient anemia, just go? *You will not make him love you*, Henry had said. Maybe, she needed more professional help than even Fr. Alexis, who had counseled her when the vampire dreams grew dangerous, could provide.

"I have to go around to the front," Melissa said. "Security locks this door after ten o'clock."

John made no reply, but he turned toward the main entrance. When they reached the building's edge, John stopped.

"I'm heading in the other direction. I'll watch until you're safely inside.

"Thanks."

Melissa held her head high as she left him, but she felt stupid, ashamed, and thoroughly crushed at the thought of never, never making contact with Professor Simotes again. Doing so was trouble, trouble on more levels than Melissa was prepared to handle. Please, please, please, Melissa wordlessly pleaded. Don't let anyone find out about tonight. I will be good. I promise. She made it all the way to the front door before yielding to the overwhelming urge to glance behind her. John had disappeared.

As she stepped into the building, Melissa sighed without meaning to do it. She nodded to the student security guard and then plodded down the deserted corridor. Yet, even as she climbed the stairs to the third floor, Melissa couldn't help smiling at the memory of the evening's final activities, but her spirits dropped when she remembered that, despite her resolution, she would not cross John's path this weekend. Melissa was going to Munsonville; he was lecturing in Thornton. The realization filled her with loneliness and a desperate longing for John. She then remembered the night Simons Mansion burned down, the night that John had killed Henry with the vampire weapons from the library. What would the estate be like without the mansion sitting at the top of the hill?

Melissa fumbled under the dim hallway lights for her key. Once inside, she avoided turning on the light. She wasn't prepared for Jill's interrogation. Instead, Melissa kicked off her shoes and lay down on her bed fully dressed, too tired for any more tasks. She'd worry about a shower in the morning.

With the highway behind them, Melissa leaned her head back into the seat as Julie turned onto the very familiar two-lane road leading into Munsonville. Although it was mid-October, the Indian summer sun beat down as warm as the foliage's bold reds, oranges, and yellows.

"Almost there," Julie said with cheerfulness. "Welcome home, Melissa."

Home? Melissa desperately wanted Simons Mansion for her home, but Simons Mansion existed only in memory.

She forced a limp smile. "It's good to be back."

Melissa couldn't help smiling in earnest, though, when Julie drove past the familiar sign: *Munsonville. Population: 386. Everyone Welcome Here.*

"That sign never changes?" Melissa asked.

"Nope. We're allowed one birth for every death. It keeps the population consistent."

That was Munsonville on its surface, predictable. The buildings dotting both sides of Main Street still resembled Western storefronts with wood signs to identify them. Sue's Diner remained dingy, squat, and gray. The black-top still looked brand-new. Julie turned left up Bass Street. That's when she told Melissa that Katie's parents, not the Daltons or Coopers, were hosting Ann and Jack's engagement party.

"How come?"

"Ever visit Katie?"

Melissa shook her head.

"The Millers own this huge house at the top of Blue Gill Road, right next to the cemetery. Ann's house is too small for a crowd, and Jack's parents live in one of the fishing cottages. They had considered shutting Sue's Diner for the night and throwing the party there, but Jack's dad didn't want to lose the revenue. So, Katie's mom and dad offered to have the party."

"That's nice of them."

"It's not like they don't have the room. Katie's the youngest of nine, all brothers, too, except for one sister two years older than she. Makes me glad I'm an only child."

"I've only got one brother. He's not too bad, now that he's getting older."

"Katie's brothers are in their twenties to late thirties, but they're still obnoxious. Her oldest has kids. I can only imagine the ruckus at Christmas. I'd rather have cats."

Melissa had never spent the night at Julie's house. The one time she and her Munsonville friends had gathered for a sleepover, everyone had wanted to stay at the servant's cottage, Melissa's home at the time. None of them had ever stayed all night on Simons Estate, especially on Halloween.

Julie's mother, short and plump with steel hair wrapped into a bun and a smiling face full of wrinkles, was washing dishes when Julie and Melissa walked through the back door. At the sight of the girls, Mrs. Drake hastily wiped her hands across her apron and reached inside the cupboard for two glasses.

"Would you like some cookies?" Mrs. Drake said, setting the glasses on the counter. "They're almost done." She opened the refrigerator and removed a carton of milk.

The Drakes' square kitchen, scarcely big enough for its round table, nevertheless felt pleasantly homey, with its polished wood floors and white walls, cupboards, and counters. The blue and white striped glass plates neatly stacked in the drying rack matched the blue and white striped canisters on the cupboard shelves and the limp towel hanging from a handle drawer. A blue teapot, ready for duty, rested on a back burner. The air smelled of cinnamon and cloves.

"Thanks, Mom. We're taking our suitcases upstairs first." Julie turned to Melissa. "I hope you don't mind sharing with me. We only have two bedrooms."

"Not at all." Melissa, who had never shared a room, except with her mother, when they had stayed in Detroit last year and at Munsonville Inn the night of the fire, was now accustomed to roommates, thanks to college. "It'll be fun."

"You won't have to sleep on the floor, either."

At the top of the stairs, Melissa saw a tiny bathroom directly in front of her with two small bedrooms on either side. The landing was so small, Melissa and Julie could not fit on it at the same time. Julie turned left, and Melissa followed her. Julie's bedroom contained the simplest of furnishings: two twin brass beds with matching brown chenille bedspreads and one tall dresser between them. A desk stood opposite on the south wall; pleated curtains matched the single beige rag rug on the floor. The roof slanted and formed a peak. Three large hooks were screwed into the wall left to the door. The room had no closet. On one of the beds, a large striped cat was curled up and either purring or snoring, Melissa could not tell which.

Melissa stood in the doorway, suitcase in hand. "Why two beds?"

"My mother bought the pair on sale. The second one came in handy whenever Katie or Ann spent the night."

"Which one's mine?"

Julie shrugged. "Doesn't matter. I've slept in both."

Melissa didn't meet Julie's father until dinner. Mr. Drake, white wispy hair hair combed over his large pink bald spot and as short and plump as his wife, took quite seriously his duty of house entertainer.

"Okay, Melissa, here's another one," Mr. Drake said, wiping his eyes. "A duck walked into a bar, asked for a martini, and told the bartender to put it on his bill."

Julie groaned and dropped her head into her hands. "Come on, Dad, Melissa doesn't want to hear your old jokes."

"Sure she does. Hey, Melissa, did you ever hear the....?"

Mrs. Drake interjected. "Sam, maybe our guest would like more chicken casserole."

"Oh not for me, please, I'm full," Melissa protested. "I will, however, take another joke."

Mr. Drake beamed. "I've been on so many blind dates I should get a free dog."

Julie and her mother exchanged pained glances. Mrs. Dalton pushed her chair away from the table and began stacking dishes. Melissa followed. Julie was already rolling cloth napkins back into their holders. Mrs. Dalton paused, looking worried.

"Girls, that's just not necessary," Mrs. Dalton said, with real distress in her voice.

"Sure it is. Take a break tonight, Mom. Melissa and I will clean up."

"Come on, Mother." Mr. Drake stood up. "I'll take you into town for an ice cream. You girls want something?"

"No, thanks, Dad. We're fine."

Melissa and Julie finished clearing the table as the Drakes prepared to leave. Melissa overheard Mr. Drake say, "Mother, I'm so glad I hired Eric Miller. He sold three cars today...."

Julie filled the sink with generic pink liquid soap and showed Melissa where to find a fresh towel.

"Thanks for being a good sport." Julie handed her the first plate to dry. "My mother takes her role as domestic goddess way too seriously."

"I don't mind. I helped all the time when my dad was sick."

"Well, I wished she'd find a hobby, now that the nature center's closed."

Melissa almost dropped the plate. "It closed! Why?"

"No money to keep it open. The stupid village invested all its resources into Simons Mansion. By the way, Eric Miller is one of Katie's brothers. He's twenty-three and a hunk! That's what I mean about this dump. He could be modeling, but he's content to work at a used car lot."

They finished the last of the dishes just as the Drakes returned. Mr. Drake opened the pantry door and pulled down a stack of board games. Julie rolled her eyes.

"It's been a full week, Dad, and we're helping Katie's mom cook tomorrow."

"Well...okay." Mr. Drake, looking disappointed, set the boxes on the kitchen table. "We hardly see you anymore."

"I'll be back in a few weeks."

Mr. Drake's face brightened. "We have a television now!"

"Not tonight, Dad."

The girls had climbed halfway up the stairs when Melissa heard Mr. Drake say, "Mother, regular checkers or Chinese?" Julie shut her bedroom door, disgust plainly showing on her face.

"What's wrong?" Melissa asked.

"Her name's Barbara," Julie dropped onto her desk chair and opened a psychology textbook. "I hate how he depersonalizes her by calling her, 'Mother.'"

Melissa wished now she hadn't completed all her homework early. What would she do all night, brood over the empty space at the top of the hill? Maybe she should have waited for student teaching before coming to Munsonville. Besides, she didn't understand Julie's annoyance.

"Your dad is cute." Melissa glanced at Julie to gauge her reaction. "He was so excited about having TV."

"If you say so. It's an eight inch black and white. If he's lucky in adjusting the rabbit ears, he can tune in two channels."

The next morning, immediately following the pancake and sausage breakfast Mrs. Dalton insisted on cooking, Melissa and Julie walked to Katie's house, a tall boxy, slightly dilapidated three-story, with gray wood siding and green shutters, where shutters remained. Chipped concrete steps led up to the front door. The back yard stretched into the woods.

Julie poked Melissa's ribs. "We've had tons of fun playing hide 'n' seek here."

Mrs. Miller, a tall, broad-shouldered, muscular woman whose tightly knotted yellow bun showed just a hint of gray, kept Julie and Melissa running to Harper's Grocery all afternoon for one item and after another. Katie, kerchief tied on her head and brandishing a feather duster, had the fun of cleaning all three stories and finished basement. That's where the Millers, Julie said on one of their many trips into town, had a recreation room that ran the entire length of their house.

Melissa and Julie had just reappeared when Mrs. Miller said, "Girls, I forgot olives. Will you go buy a couple of jars?" They set their purchases on the table and headed back to the door.

"Why didn't Mrs. Miller just sit down and make a list?" Julie complained to Melissa during their fourth trek down the hill.

Despite working around Mrs. Miller's chaos, a festive mood ruled the kitchen, interspersed with the whining and bickering of Mary, Sherry, and Harry, the three oldest kids belonging to Katie's oldest brother, Gerald Jr. Their mother, Patty, looked as young as Katie, except Patty was skinny. She also still had adolescent acne, a shiny pug nose, thinly plucked eyebrows, and dirty blonde hair caught in a high pony tail. Katie still parted her hair on the side and held it in place with a gold metal barrette. Everyone laughed and gossiped while cooking huge pots of barbecue, peeling bag after bag of potatoes for salad, and arranging trays of deviled eggs and celery with cream cheese. Melissa scraped and sliced bagfuls of carrots for the relish tray and pretended to be a Simons Mansion cook. Julie methodically cut-up chicken. Katie's older sister Cara, humming to a pop song on the radio, salted, peppered, and floured the chicken. Mrs. Miller worked the deep fryer, and, when she filled the oven, Katie ran the pans to the neighbor's house to keep the chicken pieces warm.

"How many people are coming tonight?" Melissa said, as she covered another bowl of potato salad with plastic wrap.

A loud wail came from the next room. Melissa had forgotten about Baby Larry, sleeping in a playpen in the parlor. Patty dropped the peeler, quickly pumped water over her hands, and dashed from the room.

"Oh, about eighty," Mrs. Miller said, bending over to sweep a large pile into the dustpan. Katie was washing her fifth batch of dishes. "When you're done with these, you can decorate."

Julie and Melissa spent the last hour before the party hanging leftover streamers and balloons from decades of Miller birthday parties. In the meantime, Katie decorated a

Congratulations Ann and Jack poster with brightly colored markers. They had just finished when Ann and Mrs. Cooper arrived. Ann looked the same as last year, except her for the permanent wave in her shoulder length, chestnut hair. Mrs. Cooper, a slender, petite, graying brunette with tired eyes, was carrying a large sheet cake. Soon afterward, the first guests, all middle-aged and older, poured through the door.

"Let's go up to my room," Katie said. "We can hang out there for awhile."

Julie paused at the bathroom door. "I'll be up in a sec."

Melissa and Ann followed Katie up the stairs, climbed another staircase to the two attic bedrooms at the top of the house, and then turned right to enter Katie's bedroom. Katie shut the door behind her, and the downstairs noise became muffled.

Both the slanted roof and the floors were white-painted board; pictures from hairstyling magazines covered most of the white plaster walls on one side. Each length of the room held a twin bed, its metal frame also painted white. Above each bed, a steel pole spanned the ceiling. Someone had threaded white sheets onto the poles, which could be drawn for privacy. A few hand-sewn dresses hung off those same poles beyond the foot of the beds. Both sides of the room had a tall white dresser with an attached narrow mirror. The room boasted just one window. Upon it hung a pair of white curtains fabricated from old sheets. Katie sat cross-legged on the bed farthest from the door and invited Melissa and Ann to join her. Next to her bed sat a blue-green, hard plastic traveling case: *Molly Blake School of Beauty.*

"I like your hair," Melissa said, wondering where Ann's aspirations for wealth and fancy living had gone in less than a year.

Ann's hand instinctively patted an invisible strand into place. "Katie did it, for the party."

"Have you really set a wedding date?" Melissa said.

Ann's eyes sparkled with happiness through her tortoise shell glasses. "Valentine's Day weekend. I can't wait."

"So what happened?"

"Jack invited me to a movie in Jenson right after you moved back to Grover's Park. And well, things progressed from there."

Katie giggled and wriggled with excitement. "I'm maid of honor."

The door banged open.

"Melissa!" Julie cried. "He's here!"

"Who?"

"Professor Simotes!"

"No!"

Melissa scrambled to her feet and fled to the mirror. *What was John doing here?* Wasn't he going to Thornton? Had he lied to her, or had he discovered her weekend plans and schemed to surprise her? Did that mean he really cared for her? Had Melissa a decent chance with him?

"Who's that?" Ann said, looking confused.

"He's a music professor at Jenson College and the spitting image of the painting of John Simons at the library." Julie suspiciously eyed Melissa. "Anyway, Melissa's infatuated with him."

Ann yawned and twisted her engagement ring, a mere chip attached to a thin strand of wire. "What's some old professor doing here tonight?"

Katie leaned against the wall. "He's not that old. He went to school with Al and Ben."

Melissa, heart racing, turned away from the mirror. "You met him here? In Munsonville?" She could not believe it. Hadn't John said he'd never been to Munsonville?

"No, you silly goose, not here. They'd all gone to Michigan State together, so when Ben got married last year, Professor Simotes joined the wedding party." Katie slid a pillow behind her head. "Melissa's really got a crush on him?"

"She asked him out."

Katie frowned, thinking. "Isn't he engaged? That's what Al told Mom."

"He is. He turned Melissa down."

Ann stretched and rolled off Katie's bed. "I'm going downstairs. Jack's probably looking for me."

Katie bounded after Ann. Melissa began to follow, but Julie barred the door. "I hope you're not trying anything funny tonight."

"Who, me?"

Down below, the party had already subdivided itself. Katie's brothers and their friends had congregated in the family room; their loud, boisterous voices drifted through the floor and cracks of the basement door. The Millers and other parent-types hung about most of main floor, bragging about their children and gossiping about their neighbors. The tall, bulky, and gray Mr. Miller didn't join them. He was heading for the basement with a plunger. The teens, as well as Katie's younger siblings, sat in the dining room and played cards. They drew for partners, which paired Melissa with Jack. He had filled out a bit, and his brown hair curled about his ears, but Jack still looked as cute as the first day she had seen him bussing tables at Sue's Diner. Melissa might have been jealous of Ann's good fortune, if she was not so in love with John. Julie was paired with Eric, who was definitely every bit as handsome as Julie had described, with spiky blond-brown hair, bushy black eye brows, deep blue eyes, and perfectly shaped lips. Ann played opposite Katie's youngest brother, Nate Miller, cute in a quiet, Jack Cooper way. Stocky Pete had blond-brown hair and blue eyes, but both were significantly lighter than Eric's,

They played for three solid hours until Julie threw down her cards in exasperation.

"I'm out," she said, "and hungry. I'm getting some food. How about you, Melissa?"

Melissa nodded. "I can't play anything else either. Sorry, Jack."

Making their way into the kitchen, they passed Mr. Miller. He was now traipsing up the stairs with the same plunger. Julie nudged Melissa's arm with her elbow and nodded her head. Melissa followed her gaze. John was tucking a paper napkin under his chin while balancing a full of plate of food in one hand and reaching for his beer can with the other. That wasn't the reason Melissa froze at the sight. John, dressed in jeans and a gray and blue striped, button-down shirt, looked so...good. He hadn't noticed her, but Melissa remembered her promise to acknowledge him.

"Hello," she said, prying apart a paper plate from the stack on the counter.

The basement door opened, and a rush of noise flooded the kitchen.

"Hey, Johnny!" a voice called, and without a word to Melissa, John descended into that nether region. The door shut, and the clamor once again became muffled. Melissa choked back tears.

"Sorry, Melissa," Julie said as she scooped potato salad onto her plate.

Melissa hoped she sounded nonchalant, despite her trembling lips. "About what?"

"I thought he was rude."

"It's no big deal," Melissa said in a low voice.

Disappointment strangled Melissa's throat; she couldn't swallow her food. She pushed it around her plate, pretending to eat it, and then she threw it away when no one was looking. At ten o'clock, Mrs. Miller finally decided to cut the cake.

"I forgot a knife and spatula!" Mrs. Miller clapped a hand to her forehead.

"I'll get them," Melissa offered, confident she could find the necessary items after spending so much time in the kitchen earlier in the day. She was just pushing the drawer close when she saw Professor Simotes wandering around the back yard. She strained for a closer look, but he had disappeared from view. What was he doing back there?

Last year in her Bryony dreams, during a Simons Mansion party, a woman lost her life in the gazebo. Was someone here in danger? Maybe the vampire fantasy was no delusion. Maybe Professor Simotes wanted to confuse Melissa regarding his true identity. Maybe he really was John Simons. Maybe his transformation from vampire to human was incomplete. Maybe he was planning to attack and kill a guest. With so many people gathered in one place, he could probably get away with it. No one might discover his awful deed until morning, when it would be too late. No one would even suspect John. He'd be far away, in Thornton.

She returned to the dining room. "Here's the knife, Mrs. Miller."

The guests crowded around Ann and Jack. Melissa grabbed her jacket from the hall closet and slipped out the back door, astonished at how chilly it had become. Why, the temperature must have dipped thirty degrees since the afternoon. Melissa pulled up the zipper and hugged herself even as she strained to see past the shadows of trees in the moonless night. Not a soul, not a sound. Nothing.

She turned the corner of the house where she had seen John vanish. Except for a few overgrown bushes, the area was desolate. She had let her imagination overrule sound judgment once again. Even if John had ventured outside, he was probably enjoying a nice piece of cake by now. She heard a rustle on her right, and, with a start, noticed she was only several feet away from the cemetery in her dreams, where Henry had dubbed her "food."

"Boo," said a low voice close to her ear.

Melissa jumped, whirled around, and saw John softly chuckling at her distress. Shaking, yet very much relieved immediate harm was unlikely, Melissa managed only a feeble smile. "Gosh, you scared me!"

He teetered forward, his nose almost touching hers, an impish grin spreading across his face.

Melissa blurted, "They're cutting the cake. What are you doing out here?"

"Taking a leak."

Suddenly embarrassed, Melissa looked away and wished she had stayed inside. Was John drunk? She didn't really have much experience with intoxicated people, only Jill and the idiots she had observed after the bowling fundraiser last weekend at Crossroads Tap. Steve enjoyed a cold beer after cutting the grass on a hot summer day and occasionally he and her mother split a bottle of white wine. Her father had enjoyed sipping an occasional martini.

"How much have you…?"

"Shhh." John placed a finger on her lips.

Melissa's heart nearly stopped at John's unexpected touch. Before she could respond, John took her hand and started toward Katie's driveway. "Let's go."

"Go...where?"

"I'd like a tour of Munsonville."

"Now? This late?" Melissa grew uneasy and thought of her friends waiting inside for her. What if this man was John Simons? What if he wasn't? "Can't we go tomorrow?"

"I have a seminar in Thornton, remember?"

Melissa hesitated. Was it safe? Yet, how could she miss this chance with John?

"Um, let me tell someone I'm leaving."

"Why? They'll never miss us. Munsonville can't be that big."

"It's one short street."

"Well then."

Melissa relented and allowed John to lead her as he staggered across Katie's driveway and down the hill of Blue Gill Road toward Main Street. The only gleam brightening the velvet night was the occasional living room lamp. Strangely, despite the chilly air, Melissa no longer felt cold. The warmth of John's hand crept up her arm and radiated throughout her entire body until desire for John, whoever he was, filled her being. She dared not look at him.

They had reached the deserted Main Street. Hand in hand, they walked down one side and then back, with Melissa pointing out the various buildings.

"This is the grocery store. That's Dalton's Dry Goods; Ann's dad owns that one. There's Sue's Diner, which Jack's family runs, and where, believe it or not, the food's really good."

John winked at her. "Too bad I'm not staying another day. You owe me a meal, as I recall."

Melissa blushed, glad this time for the darkness. Was John joking, or was he planning to officially see her again? He was here, now, so didn't that mean....?

Stop, Melissa told herself. Remember your promise. This time doesn't count. You didn't know he was coming to

Munsonville. Stick to the facts. John asked for a tour, not a lifetime commitment.

"There's the library. Inside is a painting of John Simons that looks just like you."

"How amusing."

Something in John's inflection jarred her. He was staring down at her as John Simons had the night he first kissed her, on the balcony at Albert Brumfeldt's home, after Melissa had panicked at the malevolent beings sharing her dream. She looked up at Professor Simotes. He *was* John Simons, wasn't he? *Wasn't he?*

"That big red brick building on the end is the school." Melissa hoped her voice didn't sound as shaky as it felt. "All twelve grades are under one roof. That's where I had the English teacher that inspired me to become one, too."

"Your reason for attending Jenson."

"Yes, well, I had won a contest that led to receiving a full scholarship."

Melissa knew she was babbling, but luckily John wasn't paying attention. Still holding her hand, he led Melissa over the bike trail and past the row of fishing cottages to the edge of Lake Munson. The murky water licked the shore with gentle, easy waves.

John leaned forward for a closer look. "I hear the fishing's good."

"It is. So are the leeches. We had a science teacher once bring a jarful to class. He collected them right from this lake."

They continued in silence along the path. At the woods, John immediately tightened his hold and increased his pace. Frightened, Melissa dug her heels into the soft earth and tugged back.

"We...we're not going in there, are we?" she timidly asked.

Images of the past whirred in her mind: a full-suited man crouching on all fours, a Newfoundland screeching with demonic fury, a thick, strangling mist.

A sudden yank caught Melissa off-balance. John had crossed the threshold and was pulling Melissa into solid blackness. John faded to a mere shadow, and Melissa stumbled, unseeing, after him. She anxiously looked around and halfheartedly attempted to reclaim her hand. No mist, thank God.

Still, she tried again. "This late? In the dark?"

John stopped and slowly, slowly looked over his shoulder. A queer glint lit his eyes; a cunning smile passed his lips. Melissa's mouth went dry.

"You're not afraid, are you, Melissa?"

Was she afraid? Was he reassuring her? Mocking her? Why did he look like that? *You're playing a dangerous game,* Henry had warned her. *Too bad it's not your game.* She shrank back, but John squeezed harder.

"I...."

Unformed words. A million objections. Terror colliding with aching, wrenching, ravenous yearning. This was John. He was real, now, in this moment. Nothing, nothing, nothing else mattered. Melissa surrendered.

John strode quickly, determinedly, into the woods. Night dropped like a heavy curtain and swallowed the blacktop. Gnarled silhouettes guarded both sides of the path; arthritic arms poised for attack, while others stretched into the sky and clasped twisted hands in macabre solidarity, a sinister outline against the coal-black sky. Winding shades swayed, taunted, and melted into pixels. John passed the entrance to Simons Mansion and continued into the deep part of the woods. They jogged to the nature center and away, on and on into endless, ageless void. Melissa stumbled, faltered, and John briefly slowed until she again steadied her pace. The woods whispered unearthly, disquieting hushes; John's footsteps pounded in her ears. A cramping spasm, a searing pain shot from side to shoulder, and Melissa yelped.

"Please, stop!" Melissa gasped out.

And John abruptly did, dropping her hand. Melissa bent over and massaged her stomach. She shuffled off the road and leaned against a tree, panting, as breathless from fright as the dash into the woods. John waded into weeds and vanished amongst the trees.

"John?"

Silence, except for the easy swishing of grasses and light rippling of leaves.

"John?"

Melissa took a hesitant step, afraid to move, afraid to remain.

"John!"

Nothing. Where was he? *Oh, God, he wasn't leaving her?*

"John!"

A snap, a splash, a grunt, and Melissa, heart racing, plunged into the weeds after John, bracing against trees and clawing through high grasses toward the sound. Gradually, the copse dwindled; Melissa's eyes widened; and her mouth dropped. John was pushing a rowboat toward the lake. He saw her, stood erect, and wiped his sleeve across his face.

"Where'd you get that?" Melissa said, hurrying to meet him, surprise momentarily displacing her fear.

"Borrowed it."

"From...where?"

Leering, John merely wagged a finger at her.

"You're not taking it out there!"

He offered his hand.

"But..." Melissa scanned the dark waters. "Isn't this dangerous?"

"Melissa, you don't trust me?"

Did she? Melissa wavered. John, hand still outstretched, wore a half-beguiling, half-wily expression. What should she do? She glanced at the ghostly trees, the opaque lake, and back to John himself. Who was she kidding? She wasn't mentally debating; she was stalling. Melissa knew what she wanted to do.

She stepped forward and slipped her hand into his. He assisted her into the boat, and, with one final push, sprang into it. The boat tipped far to one side, then back again. Melissa screamed; John shifted his balance and stifled her with a clap of his hand.

"Don't," John said, with a long and menacing look. "You'll spoil it."

He settled onto the opposite bench and assumed the oars; the boat swayed in a most erratic way and then steadied. Melissa gripped the sides and looked uncertainly at John, but he stared back, insistent and aloof, while dragging the craft into the middle of Lake Munson. Melissa remembered another boat ride on a sunny afternoon, as delectably full of promises as Bryga's picnic basket. She recalled the majestic sunset, the heavenly strokes, the searing pain.

"I learned how to row once," Melissa said and then faltered at John's dispassionate, fixed gaze.

The moon, hidden all night, now peered from behind a cloud, scattering gauzy beams across the water, and reflecting an ethereal glow over John's face. The barest hint of a smile danced on John's lips, but his eyes still gripped hers as he rowed in perfect, measured time. Melissa, drowning under John's intensity, blinked away and studied the trees, the moon, and the ripples from the oars, but all the time she sensed John's eyes drilling into her.

An eternity passed before John steered the rowboat into a cove. It stopped with a thud and a thwack. Really scared now, Melissa scrambled out on trembling hands and knees and then flopped onto her back, gasping. A slight breeze blew over the shore as John fastened the boat to a tree. Quaking from the unexpected midnight ride and the unreal scene before her, Melissa closed her eyes, told herself this was only a Bryony dream, and waited for the nightmare to end.

A hand brushed her cheek; Melissa forgot to breathe. Gentle fingers swept away strands from her face; soft lips tasted her forehead; the tip of a tongue flitted across her lashes, then to her lips, and Melissa met the mouth devouring hers. In the mystical clearing of the vampire attack of Melissa's dreams, Melissa again knew pain and blood, but this time, neither lasted long.

Moonlight, desire, and the damp, earthy fragrance of the woods at night fused together as John made love to her.

CHAPTER 6: MELISSA TAKES A LEAP OF FAITH

"Wake up!"

A rough hand shook Melissa's shoulder.

"Mmmph...." She rolled onto side and pulled John's jacket over her head. The hand yanked off the jacket and tugged her hair.

"Let's go!"

Melissa blinked back slumber and descended into warm, drowsy, silky eiderdown.

"Now!"

Melissa slowly pushed herself up and dazedly rubbed her eyes. Mauve and melon streaked the purple-black sky. She blinked, astonished at the sight. She'd slept all night in the woods!

John, crouching beside her, face twisted in irritation, again harshly shoved her, but her eyes drooped; her body swayed. Sleep....

"...Thornton by eight o'clock!"

"In a minute," Melissa mumbled, stretching stiff arms and gingerly moving numb and prickling feet.

"You're up?"

Melissa absently brushed leaves off her damp sleeves and pulled a twig from her hair.

"I'll be at the boat."

Melissa waited until he left then quickly ducked amongst the trees. Fully awake now, Melissa hurried to the shore, for she was unwilling to invoke further ire. John, pocketknife in hand, stood poised by the tree where he had tethered the boat last night.

"Get in."

She paused, bewildered at his coldness, so very different from last night.

"But...."

"Hurry!"

John pulled her to the boat. Dazed, Melissa stepped inside. John slashed the rope with one swift movement. Melissa had just sat when John leaped into the boat, seized the oars, and began furiously rowing down Lake Munson at unbelievable speed. Above her, yellow bands pushed aside the lingering remains of the nocturnal enchantment and diluted the inky waters into dusky-green. Cloudy trees appeared in the misty morning air. John's gaze darted about him as he rowed. Far too soon, the outline of the fishing cottages came into view, just as the last dew weakly sparkled and vanished. The boat headed straight for the dock. Once there, John immediately exited and began securing the craft. Melissa reluctantly stepped from the boat and waited, waited, waited.

"Well," she said, with hesitation. "Good-bye."

"Bye."

That was it? After he had made everything so wonderful? Not a kiss, nothing? With a leaden heart, Melissa set out for Bass Street, but the walk up the hill lacked the magical qualities of the one down Blue Gill Road last night. What had happened? In the woods, in the dark, everything had seemed right, perfect. Today, John's brusque attitude sent a different message. Why hadn't she heeded Henry?

By the time Melissa had reached the Drakes' house, the morning sun had swallowed up any remnants of the previous night. She tried the front door, expecting it to be locked, but the handle turned with ease. Had Julie left it opened for her? The sizzle and scent of bacon filled the air. The Sunday morning newspaper sat on the living room coffee table. Melissa slipped off her shoes and tiptoed up the stairs. A stair halfway to the second floor creaked. Melissa paused and held her breath. The hard plink of a frying pan hitting the stove drowned out any other sound. Satisfied no one heard her, Melissa continued to Julie's room and then peeped inside at her friend who, with eyes closed, lay curled into a fetal position.

Other than receiving some very strange looks from Julie across the breakfast table, Melissa heard nothing about her midnight escapade until they were driving back to Jenson College.

"Okay, what gives?"

"I don't know what you're talking about."

"Oh, come on! Both you and Professor Simotes disappeared last night. You don't think anyone noticed?"

"So what?"

"What do you mean, 'So what?' He's engaged to your literature teacher, remember? Are you trying to flunk?"

Melissa looked out the window. "He asked for a tour of Munsonville."

"If you tried really hard, you couldn't stretch a tour of Munsonville into ten minutes."

"Well, he wanted to see Simons Estate because everyone's mentioned he looks like John Simons. He passed out in the woods, and I waited until daylight to come back."

"A likely story."

"Did you see how much he had drunk?"

Julie kept silent a moment. "You left me in a hell of a bind. I waited as long as I could. Good thing my parents were sleeping, so I didn't have to invent an excuse."

"You could've just said I was spending the night at Katie's."

Julie tightly pressed her lips together and then said, "Okay, drop it."

Neither spoke for a long time. The car lapped up the miles that distanced Melissa from Munsonville and the glorious woods. She returned to classes tomorrow. How could anything be the same now that she and John had....

Julie began to giggle. "You actually spent the night with Professor Simotes!"

Melissa smiled grimly. "I wonder how long before everyone hears it."

"It won't be from me."

"Me, neither."

Julie glanced at her gauge. "I need gas," she said. "Watch for a sign, Melissa."

Five miles later, Julie pulled into a service station. A uniformed boy about their age approached her window.

"Regular, please." Julie fished in her purse for a ten dollar bill. "Listen, Melissa, I'm not trying to sound like your mother. Just be careful, okay? He doesn't belong to you."

"I know."

The realization that she still could not lay claim to John burrowed deeply into Melissa's psyche and spread its gangling poisonous fingers. Did John kiss Miss Garboldi with blazing passion? How often did they....? At her place? At his place? In the woods?

Literature class now became the place where Melissa visually stalked Miss Garboldi with obsessive ruthlessness. The lilt in her teacher's light voice, the poised stance of her tiny frame, the flourish of the diamond-topped hand all triumphantly broadcasted to the world that Miss Garboldi owned what she, Melissa, would never, ever have, and Melissa hated her for it.

Still, Melissa loitered in the halls, around corners and behind doors, waiting to accidentally, and quite by surprise, bump into John, since she didn't dare venture to the music room, and he avoided the library. By evening, Melissa scrupulously completed assignments and feverishly studied for exams, terrified of losing her scholarship to Jenson College. At night, Melissa silently cried hot tears into her pillow, berated her lack of sound judgment, and prayed Miss Garboldi would drive off a cliff. Melissa's misery was her own fault, and Melissa knew that, too. She had gone too far, but she couldn't help it. She wanted John, John, John, and only John. Emotionally exhausted, Melissa would jerk into restless, broken sleep and dream troubling dreams of the love-struck teachers.

That's it, Melissa told herself late one Friday afternoon with a sudden resolve as she stamped cards, shelved books, and pocketed new arrivals. I'm through with Professor Simotes forever. I'm through with *vampire* fantasies forever. She got off lucky this time. No school gossip, only a badly damaged heart. Although it seemed unlikely Melissa would ever cross paths with John again, she vowed that, if she ever again felt tempted to see him, she'd immediately call her mother and beg for professional help. Melissa had to stop, now, before her insane notions caused irreparable harm.

"Are you ill, Melissa?"

Mr. Schmidt's voice startled her, and she nicked the side of his desk with her cart.

"No, I...." Melissa faltered and tugged her thoughts back to the present. "Just a little tired."

"You look exhausted. Clock out and get some rest."

"But...."

"It's slow tonight, anyway."

Now that she'd made the right decision, the tension relaxed. Melissa felt only weary heaviness and deep sadness. An opportunity to sleep for hours seemed like the best deal she'd been offered in a long time.

"Thanks, Mr. Schmidt."

As Melissa stepped outside the library's front door, she saw Professor Simotes waiting on the sidewalk. All resolve melted at the sight of him. A thousand and four imagined reasons why John had not contacted her deluged her. Melissa pardoned him on the spot. *Oh, God, she had missed him!*

How to respond? Should she be nice to him? Shut him down? Dealing with Jason Frye had been simple, but Jason was only a boy. What would Bryony do? How could she think with John staring at her?

"Good day, Professor," Melissa said in her most sophisticated, yet offhand, voice.

John grinned. "That's a little formal, don't you think, considering?"

Melissa blushed, but she forged ahead. "Do you generally hang around the outside of libraries?"

"I'm not hanging anywhere. I'm heading to my apartment for a quick sandwich and hoped you might walk with me."

"You're done teaching for the night?"

"Yes and no. I've mounds of homework to correct. Anyway, I'm rushed. Will you accompany me or not?"

Would she! Her conscience pricked her and whispered stern reminders of self-made promises, but Melissa disregarded the clamor. The invitation thrilled her, yet she wouldn't show that to John.

"I guess so." Melissa then added with a playful smile, "I've already finished *my* homework."

"Minx."

Not until they rounded the corner and walked toward the stately houses behind Jenson College did John take Melissa's hand. Was it merely coincidence that he waited until they were removed from sight? Melissa internally sighed. How long until she stopped second-guessing John's every move?

"Do you own one of these houses?"

"No. I rent a second floor studio."

"That's not very big."

"It's fine for the present. I'm looking to buy."

Melissa's face burned. Of course, he wanted to buy a house. He's getting married. Inwardly groaning at that glaring reminder, Melissa only said, "Around here?"

"Most likely. It's close to work, and I prefer old homes. There's much history to them."

John led Melissa up the stone steps of an grey Queen Anne. A gazebo-like deck encased the front porch on two sides. Right of the porch, three stories extended to a peaked roof. A second roof capped the back of the house, just two levels high. John unlocked the front door, and Melissa stepped into the foyer, dim, but with sufficient light to see the oak floors and gold-scrolled gray-blue wallpaper.

"I'm on the second floor."

Still grasping her hand, John led her up the stairs. Melissa's mouth went dry with nervous excitement. For weeks, she had fretted and grieved, but she never once imagined John would actually bring her here. John slid a long bronze key into a large brass keyhole, pushed open the door, and snapped on the overhead light. She saw the bathroom opposite the threshold and the kitchen on her left. Another room lay beyond. John walked her into the far room, ruled by a baby grand piano.

"Well," John said "This is it."

"It's very nice."

One glance and Melissa could tell this apartment belonged to a bachelor musician. A hastily made, wrought-iron, four-poster bed occupied one end of the room; sagging shelves overcome with heavy books claimed the other. Sheet music covered every empty spot.

"I'll be back," John said. "Make yourself at home."

Fairly shaking with nervous excitement, Melissa walked to the window overlooking the neighborhood and peeped around the drawn curtains. She could see why John liked living here. Old houses lined the street, bordered by the ancient trees that shaded them. Melissa jumped at the string of chords. John had returned. He was biting into a bologna sandwich and closing the piano lid with the other hand. The image of John eating Brian's favorite lunch food clashed with his shirt and tie and the memory of multicourse feasts at Simons Mansion.

"My little brother eats that stuff, too."

He shrugged. "It serves the purpose."

Melissa smiled archly. "Is that a Schwechten?"

"Steinway."

Engaging John in conversation, even in his territory, still proved to be an arduous task. Melissa tried again.

"How'd you get a piano up here? The door doesn't seem wide enough."

"It isn't." John stuffed the last bite into his mouth. "Ready?"

"Sure," Melissa said in dismay. She had not expected to leave quite so soon.

Instead of leading her away, John slid both hands under her sweater and pulled it over her head. Surprised at his brusque lack of romantic prologue, Melissa grabbed his wrists. "Wait."

"What?" John was unbuttoning her blouse. Melissa pried off his fingers. John looked annoyed. "What's the problem?"

"I don't know," she said. "I just thought...."

"I didn't invite you here to watch TV. I can take you back to your dor...."

"No!"

Blouse on the floor, John cupped her shoulders, bent over her neck, and covered it with light kisses and tiny bites. His breath, warm and gentle, swept over her skin. Melissa untied his tie and started to remove his shirt, but John tapped her hand.

"What?"

"The shirt stays." John moved lower.

Was he joking? Melissa tried again, but John thrust her hands aside. Melissa pulled back, incredulous. John raised his head and an eyebrow, but this time Melissa persisted.

"You'll take off all your clothes except your shirt."

"You're getting the best parts."

She folded her arms across her chest. "I want an explanation."

"I'd rather not provide one, but since you insist...." John sighed deeply and looked at the floor. "Bad acne left deep scars on my back and shoulders." John fixed cold eyes on hers. "The shirt does not come off."

Perplexed, Melissa acquiesced, and John lay her down on his bed. Later, as he slept, Melissa lightly ran her fingers over his shirt and felt deep grooves in his back and shoulders, marks too deep for acne.

Melissa saw John only twice over the next couple of weeks. Each time, he waited for her outside the library door, and each time he took her to his apartment. Melissa's erratic absences did not escape her roommate's notice.

"Where've you been hanging out, Melissa?" Jill said one evening.

Melissa closed her history book and yawned. "I don't know what you mean."

"Yeah, you do. Who's the guy?"

"Not telling."

"Why not?"

"Keeps one safe from you."

"That's cold!"

"Whatever."

Jill's incessant questioning bothered Melissa less than the vague, harboring anxiety that had flared into full-fledged fear. Several weeks had passed since Ann and Jack's engagement party, and that was way too long. Melissa fell into an uneasy sleep, only to awaken at two o'clock by an inferno lighting up her room. Deafening thunder followed. Her wind-up desk clock—her insurance policy against electrical failure-- mocked her as it ticked out each second.

Late. Late. Late. Late. Late. Late. Late. Late. Late. Late. Late. Late. Late. Late.

The ticking merged with the battering monsoon against the window pane until it thudded into the beating of John Simons' undead heart. Through closed eyelids, Melissa sensed his presence as he drifted out of the mist and glided nearer, bent closer, and rammed his fangs into her neck. She screamed soundless cries, but still John drank hard and deep, tearing into her wounds for more, never minding the overflowing draught streaming down her legs until she was lying in a pool of blood. Melissa awoke with a jolt, discovered the blood, and happily yelped, jarring her roommate from peaceful slumber.

"Holy, crap!" Jill bolted awake, breathing hard and searching around. She shot an angry glance at Melissa and threw the blanket over her head. "Shut up. My class isn't 'til ten."

"Sorry."

The week passed in flawless joy. On Thursday, Melissa worked the lunch hour for Pat, sick with a stomach bug. Then she stayed an extra half hour because the counter grew busy. At one-thirty, Mr. Schmidt relieved Melissa of her duties.

"I'll be back at six o'clock," Melissa promised, as she left circulation.

She walked outside in time to see Professor Simotes cross the street. Dodging him was impossible. He smiled, approached her, and said, "Long time."

"I guess," Melissa said, carefully avoiding his eyes.

Not one peek, she told herself. Not one peek.

"Walk with me. I left something at the apartment."

"Um...."

His invitation caught her off guard. She had not expected it, not this early in the day. She did not know how to refuse him without inviting a discussion about the particulars of the refusal. Feeling spineless, Melissa accepted his outstretched hand, the first time John had offered it to her within such proximity of the college. She averted her eyes.

"Work an extra shift?"

"Sort of. Just through lunch. Someone got sick."

She offered no further conversation. For once, John noticed.

"You're quiet today, Melissa."

"Just tired."

They walked in silence to John's apartment. Melissa's control evaporated the second she stepped into the foyer. She could not, *must not,* go upstairs.

Aloud she gasped, "I can't stay!" She spun around and started for the door.

"What?"

"I'm done," Melissa choked, turning the knob. John must not see her crying.

John slipped between her and the door and tilted up her chin. Tears poured down her face. She attempted to jerk her away from him, but John remained firm.

"Melissa, what's the problem?"

"Nothing."

"This is considerable commotion for nothing."

"What difference it make?" Melissa said, her voice bitter with disappointment.

"It matters to me. What's troubling you?"

John's fingers closed around her. Melissa took a deep breath, bravely looked him in the eye, and said, "I was late...and I thought...."

Alarm crossed John's face, and she hastened to reassure him.

"I'm not. I mean, I started. But I'm not going through this again. I do mean it. I'm done."

John faced her with placid determination. "We'll get married."

His words doused Melissa like ice water. "What!"

"I'm not ready to end it. Since pregnancy concerns you, we'll....

This was incomprehensible! "Married?"

"Yes."

"What about Miss Garboldi?"

"What about her?"

"I thought you guys were...well...."

"We broke up."

"Oh...I...."

In disbelief, John said, "You thought I'd go from her to you to her again?"

Melissa had not known what to think, especially after Jill's remarks regarding the professor's escapades. Could the scandal simply be vicious rumors?

"But...I'm not pregnant."

"So, you'll only marry me if you're pregnant?"

The question confused Melissa. Hadn't John offered marriage to her because it seemed proper under certain circumstances? Did John really wish to spend the rest of their lives together? As husband and wife? She turned full eyes up at John, never minding the now falling tears.

John's features relaxed. "Luckily, that's easily managed."

When Melissa awakened, John's side of the bed was empty. His desk clock read seven o'clock. Melissa sat up, stunned. Not only had she missed dinner, she was late for work. She had never done such a thing.

Melissa dressed with a speed that threatened to break time barriers. She flew to the door, and then, remembering she hadn't eaten since breakfast, decided to check out John's refrigerator. With her luck, she'd pass out right in the middle of the library. She found some lunchmeat and a package of cheese; John had left an open bag of bread on the counter. As an afterthought, Melissa grabbed an apple from a bowl on the table. She ate the sandwich while racing down the stairs and munched the apple as she flew to the library, wondering what she would tell Mr. Schmidt, hoping he would not fire her, praying she didn't choke along the way. She tossed the core into the garbage can by the library's front door, said a quick prayer, and walked inside. A girl Melissa had not met stood at the counter.

She hurried past the circulation desk and approached Mr. Schmidt, who merely said, "Is there a problem?"

"No problem. I fell asleep this afternoon and forgot to set my alarm. I'm really sorry. It won't happen again."

"I can overlook one transgression, as long as it's not habitual. You've not disappointed me in the past. I appreciated your extra hours this afternoon."

"I'm not working tonight?"

"I've got tonight covered. Get some rest. You still look like you could use it."

"Thank you very much, Mr. Schmidt, for understanding."

"Have a good night, Melissa."

She walked on air all the way back to her dorm room. She could not absorb the wonderful thing that had happened this afternoon. John Simotes asked her to marry him! Never mind the rumors surrounding him and the other students. Never mind Miss Garboldi. Never mind *Bryony*. Who cared now? Melissa had won the prize.

Standing outside her dorm room, Melissa considered the previous ridicule she'd endured. She recalled Julie's lecture, delivered with a dose of superiority that had nettled Melissa.

This time, the joke was on them, and Melissa would laugh last.

And, oh, how she would enjoy it!

CHAPTER 7: NEW HORIZONS

Time crept and flew Friday as Melissa vacillated between disbelief that John had sincerely proposed marriage and total rapture at becoming his wife. In between, Melisa felt moments of panic. What if John Simotes was not John Simons? What if marrying him would be a horrible mistake? She half-hoped, half-assumed John would visit her at the library that night, perhaps feeling just as flustered as she, but Melissa neither saw nor heard from him.

At closing time, the door opened one final time. Melissa's heart soared, but only Julie and Tracy entered.

"Come on, slave," Julie said with a wicked grin. "We're going skating."

Melissa looked blank.

"You do skate, don't you?" Julie said, "Unless you'd rather bowl."

"I skate about as well as I bowl. There's a rink in Jenson?"

"Shelby has one," Tracy said, "and it's open until midnight."

"We'll stop by your room first and get your stuff," Julie said.

Tracy leaned her elbows on the counter. "I mean, why risk walking into...."

Melissa contemplated her overflowing laundry basket while squelching the image of Jill cavorting with her latest cohort. "I know, I know."

Roller skating proved the perfect activity, and Melissa twice thanked the girls for inviting her. The loud music, coupled with the monotonous circling around the rink, allowed Melissa to unravel her feelings of the last few weeks' events.

John behaved unpredictably and contradictorily. He rebuffed her invitation and then treated her to dinner. No one witnessed Melissa's conversation with the professor on the stairs the day she had asked him out. Only one person could have promulgated that fact around school: John. But...why?

Since that first date, Melissa's time with John had been sporadic, spontaneous, and only when John chose to initiate it. Had he really broken up with Miss Garboldi? Why hadn't *that* piece of information circulated through Jenson College? Perhaps because it wasn't true?

Yesterday, John had proposed marriage, yet never had he declared his love for her, so why else did he want to marry her? To get her upstairs? Surely, John would know that trick could only work once. If all he wanted was sex, then why her? What possible advantage could such a relationship have for John?

Furthermore, if John really intended marriage, why had he not contacted her today? Wouldn't he be eager to see her? Do men usually ask girls to marry them and then disappear?

Melissa felt a tap on her shoulder.

"Last song," Tracy said. "Couples only."

They skated to the carpet and bumped onto the floor. Melissa wobbled but held her balance.

"Hey, look!" Tracy pointed to the boy and girl at the far end of the rink.

Julie and that David from her Psych One class, heads close and hands clasped, skated together with synchronized ease. Melissa, slightly jealous at Julie's prospect, watched them and wished John needed more presence in her life. Julie and David looked so darned happy together. After the song concluded, the girls purchased pizza slices from the concession stand and carried them out to Julie's car. Tracy teased Julie about the couples skate during the ride home.

"I told you he had a crush on me," Julie said, driving with one hand and eating pizza with the other.

"You seemed pretty friendly with him, too."

"Why not? He's shy, but nice."

"Did he ask you out?"

A passing car lit up Julie's face long enough for Melissa to see her friend smile.

"Actually, I invited him to the movies tomorrow night. I'm tired of waiting for him to make a move."

Despite her late night, Melissa stormed the laundry room early the next morning, before the other residents had the same idea. Luckily, she didn't work until afternoon. As her laundry spun round and round, Melissa sipped a vending machine iced tea, balanced homework on her lap, and brooded over why John had not called. As Melissa lugged her first basket back to her dorm room, she heard an incessant ringing. Hadn't Jill returned to the dorm last night? The second Melissa turned the lock, the phone stopped. She opened the door, and Jill thrust the receiver in her face.

"Here! Some guy's been calling for you all morning!"

Jill flounced to her bed, rubbed her swollen eyes, tucked up her legs under her, listening and sulking. In wonderment, Melissa put the phone to her ear. "Hello?"

"Did you know it's improper for engaged women to gallivant around town all night? I've been attempting to reach you for twelve straight hours."

Melissa glanced at Jill who listened with full, unabashed attention.

"Um...I never stay here on weekends. The room is usually, well, full."

"You didn't tell me, why?"

"I didn't see you."

"The phone works both ways. Can you be ready in an hour?"

Could she! Melissa opened the door and pulled the long cord behind her into the hall.

"Sure. Any special reason?"

"I want to drive into Shelby and look at rings."

Rings! So John *was* serious.

"Uh, yeah. I'll see you then."

"Cafeteria door." John hung up.

Melissa quickly called Pat and asked if she could sub for her this afternoon.

"Something's come up," Melissa cried breathlessly into the receiver while sensing Jill's impatience for details.

Pat reluctantly agreed. Melissa zipped around the room, shoving clean clothes into drawers and collecting shower paraphernalia.

She had just reached the door when Jill stopped her with a loud, "Ahem!"

With a start, Melissa turned to face her.

Jill learned forward with suppressed eagerness.

"Come on, Melissa, don't be secretive. Who's the guy? He sounds hot."

"Wrong number."

Grinning with bubbling delight, Melissa cranked up the hot water and narrowed the spray. John really *had* tried contacting her last night. She rinsed uncertainty and disappointment into the swirling drain, where they belonged.

Pelting streams smarted against her skin, but, inside, Melissa glowed with warm, overflowing happiness. John had missed her!

Despite her haste, Melissa heard the familiar motor as she neared the cafeteria door. John leaned over and pushed open the door. After she fastened her seatbelt, John handed her a folded slip of paper. Puzzled, she unfolded it and then smiled at its contents.

"Make sure you use it." John moved away from the building and toward the street. "I realized after hanging up that you didn't have my number."

"Are we really looking at rings?"

"You don't want one?"

"Of course I do. You surprised me. It seems so public."

John looked perplexed. "And?"

"Well...I...I...." Damn! Hadn't John acted ashamed of their relationship? Why did he only meet her behind the building? "I thought you didn't want people to know."

"Why on earth not?"

"I don't know." Melissa studied the glove box. How had she trapped herself into a losing discussion? "It...it just seemed that way to me."

John swerved onto a side street and parked under the first tree. As Melissa tried processing the abrupt detour, he leaned as near as the center console allowed, removed his sunglasses, and gently guided her face to meet him.

"Remember when I said I felt we'd previously met?"

Unease crept into her mind and picked apart her fading bliss, despite the delectable sensation of John holding her cheeks in his hand. Melissa stiffly nodded. *Now, what?*

"That was no line. It's true we haven't dated long. I agree a huge disparity exists between our ages and interests. I know nearly nothing about you, and you know less regarding me, and yet...."

Strangled by fear, paralyzed by hope, Melissa could only gaze up at John. Was he breaking off the engagement before it scarcely started?

"...I believe we're destined for each other, and I trusted you felt the same. What am I misunderstanding?"

She felt too stunned to reply, so John did it for her, with a warm, parted mouth and a soft, lazy kiss that nearly stopped her heart. He had closed his eyes, but when Melissa set a timid hand on his cheek, he opened them slightly, electric blue eyes peering from beneath tangled brown lashes. He paused, his lips resting on hers.

A screen door banged. "Ma! Angie says...." A lawn mower drowned out the rest.

John's lips moved in an easy half-smile, as he delivered one final, gentle peck.

Melissa swallowed, hard.

"This," John murmured, "is not getting you a ring."

He slid back to the driver's seat, and once again joy surged inside Melissa as she said, "Where in Shelby are we going?"

"Overbeck and Rogers. They do beautiful work."

Melissa's heart sank a little at John's words. How did he know? Is that where he bought Miss Garboldi's ring? She shook her head to clear the thought. John looked, and Melissa blushed. Stop thinking so negatively, she told herself. Miss Garboldi is out of the picture, so who cares where John bought her ring?

John drove in silence, and Melissa pretended to stare ahead while stealing peeks at John. His blond hair scattered past his shoulders and down his back, but his expression appeared serene. John steered with a relaxed left hand; his right hovered between his knee and the gear stick, and he casually monitored the road as if surveying his kingdom. Melissa couldn't help smiling at the sight. Surely, these actions proved John Simotes *was* John Simons.

The jewelry store was located in a one-story yellow brick building in the middle of Shelby's downtown area. A weathered wood sign with painted black letters *Overbeck* and *Rogers* hung above the entranceway. John opened the door for Melissa, and she stepped inside the store feeling as happy as if she had just entered a nineteenth century concert hall. Vintage photographs and gas lights hung on the walls; rows of displays flashed their contents. Melissa sidled up to one of the cases, but she saw no prices. How, Melissa anxiously thought, should she select? Would John think her cheap if she gravitated toward something simple? Would it wreck his budget if she selected a more spectacular ring? How much fortune did John Simons still possess?

John noticed her dilemma. "Melissa, come see."

He pointed to a platinum band with one medium-sized diamond in its center and seven smaller diamonds arching down each side of the band. The jeweler, a stocky man with balding, tightly curled brown hair and round glasses, removed the ring and showcased its splendor on a piece of black velvet. The smallest stones twinkled beseechingly, while the larger one radiated a hypnotizing, dazzling brilliancy.

"It's lovely!" Melissa breathed in awe. She could not imagine anything so elegant occupying her finger.

John glanced up at the jeweler. "How soon can you have it ready for her?"

"Three to five business days."

"No good. She needs it Monday. We'll return tomorrow morning."

"Sir, we're closed on Sundays."

"I'll pay double for it."

The jeweler looked mildly surprised. "Double for the adjustment?"

"Double for the ring."

The jeweler's eyes opened wide, and his jaw fell. "Sir, you've got yourself a deal! I'll be right back." He left the counter and withdrew to the back room.

Melissa tugged John's sleeve.

"John," she whispered. "I can wait."

"Nonsense. You think I'm ashamed when I'm actually proud. You've agreed to marry me. The world might as well know it."

"It's too much money."

"It's worth it to me."

The jeweler reappeared with his sizing rings and proceeded to test them on Melissa's finger. Melissa floated in a dream world and hoped never to wake up.

At the car, John asked, "Are you in a hurry to return to school?"

"I'm free all day." Melissa lied. "Why?"

"Good."

John did not speak again until he pulled into Keppler Brothers in Jenson, a supermarket on the opposite side of town from the college. It amazed Melissa to see John pushing a grocery cart. Shopping seemed so normal, so average. It occurred to her with sudden realization that this scene would replay itself a thousand times once she and John were married.

Married.

Melissa's heart leaped into her throat. Marriage was such a lovely word, and it now belonged to her and John.

"Do you like lasagna?"

His words pulled her back. "I'm sorry?"

"Lasagna. Do you like it?"

"Well, um, sure."

"Wonderful. I make excellent lasagna. We'll have that tonight."

Tonight? The concept of John cooking dinner for them suggested an intimacy she had not fully considered. John casually tossed ground meat, noodles, and ricotta cheese into the cart and proceeded to check-out.

"I have everything else at home," John said.

Home.

Just days ago, Melissa had agonized over John's infrequent appearances in her life. Today, he would prepare a meal for them, and tomorrow she would wear an engagement ring he had purchased. In a haze of unreality, Melissa followed John to checkout.

John, Melissa discovered, moved as proficiently in the kitchen as Steve did. She unloaded the few groceries while John expertly chopped onions, minced garlic, and diced tomatoes. The fragrance of olive oil and browning meat filled the kitchen. John uncorked a bottle of red wine sitting on the counter.

"Grab two glasses, Melissa. First cupboard on your left."

She marveled at John's delivery of those instructions. With near reverence, Melissa opened the cupboard door, grateful for admittance into the inner room, the private life of

John Simotes. At first she felt invasive until she remembered who had invited her. She selected two glasses and handed them to John.

"Not too much for me." Melissa watched, with apprehension, the burgundy liquid flowing into her glass. "I'm lightweight."

"That's why I poured yours half full. Tonight won't be a celebration if your head's hanging over my commode."

Melissa cringed at the reference to Crossroads Tap and then fingered the stem of her glass, contemplating John's other words. *Tonight. Celebration.* She took a sip. The sweet white wines Darlene sometimes served seem almost anemic compared to this wine's dry, almost carnal, taste.

John drained the pasta and began assembling the lasagna, while Melissa, recalling the bologna sandwich, watched, fascinated.

"I didn't know you could cook."

He spread sauce over the first layer. "It's either that or starve."

"My step-dad and little brother cook all the time," Melissa said. "But I'd heard single guys can't cook."

"Untrue."

John placed the lasagna inside the oven. Next he mixed an aromatic olive oil and a pungent red wine vinegar, adding a dash of this and a pinch of that from the glass jars on his counter.

"My mother not only cooks, she grows and dries herbs, so she keeps my kitchen well-stocked." John paused as a shadow passed over his face. He then looked intently at Melissa. "I'm sure you will like my parents."

Parents? Melissa leaned weakly against the counter and watched John as he tasted a drop from his finger, added a final ingredient, and pushed the cruet aside. He brought forth romaine lettuce, spinach, and two other greens Melissa could not identify. This *was* John Simons, wasn't it? *So how could he have parents?*

John noticed her panic. "Watercress and dandelion. I trust they're not too bitter for you. I like intense food."

Melissa closed her eyes. John's voice, his touch, and, for God's sake, even his *scent,* matched the John Simons of her dreams. The way he had kissed her in the parking lot, wasn't that how she remembered the other kisses, at Simons Mansion and inside the carriage, on their way to the wedding reception?

She reopened her eyes. "I'm sure the salad will be delicious."

"Would you like to hear my new piece?"

"Sure!"

John poured himself a refill, and Melissa trailed him into the front room, feeling very sophisticated holding a wine glass while standing near the gleaming piano.

"It looks old," Melissa said, wondering if it was from the Victorian era.

"Nineteen thirty-three." He played a cacophony of chords and then grinned sheepishly at her. "Warm up."

For the next five minutes, John filled the room with silvery, clear tones. Melissa, enchanted, reveled in John's manipulation of each note. She could never, ever acquire that enviable skill, even if she practiced from now to eternity.

"That was very nice," she said with a knowing smile.

"Liar. You can't discern a bad arrangement from a good composition."

Melissa blushed into her glass and dropped the facade. "I guess that's true, but it still sounded nice."

John patted the bench. Feigning nonchalance, Melissa eased onto the seat and took another sip, but John lowered the glass. Slowly, deliberately, he swept her lips with his tongue. Melissa closed her eyes and waited, quivering, for the inevitable kiss, but instead John muttered darkly, "And I shall taste no other wine tonight."

Stunned, Melissa's eyes flew open, but John, composed, had already returned to the keys. Nothing in his expression suggested malevolence. Had she imagined it? She blamed the wine. Good thing John had taken it away.

"It's time for our first lesson. I shall train your ear to discriminate between fine and shabby music."

Half an hour later, Melissa's still hadn't developed any ability to distinguish quality from trash nor did she care. John's enigmatic comment had blunted her paradise and evoked memories of another John, one who visited her by night and raised a sleeve to wipe away her blood.

"It's time to toss the salad," John closed the piano lid. "The lasagna is nearly done."

How did one eat while sitting across from a handsome man? Although the food tasted delicious, Melissa could only push small bites past her narrow throat. John's silence didn't help.

"The salad's not bitter," Melissa said, attempting light conversation, "and I really like the dressing. What's in it?"

"I don't recall."

She cocked her head and smiled coquettishly.

"No trade secret. I really don't remember. Just an instinct for taste, I suppose. Will you be happy with a small wedding?"

Unprepared for the question, Melissa stammered, "I...I haven't given it much thought."

"Well, I have. If we get married New Year's Eve, we have two weeks before school begins. During that time, I have a conference in Chicago, so we could combine it with a honeymoon. I found a house in this neighborhood I think you will like. We could close on it before the Christmas holidays."

Melissa's head spun. So much information! She set down her fork and sighed. Being engaged seemed so romantic, but John's speech reminded her of the permanent and lifelong journey upon which she was embarking. John pushed back his chair, knelt beside her, and laid one hand on her knee.

"Listen, Melissa, you probably think I'm hasty, and you have every reason to believe it, but at thirty-two, I know what I want and prefer not to play ridiculous games to get it. Bluntly speaking, this is my second marriage, and I won't repeat a splashy affair. I want to begin nineteen seventy-seven with you as my wife, decorating our home, and beginning a family. If you feel I'm cheating you, let's address it now. Otherwise, I prefer to go forward with our plans."

"You want to elope?"

"Of course not. I want the ceremony, the nice clothes, the flowers, the rings. I want to flaunt you before our family and friends, but I want to keep it simple, and I want to do it soon."

John looked so open, Melissa's awkwardness at his close presence dwindled. Her hesitant fingers moved through his abundant hair and over his face, touching first his forehead and then tracing the gentle arch of his eyebrows, his full eyelashes, aquiline nose, and thin, but perfectly curved, lips. *John was offering himself to her!*

Yet, it was the blue in John's irises, icy, sparking Tesla coils, gazing at her from the depths of a time long past, that said this: somewhere, deep inside this man, lost in buried memories of the present, lived John Simons the vampire, and he had not changed. John's all-too-familiar air of triumph and apparent condescension, this asking of Melissa's opinion, was mere formality. Melissa blinked; the beastly image vanished, and John gazed at her with peaceful sincerity. In all her moments of playing Bryony, Melissa had yearned for this moment, and it now belonged to her for the taking. She refused to squash it with specters of the past. She and John had a future, together. Her true purpose for living had begun; she need only claim it.

So, Melissa nodded.

John stood up. "For an aspiring English teacher, your acceptance speech is highly amusing. Dessert?"

She blinked at the brisk change in subject. "I beg your pardon?"

"Are you ready for dessert?"

"What's for dessert?"

John opened the freezer and held up two containers. "Chocolate or vanilla?"

Melissa laughed out loud. "Ice cream?"

"My one vice. Can't go a day without it. I make it myself from an old family recipe."

"Chocolate."

"Good. There's only enough vanilla for me. But you may have two scoops."

"And still fit in a wedding dress?"

John shrugged and tossed her a cloth napkin. "Dresses come in all sizes. Follow me; I want to catch the news."

They crowded together on the small couch John kept in the corner at the foot of the bed, before a tiny black and white television perched atop an upside-down wooden orange crate. Twice John adjusted the rabbit ears.

"I take it you don't spend many nights watching TV." Melissa bit into her cone.

"You have ice cream on your nose."

John moved his napkin close to Melissa's face as if to wipe it and then abruptly stuck the tip of his tongue on her nose and slowly, slowly licked off the chocolate. Instinctively, Melissa's hand smacked the bottom of his cone, which covered John's face in ice cream. A tug, and John had both napkins shoved behind his back.

"You shouldn't have done that, Melissa." A broad grin spread over his face.

He had just moved her to his bed, all the while kissing her with increasing ardency, when John suddenly paused, lifted his head, and said, "This is the last time."

Melissa tried kissing him back, but John pulled away. Perplexed, Melissa said, "The last time for what?"

"This. Until we're married."

"I...I don't understand."

"Not necessary."

"But why?"

"Because." John proceeded as if nothing had happened.

Plaintive melodies haunted her nighttime fancies and awakened Melissa to firelight's dancing shadows. Magnetized by the piano's mournful call, Melissa rhythmically descended Simons Mansion's grand staircase and followed the dirge to the music room. John, aristocratic in white tails, swayed to halting melancholic notes, chipper trills now waltzing bittersweet and then cascading into doleful tones spilling from her eyes, streaking across her cheeks, and splashing the lace collar of her rose print tea gown. Death, death, all of Melissa's heart-felt wishes must end in death.

Melissa rolled onto one side, hardly surprised by the musical lament or her wet face, which she wiped dry with the sheet. John, in shorts and the same T-shirt he had refused to remove all night, hair streaming down his back, worked the pedals in bare feet. The morning sun seeped through the cracks of the heavy drapery John had not yet parted. She lay and listened as long as she could and then padded to the bathroom. She studied her reflection while splashing water on her face. How could she look the same with her future so irrevocably altered?

The music ended. Melissa opened the door. John stood in the kitchen pouring a mug of coffee, which he gestured toward her. "Want some?"

Melissa shook her head.

"Hungry?"

"A little."

"I'll scramble some eggs before I take you back to school. The jeweler called me this morning. Your ring is ready."

Her eyes flew to the clock. Half past ten! "Why'd you let me sleep so long?"

John chuckled. "You seemed like you needed the rest." He removed a homemade loaf from the bread box. "One slice or two?"

"John, about what you said last night...."

"It's not a debatable subject."

"But...."

John set down the knife and faced her. "I regret our inappropriate beginning

"Are you saying that....?"

"We have time." John's face darkened, and he looked away. "Time," he repeated under his breath. He turned toward the stove. "Melissa, bring the eggs."

John's engagement ring couldn't have fit better. Melissa reverently moved it this way and that, watching it capture the light and scatter its rays into glittering sparkles. What a marvelous symbol of John's promise to marry her in two short months!

Melissa retreated to John's apartment for the rest of the evening and did not return to the dorm until bedtime. She ate breakfast with her hand under the table and avoided Julie and Tracy's questions regarding her weekend whereabouts. They were about to climb the stairs to class when John Simotes, clad in his customary three-piece suit and carrying his briefcase, strode in through the main entrance and embraced Melissa in front of her friends. They stood gaping as John clasped Melissa's wrist and ascended the staircase with her.

John's fingers slid down to her hand and squeezed it. "Everyone's staring at us."

"I...I know," Melissa said, uncertainly glancing up at him.

He looked grave. "Now what's wrong?"

"Miss Brenda Garboldi."

"What about her?"

"I have her class in five minutes."

"So?"

"What do you mean, 'So?' She's going to hate me!"

"She'll get over it."

"She might flunk me!"

John frowned, but he did not otherwise look concerned. "She'd better not."

If Brenda Garboldi held any animosity toward Melissa, she did not display it in the classroom. Her third finger no longer wore an engagement ring. Yet, despite the star status accompanying this first sharing of Melissa's euphoric news, a storm cloud hung over day. Melissa had a bigger hurdle to overcome than Miss Garboldi.

After classes ended, Melissa trudged to her dorm room, methodically arranged her books on her desk, and even retrieved the stray pencil that had fallen from her notebook. Finally, Melissa could delay it no longer. On the third ring, Melissa heard the friendly, "Barnes residence."

"Mom?" Melissa began, then faltered. She took a deep breath. "I think you'd better sit down. There's something I have to tell you."

CHAPTER 8: FOREVER YOURS

At closing time Monday night, John walked up to the circulation desk where Melissa was preparing to clock out. Mr. Schmidt was elsewhere in the building, switching off lights.

"Did you talk with your mother?"

Melissa punched the time card. "Yes."

"And?"

"Not good."

"Will she see us?"

"She says you will stay in a motel," Melissa reached for her jacket.

"I planned on it."

Melissa looked up, astonished. "Really?"

"I told you. We're done until after the wedding. I considered how upset you felt that day you broke up with me, and I agree with you. Things got out of hand, and I let them.

We have an entire lifetime together. Shall we go for a sandwich? At Berkley's, not my apartment."

Melissa hesitated. She didn't quite trust the sincerity behind John's offer, and she had plenty of homework waiting for her.

"We won't be long," John said. "I want to discuss our house."

House? Leaving the library with John, Melissa thought, If I'm married to him a thousand years, I don't think I'll ever understand him.

At Berkley's, John ordered Monday's chili for two and held up his cup, but Melissa quickly turned hers over and said, "Iced tea, please."

The waitress nodded and moved away. John took a sip and told her about the house: a bungalow, four blocks from school, three bedrooms, one bath, living and dining rooms, large kitchen, unfinished basement, two-car garage, reasonable price, and low taxes.

"The owner is anxious to sell," John said. "His wife died last fall, and he wants to retire to Florida. We could purchase a more lavish house, but I prefer to spend prudently, so I can buy you a car. Unless, of course, you would rather learn to drive stick."

He sipped again and winked at her from over his coffee cup. Melissa couldn't help smiling.

"I'll pass on the stick shift," she said. "When can I see it?"

"When do your classes end tomorrow?"

"Noon."

"Excellent. I'm free at two o'clock. I'll ask the realtor to meet us."

The next afternoon, standing outside the little red brick house with John, Melissa realized she might be seeing hers and John's first home. From across the street, children's laughter rang in the air, and Melissa imagined her children frolicking in the yard.

"....move in condition, the washer and dryer, along with the refrigerator and stove stay," the realtor said as he walked up the front steps with them. "The owner has already left town."

Melissa followed them inside. The combination living/dining rooms ruled the center of the house. A small bedroom was on her right. Beyond the short hall off the dining room were two tiny bedrooms with a bathroom between them. The kitchen, with windows on two sides, was in the back. One door led to the yard, bordered with ancient rose bushes; another opened to the basement. The rear porch had a small deck. John closed on the house forty-eight hours later. This way, John reasoned, they could gradually move their belongings and be settled by the first of January. Melissa could not wait.

Wednesday's drive to Grover's Park was a tense one. John had taken the day off work to beat the Thanksgiving traffic, and Melissa, who had cut classes, studied in the car, but as home loomed nearer, Melissa grew more uneasy. John, as usual, had little to say.

"Nervous?" John asked once as they neared the exit leading to Grover's Park.

"Yes! Aren't you?"

"Why would I be? I believe in us."

"But, John...."

"And your parents will, too."

All too soon, John pulled the car into the familiar driveway, where Melissa had loaded Steve's work van with her college bundles. Had it only been three months?

John walked around the car to open Melissa's door. She stayed, even after John extended his hand and said, "Joining me?"

Soberly, Melissa asked, "Do I have to?"

With a soft chuckle, John helped her out of the car.

"Don't be apprehensive, Melissa; believe in us."

"But...."

"You mustn't be afraid."

Something in John's words stirred a vague, unsettling memory, but Melissa had no chance to dwell on it, for Steve had opened the front door with a cheerful, "Welcome, home!"

and soon enveloped Melissa in a giant hug with one hand while he shook John's hand with the other.

"John," Steve said with a friendly smile. "It's a pleasure to meet you."

Steve motioned them into the house just as Melissa's mother walked out of the kitchen.

"John, I'd like you to meet my wife, Darlene."

John took one of her mother's small hands into both his larger ones, gazed deeply and sincerely into her eyes, and spoke with unusual warmth in his voice.

"Mrs. Barnes, I fully comprehend why you're angry with me, and I'm humbled you've received me into your home. Thank you for the opportunity to prove my good intentions toward your daughter."

Darlene took a deep breath and pressed her lips together before speaking.

"John, I'll be blunt with you. My first husband was twenty-five years older than me, and we had twenty happy years together. Your age does not concern me as much as Melissa's inexperience and her hastiness in making such an important decision."

"I completely understand."

He did not break his gaze.

"I don't think you do. However, my husband and I have discussed this at length, and, for Melissa's sake," Darlene glanced at Steve, "we fully intend to accept you with open arms into our family."

"I do appreciate it."

"That said, if you ever hurt Melissa, I will personally castrate you."

"Mom!"

John grinned, but his eyes shone blue and piercing. "Deal!" he agreed.

By now, Brian had paused halfway down the stairs and stood glaring at John. Steve noticed him, too.

"Brian, come meet your sister's fiancé.'"

Obediently, but most reluctantly, Brian plodded into the room, verbally acknowledged John, but refused his hand.

"Very admirable," John said, "to act so protective of your sister."

Brian's eyes narrowed, but he met John's with an unwavering stare. "That doesn't work on me." He looked at Darlene with a polite expression. "Shall I set the table?"

During dinner, Steve and Darlene donned their best company manners, and John accepted their food and hospitality with such humble grace that Melissa burst with pride at him. Moreover, John did not overstay his visit. After Steve agreed to John's invitation for breakfast, Steve, in turn, asked John to spend that morning with him cleaning offices. To Melissa's surprise, John responded with enthusiasm. No one, Melissa thought, at Jenson College would ever believe Professor Simotes went away for the weekend to play janitor.

All too soon, John excused himself from the table.

"I haven't yet checked into my room," he said. "Thank you again for the kind reception."

Steve rose, too, and again shook John's hand as he said, "I'll pick you up at seven."

"I look forward to it. Do you mind if Melissa accompanies me to the car? I'd like to briefly speak with her."

"Not at all."

Once outside, Melissa grabbed John's arm and beamed at him, marveling at the instantaneous bond between John and her stepfather. When they reached his car, she stood on tiptoe and happily kissed him. John drew back and absently kissed the top of her head.

His indifferent reaction baffled Melissa. "What's wrong?" she asked nervously.

John gently bent her head in the direction of the front upstairs window. The curtain moved with a slight quiver.

"Your little brother is monitoring us," he said.

Aghast, Melissa started to object, but John's finger touched her lips. "Shh. Let him alone. He's merely cautious. Besides, we're here this weekend to ease your parents' minds. Let's be subtle and offer no cause for worry."

Melissa remained in the driveway until John's car disappeared from sight. Inside the house, Steve and Brian were washing the dinner dishes, while Darlene was covering containers of left-over food. How could Melissa summarize her overwhelming gratitude for their cordial reception of John?

"Thanks, Mom." Melissa hoped her mother understood. "For, well, you know, everything."

Darlene shut the refrigerator door, and, not smiling, contemplated her daughter.

"I'm not arguing during your first night home, so I'll keep this brief. For many reasons, I do not approve of your decision to marry this man, and I think you will soon regret it. However," Darlene added, with a backward look at Steve, "because you're my daughter, and I love you, I will support your decision, although I feel it's a poor one."

Relieved at the absence of a dramatic scene and feeling it unwise to press the issue, Melissa instead studied the mess and asked, "Where should I help?"

"Go upstairs, take a shower, and relax. It's late, and I'm sure you've had a long day."

The next morning, when Melissa skipped downstairs to prepare breakfast, she found Steve had already left to collect John. Her mother was typing in her office, and Brian was lounging in the family room chomping on a bowl of cereal and watching a televised parade. For the first time in many months, Melissa felt at odds. No homework, no job, no friends, and, worst of all, no John. How would she fill the day? Maybe she could reconnect with Brian.

Melissa poured herself a bowl of the same junk and joined him on the couch.

Brian's face twisted in annoyance. "Don't you have anything better to do?"

"No, I'm hanging out here this weekend. What are you watching?"

Brian flipped the TV guide at her. Melissa took a deep breath and tossed it on the coffee table.

"Why are you acting like a jerk?" she asked.

"Scram."

Melissa marched to the television and switched it off. Brian ate his cereal with mock calmness. Melissa reached for his bowl, but Brian moved it away. Melissa's patience shattered.

"Lose the attitude. I'm leaving tomorrow and getting married in a couple of months. Then I'll never come back."

Brian made a face and twirled crazy signs around his head. Understanding dawned on Melissa.

"So that's it," she said. "You're jealous!"

He turned to her with an incredulous expression. "Jealous? Of that old creep? You need to have your head examined." Brian stalked out of the room, taking his bowl with him.

At noon, Darlene abandoned her work and invited Melissa to join her for lunch.

"Besides," her mother added, "we're overdue for a nice talk. Tell me about school."

Grateful her mother avoided the topic of Professor Simotes, Melissa chattered about all her classes, professors, roommates, and her job at the library. Darlene laughed on cue at Melissa's descriptive depiction of Mr. Schmidt, but when her smile faded and she regarded her daughter with soberness, Melissa knew the lighthearted conversation and mirth-making had ended.

"Tell me," Darlene said, "how you became involved with this professor when you aren't even taking music classes."

After a little pause, Melissa shared with her mother how she fell in love with John during orientation weekend, without knowing either his age or his teaching position at Jenson College. Melissa even admitted making the first move and did not leave out his subsequent rebuff and sudden change of heart. She did not mention Professor Simotes' resemblance to John Simons.

"I can't explain it, Mom. I love him, just like you loved Daddy. You didn't know him that long, either, and he was twenty-five years older than you were!"

"Melissa, I had already graduated from…."

"Mom, come on! Four years? That's not much of an age difference."

Darlene sighed and brushed the hair away from Melissa's indignant face. "No, dear, I suppose not. But a good deal of maturation happens in those four years between eighteen and twenty-two. Marrying John is different from going steady with Jason. You shouldn't take this lightly."

"I'm not!"

Her mother said nothing, so Melissa persisted. "What did your parents say when you married Daddy?"

Darlene laughed out loud. "Not only did they try talking me out of it, my best friend berated me for wanting to spend my life with an old man." Her tone grew serious. "Honey, I want what's best for you."

"This is best. I promise."

"What about your education and dream to become an English teacher?"

"I'm not dropping out of school, if that's what you mean. Because John's staff, my tuition will be free."

Darlene sighed and left the room. She returned with a pen and pad of paper.

"Well," she said slowly, "I guess we have a wedding to plan."

With heads together, Melissa and her mother spent the rest of the afternoon making tentative arrangements. The work so absorbed them, neither heard the back door rattle, until Steve called out, "Can you lovely ladies help a couple of overburdened men?"

He and John stood at the porch, arms full of brown paper sacks. Melissa rushed to the door and opened it for them.

"Wow, what a feast!" Melissa peered into the bags as Steve and John walked past her into the kitchen.

John set his bags down on the counter next to Steve's bundles. Steve winked at Melissa and said, "Well, let us know when dinner's ready. John and I are going to watch the game."

Darlene looked shocked, and Steve chuckled. "Just kidding. However, I will ask the two of you to vacate my kitchen. John and I have plenty of work to do."

Melissa lingered after Darlene left the room, watching John empty his purchases and organize ingredients. Steve set a roll of wax paper by John, then opened a drawer and brought him a mallet and rolling pin. John unrolled the white butcher paper.

"What's that?" Melissa said, looking at the pale, pink meat. "Pork chops?"

"Veal."

"We always have turkey for Thanksgiving. I've never eaten veal."

"You will tonight."

At dinner, each of them shared that for which he or she felt especially thankful. Every year, John topped Melissa's list, and every year, she contrived creative ways of expressing it. The first year, Melissa had said, "New beginnings." This time, Melissa, heart overflowing with the joy of desires soon to be met, freely spoke the plain truth.

More than once, Darlene praised the dinner Steve and John had prepared. Brian's eyes remained glued to his plate throughout the entire meal. Steve modestly admitted playing kitchen assistant to John's finer talents and pronounced John a fitting culinary accomplice.

Darlene smiled at John. "The last time I ate veal escalopes was with Frank, before Melissa was born."

Melissa scraped the mushroom sauce off her meat. John returned Darlene's smile.

"I'm glad you enjoyed it. I hadn't prepared this dish in a long time and must confess, did worry over its outcome."

"No, it's excellent. Where did you learn to make it?"

"My mother. She was an excellent cook." John gestured to the pile of mushrooms at the rim of Melissa's plate. "No dessert unless you finish."

"Don't worry. I'll clean my plate." Melissa planned to scrape the remnants into the garbage when John wasn't looking.

Darlene changed the subject. "John, this afternoon Melissa and I discussed the wedding. With less than two months to plan, your idea of a small wedding seems perfectly reasonable. Did you want it here or in Jenson?"

"Whatever Melissa wants. My family lives in Cleveland, so either way, they must travel. Also, please understand I will pay the expenses."

Melissa noticed her mother and Steve exchange glances, but John continued.

"I never expected for you to assume financial responsibility for my wedding. We are the ones being abrupt. Nevertheless, I do appreciate your assistance with the planning."

"Well, then," Steve said, "I nominate Jenson as the location. We have no extended family in Grover's Park, and my close friends live in Munsonville. Melissa does have a couple of good childhood friends, but they're away at college. We don't mind traveling. Besides, Jenson makes it easier for Melissa's college friends, as well as the friends and colleagues you, John, would want to invite."

As Melissa pondered Steve's words, a bold idea popped into her head. "What about the congregational church in Munsonville? That seems like a nice place for a wedding."

"No!" John's eyes swept around the table at the four shocked expressions staring at him. "I don't believe in God," he added in a milder tone.

"That's okay," Darlene said soothingly. "Melissa's father didn't, either, and we aren't church-goers. What about the college? Does it have a hall we could rent?"

Melissa tuned them out. Maybe John did not believe in God, but Melissa doubted John had stated his true reason for declining a religious ceremony. I'll bet, Melissa thought, sudden bitterness filling her heart, John won't marry me in the place he married Bryony. Would she ever step away from the penumbra of Bryony's memory?

"....so I'm fine with anything you and Melissa decide. My only requests are: no church, simple, and the first of January. Other than that, make the plans, keep me informed about my role, and send me the bills."

The next few weeks flew past under a cloud of happy anticipation, for John had begun transferring his possessions into the bungalow, a sure sign he intended to move forward with the blissful nuptials. Melissa couldn't wait to see John gazing at her, full of love, and saying those two magical words, "I do."

In the meantime, several staff members offered the engaged couple various items for their new home. An art teacher purchased new lamps for her house; would John and Melissa like her old ones? The math teacher's grandmother died; could they use any living room furniture? The secretary in the financial aid office found a bargain of an antique dresser at a garage sale and bought it for Melissa.

As children, Melissa and Shelly had solemnly promised to serve as each other's maids of honors at their respective weddings. Shelly nearly fainted when Melissa called her at school and reminded her friend of that pact, which Shelly, marveling at the whirlwind romance, couldn't wait to keep.

"I always wondered who'd go first. What about a dress?"

"John said pick out something you like and send me the bill. You're the only bridesmaid."

"Is yellow okay? It's my favorite color."

"Yellow's fine," Melissa said, but her mind stood before John, hearing him say the loving words he once had said to Bryony.

Melissa, with her disdain for clothes shopping, circumvented the wedding dress dilemma by asking to wear her mother's wedding dress, the one she wore when she married Melissa's father.

"You still have it, don't you?" Melissa asked anxiously.

"For goodness sakes, why?"

Melissa's voice broke. "So Daddy can be part of the day, too."

"Oh, honey!"

Melissa began to cry. "He *will* be there, won't he, Mommy?" She felt like a baby now and didn't care.

"Of course." Darlene took Melissa into her arms and stroked her hair. "Wherever your father is, I'm sure he's proud of you."

John obtained permission to utilize the entire music department, nearly half the fourth floor, for the wedding and then asked the Berkleys to cater the reception. Jenny solicited her aunt, a professional baker, to provide the cake, and suggested holding the ceremony at midnight.

"With everyone in town anyway, just do things in reverse. Host a private New Year's Eve party on the fourth floor and conclude with your wedding. Wouldn't that be far out?"

Melissa liked the idea, and, to her astonishment, so did John, whom Melissa hardly saw during the early part of December. Both were drowning under the load of final exam preparations. The combination of John's absence with the whisperings from the other students as she passed them in the halls or weaved her way through the cafeteria created a tenth and isolating level of hell for Melissa. When the passage from Melissa Marchells to Melissa Simotes grew a little too warm, she gazed down at the talisman sparkling on her left hand and focused on the impending reward.

Even Julie appeared to have forsaken her. She had taken the news of Melissa's engagement rather coolly. This surprised Melissa since she had assumed she had found an ally in the free-thinking, goal-oriented, independent, "cut off my braids for a page boy" Julie. On the contrary, Julie had distanced herself since the day John had kissed Melissa in front of her friends and led her up the stairs. Melissa still ate lunch with Julie and Tracy, but any strained conversation Melissa attempted between bites of food faltered under Julie's stony disapproval.

Only Jenny supported Melissa, and she did so with staunch, unwavering loyalty. Many evenings, Melissa and her schoolbooks found solace in Jenny's comfortable, albeit messy, dorm room. Jenny had filled her walls with black light posters, smothered her bed with ratty stuffed animals, piled weeks of dirty clothes in front of her closet door, and hoarded stacks of fashion magazines. With eyes round with awe and a mouth formed into a perfect "o," Jenny reveled in each of Melissa's plans for her wedding and new life with John with a fascination bordering on reverence. She "pooh-poohed" their classmates' scorn.

"They're just jealous," Jenny insisted. "You could look a long time, and you'd never find anyone as sexy as Professor Simotes. He's well-established here, too. While the rest of us will struggle to start our careers, you're set for life."

The week of exams arrived and with great relief, Melissa completed the test she dreaded the most, momentarily wondered if Miss Garboldi might vindictively grade it, and then nearly pranced to blessed freedom. Never again would Melissa have to cross its threshold.

Her exit, however, lacked the hoped-for smooth ending. As Melissa reached the door, a sweet, musical voice announced, "Melissa, please remain inside the classroom. I wish to speak with you."

Melissa's stomach flip-flopped and then turned to stone. She would not avoid Miss Garboldi's wrath. Melissa stepped aside, nervousness increasing with each second, until the other students filed into the hall. Miss Garboldi's seemingly innocuous words unsettled Melissa as the she began understanding the weight behind them. She had greatly deluded herself. Miss Garboldi's silence during the remainder of the semester was not meek abdication of her man. It was methodical, calculated revenge.

After what seemed a very long time, Miss Garboldi slid the papers into her briefcase and faced the Melissa. Her expression appeared nonchalant, but her voice came straight from the freezer.

"Never in my brief career as an educator have I experienced a student as brass as you. I suggest you raise your standards of behavior and develop a sense of professionalism before you consider entering a classroom."

Melissa's face grew hot. "Miss Garboldi, I...."

How could Melissa convince her teacher that Melissa had not interfered, that Melissa had nothing to do with the breakup, that she and John were simply destined for each other?

"Furthermore, I intend to pass you with a high grade, regardless of how you performed on this test. I never want to see you in my classroom again. Your affair with my fiancé made this a most uncomfortable semester. You're free to go."

So, Miss Garboldi would not hear Melissa's side. Subdued, Melissa turned to leave. She had nearly reached the door when she heard, "One more thing, Melissa."

Melissa stopped.

"Remember, what goes around, often comes around."

Melissa fled to her American history final. Miss Garboldi's confrontation upset Melissa more than she would at first admit. John downplayed the scene, reminding Melissa that contact with her teacher had ended with the final exam. Ironically, it was Jill who unwittingly provided Melissa with much-needed reassurance.

Jill had been lying on the bed watching Melissa pack up her possessions. "Since when did you become the femme fatale?"

Melissa dumped her top drawer into a suitcase.

"What's your hold on Professor Simotes?"

Melissa snapped the case shut. "My hold?"

"You do know he flunked three female students this semester."

"So what?"

"Pretty girls with bad grades don't flunk his classes, if you know what I mean."

A knock on the door ended the conversation. John had arrived. They were moving most of her possessions to the bungalow. Melissa couldn't wait to leave. Jill and her petty insinuations made her sick. Look at how Miss Garboldi had acted the day of finals. If John really had slept around as much as Jill claimed, Miss Garboldi would never have tolerated it. As she followed John out the door, Melissa threw her trashy roommate a gloating look. Jill was jealous, that's all, because she couldn't score with anything except garbage. Melissa never wanted lay eyes on her again.

Melissa's secret hope that John might spend Christmas with her collapsed when John's father caught the flu, which quickly developed into pneumonia. Without first discussing it with Melissa, John called Steve and asked him to bring Melissa home. This left John free to drive straight to Cleveland. John shared that news to Melissa when she met him for dinner in the music room one night, a dinner he quickly cancelled.

Although she didn't like the change, Melissa hid her disappointment under a cloak of diplomacy.

"I totally understand. We went through this all the time with my dad."

"I appreciate it, Melissa," John said quietly.

He continued grading papers and did not look up.

Melissa spent a sober Christmas Day in Grover's Park. The day seemed bleak and gray without John present to spend it with her. She waited until Christmas evening to try on Darlene's wedding gown. Gauzy, filmy, and white, the dress reached Melissa's ankles; the short veil skimmed her waist, where the fabric pinched. Darlene laughed at Melissa holding her breath.

"Believe it or not, Melissa, the dress was too big on me, so I added a couple of stitches. I can take them out."

Melissa swished back and forth before the large mirror in her former bedroom, recalling a certain Halloween night, just a year ago, when she had donned a Victorian-style dress to play-act Bryony Simons. In less than seven days, Melissa, in her mother's wedding dress, would marry the man she hoped was John Simons. She ceased twirling when she remembered John's final request wedding request. For someone who had wanted "simple," John had many final requests. For instance, he wanted no vows.

She had argued the point with him. "But why not? It's traditional."

"It's also foolish. Spouses frequently break vows. Prattle means nothing to me. I'd rather incorporate something more ancient and binding."

Another blow! No church, and now, no "I do" either. Why have a wedding with no vows? And what did John mean, "Spouses frequently break vows?" Did John refer to his own past behavior, as interpreted by Henry, when John Simotes lived as John Simons? Or had John simply recalled Henry and Bryony's adulterous liaison? Maybe John feared Melissa might also cheat on him, so instituting a "no vows" policy insulated his heart. Maybe Melissa needed more understanding. If she was mature enough to marry, she ought to be mature enough to respect her future husband's point of view.

So, instead of expressing the letdown she felt, Melissa tried sounding intrigued and interested.

"What did you have in mind?"

"A secret."

Damn! John was frustrating!

"Have you talked to the minister? Is he okay with it?"

"Yes. He's generic."

John also vetoed Melissa's suggestion to spend their wedding night at Munsonville Inn, something Melissa had intended as a surprise for John. The surprise backfired. John had discovered her arrangements, canceled them, and then coldly accused her of deception.

Stunned, Melissa had vehemently protested her innocence and defended the lodging as a quaint romantic venue for their first night of married life together. As she continued to jabber, Melissa watched the fury on John's face settle into a maddening, condescending calmness.

Not until she sputtered into silence did John speak. "What is your preoccupation with that village?"

Melissa's face turned pink. "I used to live there, remember?"

"For what, three or four months?"

"I just have good memories of the place, that's all." She tried reversing the debate, hoping John might change his mind. "Why do you want to stay in Jenson on our wedding night?"

"For good luck. We christen ships with champagne. Well, we shall christen our new home."

"You have some very strange ideas."

"We'll have champagne, too."

Two days before the wedding, Melissa and her family returned to Jenson and checked into the same bed and breakfast they had stayed four months ago. They spent a full day finalizing preparations and moving Melissa's remaining items in the bungalow. That included steamer trunk full of her Munsonville treasures, *The Best-Loved Compositions of John Simons, Creatures of the Night: Witches, Werewolves, and Vampires, Nocturnal Lore: The Collected Tales of Henry Matthew,* as well as Bryony's broken music box, which

Melissa stored in the back of the guest room closet. As they left, Melissa noticed the hum of the refrigerator. Curious, she peeked inside the freezer and found it empty, except for several cartons of natural vanilla ice cream.

Despite the distracting activity, Darlene acted noticeably jittery, and Brian appeared aloof and withdrawn. Only Steve retained his usual warm, easy-going self, and for this Melissa felt thankful.

Julie called at bedtime begging Melissa to rethink her decision. The abruptness of the plea took Melissa aback. Since Julie had not yet voiced her objections, Melissa had assumed she never would.

"Julie," Melissa said, confident she could make Julie see reason. "You don't understand. I love him."

"You're making a horrible mistake."

"Julie...."

"I'm not talking about his position, his reputation, or even the fact that, until a few short weeks ago, he was engaged to your literature teacher."

"Then what?"

"Not that those aren't good enough reasons."

Melissa grew tired of Julie's superior stance. "Are you going to tell me, because if not...."

Julie took a deep breath and then blurted out, "I don't think you've accepted your father's death. You're trying to replace him with Professor Simotes. You don't want a husband. You want a daddy."

The nerve of Julie practicing psychology homework on her! In Julie's efforts to succeed in life and break out of the village she scorned, Julie had resorted to pegging Melissa into theories. Melissa didn't know whether to laugh, cry, or tell Julie off.

"I think you're envious of my good fortune," Melissa said. "I'm sorry that John and I aren't stamped and dyed like you and David. Every relationship is different."

"I can't stop you from having a different relationship, Melissa."

"Good, I'm glad you finally...."

"But I won't witness it. Good night."

New Year's Eve heralded the grand day with a biting wind and deathly ashen skies. The weatherman forecasted no snow, yet Melissa nurtured a secret wish the skies would defy his predictions. She wondered if John Simotes enjoyed sleigh riding.

John was not scheduled to arrive at the Chicago convention until Thursday evening, so Melissa could spend two entire days in John's presence without outside distractions. Although John had forbidden it, Melissa had sneaked into the music room that afternoon and peeked at the festive decorations. John had solicited the services of the art department and those students, armed with ribbon, candles, and flowers, had transformed the fourth floor into a place of neo-Victorian beauty. The tables rivaled any nineteenth century reception with their white cloths, candelabras, and mulberry silk flowers. Melissa smiled smugly. Whether or not the professor knew it, something of the historic John Simons still lurked inside him, and now he belonged to her forever. The best of the bargain was yet to come.

She met John coming down the stairs. When John saw Melissa, he frowned, and she steeled herself for the inevitable lecture.

"My parents aren't coming," John said. "My father had a relapse."

Melissa feigned shock. Surely John was dodging the fact his parents had died nearly a century ago. They both knew John had no parents to bring to the wedding, but Melissa felt helpless to address it. If only he'd stop pretending!

"Oh, John, I'm so sorry. Is he in the hospital?"

"No," John said. "The doctor confined him to bed."

Melissa reached out to hug John, but he sidestepped her embrace and continued up the stairs.

"First opportunity," John said, "we drive to Cleveland."

By eight o'clock, the music department swarmed with guests. Some lined up at the lavishly filled buffet tables; others milled about the bar area; and still more grouped in semicircles, drink in hand, sharing the latest gossip. Melissa overheard Mr. Berkley refuse any payment for the food, except the costs of the ingredients.

"We would not have such a successful business without the support of college people like you," Mr. Berkley said with a smile. "Please accept our token of appreciation."

Melissa watched people carrying heaping plates past her and toward the rows of tables. If anyone goes hungry tonight, Melissa thought, it's his own fault.

Side Effect, the band that had played orientation weekend, began at nine o'clock, only this time, they worked off a dance set list. More than once, Brad Eaton tried coaxing John onstage, and, each time, John refused.

"Johnny," Brad stepped back in total amazement. "You never turn down a chance to play."

"I have one official business tonight," John said. "No exceptions."

Melissa overheard that remark, and her heart soared. Although she mingled with the guests as much as John did, her mind never strayed from her soon to be husband. John, clad in the pewter suit he had worn for their first date at Rudys, took away her breath each time she peeped at him. If he wasn't John Simons....

She quickly dismissed the thought. Of course Professor Simotes was John Simons.

At ten o'clock Melissa, accompanied by Darlene, left the music department and descended to Jenny's room to get ready. Jenny had spread Darlene's wedding garment over her bed and then had taken Shelly to a friend's room on the other side of the floor to change, too.

Melissa dressed slowly, prolonging the anticipation, relishing each moment that brought her nearer to eternity with John. As Darlene slipped the wedding dress over Melissa's head, Melissa allowed her fingers the sensuous pleasure of gliding over the sleek material. She could almost feel John's fingers around her waist, leading her in a waltz. She stood before Jenny's mirror, noting her mother's shimmering satin gown and her mother's worried reflection.

"Mom?"

"Melissa, are you *sure*?"

After indulging a last, lingering look in the mirror, she turned to Darlene. Melissa had never felt so grown-up. With exaggerated patience and a confident smile, as if speaking to a child, Melissa said, "Mom, John is the one."

Nevertheless, Darlene cried as she fussed with Melissa's hair and make-up. She was adjusting the veil when Shelly stepped inside. Melissa's only attendant wore a pale yellow dress with a fluted collar, sleeves meeting her wrists, a gathered skirt, and rows of ruffles sweeping the floor. With a start, Melissa realized Shelly's dress closely resembled the gown worn by the woman John had killed in the gazebo.

"Ooh, Melissa," Shelly said with a gasp. "You look *so* pretty!"

Melissa heard a knock and then Steve's voice saying, "Melissa, are you ready? Everyone's waiting."

This time, Melissa wavered. If Steve only realized the enormity of his question. *Was* she ready? In a few minutes, Melissa would participate in a ceremony that would cleave her to John Simotes for the rest of her life. Destiny summoned her with a long finger. Was she ready?

"Come in," Melissa called back. "I am ready."

Steve entered, holding out a bouquet of white and red roses. Its sweet perfume filled the room and instantly carried Melissa back to Henry's study, the place where Melissa had filled many frustrating hours longing for John, while enduring Henry's scoffing, and eventually stirring up the audacity to ask Henry....

"From John," Steve said.

Melissa, heart overflowing with desire and hope, gingerly accepted the flowers and remembered the abundant rose gardens at Simons Mansion, especially the bushes that were not purple. Was that where John had developed his fondness for roses? Had Bryony carried roses down the aisle on her wedding day? Melissa lightly stroked a velvety petal. Bryony...Henry...none of them mattered now. John was hers.

Darlene dabbed at her eyes and then lightly pressed her lips on Melissa's forehead. Shelly blew Melissa a kiss as she walked out of the room with Darlene. Steve closed the door and stood in front of Melissa.

"You know, I could not feel any prouder of you today than if you were my own daughter."

A lump rose in Melissa's throat, and she fought back tears. She had not expected this from Steve.

"And I want you to know that if, for some reason, this marriage does not work out, you may always return home, no questions asked."

"Steve," Melissa began.

"I'm not saying you'll have trouble. I wish you all the joy and love I share with your ma and then some. But I'm here for you. Always. That's a promise. Okay?"

Melissa nodded, her eyes and heart too full for words. After fielding tremendous criticism for her decision to marry John, she had not anticipated such unconditional support. She waited for the wave to pass before asking, "Steve, you don't think I'm making a mistake, do you?"

Steve hesitated. The dim dormitory room lighting shone brightly enough to reveal the concern in Steve's gray eyes.

"I think," Steve began and then stopped, fumbling for words. "I think only you can answer that question. If this is the right decision for you, I'll back it one hundred percent. If you later change your mind...."

"Oh, Steve, I've never felt so sure in my life!"

Steve smiled softly, but the worry lines remained.

"Well then, young lady," he said. "I think you have some place to go."

He offered Melissa his arm and led her back upstairs. At the sight of Melissa standing in the doorway, the substitute keyboardist for the band winked at her and began playing a clumsy version of Pachelbel's *Canon*. Shelly walked down the center of the room, followed by Steve and Melissa. A man dressed in a brown suit, whom Melissa later learned was Katie's brother Don, not Henry, took his place by John.

The minister, short with thinning dishwater hair, clutched his service book and motioned John to stand near Melissa.. Then he said, "Dearly beloved, we are gathered here today...."

At once, the oft-repeated words sounded stale to Melissa, especially while standing next to a man teeming with life because of her blood. Nothing about her relationship with John was conventional, so why should their wedding ceremony conform to mediocre standards? For the first time, she pondered John's stance regarding empty syllables, clichéd vows, and keeping his vision for the ceremony hidden. Intensely curious, Melissa waited for John's plans to unfold.

The minister rambled a few prayers and then explained to those present how the next portion of the service would break from popular custom.

"We'll perform several different ceremonies," the minister said, "and each symbolizes Melissa's and John's union. Instead of making promises, they will bind themselves to each other in everlasting and irrevocable ways."

He gave a white, taper candle to Melissa, and then he gave one to John. By turns, the minister lit each wick, which Melissa and John used to simultaneously light the one, single, large candle on the small table before them. Melissa did not understand why John considered lighting a common candle a big deal. Many people did this at weddings.

Don held out a white satin pillow. Two splendid rings sat on it. The ribbon of diamonds on Melissa's ring contrasted beautifully with John's plain platinum band. The minister prayed a blessing and then gestured to John.

With steady fingers, John picked up Melissa's ring. Ardent eyes gripped hers as John slowly slid the ring onto her finger, pausing, watching, before gradually allowing his hand to slip away. Melissa's heart followed that hand, and the minister had to nod at Melissa to repeat the maneuver for John.

Although unembellished, the weight of John's ring stunned her, and Melissa, already nervous about touching John, officially, in front of so many people, nearly dropped it. With cold, trembling fingers, Melissa managed to fit the ring onto John's finger. She felt his eyes studying each movement, but she avoided his gaze, terrified of sabotaging her task if she saw the depths of his passion.

The minister handed John a silver goblet. As John brought the chalice to Melissa's lips, she spied the crimson wine inside the bowl and smelled its potent fragrance of grape, cedar, and violet. Melissa obediently opened her lips, and John trickled its dry, full taste down her throat. She drank deeply because John offered it. She then raised the cup to John. His face appeared composed, but the stare over the rim revealed an inner, raging tempest.

After setting down the goblet, the minister produced a length of white ribbon and loosely bound Melissa's and John's hands together. He then took scissors, snipped a piece of John's hair, which he placed between Melissa's fingers, then repeated the same on Melissa's head, giving the lock to John. During this exchange, no one uttered a sound, not even a single clearing of the throat. Melissa glanced at the bonds joining her and John, in this moment and for all eternity. The alabaster cord had finally accomplished what Melissa's blood had begun. They were one.

The minister cut the ribbon from their hands. He smiled at John and spoke for first time since the atypical ceremony had begun.

"You may now kiss the bride."

John tucked Melissa's hair into his trousers pocket. He lightly slid a hand under her chin and raised it, so Melissa, who felt too overwhelmed for even a gasp, would face him. Was it the room's subtle lighting or had some buried emotion broken loose inside John? For one fleeting moment, Melissa thought she had glimpsed something in John's eyes, a meld of ownership, entitlement, and victory. Melissa knew that look. John Simons had worn it right before he kissed Bryony in front of Reverend Marseilles. In Melissa's mind, there was only a single reason for it.

He does love me, Melissa thought happily. John may never have said it, but, somewhere deep within him, John cares.

John bent toward Melissa and greeted her lips with unparalleled gentleness. He moved back only far enough to brush her cheek with the tips of his fingers; his gaze penetrated the depths of her soul.

"Congratulations," John softly said, "Mrs. Simotes."

CHAPTER 9: BECOMING ONE FLESH

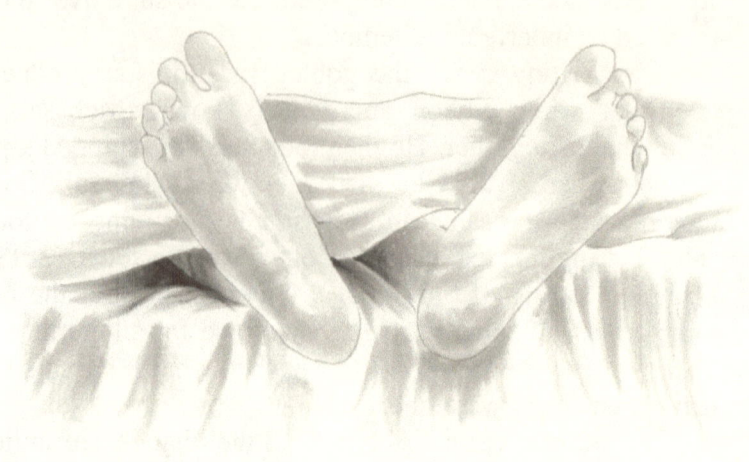

From that moment onward, Melissa perceived a subtle change in John, although she could not decide if she liked it, since she did not immediately discern the transformation's full extent.

She first sensed it when they cut through the frosting's satiny sheen and straight through the cake's four layers. John had slightly relaxed, similar to when one overcomes a monumental challenge and brandishes the trophy.

Before John fed Melissa a morsel of cake, he topped it with one of the lifelike icing roses. His fingers pushed past her lips along with the pastry, and he rested the tips of his other hand against the base of her neck. While the rose melted in Melissa's mouth, John softly kissed her, lightly pressing his fingers into her throat, and seeking her reaction with eyes of fire. She remembered fully how John had once drunk from her neck, a virtual fountain of youth for the human life he again knew. Through it, Melissa had become both the source and fulfillment of John's future.

John stood erect and waited for Melissa to feed him. As her fingers touched John's mouth, he captured them with his lips and held them fast until he finished swallowing. Brad chuckled at them as he headed for the men's room.

"Break it up; break it up," Brad good-naturedly muttered.

Together, Melissa and John cut and distributed the rest of the cake. Head down, Brian approached the dessert table, but Melissa slid the coveted plate back an inch as he reached for it.

"Come on, Brian," she whispered to him. "Be happy for me."

Brian shook his head. "I can't. You're making a huge mistake."

He selected a different piece, stuck a plastic fork between his teeth, and stalked away.

By two o'clock, the guests had begun to disperse. John linked his arm around Melissa's waist and murmured into her ear, "Ready to go home?"

Home? For Melissa's entire life, the word implied a dwelling she shared with her parents and Brian. Now, that word meant something else, the place where she would build a life with John. *Home!*

She gazed up at John with glistening eyes. "I want to say good-bye to my family first."

John's kiss felt more possessive then understanding of Melissa's wishes, but Melissa decided fatigue had blunted her judgment. As John joined the other band members near the exit, Melissa eased her way past the lingering guests, all the while accepting their congratulations and well-wishes for a happy future.

Steve and Darlene sat talking with the Daltons at the farthest end of the room, but they both rose as Melissa approached. The look of bleak desolation on her mother's face shot straight through Melissa's heart.

"Oh, Mom!" Melissa threw her arms around her mother's neck and kissed her wet cheek. "Thank you. For everything. I mean it."

"Keep in touch, hon. *Please.*"

"Mom! I'm married. I haven't left the family."

Darlene sniffed and reached inside her pocket for a waded tissue. "I know."

Melissa turned to Steve, and he wrapped her in a tight embrace and patted her back.

"Remember what I promised," he whispered in her ear.

"I will, Steve," Melissa said. "Always."

As Melissa walked away, she overheard her mother say, "And I thought it hurt when Melissa left for college...."

She found John talking with two band members. Brian loitered at the dessert table, helping himself to a second piece of cake. He looked up as Melissa passed him.

"Hey, Liss."

Melissa paused and then retraced her steps. Brian set down the plate, and, to Melissa's astonishment, hugged her.

"I really do wish you all the happiness in the world," Brian said. "I just don't think you'll get it with him." He jerked his head in John's direction.

"You're wrong, Brian. You'll see.

"I hope so, Liss," Brian said, as picked up his cake. "For your sake, I really hope so."

Family obligations satisfied, Melissa hurried to meet John. He noticed her approach and immediately ceased speaking.

"Now that you've gotten romance out of your system," Brad said, "remember band practice resumes next month."

John pulled Melissa to him and fervently kissed her.

"Ready?" he murmured.

"Yes, oh, yes!"

Melissa insisted they stop at Jenny's room. John seemed annoyed at the further delay, but Melissa giggled as she retrieved the bag. She couldn't wait to show John!

Twice on the way to the bungalow, John stopped the car in the middle of the road to kiss Melissa, and, twice, Melissa tasted the lingering flavor of the wine that had sealed their covenant. When they reached their home, John carried Melissa, who still clutched the package, up the back deck. He stopped to kiss her again, longer and harder than he had all night, enough for Melissa to wonder if they'd ever make it inside the house. Once, Melissa opened her eyes to watch him. John's were tightly closed, and his rigid face showed controlled, but rapidly rising, excitement.

The sky had begun to lighten, although no colors of dawn had broken through the fading black, when John finally unlocked the door. They made it as far as the dining room before John leaned Melissa against the treasured Steinway and kissed her with such unrestrained ardor, hands flying everywhere, that Melissa knew she had to stop him. John might have insisted on consummating the marriage in their bungalow, but Melissa wanted to be sure they completed it in the bedroom.

She placed her free hand on the side of his face and pulled slightly away.

"Wait," Melissa said.

John, mouth still slightly ajar, lifted only his eyes, and they were not pleased.

"It's my turn for a surprise."

Curiosity flickered and then vanished. John, slowly, reluctantly, straightened and stepped back, but his strained expression gripped hers, and he breathed fast and deep. As a child, Melissa had tossed a wind-up, plastic, potato-shaped toy back and forth with Shelly. The goal was for the other to be holding it when the buzzer discharged. The longer it ticked, the greater had grown Melissa's frenzy in handling it, knowing detonation was imminent. John was a land mine threatening to explode, and that, coupled with Melissa momentarily gaining the upper hand, filled her with inebriating confidence in that, this time, she would prevail.

She took John's hand and led him to the bedroom, then turned and smiled mysteriously at him.

"I'll be right back," Melissa promised.

Once inside the bathroom, Melissa squirmed with uncontrollable delight as she quickly shed the wedding dress and slipped the sheer, purple baby doll over her head, imagining the unabashed pleasure on John's face once she paraded herself before him. A glimpse in the mirror, even in the poorly lit room, revealed the smudged makeup and streaked mascara. A quick search in the medicine cabinet produced a bar of soap. Once she scrubbed her face, Melissa decided she'd better brush her teeth, too.

She hastily mopped the sink with the hand towel, hung the dress on the door hook, and scampered to the bedroom, already partially illuminated by the pink rays escaping through the windows. In the doorway, Melissa stopped in sudden shock. John was spread out across the bed, soundly asleep. Only his chest moved and that but barely. A strangled half-laugh, half-cry cry broke from Melissa and cut the room's stillness. Damn the loss of her fantasy wedding night, and damn her premature gloating at having controlled John. She had lost again. She leaned across John, carefully grabbed a pillow, and trudged to the living room. The lone afghan from back of the couch did little to deflect the chill, but Melissa shook more from bitter disappointment than inadequate room temperature. Her overtired limbs jerked and fought against suffocating sleep as it dragged her into its empty depths. When John's kisses awakened her, the morning sun was lighting up the room. Ecstatic at the sight of him, Melissa completely forgot about the bedroom until John, naked except for the hateful T-shirt, took her there for round two. Propped against the remaining pillow was the promised bottle of champagne. As if to compensate for his earlier omission, John confined Melissa to bed for most of the day. They made love, dozed, and made love again and again until physical hunger drove them into the kitchen. John, who had now added a pair of shorts to keep the shirt company, quickly assembled a stir-fry. They ate at the kitchen table while John showed Melissa his itinerary for the upcoming weekend.

"We leave tomorrow," John said. "I must confirm registration by four o'clock to attend the evening banquet."

An introductory, mandatory session would follow, led by someone whose name Melissa could not remember, but whose importance she deduced by the slew of letters and abbreviations succeeding his name. With pride, John pointed to the places on the agenda featuring him.

"These are the sessions I will lead," John paused. "I hope they go as planned. I never prepared for them until after finals ended."

No wonder John seemed so tired! Melissa marveled at how John juggled preparations for this conference with his full work load and their wedding arrangements. Her class and job schedule appeared ridiculously easy by comparison. Remorse for her anger toward John pricked Melissa, especially since he had acted so attentive today, and she resolved to atone for last night's lack of compassion with extra consideration during the conference.

Hoping it would promote self-confidence in his upcoming task, Melissa smiled her most encouraging smile at John and said, "I'm sure you'll do just fine."

John picked up his plate and stood. "Ice cream?"

Melissa conceded and then scanned the titles, her first real glimpse into her husband's mind: *The Role of the Professional, Classical Musician in Undergraduate Education*; *Western Classical Music in Elementary Education: Pros and Cons*; *The Marginalization of Classical Music in Contemporary Society;* and *Why Popular Music Dilutes Music Literacy.*

"You're welcome to attend, if you wish," John said, setting a dish before her, "but you will probably find it dull. I suggest you bring a good book."

Still, John had purchased tickets to several musical events in the city for after the conference's end. Melissa basked in the joys that lay ahead in the near future and looked forward to her first, comprehensive lessons into the world of the man she had married.

Melissa ignored John's advice to pack literary distractions and instead chose to attend his lectures. Both the concepts he purported and the rhetoric he spurted lay beyond Melissa's comprehension, but she gave him her polite attention anyway. Although she listened with great patience and feigned interest, Melissa left each meeting room with no further understanding of the presented subject matter than when she had entered it.

Nor did the scholarly orations end with John's morning and afternoon sessions. The musical masses in attendance gathered round their hotel dinner table, hoping John would expound or debate. With as much civility as she could muster under the circumstances, Melissa deferred to the vultures. Such circumstances also taught Melissa volumes about John and his life as a classical musician, a life in which she now participated and must also now accept.

Melissa's reward began on Monday, when room service woke her with the breakfast trays John had ordered. With that act, their honeymoon assumed a regularity that enraptured Melissa and more than recompensed the sacrifices she made for John during his shining moments.

Each day began at night with a mutual shower, although to Melissa's amusement John's shirt remained in place, and ended with dinner at a fine restaurant followed by a concert. Once they returned to their hotel, John kept room service hopping with outrageous orders, which enabled them to remain between the sheets. They slept only when exhaustion overcame them, and then they wakened to begin anew.

The passionate whirlwind lasted only until Friday morning, the day the Simotes' packed their bags for home. School began again on Monday morning. John especially faced the distasteful task of repairing strained professional relationships. During the drive back to Jenson, John told Melissa his superiors had delivered quite the castigation for his relationship to her. The news alarmed Melissa. Why had not John mentioned it before their marriage?

As if he read her mind, John glanced at her and said, "I wanted you to know the depth of my commitment to you."

Reassured, Melissa leaned back into the seat and contemplated the open road. She meant so much to John, he would take a metaphoric bullet for her. He really belonged to her. Never had Melissa's future felt so bright.

Stepping inside the front door to her new home initiated a symbolic bell-ringing inside Melissa's head, similar to the manner in which her alarm clock once reversed her hallucinatory existence as Bryony and returned her to reality. During their brief engagement, Melissa's deliberations centered on the exultation that her greatest wish, union with John Simons forever, had finally come true. She had given little consideration to what marriage to John might actually mean in terms of daily life.

To Melissa's dismay, their lifestyle revolved not around home, but on Jenson College, where John and Melissa both worked and where Melissa still attended school fulltime. Because they lived two blocks farther away from school than John's former apartment, she ate many free meals inside the school's cafeteria rather than waste time with a trip home. John scorned cafeteria food and packed food. This meant they rarely ate together since John's perfectionist work habits often compelled him to arrive at school before dawn to prepare for his first class. However, he also dissuaded Melissa from awakening that early in the morning simply to join him.

Melissa, lonesome without John, often begged to accompany him. John merely pointed to the car he had bought for her. Because Melissa loathed coming home to an empty house knowing John occupied the college's music room, she usually elected to study and complete homework inside the school library, until she could follow John home.

Those boundaries proved their advantage to Melissa: she focused better on her work and scored top grades. For John, evenings meant piano practice, shower, and sleep. Several nights a week, John remained at school until late, teaching private piano students. On weekends, he corrected homework and played or composed. Neither she nor John enjoyed television, but Melissa, who relished a good book, found even that simple pleasure growing old.

Their social lives revealed the largest gap of their ages and interests. Melissa felt awkward at cocktail gatherings for other Jenson College staff members, especially when they included Brenda Garboldi. John simply didn't fit as a member of Melissa's teen group, nor did he try. If Melissa went out with her friends, John always found work to keep him busy at school.

None of these situations posed insurmountable challenges to Melissa. She knew firsthand from years of observing Darlene's care for Frank that marriage often required renunciation of petty differences and a resolve to put the beloved's needs and interest before one's own. Melissa committed herself to both. Nothing, even her goal of becoming an English teacher, mattered more to her than this marriage to John Simotes, but John's inability to separate the man from the musician baffled Melissa beyond all comprehension. John's entire identity depended upon music, and he manifested this quirk to its highest degree in the bedroom. The discipline and self-control John developed by sitting at a piano spilled into his style of lovemaking.

Although Henry's opinion that John Simons would rather touch a piano than a woman might have been true, John Simotes excelled in both women and music, perhaps because his approach to them was identical. He treated Melissa with the same methodical finesse as he would a new composition piece. John carefully studied Melissa's movements, and, with an uncanny instinct for tempo and beat, as well as the nuances of her flats and sharps, played every note and chord to perfection. What annoyed Melissa was the way John treated her like a beginning piano student. He provided step by step instructions, monitored every move, and assigned practice lessons. That said, John never failed to bring the piece to its proper conclusion and always waited until he experienced Melissa's applause before he himself took a bow, even if that first required an intermission on his part. No exceptions, not that Melissa didn't try.

"We don't have to do it your way all the time, you know," Melissa had once grumbled. "It's okay for me to make a suggestion or two."

"I know how to do this, Melissa."

She could not argue with his logic. Although she longed for him to soften his stance and approach their time together as a duet rather than a solo performance to a captive audience, and a few verbal expressions of affection would have been nice, too, Melissa, deep down, could not resent John's mechanical, often silent approach to lovemaking. He achieved remarkable results.

Just once did John relinquish his role of maestro. Melissa had wakened one night as John, who played into the small hours of the night once again, climbed into bed, in obvious need, but too fatigued to make any effort to satisfy it. He lay there passive and submissive while Melissa assumed control of him, the first time she ever watched his facial muscles slacken, his customary vigilance absent. Yet, not once did he open his eyes and acknowledge her. John offered no assistance of any kind, so Melissa relied on subtle clues to tell her if she affected him: a slight twitch of a cheek, a faint parting of his lips, an involuntary shudder. Yet, when he finally gave it up, he did so with almost primal abandon.

However, John's fixation with music and its resultant spill into the bedroom was not the greatest of Melissa's worries. John owned another obsession, one that caused Melissa much anguish. That was his manic insistence that he and Melissa conceive a baby as soon as possible.

CHAPTER 10: AND BABY MAKES TWO

MAY 1977

On the Saturday before Valentine's Day, Melissa and John drove to Munsonville for the grand Dalton/Cooper wedding.

Melissa had secretly hoped she could persuade John to leave on Friday night and spend the night in the village instead of just visiting Munsonville for the day, but, at the last minute, John scheduled a make-up class for a student recovering from a stomach bug. However, on Thursday, Melissa caught John reserving a room for Saturday night at Munsonville Inn. He noticed her standing in the doorway as he hung up the phone.

"Satisfied?"

Melissa ran to hug him. "Oh, John, thank you!"

Finally, she would finally spend an entire weekend in Munsonville with John, the place where it had all begun for them. Perhaps it would trigger happy memories of the past, not Bryony's past, but their past, the night of the engagement party last fall that ended happily inside Simons Woods.

Then her period began after dinner and ruined it all.

John leaned against the door frame, bristling at the sight of Melissa fishing in the bathroom cabinet.

"It's impossible," he fumed. "We've been together almost every night."

"We've hardly been married a month," Melissa said, turning, astonished at John's irritation. "Do you know the odds of getting pregnant right away?"

"One hundred percent if we wanted to avoid it."

John coldly withdrew from her the entire evening and continued playing long after Melissa had gone to bed. He was still sulking the next morning and left for school without speaking to her. Melissa moped at John's rebuff. By that afternoon, when Melissa packed her suitcase, she almost wished they were staying home. Once they departed from Jenson, however, John's brooding mood lightened slightly, and Melissa felt better about the trip. She decided the changed surroundings accomplished it. Take John away from painful reminders of this month's barrenness, and he once again became a happy man. Perhaps, little by little, she could peel away the mystique and understand his many moods. Anyway, tonight, Melissa wanted no interferences in their utopian weekend, no sadness regarding Bryony, no fixation on achieving a pregnancy, and she would do her part to guarantee it.

John parked behind Munsonville Inn. In silence, he and Melissa joined the villagers as they streamed from the hill under the blanket of an overcast sky on their way to church. Not a shop in Munsvonville remained open. Even Sue's Diner closed for the day since most of its potential customers would be eating at the reception. The nave appeared the way Melissa remembered it from her Bryony dreams: whitewashed walls, board floors worn smooth with the years, and straight block pews. The only difference was the hint of carnations. The alter area, a simple raised platform, contained only a podium and unadorned wood cross. To the right stood an old piano and sitting at that piano was Julie, classy in a copper cocktail dress. Nate Miller, in a black suit with a white carnation at his lapel, stepped into the room followed by Jack Cooper, in similar dress. An excited hush ran through the room, and Melissa followed the crowd's gaze. Julie began the wedding march, and Katie, bursting the seams of her gauzy pink bridesmaid dress, despite the efforts of the wide bow that ran around her waist to hide it, stiffly held a bouquet of pink and white carnations as she minced down the aisle. An overweight Reverend Brown stood panting at the front end of the church and clutching his service book to his chest. His tousled brown hair reminded Melissa of his son Joey, her former classmate. Ann, flushed and beaming in a fitted plain white dress and equally plain long veil, grasped the arm of Mr. Dalton as they moved down the aisle in unconscious time to the music. Julie added a fancy flourish to the end of the march as Ann took her final step, then grinned and sat back to watch the show.

"Dearly beloved," Reverend Brown wheezed, "we gather today in this church to witness the ultimate celebration in the human family, the uniting of a man and woman in holy matrimony."

As Ann and Jack mechanically vowed their lives to each other, Melissa occasionally glanced up at John, hoping he'd return the look, along with a reminiscent smile, to let Melissa know he fondly remembered their own ceremony, just six weeks earlier. But John's gaze never wavered from the couple, which caused Melissa to uneasily wonder: Was John thinking back to Bryony, whom he married eight decades ago in this very church? Or was he waiting for Melissa to signal her feelings for him?

Melissa squeezed John's hand. He looked at her, puzzled, yet distant.

"I'll tell you later," she whispered to him, but his indifferent attitude dampened her mood. She saw in his eyes what she had not wanted to see. John was not thinking about her at all.

I hope he doesn't miss her too much, Melissa thought, as Jack obediently obeyed the prompt, "You may now kiss the bride." She peeked up at John and silently pleaded, Don't think about Bryony. Not now and especially not tonight.

Soon Melissa was throwing rice onto the newly married couple as they paraded through the front door of the church into the crisp, cold air, but only half-heartedly, for John still seemed aloof. A beaming Jack clutched Ann's hand. Ann's eyes sparkled; her face shone rosy with excitement; a giddy smile overtook her face. Only John abstained from the crowd's festivities. Melissa turned a questioning gaze at him.

John bent near her ear. "Let's go," he whispered.

Before Melissa could reply, he took her hand and guided her through the crowds. With brisk steps, John walked Melissa away from the church.

"Where are we going?"

"To check into our room."

"We can't do that later?"

"No."

Melissa glanced back, wishing John hadn't broken away so soon, disappointed he lacked her sense of nostalgia for their wedding. She tried humor.

"I don't think anyone will be beating down doors to get into Munsonville Inn."

John said nothing.

As Melissa had predicted, the inn had plenty of empty rooms. John signed the register, accepted the key from the clerk, and led Melissa to the elevator, but she hesitated. She had to know. Was John consumed with memories of Bryony? Is that why he deliberately avoided spending any significant time at the church?

"Now where are we going?" Melissa asked.

"To ensure the room is suitable."

"We'll be late for the reception."

"They're probably taking pictures."

On its ride to the third floor, the musty elevator steadily hummed and produced only an occasional clank. John, predictably quiet, stared ahead. A step inside Room 304, however, renewed Melissa's hopes for a romantic evening. Could anything be more Munsonville? She scanned the wallpaper, white with pale blue and salmon flecks, and the worn beige carpet. A white-patterned quilt and blue pillows on a large dark walnut bed graced the center of the room. Matching night stands holding white lamps replete with ornate silver fixtures and cornflower embellishments flanked both sides. A large dresser with a hanging mirror and a small television with large rabbit ears stood opposite the bed; a roll top desk with a high back chair sat a few feet away from the dresser, closer to the large bay window. Each open surface displayed a glass bowl of dried brown petals, which lent an earthy redolence to the feminine room. While John performed a thorough search of their quarters, Melissa smoothed aside the lace curtains, gazed at the Lake Munson's black water under the steel sky, and breathed silent wishes. She sensed John behind her, so she said, "It looks like snow."

John did not answer, not with words, proving Melissa right. They did arrive late to the reception. By then, guests had filled the school lunchroom to the door, necessitating a good amount of weaving amongst the people to reach the end of the buffet table. Fish and black coffee heavily scented the air. Servers kept the tables filled with plain food: fried perch sandwiches, macaroni salad, and cole slaw. Mrs. Cooper's modest wedding cake had three perilously leaning tiers propped up by short pillars. On the top stood a smiling, plastic bride and groom.. A young man, tight curly yellow hair crowning a long face with Dudley Do-Right chin, ran back and forth from the kitchen to the buffet, removing and replacing large stainless steel pans. Katie cut in line to grab a fish sandwich, and the man lightly slapped her hand.

"Another brother?" Melissa said, as Katie turned back to the head table.

"Yeah, that's Russ. He's helping the Coopers tonight since they obviously don't have Jack. You missed Nate's toast. Where were you?"

"John wanted to check in first."

"That long?"

Someone called out, "Katie," and she dashed away, thankfully, before Melissa could answer. She and John ate while Jack and Ann cut the cake, and Donny Nelson and the Turn Tables played the initial songs. Katie's sister Cara, the group's lead vocalist, sang in silvery high notes the lyrics of *Muskrat Love* for Ann and Jack's first married dance:

To Melissa's surprise, John held out his hand, and that act transported her back into a ballroom of another era. She closed her eyes and once again swooned to the pressure of John's hands, without the barrier of white gloves, and the moving of his legs as he eased her about the floor. How many times had she danced with John Simons in his past? She hadn't been wrong about the real identity of John Simotes. She knew her vampire by touch; she knew him by heart.

Melissa opened her eyes again and looked at John. His face remained impassive.

"You don't have to do this," she said in a low voice. "This music is truly awful." She raised her voice a notch. "See? I did pay attention to your music appreciation lessons."

"Let's congratulate your friends and find another amusement."

Julie and David swayed on the dance floor, wrapped in each other's arms, oblivious to the crowd surrounding them. Except for a polite "hello," Julie had avoided Melissa all evening. A beer in one hand, Jack leaned against the makeshift bar and talked to two men, whom John introduced as Al Miller and Ben Miller. Al, a math teacher at Jenson High School had Russ' long face, a brown Van Dyke beard covering the prominent chin, brownish-blond hair graying at the temples, and transparent blue eyes. Ben also had a long face, but it was smooth like a baby's, and his light hair had faded to sterling. He served as assistant principal at Jenson Junior High School and the school's eighth grade history teacher. Just how many brothers did Katie have? Certainly, too many to remember!

Al slapped John on the back, passed him a beer, and said, "Good talking to you tonight. Remember, marriage doesn't mean you drop out of society!"

Melissa shuffled uneasily, and a twinge of doubt pricked her. Al seemed to know John well. Katie had said he and Ben had attended college with John. What if he really wasn't John Simons? She recalled her dance with John. Melissa didn't care how Katie's brothers had become acquainted with John. She felt certain of one fact. Somehow, John Simons lived again as Professor Simotes. She needed to trust her gut on this one.

John merely set the plastic cup on the counter ledge and shook Jack's hand. "Life grows busy, as this young man will soon discover."

Jack heartily returned John's greeting. "True, but all work and no play will soon make me a dull boy." Jack looked sideways at Ben and winked. "And that would not be good for Ann."

Melissa studied this semi-adult Jack and decided John granted the better bargain. Born and raised in Munsonville, Jack only knew this village as home even as he only knew Sue's Diner as his lifelong place of employment. With sudden clarity, Melissa realized Ann and Jack had mapped their entire future without even realizing it.

As if gazing into a crystal ball, Melissa saw the life Ann would lead as Jack's wife. She would waitress and keep house, raise children who would attend Munsonville School, and hang out on weekends with her girl friends while Jack fished with his dad, his uncle, and maybe a couple of buddies. He might drink a little too much on Saturday nights, which Ann would forgive because after all Jack was a steady, albeit dull, husband. Although Melissa doubted she would ever understand John in his totality, she knew life with John would never bore her.

She smiled politely at her former schoolmate and said, "Congratulations, Jack."

"Hey, thanks, Melissa."

John lingered by the bar, talking to Al and Ben, while Melissa sought out Ann. Still in her wedding dress, probably bought at a bargain-basement price through her parents' connections with their dry goods store, Ann sat at a table with Katie, who was bemoaning her lack of escort for the night.

"No, don't get up," Melissa said as Ann began to rise from her chair. "I'm leaving. I just want to wish you many years of happiness."

Ann stood anyway and tightly hugged Melissa. "Thanks, Melissa. Please come visit me sometime. We live so close to each other now."

"You, too."

"I will."

John stayed so quiet and reserved during the short trek back to the inn that he surprised Melissa when his passion ignited the second they stepped through the motel room door. John tossed the key onto the dresser and kissed her as if he were starving. She responded with equal intensity and instinctively slid her hands underneath John's shirt. She immediately felt John's muscles tense. He pulled away and began refastening his belt. Melissa flinched as if she had been slapped.

"John," she said uneasily. "What's wrong?"

He retrieved the key and headed for the door. Melissa's face grew hot.

"You mean the shirt? Seriously? John, we're married now!"

"Your point?"

"I assumed that...."

She frantically grabbed his sleeve to prevent him from leaving. Oh, he couldn't! No! Not tonight!

He shook off her arm.

"John, don't you trust me?"

"It's not about trust."

"And if I wanted to keep my shirt on?"

"I'd respect it."

"Respect?" Melissa cried in desperation. "That's a laugh, when you're pressuring me to have a baby!"

The words had escaped before she could stop them. Melissa's hand flew up to her mouth, but John's face contorted with repressed rage.

"How *dare* you compare the two?"

"John...."

He slammed the door behind him. *No!* Melissa flung open the door, but John was gone. Billows of despair overcame Melissa; their stormy waves beat her down, and she choked and gasped against the gale of hot tears drowning the colossal hopes she had pinned on this weekend. Why, oh why, did John treat her this way? Why, oh why, did she let him? She closed the door, collapsed onto the carpet, and, repeatedly, mutely shrieked, *"John!"*

How long she lay there, Melissa had no clue, but eventually exhaustion beat back the tempest. Shivering, Melissa crept across the room and crawled into bed, ignoring the flurry thickly falling past the window. She pulled the covers high above her head and curled into a fetal position, but that reminded Melisa about John's preoccupation with having a baby, which precipitated a fresh torrent.

A click in the lock jerked Melissa awake, and she threw off the blanket. John was hanging his wet overcoat over the back of the desk chair, and the entire room smelled of clean, new snow. John kicked off his shoes and eased into bed next to Melissa.

"Let's talk," he said in a strained voice.

Melissa tried scrambling away, but John moved closer, lifted her hand, and slid it under his shirt. She tried to pull away, but John pressed her fingers into the deep, indented lines that crossed his back. So John hadn't been lying about acne! Didn't Victorians know how to treat it? How much pride had John swallowed to allow her to touch him there?

Forgetting her anguish and engulfed in shame at insisting he humble himself, Melissa kissed her husband on the cheek and said, "I'm sorry, John. I shouldn't have...."

"No, you should have. You're my wife. I'm the one who can't."

He tucked the blankets around Melissa, settled her onto the pillows, and lay next to her, propped by an arm. "So, you don't wish to have my baby."

"John! Of course, I do! I don't understand your hurry. We have a lifetime together, and, besides...."

He placidly waited, eyes expectant.

"I'm only nineteen."

"I'm not."

Melissa's throat tightened. A rush of reasons flew into her head; how could she verbalize them? Nature had not endowed her with John's talent and accomplishments, but she still dreamed her own dreams and set her own goals. She wanted to carry a portion of Henry Matthews inside her. She wanted to inspire as an English teacher. She longed to instill the beauty and poetry of the world's greatest literature into the minds of the next generation. Wasn't that as valid as John's vision for musical immortality? A baby at this time would abort those ambitions. Her life would become as dead-end as Ann's.

She looked away from him. "I want to finish school first."

John's ensuing chuckle might have hurt Melissa's feelings had it not emerged softly and accompanied by his warm, strong hand stroking her cheek.

"Whoever suggested dropping out of school?"

Confusion jumbled Melissa's thoughts as she turned toward John. "But...I thought....don't you mean...."

His eyes locked onto hers. "When we have a baby together, we will raise that baby together. My ambitions do not precede yours." John kissed the corner of Melissa's mouth. "Is creating a baby with you such a bad thing to want?"

How marvelous those words sounded coming from John. Melissa started to tell John that very thing, but he was now working on the opposite corner of her mouth. That night, and for days afterwards, Melissa reeled under the cover of romanticism, for John's attentive mood continued even after they returned home.

Until the night John exploded when Melissa shared her reason for a quick trip to the drugstore.

"This doesn't make sense." He eyed her with suspicion. "Are you sure you're not taking the pill?"

"Of course not! You have a lot of nerve asking!"

John turned back to the piano. "You should be pregnant."

On Saturday afternoon, Melissa was studying at the kitchen table when John, home later than usual from the youth classes he taught on the weekends, stumbled through the back door holding a book before his face. She wondered what music text engrossed him until she noticed its title.

"John, you're reading about infertility?"

"Some studies suggest limiting sexual activity to maximize the chances of conception."

He jotted a few notes on the wall calendar while Melissa watched.

"What are you doing?"

"Compiling a schedule."

"Are you *kidding*?"

John turned around, still thinking. "You're right. I hadn't considered compositions and exams. Bring me your syllabus."

With a rueful smile, despite feeling insulted, Melissa left to fetch her notebook. Once John created the timetable, he maintained rigid obedience to it, despite any tempting distractions Melissa offered, just to see if she could sway him. So when Melissa did not conceive in April, John bought another book, one providing detailed instructions for pinpointing ovulation. With the precision of a biologist, John charted Melissa's menstrual cycles, monitored her daily temperature, and studied the efficacy of various positions before updating the spreadsheet. Melissa felt like a chance bystander and told John so.

'How can I enjoy it when you're obsessed with having a baby?"

"Our lack of success doesn't bother you?"

"I'm saying quit trying so hard. If it's going to happen, it will happen."

John's eyes narrowed into menacing slits. " '*If?* '"

"Okay, okay. '*When.* '"

When Melissa's period appeared in May, during the week of final exams, she initially refrained from mentioning it, sparing them both the stress of John's overreaction to the incident.

He exploded when the truth came out. "You lied!"

"I wasn't dishonest. I just delayed telling you, that's all."

"Same thing," John said, glaring and heading for the back door.

Uneasily, Melissa said in a low voice, "John, where are you going?"

"I'll be home within the hour."

A grim John returned in fifty-nine minutes carrying yet another book on infertility, which he consumed over dinner.

"John, you're being extreme."

He peered over the page. "Are you getting enough rest? You look tired."

Melissa dropped her fork in frustration. "Of course I'm tired. We both just came off finals. Aren't you tired?"

"A few lifestyle changes are in order."

"Like what?"

"What are your plans for summer?"

"I'm working fulltime at the library and taking two classes."

"Could you work part time and take only one class?"

"No!"

"Well, I shall lead by example."

John cancelled all evening and weekend classes for the next three months and hired a cleaning woman so neither one had to waste precious energy in household chores. This time, his dedication to fathering a baby deeply touched Melissa, and she decided to stop her selfish resistance. How many men would adjust their life's vocation to expand their family?

The next day, feeling guilty that John had more devotion to this noble task than she did, Melissa approached Mr. Schmidt and requested a schedule adjustment. She then marched into the registrar's office and dropped her speech class.

During Sunday breakfast, John announced he could no longer dodge band members' frequent requests to attend practice sessions. Melissa had forgotten John had even played with a band.

"I'm attending rehearsal this afternoon. Would you like to accompany me?"

"This I've got to see. Professor Simotes in dire need of rock band practice."

"You're hilarious."

Melissa slid her fork into a crepe. "Then why are you going?"

"Because they committed to a slew of summer festivals."

"So everyone needs to practice? By the way, these crepes are good. Is this your mother's recipe, too?"

"*They* need to practice. I'm checking the set list so I can cover their mistakes."

"So, why play with them if they're so terrible?"

"Because Greg is my friend, and I value friendship."

Melissa, bursting with pride at that statement, set down her knife and fork. "John, that is so admirable!"

"The additional community exposure doesn't hurt either."

As soon as the Simotes' entered the basement where the band was setting up for practice, Greg offered a bottle of beer. John waved it away and said, "Melissa's also not drinking."

Greg snatched the bottle from Melissa's outstretched hand, and she felt like an idiot standing there with an open palm. She leaned close to John. "Can I talk to you?"

John ignored her. "If you don't have juice, we'll take ice water."

The guitarist stopped adjusting his amp to gape at John. "What gives, Johnny? Are you ill?"

"Special diet. Doctor's orders."

A buxom woman with shoulder-length, bleached-white hair brushed Melissa's arm.

"Come into the kitchen, sweetie," the woman said. "I'll fix you up."

Melissa followed her up the carpeted stairs. The woman opened the kitchen cabinet and brought forth two clear glasses.

"I'm Adrienne, Greg's wife. Do you like apple juice? My boys love it. That's all they'll drink."

"Uh, sure."

Adrienne poured the juice from a battered, pink, plastic pitcher from the refrigerator.

"Not trying to be nosy, but what kind of special diet are you on?"

"We had some nasty virus." Melissa tasted the watered-down juice and tried not to make a face. "The doctor felt our resistance was low due to stress over finals, so he told us to cut out junk food and eat really healthy for a couple of weeks."

"Wow, you're lucky John is so cooperative. Greg won't eat anything nutritious."

For the next three hours, Melissa braved the noise this amateurish group defined as music. Maybe her sense of good taste really had improved. Anyhow, John would be pleased with her assessment of the band. At five o'clock, John rose from the bench and bid everyone a good evening.

The lead singer spun around. "You're not leaving?"

"Doctor's orders," Melissa said.

An impish grin crept across John's face. Empowered by his approval, Melissa added, "We're run down with school, the wedding, work, you know, everything. We need to take it easy for a few weeks."

As soon as they pulled away from the house, however, Melissa demanded, "Okay, what gives?"

"About?"

"Apple juice?"

John slowed and checked for oncoming traffic. "Alcohol might lower sperm count."

"I don't think that's my problem."

"It's also incompatible with a healthy pregnancy. Why risk damaging the baby?"

Was conceiving a baby this complicated for all newlyweds? For now, John had assumed the position of Melissa's personal chef. He packed the refrigerator full of organic fruits and vegetables, served only whole grains, and selected the finest grades of grass-fed and free-range meat. For the first time in their marriage, the freezer contained no ice cream.

Moreover, John perused labels on all packaged foods for chemicals, artificial colors, and preservatives with a ferocity generally reserved for warfare. He tossed leftovers into the garbage lest they lose their nutritional value overnight and purchased all-natural multivitamins for them both. He

163

cancelled every social activity and even limited his personal piano practice, so they both could get to bed early each night.

June came and so did Melissa's period.

"Damn!"

"John...I....I," Melissa stammered, wondering why her body was waging war against her. "I don't know what to say."

"Neither do I. But I shall fix it."

The next afternoon, John stalked through the back door laden with his customary groceries and flipped a business card onto the kitchen table.

"I hope you have no plans for Friday night." John set the bags on the counter.

"I didn't. Why?"

"I scheduled an appointment with a Dr. Jorgenson in Thornton. He's a fertility specialist."

CHAPTER 11: KICKED

Melissa picked up the card and read it with exasperation.

"Aren't you being hasty? Your books recommended not worrying until we've tried an entire year. We've only been married six months."

"That's six months of wasted time. Let's determine the problem, remedy it, and begin our family." As John walked out of the room, he tossed over his shoulder, "The appointment is at seven o'clock. We'll leave at five. Be ready."

Melissa sighed and shut the book. As much sex as she and John had within the last few months, why wasn't she pregnant? If she and John were dating, she would have conceived ten times by now. Could they really be trying too hard? Melissa was young and healthy; except for John-induced anemia, she had never experienced a chronic illness. Perhaps once Dr. Jorgenson reassured them, John would relax. Besides, she knew the true cause of John's baby fever.

Henry Matthews.

Had John suspected his baby's possible illegitimacy? Did he still grieve the loss of that child, along with its mother, and desperately sought a replacement? Was John tormenting himself with eighty years of "what if's" and regrets. Last year, Melissa had readily played host to John's vampire state so she could live a fantasy. Now, as John's wife, Melissa shrank at being reduced to womb space simply to satisfy John's archaic fatherhood urges and soothe his bitter memories from the past. Yet, through all his badgering, she now realized he had stirred something inside her, a shared desire to make a baby of their own.

Damn!

A cool breeze blew through the partially open window, fluttering the curtains and briefly scenting the air with roses. Instantly, Melissa awoke inside Henry's study, yet, underneath the pleasant fragrance, she sensed an oppressing heaviness: the dominating, manipulative tactics of a ravenous vampire.

Melissa stacked her books. She needed space to think.

"John, I'm going for a walk!"

The screen door slammed behind her, and she bounded down the stairs. She did not wait for John's reply. For the past few months, John's dogged attempts to impregnate her overshadowed Melissa's need to reflect about babies, parenthood, and their newly formed marriage, vague concepts she had not developed. Even during the months she had pined for John, Melissa never considered what marrying him might really mean.

She considered it now.

Despite the intoxicating euphoria of finally possessing John, a spidery truth wove itself around her, which, because she had so desperately wanted him, she had shunned and ignored. Now, Melissa could no longer escape it.

Not once had John told Melissa he loved her, not even at their wedding.

Melissa stopped. A fat man in a red convertible zoomed through the intersection.

She crossed the street and thought: Steve freely said those three words to her mother. Jack probably had told Ann. So, maybe, if she and John sealed their marriage with a baby, it would uncover John's latent feelings of love for her.

If he had any.

She turned the corner to avoid the apartment where John had once lived. Its sight stirred unsettling memories of time spent there with John. Instead, Melissa thought about babies from her past: her little brother, a distant cousin, the next door neighbor. She remembered the first time she saw Brian, a tiny little bundle wrapped inside a blanket. Frank had ushered Melissa to the sofa and placed a pillow on her lap to support the baby. With her mother sitting at one side of her and her father on the other, Melissa marveled at Brian's liquid dark eyes, tiny pink nose, pursed lips, round cheeks, and the dimples when he yawned. She recalled stroking one cheek with a finger. She had never touched anything so soft. The feathery strands on Brian's head had felt lighter than air. She had bent to kiss his forehead and inhaled sweet, new-baby scent. Melissa wanted similar experiences with John, but did she want them yet? At nineteen, could she be a mother? Should she be a mother? And now, after these months of trying for a baby with no success, would motherhood simply forsake her? Of course, the phone call Melissa received earlier in the day, the one she "forgot" to share with John, heavily influenced this ponderous mood.

"Melissa," Ann had cried. "Jack and I are going to have a baby!"

"That's great," Melissa said with an enthusiasm she did not feel and realizing, for the first time, how much she shared John's discouragement. "When are you due?"

"End of January." Ann sighed. "I'll be as big as house for the holidays."

167

"You'll look great."

"We'll talk later. I have more people to call. I just wanted to let you know."

"Tell Jack, 'Congratulations.'"

"I will."

A small boy on a tricycle sped off his driveway onto the sidewalk. Melissa jumped and the little boy stuck out his tongue. The man kneeling in his front yard cutting dandelions by their roots looked up and shouted, "Timmy!"

John was stirring something on the stove when Melissa returned. He did not look up, but he did say, "We'll work it out, Melissa."

"I know."

She picked up her books and carried them to the bedroom.

On Friday, Melissa had just reached the library when she heard John calling her name. Melissa stopped and waited for John to catch up.

After a quick, absent-minded kiss, he said, "Can you stay at the library after work and study?"

"I guess so. Why?"

"Let's leave early. I'll take you to dinner before we see Dr. Jorgenson."

"Tired of cooking?"

"Hardly, but I am tired of the tension."

Melissa started at the almost sad tone in his voice. "John, are you okay?"

John straightened and blinked against the noon sun. "I am confident this doctor will have answers for us, if that's what you implied."

"Oh."

"Tonight I just want…time."

John said that last word with such wistfulness that Melissa's heart softened, and she smiled to show her sympathy.

"No problem. I'll get my homework out of the way."

During the ride to Thornton and subsequent dinner at a steak and seafood house, John tried hard to be friendly, attentive, and accommodating to Melissa, but he floundered with small talk, absently rattled the silverware, and fidgeted with the salt and pepper shakers.

"Professor, you get an 'A' for effort." Melissa reached out to stroke his hand. "It's okay to be nervous about tonight."

"I am absolutely not nervous. I have faith in modern medicine. Sources say he's the best."

A number of trucks, all reading *Moretti's Construction,* were parked across the street from Dr. Jorgenson's office. The site seemed five times the size of any other building on the street. Who needed that much office space?

Inside Dr. Jorgenson's waiting area, a large square with floral wallpaper on four walls, pale pink carpet, a tall green plant in each corner, and sunlight streaming through quaint casement windows, the receptionist handed each of them a clipboard of thick paperwork.

"Fill out everything to the best of your ability," she said, raising her voice over the din of the machines, "but don't worry if you can't answer a question. The more information Doctor has about your medical history, the better he can help you."

Melissa selected a pen from the desk canister. "Do you know what they're building?"

"I hear it's a funeral home." The receptionist turned her attention to the next couple.

Troubled, Melissa settled next to John in the waiting room. She answered numerous questions about family health history and sexual habits, but, as Melissa wrote, a vague unsettledness chilled her, despite the brightness of the room. There was something unnatural about a funeral home across the street from an infertility specialist.

She leaned close to John and dropped her voice. "I feel like I'm in some weird genealogy class."

John flipped a page and kept writing.

Melissa liked the tall and plump Dr. Jorgenson on sight. With his easy smile, white goatee, and balding head, Melissa thought he looked more like a friendly, nursery school principal than a medical doctor, and she instantly relaxed in his presence. A secretary joined them, pen poised for note-taking.

Hands clasped behind his head, Dr Jorgenson leaned backward in his chair, closed his eyes, and attentively listened as John, methodically and bluntly, recounted their efforts from January until now. From the window behind his desk, Melissa watched a bulldozer push away a mountain of black dirt and leave an enormous gaping hole. Did the area require a huge facility just to bury their dead? She doubted that many people lived in the entire county.

"Anything else?" Dr. Jorgenson said when John had finished. "Melissa?"

Self-conscious, Melissa studied her shoes and shook her head, glad John had done the talking.

"Well, then, my advice is to go home and wait another six months. The odds are you won't return to see me." He looked intently at John. "My hunch, though, is that you'd rather proceed with testing."

"Correct," John said.

Dr. Jorgenson sat up and scribbled on a piece of paper. He tore it off the pad and handed it to Melissa. He repeated the process with John.

"Schedule a second appointment with me for physical exams. In the meantime, get these lab tests done at your local hospital. If we uncover nothing, which I'm confident will be the case, I really would advise waiting before we try anything complex."

The receptionist, however, had bad news. Dr. Jorgenson had no openings until July seventh.

John scowled. "Unacceptable. We need an earlier date."

The receptionist remained unperturbed. "Dr. Jorgenson is a very busy man. I can put your names on our cancellation list."

"We'll take July seventh," Melissa said with haste.

John snatched his appointment card and marched out ahead of Melissa, abandoning all earlier pretense of the considerate husband. He was sitting in the car, smoldering, but composed, and staring at the commotion across the street. For the drive home, Melissa mentally rehearsed retorts in case John began an argument, but as they approached Jenson, the severe lines on John's face mellowed, and then disappeared, once he turned down their street.

He parked the car in front of the garage, but before Melissa could open her door, John said, "Would you like to go to Cleveland next week?"

"Cleveland? Why?"

"Well, not exactly Cleveland. Bradford Heights. You haven't met my parents, and they'd like to see me for my birthday, if you feel like celebrating with a tyrant."

Parents? So Professor Simotes really *did* have parents? But how...."

"Just a weekend so it doesn't interfere with our school schedules."

Parents? Just who was this man she had married? If he wasn't John Simons...oh, what an awful mistake she had made!

John moved Melissa's head onto his shoulder, stroked her hair, and said, "Three weeks is too long to wait." He had misinterpreted her stunned look, but how could Melissa correct him? She couldn't blurt out, "Weren't you once a vampire?

Instead, Melissa sighed and leaned weakly into John. "I know."

The next day, Melissa suggested delaying the lab work until they returned from Cleveland, citing the turmoil surrounding the Munsonville trip earlier in the year and expressing her need for a weekend with John without high drama. As she spoke, Melissa formulated what she would tell her mother and pondered how much a divorce might cost. She held her breath while waiting for John's reply, but he off-handedly agreed with Melissa's plan. He then informed Melissa he was playing Shelby's summer festival that night with the band, and Melissa was not invited.

"It's a late night," John said as Melissa, feeling the sting of exclusion, opened her mouth to heatedly object. "You need your rest."

"What about your rest?"

"I'll get mine."

To compensate for that disappointment, John treated Melissa with especial consideration for the rest of the week but Melissa, feeling awkward and distant, buried herself in her studies, giving, "I don't want to do homework in Bradford Heights," as her reason for dodging him. On Friday, John cut short his afternoon class schedule to get an early start. Nevertheless, John drove only halfway before he exited the highway. Melissa, startled, looked up from her book.

"John, is something wrong?"

"We're stopping for the night."

The sun shone with glaring brilliance through the car window, warming Melissa's face and arms. John, for Pete's sake, was still wearing his sunglasses.

"John, it's not even dusk."

"We haven't eaten yet. Sufficient rest, remember?"

John checked into a hotel and left the bags in the car until after dinner. The hotel dining room's pleasant atmosphere relaxed Melissa, and its delicious food cheered her. John, sitting across from her, engulfed in thought, noticed neither the room nor the food. He remained preoccupied even after they had settled for the night, but, for once, Melissa preferred it that way. She showered and returned to find John stretched across one of the beds, fully clothed, sound asleep. The room felt brutally cold. Melissa laid the spread from the second bed across John to keep him warm and then checked the air conditioning unit. If Professor Simotes was not John Simons, perhaps they should sleep in separate beds.

"What idiot turned it to sub-zero?" Melissa muttered in disgust and adjusted the dial.

Her glance fell on the little travel clock on the night table between the two beds. John had set the alarm at four o'clock, so she'd better get some sleep. Lying in the dark, wide awake, slumber merely taunted her, and impressions of the brief conversation on the road ticked in her mind like bullet points.

Parents: Marvin and Carol Simotes

Suburban home.

Only child.

Little league.

Piano lessons, paid by cutting grass on the weekends.

Melissa shivered, and her breath curled in the icy air. What had happened to the air conditioner? She started to climb out of bed, but to her horror, the mist snaked under the door, looped around the curtains, and fanned into the room. Not since encountering Kellen Weschler deep in Simons Woods had Melissa seen that horrifying fog. She opened her mouth to scream, and the mist rolled in, weaving around her throat, lacing it shut, and shrieking her name. Melissa bolted up, tearing frantically at her neck, and then paused and relaxed. The clock, reading four-ten, was incessantly jangling. John's bed was empty. Melissa leaned forward to silence the alarm, and sudden light bathed the room. John had opened the bathroom door and was walking into the bedroom, carrying his toothbrush. He wore clean jeans and a fresh shirt. His hair hung in limp, wet strands over his shoulders and down his back.

"Sorry," John bent down to kiss Melissa. He smelled of soap. "I didn't hear it."

They arrived around noon in Bradford Heights, stopping once along the way for breakfast at a roadside diner. While John ate, Melissa examined him with the precision of a forensic scientist and extinguished all notions of ending her marriage. *He was so John Simons!* What if....?

She developed her hypothesis during the drive, while pretending to read. Okay, the idea seemed bizarre, but no less extraordinary than making a pact with a century-old vampire. *What if* John Simons had been reborn through some twisted time warp? In that case, John would have no knowledge of his true identity. Wouldn't that absolve him of any suspected deceit? Melissa believed it might. Furthermore, she would not allow a bout of overwrought nerves, activated by weeks of frenzied baby-making, detonate the marital relationship she was building with John. He was most definitely John Simons. He belonged to her now.

"Melissa."

"What?" Melissa sat up, blinking and rubbing her eyes. When had she fallen asleep? "Why didn't you wake me?"

"I did. We're almost there."

John turned the car down a shaded, residential street of nineteen-fiftyish, ranch-style houses. The Simotes' owned a yellow-brick home with a matching, attached garage; an olive-green car as old as the house dominated the driveway. A spasm shot through Melissa as John pulled next to the car. John *really* had parents, and she had to meet them.

As John opened his car door, Melissa clutched his arm. "I can't do it. What if they don't like me?"

He kissed her cheek in reassurance and softly laughed. "They're great people. They'll like you."

With brisk steps, John strode to the front door and then turned around, an amused, but encouraging, smile spreading across his face. When Melissa finally reached the porch, John took a tight hold of her cold hand and said, "Melissa, it will be fine."

John opened the screen door and escorted Melissa inside. The large windows admitting plenty of sunlight belied the dullness of the living room. Wherever an open surface could be found, John's mother had filled it with a half-dead houseplant. An occasional blue throw rug covered the black and gray tile floor. The modular couch, love seat, and chairs matched, all gray; the coffee and end tables also matched, wood laminate. Something was missing, Melissa, thought as she looked around the area, but she couldn't quite decipher it. Had John really grown up here? At that moment, a tall white-haired woman briskly stepped into the room and rushed over to them.

"John!"

He returned the woman's embrace with feigned enthusiasm. She smiled up at him a long time, all the while patting his cheek. "Well, I can see marriage certainly agrees with you."

"Mom, this is Melissa."

Carol Simotes enthusiastically threw her arms around her. Melissa clumsily reciprocated, but she looked at John, who nodded with approval. Melissa felt her time warp theory ebbing, but she didn't have a better one to replace it. The whole scene felt wrong. No way had this woman, in stretchy pink pants with a rose print blouse and white tennis shoes, given birth to John.

"I'll call your father." She walked into the next room, and Melissa heard her shout out, "Marvin! John's home!"

Melissa saw John smother a smile as he, still holding her hand, led her into the kitchen, even more hideous than the living room. With its large windows, this room, too, boasted plenty of natural light, but its black and white metal frame furniture, flanked with bits of red--a tea pot, placemats, and a macramé wall-hanging--made Melissa wish for a darker room.

The back door opened and a tall, thin, white-haired man took halting steps inside the kitchen. John pulled a chair away from the table, but the old man stopped and leaned on his cane.

"I'm not ready for the nursing home yet," Marvin Simotes said, waving John away. He looked at Melissa, questioning.

Carol set down a bright green plastic pitcher of lemonade and a stack of four slim identical plastic cups on the table. Melissa noticed the table slightly jiggle.

"Dear, this is John's wife, Melissa."

Marvin looked down at Carol. "Melissa, you say?"

"Remember? We missed the wedding because you were sick?"

He nodded. "Gotcha. John, where are your manners? Pull up a chair for the gal."

Carol busied herself at the counter, assembling the ingredients for bacon, lettuce, and tomato sandwiches. John poured lemonade. Marvin stared at Melissa and said, "So how did you meet this boy of mine?"

Melissa hesitated, uncertain of what to say to him.

"Jenson College," John said.

"Oh, that's right. You're the English teacher."

Melissa reddened as she remembered Miss Garboldi and quickly sipped her lemonade to hide it.

"Dad, she's still a student."

"You don't say? Why I had thought...."

"They broke up, dear," Carol quickly interjected.

Marvin peered at her over his glass and then closely examined Melissa. "A bit young for graduate school, aren't you?"

"She's a freshman, Dad. Jenson has no masters programs."

"A freshman, hey? Boy, aren't you robbing the cradle a little?"

Melissa blushed, but John didn't even blink. "And you wonder why I stay away?"

Carol, with a warning look, handed John a plate of sandwiches. "Now Marvin, we talked about this," she said.

"Dear, you're absolutely right. I'm forgetting my manners." Marvin held out his hand. "Welcome to the family, Melissa."

"Thank you, sir."

"She's lovely, John. It's no wonder you like her."

Soon Carol returned with four small black and white plates, each boasting a single, large painted red apple in the middle, and distributed them around the table. John passed the plate of sandwiches.

Carol sat beside Marvin and smiled at Melissa. "John says you're an *aspiring* English teacher."

"Yes, ma'am."

Melissa bit into her sandwich and mayonnaise dripped onto her plate. The bacon, cold and burnt, obviously leftover from another meal, and the tomatoes, underripe and woody, hardly boasted this woman's best culinary skills. Didn't John say his mother had taught him to cook?

"Wonderful," Carol said. "John, are you still writing music?"

They discussed John's job, Carol's volunteer work, and Marvin's tomato plants. Carol asked John if he remembered Mrs. Dellspring? No? Well, she had lung cancer.

"Old man Belfner finally passed away," Marvin said.

"Such a pleasant service," Carol said, "and he looked so alive. Do you remember, Marvin?"

"I do," Marvin said. "Grayson's new assistant does quite the makeup job. Italian chap, isn't he?"

"No, dear," Carol said. "He's German."

"Confounded accents. I never could get them right."

As Melissa listened to the conversation, a lightning bolt zapped her head. The house's deficiency became apparent. Not one photograph of the family, nor any baby portraits or school photos of John, hung on the walls. Didn't they have any to display?

After lunch, John accompanied Marvin to the backyard to admire the vegetable garden. Melissa stayed inside to help Carol clean up after lunch. Carol promptly declined any assistance.

"I have a dishwasher." Carol grabbed a sponge from the sink, wrung it out, and wiped down the table and the counter. "So, is John still inflexible or has marriage sweetened him a bit?"

Melissa did not know how to answer that question, but luckily Carol did not notice.

"Even as a boy, he never gave us much trouble," Carol said. "He just forgets, from time to time, that others have opinions, too."

The opportunity presented itself, and Melissa took it.

"Mrs. Simotes, I'd love to see pictures of John when he was little."

Carol's face fell. She turned toward Melissa, crestfallen. Tears welled up in her eyes.

"Oh, Melissa, we lost everything in a house fire many years ago. Surely John must have told you. He saved his father's life."

"A...fire?"

Melissa closed her eyes, and she was banging on the library doors inside Simons Mansion. John, eyes ablaze, hurled a lighted candlestick toward her. She choked on mist and smoke. Flaming bands of crimson, gold, and orange crackled and raced to the sky.

"The lack of oxygen caused some brain damage to Marvin, but he's the lucky one because he doesn't remember it. John does. The fire terribly scarred his back. He's never gotten over it."

A fire?

So, John knew who he was, after all! But...then...how did the Simotes fit in?

John and Marvin returned, and Melissa began loading the dishwasher to hide her shock and surprise. Acne! Why had John lied to her?

"Dear," Marvin said, "John offered to drive me into town. I need stakes for the tomato plants."

"How nice, Marvin. Well, have a lovely time. Melissa and I will visit."

Melissa, restless and bored, pretended to follow the storylines of the many soap operas Carol watched all afternoon. Every quarter of an hour, Melissa anxiously checked the battery-operated clock on the mantle of the sham fireplace. How long did two men need to buy a couple of sticks?

At four o'clock, Carol, who didn't seem at all concerned with the length of time John and Marvin were absent, switched to a talk show, so Melissa simulated interest at the day's guests: a man who bred mountain goats, a woman lobbying to forbid all meat products in nursing homes, and a dating consultant. The early news had just begun when the front door opened.

"We're back!" Marvin called out cheerfully. "We had trouble finding the right ones."

Melissa stared at John, but he averted his gaze. Carol remained absorbed in her show.

"Dad," John said, "let's hammer those stakes in, and then I'll take you and Mom out to dinner."

"Why? Your birthday's not until tomorrow."

"Melissa and I will be on the road, so if we're going to celebrate, tonight's the night."

Why was John avoiding her? What had taken them so long?

"John," Melissa began.

Now Carol looked up from the television. "You won't stay for Father's Day?"

A shadow passed before John's face and was gone. He looked directly at Melissa.

"This won't take long," John promised.

And he led Marvin toward the back door.

Fury rose inside Melissa. Where had John gone, and why wouldn't he tell her? Nor was it a long drive back into town, so traffic wasn't an excuse, either. Melissa tried talking to John when he came inside, but he headed straight for the shower. That evening, they ate at a chain steakhouse, a favorite of his parents, John had murmured into Melissa's ear, but this time, it was Melissa who did not answer. The insipid conversation floated about her ears, and Melissa made an occasional polite remark, all the while biding her time until later that night, when she and John would be alone.

"Well, isn't this a coincidence?"

Melissa looked up. A tall man, taller than John, but quite stocky, broadly smiled down at them with thick lips and a mouthful of large teeth. He had a full head of slightly graying dark hair, gold wire glasses, and a suit that fitted a much smaller man. Marvin and Carol looked up, but John shifted uneasily in his chair.

"Leo Grayson," Carol said, beaming. "Why, how your ears must burn. I had just complimented the bang-up job your new assistant did at Mitch Belfner's funeral."

"That's what Marvin said when I visited with him this afternoon. However, my assistant needs to work on that thick German accent. It frightened Mitch's wife."

The smile stayed plastered on Carol's face as she repeated, "This afternoon?"

"Yes, I kept Marvin company during John's appointment with my assistant. Oops, my table's ready. Nice seeing you again."

Melissa choked hard on her steak. John absently patted her back until she could once again breathe. Despite gasping for air, Melissa glared hard at John, who hailed their waiter for another glass of water. Just wait, Melissa thought as she sipped it, just wait until we get back to the house.

She cringed at the sight of the guest bedroom: gray walls, brown and black checked carpet, and an orange twill bedspread. Appearing not to notice, John unzipped Melissa's dress, but Melissa shoved his hand away. Undaunted, John wrapped his arms around her waist and kissed the back of her neck. He stopped when Melissa did not respond and turned her around.

"Melissa, what's wrong?"

"Take off your shirt."

John stiffened and stood straight. *"No."*

Melissa whirled away from him. She yanked off her dress and dropped onto the bed to remove her shoes and nylons. John crouched next to her, but she edged away from him and pulled her nightgown over her head.

"Melissa."

She began crying without meaning to do it.

"You lied! You said those scars were from acne! Why didn't you tell me about the fire? Why no explanation for your whereabouts this afternoon? If you can't be honest, why have a baby with me?"

"Melissa."

"Lies! Lies! Lies!"

John slid close to Melissa and enfolded her into his arms. Her anger melted into tears of frustration from the last few weeks, and she poured them onto John's shoulder while he sat there and said nothing.

When Melissa's sobbing had turned to sniffling, John spoke. "Are you ready to listen?"

She buried her head into his chest, sniffed once, and nodded, but John lifted her face and held her eyes.

"Did it once occur to you, Melissa, that some things are too difficult for me to discuss, even with you?"

Melissa tried wrenching away, but John tilted her head higher. "Melissa, look at me."

Memory crashed down on Melissa like the waves pounding the shore the last time she had heard John speak similar words to her, when she played Bryony, the day he lay Melissa down in the clearing by Lake Munson and passionately took her blood. How could she not obey?

She looked at him.

"At what point will you trust me?"

"John...I...."

But John was already kissing her, and she surrendered into it, letting go instead to the long, unhurried love John made to her, the first time he had done so since their appointment with Dr. Jorgenson. Once they returned from Bradford Heights, however, John quickly grew moody and irritable. They completed the required lab work at Jenson Memorial Hospital, and John played two more festivals, without taking Melissa with him.

They did spend Fourth of July in Grover's Park, despite the fact Greg had booked three more shows. Melissa glowed when John told him to find a substitute, ecstatic that, this time, John had chosen family over music.

Steve and John barbecued all weekend, except Sunday's dinner, which Brian himself grilled. During their stay, Brian had behaved civilly towards John, but his words fairly dripped with sarcasm.

She hissed in Brian's ear as he flipped the hamburgers. "You don't have to call him, 'sir.'"

"Be happy with 'sir.' Worse names come to mind."

Darlene pulled Melissa aside as they cleaned up after Sunday's dinner. "Is everything all right?"

"Of course, Mom. Why do you ask?"

Darlene looked concerned. "I'm not sure. I don't hear from you and...I don't know... you seem different. You and John aren't having trouble, are you?"

Melissa forced her most convincing smile. "John takes great care of me. He cooks, insists I get plenty of rest, and even hired someone to clean the house."

Her mother looked doubtful. "Please call me if you have a problem."

"I will."

"Please."

"Mom, I said, 'I will.'"

On Monday, Melissa and John returned to Thornton for the lab results and physical exams. They learned from the receptionist that Dr. Jorgenson had cancelled the exam. Over John's heated objections, the nurse escorted them to Dr. Jorgenson's office. The doctor waited for them with their charts already in his hand.

"Well," Dr. Jorgenson said, looking at John and clearing his throat, "I have good news, and I have bad news."

181

Fear crawled along Melissa's skin, and the room suddenly felt very cold.

"Melissa, every one of your tests came back normal."

She smiled at John and squeezed his hand. John did not respond.

"However, John, I...."

John released Melissa's hand. She watched the optimism on John's face fade.

"If you're saying I have a low sperm count," John said, "I'm prepared to cooperate. Medication or surgery, I'm open."

"Well, yes, sometimes we can do certain procedures, depending on the issue," Dr. Jorgenson hedged.

John leaned slightly forward. "Well?"

"Well, in this case, your tests show something much rarer, something we cannot fix."

A look of foreboding crept across John's face. Melissa shielded his icy hand with both her warmer ones, but John merely fixed his eyes on Dr. Jorgenson's.

"And why not?"

Dr. Jorgenson looked uncomfortable, and he glanced up at the ceiling and around the room before he stared back at John.

"Because, John, you produce no sperm."

CHAPTER 12: A FATE WORSE THAN DEATH

John kicked down the door and charged toward the direction of the main entrance, leaving Melissa torn between apologizing to Dr. Jorgenson about her husband's behavior and chasing after John.

"I am so sorry!" Melissa gaped at the smashed and splintered mess on the floor. "I don't know what to say. He...."

The doctor sighed as he examined the broken door. "Don't worry about it, Mrs. Simotes. My staff will send you a bill."

"Thanks!"

Melissa tore down the hall, stopping first at the waiting room desk.

"I've got to go," Melissa gasped to the receptionist. "Do I need anything else?"

"I don't believe so. If we do, someone will give you a call."

John had parked by the curb. Melissa hurried into the passenger seat as John zoomed into the street in front of a passing car.

"Hold on! The door's not even shut!"

John increased his speed. Melissa slammed the door and tried to catch her breath. John weaved in and out of traffic.

"John, please slow down! Are you trying to kill us?"

"Well, Melissa, you got your wish."

"What wish?"

"Not to have my children."

"I never once said...."

John accelerated and cut off another car. The driver honked, and Melissa heard the squeal of tires.

"Listen, John, I know that you feel...."

He turned blazing eyes on her.

"Oh my God, John, look at the road!"

He leaned closer to her as he accelerated. "My driving's not good enough for you?"

"John, come on..."

He screeched the car to a halt in the middle of the lane. The vehicle behind lurched and stopped. A driver sped around John, shouting obscenities as he passed.

Melissa stared at John with disbelief. "What are you doing?"

"Sitting here until you close your mouth."

"You could get a ticket or be arrested!"

"It's your choice, Melissa."

She shut up.

John dropped her by the back door and then peeled out of the driveway. Melissa choked down a sandwich and cried herself into a fitful sleep. When she woke the next morning, she noticed John's side of the bed remained untouched. Not until dark did her sullen and silent husband stride through the back door and straight for the piano. John played far into the night, long after Melissa retreated to their bedroom and shut off the light. Thus began John's new routine. He left the house early in the morning before the alarm sounded, before Melissa began her day, and found plenty of reasons to stay away from home until late at night: the fall semester to plan, a piece for the junior high school band to compose, private students to teach, and extra gigs with Side Effect. Melissa often awakened to John's incessant piano playing and wondered when he slept. He had completely vacated the bed, which only exacerbated Melissa's loneliness for him. She wished he would open up to her, so they could share this bitter news together. She longed for him to hold her as she cried. Didn't he realize she was suffering, too?

After the first weeks of John's erratic behavior, Melissa shopped only for the most basic of foods. John no longer cooked or ate at the house, and Melissa found it easier if she frequented the college's cafeteria. Not only could she dodge meal preparations, she did not have to endure John's perpetual absence at the dinner table. At school, Melissa found an unlikely guardian angel. Julie had noticed Melissa's melancholy and kept her company more meals than not. Julie did not pry, and often she did not speak, but Melissa found Julie's presence so strangely comforting, she briefly wondered if Julie's accusation that Melissa was trying to replace her father might possess a nugget of truth. For added diversion, Melissa studied at the library, reclaimed her former work hours, and entertained the notion of asking Mr. Schmidt to increase them, just to have something extra to fill the lonely hours. She dreaded going home now that John had forsaken it.

Once, Melissa risked John's wrath by attempting to engage him in late night conversation. Perhaps if John couldn't talk about his feelings, he might discuss alternatives.

"We have options," Melissa began with gentleness.

"Not interested."

"We could adopt."

"I won't raise another man's child."

"What about artificial insemination?"

"Been there, done that."

"What do you mean, 'Been there, done that?'"

The tinkling of piano music was her answer. Melissa retreated in frustration and sadness.

Weekends proved hardest to fill. Melissa soon tired of reading, and she detested television. She hated to shop, and one couldn't study all the time. Julie and Jenny spent most of their time with their respective boyfriends. Melissa spent a great deal of her Saturdays and Sundays simply staring out the window and crying.

One Saturday, on impulse, Melissa departed for Munsonville, but once she arrived, she hadn't the heart to wander around the former Simons estate. Ann and Jack lived in a small apartment above Sue's Diner; stopping there was safer. She climbed the stairs, avoiding the rickety handrail and wondering why Jack hadn't fixed it. Ann, belly bulging under her faded blue and green plaid maternity shirt, greeted Melissa with an enormous hug.

"You look great!" Melissa cried, eyes irresistibly drawn to Ann's midsection.

"It's okay."

"Okay? You're happy about the baby, aren't you?"

"I don't know." Ann shut the door. "Let's sit in the living room. I'll show you my wedding album."

A drop leaf table with three vinyl-covered chairs separated the galley kitchen from the tiny living room, which only had room for an L-shaped couch, an antique rocking chair, two floor lamps, and a coffee table with a small television on it. A bedroom lay beyond the living room; the bathroom and a second tiny room was opposite the kitchen.

"It's very cozy," Melissa said.

They spent the afternoon poring through photos and reminiscing about former days. The conversation turned to Harold Masters and his outlandish teaching methods, which led Ann to ask Melissa a zillion questions about college.

"I envy you." Ann sighed as she closed the book and replaced it on the coffee table. "You set your sights higher than I did. I'm sure you'll make a wonderful teacher."

"Don't say that," Melissa quickly said, fighting back jealousy over Ann's impending motherhood. "What you're doing is important too. If you don't bring the next generation into the world, who will I teach?"

"Well, I guess."

"You don't know?"

Ann sighed and looked away.

"Maybe," she said slowly, "I'd feel that way if I could have babies without sex."

That last comment shocked Melissa. "You don't like sex?"

"Not really." Ann's voice sounded flat. "Men are pigs."

Jack came home, and the girls changed the subject. After popping a beer, pecking Ann on the cheek, and a "Hiyah, Melissa," Jack turned on the television and settled into the couch cushions. Ann scurried about the kitchen with dinner preparations and asked Melissa to stay for the evening meal. Melissa, even more uncomfortable in Ann's home than in her own, declined the offer.

"It's getting late. I have to go."

"I understand. Just don't be such a stranger, okay?"

"Okay." Melissa half-heartedly hugged her friend. The visit with Ann made her feel even more disconnected from the rest of the world. "Bye, Jack," she called back to the lounging figure. Jack, engrossed in the television, waved his hand.

The trouble hanging over her and John coupled with Ann's general dissatisfaction made the drive back to Jenson bleak and dismal. Twice, Melissa flipped through the radio stations for distracting music, but even the pop channels seemed to play only songs with piano instrumentation. As Melissa pulled into her driveway, the sounds of piano music drifted out. The sun had not yet set. John hadn't arrived home this early in a long time.

Melissa let the back door bang when she entered the house, signaling her return home. The music continued. Melissa ransacked the cupboards, found the last can of stew, and dumped the contents into a saucepan. The music never paused. Melissa ate, washed her few dishes, and then decided to shower. She had just passed John when the music ceased.

"Your whereabouts today?"

"Munsonville."

Melissa retreated to the bedroom. She was opening the bottom dresser drawer for her favorite nightgown when John flung the door open.

"You simply up and left?"

"What did you want me to do? You weren't home!"

Nightgown in hand, Melissa headed for the bathroom, but John barred her way. He leaned his face close to hers.

"Be careful. Remember, *you* can still conceive."

Hot fury rose inside Melissa. Of all the nerve!

"*You* be careful," Melissa shot back, trying to push past.

John took a step closer, but Melissa did not back down.

"You've insulted us both," she added.

John spun on his heel and left. Melissa showered. He stayed away all weekend.

On Monday, Julie hailed Melissa in the hallway and pulled her to one side with a terse, "What's up with John?"

Melissa averted her eyes. "Nothing. Why?"

"Well, tell him to knock off his attitude. He's been snapping at students left and right. He even told a senior to get her effing head out of her ass. She says she'll report him if he barks one more nasty thing to her."

That did it. What was John trying to do, get fired? She mentally prepared herself for a showdown that evening. Melissa even delayed bedtime as long as possible, but John still did not come home. She awakened to the eerie strains of John's piano and bolted upright. The dissonant chords produced a macabre melody of music such as one might hear in a B-grade horror flick. Melissa cracked open the bedroom door. John, showered and in T-shirt and shorts, wielded the pedals with bare feet. The chaotic notes bounced off the walls as John pounded the keys. Melissa took a deep breath to stuff down her uncertainty and then strode to the piano.

"Enough. Tonight, we talk."

Leering at her, John ended with a sickening string of discordant notes.

"You're not the first man who couldn't father a child."

Silence.

Furious, Melissa banged on the keys. John grabbed her wrists and held them fast, but at least he wasn't playing.

"It's not the end of the world," Melissa pleaded hotly. "We have our whole lives ahead of us. Why can't you just accept it, so we can move on?"

John's fingers tightened.

"Fine! Don't talk to me. Just sit there, miserable, feeling sorry for yourself, wallowing in pity…."

"Melissa, shut up."

"I will NOT shut up! I want…."

John dropped her wrists, grabbed two handfuls of her hair, and yanked her up. Melissa gasped for breath under bruising kisses, and, before she knew it, John had her on the floor and was soon rolling off her almost as swiftly as he had mounted her. For a long time, he lay, unmoving, on the carpet next to her. Was he all right? Melissa sat up and touched his shoulder.

"John?"

He did not stir, but his breathing slowed.

"John?"

She heard the gurgle in his throat. He was snoring! Melissa leaped off the floor and ran to the bathroom, grabbing a towel from the hall closet on the way. Bitter anger filled her throat and spilled out with the same heat as the hot water spraying the shower doors and filling the room with steam. She wrenched her nightgown over her head, once a surprise for John on their wedding night, and flung it behind the toilet. Melissa scrubbed soap over her body, but she couldn't wash away the feelings of deluging desolation. She leaned her head on the wall of the shower and sobbed great, choking sobs of anguish. Ann is right, Melissa thought as she rinsed her hair. After all those weeks ignoring her, of wrapping himself in a cocoon of misery, John could treat her like this. Men *are* pigs.

She wrapped the towel around her and picked up the abandoned nightgown. She never wanted to lay eyes on it ever again. Walking toward the kitchen, she deflected her eyes away from John, still sleeping spread eagle on the floor.

She opened the garbage can and threw the nightgown inside, shoving it to the bottom, so John would not see.

"Good riddance!" she said aloud.

Melissa woke at dawn the next morning. She dressed in haste, hoping to leave the house before John awakened. She slid her books off the dresser and grabbed her car keys before gently opening the bedroom door. She glanced at the living room on her way to the kitchen. The room was empty. She looked behind her. The bathroom door hung wide open. The piano sat silent. Where had he gone?

With light, quick footsteps, Melissa hurried to the kitchen, hoping to slip unnoticed through the back door. John leaned against the kitchen counter, sipping a mug of coffee and following her movements with his eyes. She reached for the door handle.

"Melissa."

Her hand froze in mid-air. Something in John's voice forced her to turn and look at him. She mustered her coldest expression. She watched John swallow, hard, but she refused to yield to the misery on his face.

"I'm sorry," John said.

No! He would not do this to her, *not this time*. His actions were inexcusable, unforgivable.

"Okay, whatever." Melissa opened the back door.

"I was completely out of line."

She changed her mind and decided to face him after all. So what if John felt bad? He'd made her feel worse. He deserved to see her most withering look.

"You know what? Ann's right. Men *are* pigs."

John visibly winced. "That's unfair."

"No, you're unfair! You've been nothing but mean to me this whole time! Okay, so maybe you don't care if we can't have children, but I care! You don't think I haven't figured out that the only reason you tried so hard to be good in the bedroom was to get me on your side, so we'd have kids right away? And now that we can't, there's no reason for you to try anymore!"

"Thank *you*, Melissa."

"My pleasure!"

She slammed the door and sped to her car.

"I hate him," Melissa muttered, as she started the engine, tears falling faster than she could check them. She refused to waste any more time crying over John.

Her resolve lasted until philosophy class. When Melissa announced the wrong answer to the instructor's question, she burst into tears and rushed out of the classroom. Jenny followed her all the way to the women's restroom where Melissa leaned her head on the cold tile wall and wept.

"Melissa?" Jenny softly touched her friend's shoulder. "Hey, Melissa."

Without warning, Melissa spun around and flung herself on Jenny's neck. Jenny patted her back and murmured soothing sounds. "Talk to me, Melissa. What's wrong?"

Melissa hadn't meant to tell her, but, somehow, the words tumbled from her mouth. Without revealing her misgivings about John's possible past, Melissa relayed to Jenny the events of the past few months, beginning with John's obsession about having a baby and then ending with Dr. Jorgenson's news and John's insane reaction to it.

Jenny waited until Melissa's tears subsided into exhausted heaves before she spoke. "I'm sorry you're going through this. I wish I knew how to help."

"Me, too." Melissa wiped her wet cheek with the back of her hand.

"Can you try talking to him again? Without fighting, I mean?"

"Jenny, I've tried. He won't."

"He's hurting, too, Melissa."

Somehow, Melissa made it through the rest of her classes. She ate dinner in the cafeteria that night. She did not once see John. Mr. Schmidt noticed her wan appearance, asked if she felt well, and did she want the rest of the night off? Melissa thanked him for his kindness, but she refrained from accepting it.

"I need to stay late, anyway," Melissa said. "I'm studying for a big test tomorrow."

"Well, try not to work too hard."

Once home, Melissa, slightly buoyed by Jenny's sympathy, harnessed her courage and approached John at the piano.

"I'm sorry." Melissa kissed the top of his head. "Please come to bed. I miss you."

He did not respond.

She tried again. "I know this is hard for you. Please can't we talk about it?"

The music grew louder.

Tears burned Melissa's eyes. She couldn't stand much more of John's stony silence. Crushed and broken, Melissa readied for bed and prayed for quick, dreamless sleep. Instead she saw John marking the calendar, controlling her food intake, and kicking down Dr. Jorgenson's door. The quiet room was deafening. The music had stopped.

A few moments later, the door creaked. John had entered the bedroom. She felt him climb into bed. She sensed his rigid body. He did not budge. He did not speak. Every fiber in Melissa stood guard.

They lay together in the dark, neither one speaking a word. Melissa watched the shadows on the wall lengthen and then disappear. The numbers on the clock moved to single digits as evening melted into the wee hours of the night. Melissa considered tomorrow's history test. She needed sleep; she couldn't sleep; she had to sleep.

She practiced deep relaxation, and soon drowsiness transported Melissa to the sidewalk in front of her childhood home. She was proudly sitting on her bike, training wheels removed, seat adjusted, balance found. Melissa's father gave a gentle push, and she soared through the sleepy air. A little girl in a dove-colored gown with a high-neck collar and cuffs at the wrists stepped onto the path. She held out a doll and leered under dirty-dishwater, blunt-cut bangs. Melissa veered sharply to the right to avoid her and tumbled down, down, down. Her limbs jerked; the doll hit the ground beside her. Its tiny black eyes glinted under a pair of bushy red eyebrows. A thatch of wild red hair strayed from the bonnet.

John's voice broke into her vision. "Shall I really state what I'm thinking?"

Dream waves halted, Melissa rolled over to face John. Just enough moonlight filtered through the curtains to reveal John lying on his back, motionless, jaw set, and staring at the ceiling with unblinking, savage eyes.

"I wish I'd used that stake and blade a little sooner, a little lower."

CHAPTER 13: FLASHBACK/FLASH FORWARD

Melissa stirred and sank into sleep, but the sunlight, strong and insistent, seeped through her still-closed eyes.

Sunlight!

She squinted. Both alarm clock hands pointed to twelve. Noon! She'd missed her test!

Within fifteen minutes, Melissa was locking the back door and rushing toward her car. Ten minutes after that,

Melissa was scurrying down the hall to Raymond Barker's office. Through the slightly open door, Melissa saw Mr. Barker sitting at his desk. She paused before knocking and closed her eyes, praying he'd understand.

She rapped her knuckles on his door. Mr. Barker looked up from the papers he was correcting, probably the test, Melissa thought with a sinking heart.

With an inviting smile, Mr. Barker called out, "Melissa, come in!"

Taking a deep breath, Melissa pushed opened the door. "Mr. Barker, I am so sorry about this morning's test. I overslept and...."

Still smiling, Mr. Barker said, "Melissa, there's no need to explain. Jenny already talked to me. Do you have some free time tomorrow afternoon? You may take a make-up test, here, in my office."

"Um, sure," Melissa stammered, hoping Mr. Schmidt would understand, too. "I only have morning classes."

"Come at one, then."

At the library, Melissa poured out an abridged version of the story she'd related to Jenny, but Mr. Schmidt didn't seem surprised, almost as if he'd already heard it. Melissa vowed to do something really nice for Jenny soon. Walking back to Mr. Barker's office, Melissa indulged the luxury of thinking about *last night. John had finally told her!* She couldn't wait to talk with him!

Yet, in the immediate days following John's disclosure, he did not again bring up the subject, and Melissa felt too cowardly to introduce it. Still, neither could deny the truth. Melissa *had* witnessed John Simons' slaying of Henry Matthews in the mansion's library. He *had* used the silver knife with the black handle and an oak beam hanging over his desk, the items Melissa had noticed her very first day actually inside the nineteenth century version of Simons Mansion. *Of course* John wished he had used them sooner. If he had destroyed Henry instead of leaving Bryony in his care, Bryony might never have died. Night after sleepless night, she and John lay in the black room, not talking, not moving, until daylight merged the night into gray shadows and gradually dispelled them into the jangling of the alarm clock. Melissa usually fell asleep before John had finished dressing for work, which meant, more than once, Melissa arrived late for school. Still, nothing could surpass the hopeful bliss simmering inside her, not even the "A" Melissa earned on the missed test.

For John had curtailed his late nights. He came home each afternoon to cook dinner, but he no longer monitored Melissa's every forkful. Yes, the time he spent at home consisted of correcting schoolwork, preparing quizzes, and practicing, but he always came to bed whenever Melissa prepared, in theory, for sleep. Together, they kept silent vigil of the night, yet each morning when Melissa awakened, John's side of the bed was already cold.

One Saturday morning, after a taking brief phone call, John told Melissa she'd have to attend *Bowling for the Arts* without him.

"Greg is meeting with the representative of a small record label, and he wants me there. I found subs for us, but I think you should go. Can Julie accommodate you?"

Stifling a sigh, Melissa doused her vivid fantasies about recreating last year's bowling fundraiser, where John would bestow similar attention and affection on her as he had on Miss Garboldi. She refused to kill their polite truce on an argument, but she also felt reluctant to invite herself onto Julie's team. Although she and Julie had renewed their friendship, it possessed a certain guardedness that intimidated Melissa. Nevertheless, because John wanted it, Melissa obediently picked up the telephone and called Julie.

"Do you have room for one more on your team? John isn't bowling."

"Sure!" Julie said with surprising and open friendliness. "I would've asked you, but I thought you were bowling with staff."

"The band needs John tonight, but he wants me to represent him at the benefit."

"You don't need a ride, do you? David is picking me up."

"No, I've got my car."

At Starlight Bowl, Melissa hurried through check-in and quickly gathered rented shoes and a house ball before heading down to Lane Nine where Julie's team was bowling. David looked up, noticed Melissa, and waved. Julie's eyes followed David's hand. Her face lit up when she saw Melissa.

"Hey, long time, no see. Hurry up, and get those shoes on. We've finished practice bowling."

Tracy, looking especially pretty in a turquoise shirt layered over a white blouse, leaned an elbow on the counter and chatted to the same friend David had brought last year. Melissa approached the lane, aimed the ball in a haphazard way, and gave her arm a carefree swing. The ball rolled into the gutter. No surprise there.

Melissa plodded to the bar and ordered an iced tea, taking her time returning to the couples-only group. Despite her married status, she felt like the lone amoeba in Noah's Ark. She returned to the group in time to see David's friend bowl a strike.

"That's a double!" Tracy's danced as she enthusiastically clapped her hands. "Hey, Melissa, you're up."

Melissa dragged her feet to the return, fumbled for her ball, and carried it to the approach line. As she moved her arm backward, someone called out, "Wait!"

The boy who had just struck a double, the same one talking to Tracy, now stood behind her, smiling and oozing genuine friendliness.

"Hold the ball like this." The boy crooked Melissa's arm into an unnatural position and turned her wrist. "Now, you'll throw it like that." He guided her arm back and forth several times. "Now you try it. Just make sure you follow through."

Melissa tossed her ball, and it once more rolled into the gutter. The boy did not move.

"That's okay," he said. "You'll get the hang of it, with practice. Here, I'll show you again."

He repeated the motions with Melissa and then stepped back. Melissa swung and knocked down five pins.

The boy grinned. "See? It'll come."

She flushed both from the thrill of pleasing him as well as success. It felt good to get something right. "Thanks!"

That's when Melissa noticed Tracy watching her with an odd expression Melissa immediately recognized. She had seen it just once in her direction long ago, on Lisa Harding's face at the Smythe's dinner party, when Kellen had taunted Melissa. Melissa almost laughed aloud at Tracy's jealousy. Melissa had married the college's star music professor. Tracy could have the kid.

After the boy bowled, he lingered by the ball return, and Melissa's heart beat fast as she brushed past him to pick up her ball. For a kid, he sure seemed nice. He remained standing there, observing Melissa's technique as she swung and knocked down nine pins.

"Hurray!" Melissa, shocked at her loudness, blushed and covered her mouth.

The boy beamed. "Here, I'll show you how to pick up that spare."

He knelt on the floor beside Melissa, eased her feet to the appropriate floor boards, and showed her where to aim the ball.

"Don't watch the pins," he said. "Just line the ball up with that board."

She knocked down the spare down, too. Melissa broke a hundred and thirty for both games, the best she'd ever bowled. She walked back to her seat for the forgotten iced tea. The boy followed her and held out his hand.

"I'm Lyle Fleming," he said. "David's roommate."

Melissa returned the smile. "Nice to meet you, Lyle. Thanks for all the help. I couldn't have done it without you."

"Happy to help. And you are....?"

"Oh, I'm Melissa."

"Melissa...."

"Simotes. Melissa Simotes."

Lyle scrunched his face in thought. "As in Professor Simotes, the music teacher?"

Melissa nodded. "That's my husband."

The smile vanished and a look of sympathy replaced it. "Oh, I'm so sorry. The professor told me about your loss."

"Loss?"

"I'm a music major," Lyle said. He leaned closer, in a confiding way. "You know, I'm a laid-back guy, and I understand a little irritability now and then, but the professor's been downright insulting. When I finally blew up at him, he backed off and told me about the miscarriage. Boy, did I feel stupid."

Miscarriage?

Julie nudged Melissa. "Coming with us to Crossroads Tap?"

Head spinning, flustered, Melissa could only sputter, "Tired. Going home."

Miscarriage?

"Come *on*, Melissa. One drink."

"Julie, if Melissa needs rest, I don't think you should interfere," Tracy said smoothly.

But Julie persisted. "We never hang out anymore."

Melissa tottered; her breath caught in her throat. *Miscarriage!* Think, think, she needed to think, but Tracy's suspicious attitude piqued her.

"Sure," Melissa said, dully, barely aware of the words. "One drink."

Tracy looped her arm through Lyle's and led him away. Julie, David by her side, walked with Melissa and praised her bowling. Melissa suddenly remembered she was still wearing rental shoes and hung back to take them off.

"We'll be at the bar," Julie called over her shoulder.

Melissa quickly returned the shoes and had just stepped through the entrance of Crossroads Tap when Julie, David behind her, came rushing her out.

"Hey, glad I caught you," Julie said with an overly exuberant smile. "We're going someplace else."

"Why?" Curious, Melissa started for the door, but Julie blocked it.

"Really, Melissa, don't go in there."

Melissa pushed past Julie and into the noisy room. Greg stood at the back of the bar. As her eyes adjusted to the dim lighting, Melissa noticed the other band members milling about the room. Was this the meeting place? Had they played that night? Were they taking a break? As the crowds shifted,

Melissa saw John bend to kiss a dark-haired woman holding a drink in her outstretched hand.

Without hesitation, Melissa charged across the room and into that drink, spilling it over the woman and John. The woman squealed and dropped the glass. Ignoring the shatters, Melissa turned and fled into the parking lot. Her heart thudded as she dug in her pocket for her car keys. Melissa swung the car door open; another hand slammed it shut.

"You bitch!"

Melissa whirled around. "Oh, look! You came up for air!"

John's face flushed hot with rage. "That's the label's president! You ruined a good deal for the guys!"

"The guys!" John's cavalier words appalled Melissa. "What about us? We're married, or have you forgotten that?"

"This is business."

"Business!" Melissa's head reeled. "Well, since you're into compromise, you might as well offer yourself to Kellen Wechsler again!"

John blanched and recoiled at her words. Henry had told Melissa about the host relationship John once had with Kellen Weschler, his former manager, who had traded John's blood for money and notoriety, but John didn't know Melissa knew it. Well, *good!* Melissa hoped her words stung hard.

"I'm doing what I have to do," John said in a low voice.

"Then I hope you fail!"

John didn't speak to Melissa the following week, which was fine with her, because she didn't want to speak to him, either, not until John was prepared to answer a few questions. So Professor Johnny Simotes *was* the nineteenth century pianist and composer John Simons, and John most certainly knew it. So how did Marvin and Carol fit into the picture, and what did John want from Melissa? Certainly, not love, romance, and a life built together, the things Melissa wanted from him. If he had married her only to replace a dead baby, why hadn't he dumped her?

Miscarriage!

On Saturday, John broke the silence. Melissa was heading toward the back door to study at the library. Spending an entire day in the same house as cold and heartless John was unthinkable. As she zipped past him, he, coffee mug in hand, said, "The school told me to play its black tie fundraiser next Saturday."

Melissa opened the door. "Have a good time," she said and started out.

In a flash, John slammed the door. Melissa pulled her fingers back just in time and groped for the knob. John learned against the door. "You're going."

"That's what you think."

"And I said you're going. It won't look right if you don't. This job still supplies the money that supports us both."

Melissa glared at John. "Just tell everyone I'm still recovering from the miscarriage."

"The *what?*"

"You heard me."

John leaned closer. "Explain yourself now."

"What's the matter, John, can't you keep your stories straight?" Melissa tugged the doorknob to no avail.

John slid a hand under Melissa's chin and lifted her face. *"Now."*

Defiantly, Melissa raised her head higher, so mad she struggled to find words.

"Tracy's friend Lyle said you told him I had a miscarriage. What'd you do, tell the whole school, like you did when I asked you out?"

She had gambled on this last, but Melissa watched John closely for his reaction. Instead of growing angry, John's expression softened, but his gaze remained steady.

"Melissa, I didn't tell anyone you had a miscarriage. If that imbecile Lyle had repeated the story correctly, he would have told you I said we lost a baby."

"Same thing!"

"Not to me it isn't. We lost the baby we will never have."

Melissa blinked at the tone in John's voice. Was that a grieved look in his eyes? If so, it vanished as quickly as it came. As John released Melissa and opened the door, the apathy returned.

"The event is a costume party. The theater department reserved several items for you to try. Go there Monday."

"Whatever." She began to slip out, but John seized her arm and fixed cold eyes on her. Melissa looked away, took a breath, and then stared back at him.

"Fine. I'll go. What's the theme?"

"Victorian Nights."

She banged the door behind her. *Victorian Nights?* Was that a joke?

It was no joke. On Monday, in the hour after classes and before Melissa clocked in at work, she walked over to the theater, the only structure on campus built from scratch. Someone had tacked a note on the backstage door: *Melissa, I set two dresses in my office for you. Elaine Beck.*

Who was Elaine Beck?

The door stood ajar. Leaning on it to further open the door, Melissa poked her head around it to see if anyone could help her. "Hello?" The words bounced off the walls of the empty rooms. "Hello?"

She stepped backstage without closing the door behind her, just in case. Her footsteps echoed on the old wood floor as she lightly treaded to the row of office doors. The last one bore a metal plate: Elaine Beck.

Melissa tried the handle. It swung open. Elaine Beck, whoever she was, had laid two Victorian-style frocks on the faded, brown-tweed couch, although neither dress could be classified as a ball gown. Certainly, they did not resemble anything Melissa had worn in her Bryony dreams. A pair of long, white gloves rested on the end table next to the couch. A lined, black cape draped over the back of an armchair. One dress, pale green, trimmed in pink, with white ruffles at the neckline, cuffs, and skirt, reminded Melissa of the Bryony weeds at Simons Mansion. The second was gold, speckled with tiny white flowers, and also trimmed in white lace. Melissa scooped both dresses in her arms and stepped into the room's private bathroom, locking the door behind her.

Melissa hung the dresses on the claw hook on the back of the door, slid out of her skirt and blouse, and then tossed them onto the bathroom sink. The bodice of the green dress pinched her shoulders; its bustle slid off her shoulders. Wearing it, Melissa felt like Bertha Parks, nineteenth century

Munsonville's chief gossip and housekeeper to Bryony's father, the Reverend Galien Marseilles. She hoped the yellow dress fit. Actually, the yellow dress not only suited Melissa's tastes, it conformed to her body shape as naturally as if a dressmaker had crafted it to her exact measurements. Pleased, Melissa returned the green dress to the couch, picked up the gloves and cape, and shut the office door behind her. How ironic to be attending a Victorian-themed fundraiser with John. Two years ago, Melissa had played Bryony. Now it was John's turn to masquerade the era that once belonged to him. She wondered how he felt about it.

At dinner, John broke the silence only once. "Did you try on those dresses?"

"Yep."

"And?"

"I found one that fits."

He did not speak to her again. Melissa retreated to the couch after dinner and remained there all evening, reading a book. She fell asleep while pretending to ignore the piano music. The rest of the week passed in a similar manner. John maintained his distance, but so did Melissa. Conversation stayed short and on topic.

Friday evening when John did not come home, Melissa, feeling forlorn and forsaken, flung herself back into a time that merged her past with Bryony's. After first locking the spare bedroom door to ensure privacy lest John enter, Melissa knelt before her steamer trunk and brought forth her Munsonville treasures, the first time she had exposed them to her Jenson home. How hopeful Melissa had felt the first time she had read *Creatures of the Night: Witches, Werewolves, and Vampires*, her textbook to vampire behavior when she first made her bargain with John. The rose petals she fingered inside the manila envelope checked that hope and reminded Melissa that she could have avoided her current suffering, if only she had listened to Henry. Reverently, Melissa lifted up Bryony's music box and opened the lid, half-expecting to hear its now silent notes. The temptation to bring the cherry wood box into the living room and place *The Best-Loved Compositions of John Simons* on the stereo engulfed her.

Only the real fear that John might walk through the door at any moment prevented Melissa from relenting to it. Two years ago and tired of reliving Bryony's relationship with John, Melissa had pined for the day when John Simons would be hers alone. Today, now that she had him, Melissa much preferred the John of her imagination. At least then, Melissa could pretend he attended to her needs. With a little of sigh despair and defeat, Melissa replaced her coveted items and went to bed.

On Saturday, Melissa, with a full and heavy heart and no Trudi to help her, donned the garments John wanted her to wear. The entire affair mocked the Bryony bliss Melissa had lived just a short time ago. After all Melissa had done for John, it felt very unfair. Following a brief look in the guest room mirror, Melissa walked to the bedroom to see if John had completed dressing. He, too, stood in front of a mirror, adjusting the vest of his black tie and tails. Her heart sank when she saw him, and that's when Melissa realized she'd hoped all along for a symbolic return to the past.

"You're not wearing white?" she said in nearly a whisper. She had secretly hoped he might.

John turned and inspected his reflection from the side. "Too garish for the school gym."

If Melissa didn't change the subject quickly, she'd cry. "Who's Elaine Beck?"

"Theater department chair." He adjusted his collar and analyzed his appearance in the mirror for the final time. "Ready?"

Melissa nodded, biting the inside of her lip, but with that act, pride suddenly welled up inside her, and she vowed on the spot: *John would not spoil this evening for her.* Tickets, Julie had told her, started at a hundred dollars a plate. Why, she was attending an event her friends could only dream of attending, the type of event Ann, once upon a time, desired as common in her life. So what if John's attention would be cursory at best? Tonight, Melissa, as Professor Simotes' wife, could ride on the coattails of his reputation and enjoy a real-life Bryony experience. If John didn't like it, too bad. He couldn't do anything about it.

With the composure of royalty, Melissa strolled to the car. She diverted her eyes from John's face during the short ride, stoically resisting even a single peek, lest she endanger her resolve. John and formalwear forged a breathtaking combination.

Then, a block away from the school, John said, "Remember that first night, when we made our bargain?"

Melissa nodded, but said nothing.

"Why ever did you ever agree to it?"

Melissa's heart caught in her throat. She had not expected this from John. Don't look, she told herself. "I wanted to be Bryony."

"Because?"

"She was special."

"No other reason?"

Insides now trembling, Melissa tightly squeezed her eyes shut. "I believed in your goodness."

"Although I appeared hideous?"

"I saw through it. Anyway, that part didn't last long."

"And now?"

Melissa could not answer him. She would definitely cry if she did. The entire first floor of Jenson College blazed in light. John left her at the gym door and drove away to find parking. The cape did little to deflect the chilly November night, but Melissa hardly noticed. John's questions had sparked the warm glow of hope inside her, as new as the moon above her, and she felt as excited as Bryony at her first ball. She breathed a single word, *"Please."*

John was now walking toward her with brisk steps. He reached for the handle, and then hesitated and leaned in.

"Melissa," John said in a voice so hushed, Melissa barely heard him. He edged closer, caught himself, and opened the door. "Let's go. We're late."

Although the wait staff served the food in a style similar to the Smythe dinner party, none of it resembled the traditional Victorian fare Melissa had eaten as Bryony, a relief for Melissa, since she had brought an appetite with her tonight. John spoke to the man on his right and then took note of the menu.

"Damn!" John said in a low voice.

Alarmed, Melissa whispered back, "What's wrong?"

"No tongue." John pulled Melissa close and added, "Yet."

Melissa's heart skipped an unexpected beat, but before she could either respond or react, an obese, but stylish, gray-haired woman on Melissa's left said, "I see you found the dresses all right."

"I did, thank you. You left them for me?"

"Yes, in my office."

So this was Elaine Beck!

After John hurried through the main courses, he excused himself from the table to assume his place at the grand piano stationed at the gym's farthest end. As the first melodies floated past her, Melissa realized that, for all the familiarity of John sitting at a piano at home, this was the first moment she had experienced his playing, in real time, at a formal setting. Sharp yearning for John broke through her composed exterior and nearly overflowed. Through blurry eyes, she watched John play with both animation and ease; she knew each patron sat spellbound at his performance. Who was she kidding? She wanted John and only John, but would she ever really have him?

Not until the enthusiastic clapping ended did John begin the final selection. Melissa gave a little bleat and quickly covered her mouth, but the tears flowed anyway, and it took all her strength not to sob aloud. She had not expected to hear *Bryony* tonight.

Elaine Beck handed Melissa a napkin. "Your husband plays beautiful music."

The crowd delivered a standing ovation. Head low, John sat motionless at the keyboard. Then, slowly, he closed the lid, stood, smiled, and bowed once before exiting the makeshift stage. A dance band soon claimed the area. It took John nearly an hour to make his way back to the table he shared with Melissa. Everyone wanted to talk to him.

"I'm tired," Melissa said, when John finally returned. It was no lie. She felt exhausted. "Can we leave?"

John took her hand and led her to the exit, pausing now and then to speak to another admirer. He continued holding her hand even after they had left the school and were walking to the car, but since they passed an occasional guest, Melissa decided John was simply showing off.

When they had moved away from the last person, Melissa finally spoke. "You played wonderfully tonight." She paused, uncertain how to continue. "Especially 'Bryony.' I know how much you miss her."

John stopped and looked steadily at her. "Melissa, I wasn't paying tribute to her."

She gave a weary sigh. "John, we both know the truth. Why pretend any....?"

"I was saying, 'Good-bye.'"

Melissa, beating back sudden waves of happiness, looked incredulously up at John. "Good-bye?"

John cupped her face in his hands and moved close, so very close. Don't hope, Melissa told herself over the frantic thudding of her heart. *Don't hope. Don't hope. Don't hope.*

"I won't waste an opportunity at human life in self-pity. I'm moving forward, and I want you to come with me."

"John, I...I...."

He tightened his hold on her. "Will you?"

Was he sincere? Could she believe him? Should she believe him? The passion in his eyes disturbed and frightened her. Now, John was breathing fast, too.

"No more secrets?" Melissa asked in a small, but determined voice.

John's fingers gripped her cheeks. He bore down on her with hard and riveting eyes. "No more secrets."

Melissa, throat tight, could only nod. John held open her car door, and Melissa, legs weak and buckling, all tension and heartache melting away, dropped into the seat. Long before John left the parking lot, sleep had overpowered Melissa in strong, flooding currents. She yawned and sat up straight, unwilling to miss a second of the magical aftermath of what John had just promised to her. To her delight, John was watching her. Finally, oh, finally! John was putting the past behind him; in a twinkling, Melissa had won the prize. Joy exploded into fragments of fairy dust and spooled Melissa into mellow slumber.

"Go to sleep." John's voice floated away in ripples.

She slept so soundly, John had to rouse her when they reached home. With the tenderness of a mother, John led her from the car and up the back steps. He maintained a firm hold on her as he fumbled for the house key and swung open the door.

Melissa stumbled through the house to the bedroom. She quickly shed her clothes and tossed them onto a chair before rummaging in the bottom drawer for a nightgown. She fell asleep drawing the comforter up to her neck.

"Melissa."

The whispered words echoed in her dreams and bounced off her mind. She felt a foot nudge her ribs. John's voice was firm and insistent. *"Melissa."*

Melissa struggled to regain consciousness. She cracked open her eyes. John stood at the side of the bed, one foot on top of the sheets by her waist. He wore only a broad grin. Even the shirt was gone.

"Touch me," he said.

In an instant, Melissa sprung fully awake. Unlike that first time she heard those words, long ago in the servant's cottage, there was absolutely nothing cold about John at all. Even better, and also unlike that first time, Melissa knew exactly where John would take her. They had not been *really* together, in the right way, since they received Dr. Jorgenson's bad news.

With a willing and ecstatic heart, Melissa followed.

CHAPTER 14: BLOOD DONOR

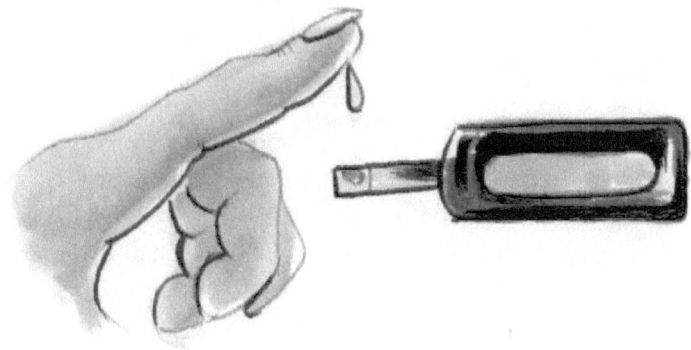

John's slow easy breathing signaled near sleep, but Melissa switched on the light anyway and said, "Roll over."

He cracked opened an eye. "Whatever for?"

"I want a good look at your back."

To Melissa's surprise, John complied. Melissa almost wished he had again refused. She had not prepared for the many horrifying slashes in John's neck and shoulders, deep furrows that extended down his back.

"The fire?" Melissa asked timidly.

"Henry Matthews."

"Henry?"

Melissa felt instantly transported to the basement of Simons Mansion, the night Henry had confessed his sins to her. *I killed him in the presence of her image and hung myself,* Henry had said, but never in Melissa's most rampant suppositions had she ever considered that Henry Matthews, always the consummate gentleman, could be capable of such savagery. Chaperone or teacher, vampire or man, Henry obviously possessed another side to him. His past advice to her now seemed less sterling, more tarnished. Just *why* had Henry feigned such concern for her?

Gingerly, Melissa gingerly traced her fingers along one groove. "It's the work of a madman." She shuddered at the thought of Henry wielding repeated blows on John.

"The old boy did a good job on me, didn't he?" John said. When Melissa did not answer, he added, "And that's the man you wish to emulate?"

Melissa shuddered again and turned off the light, Her desire to become an English teacher and teach in Munsonville School began to recede. An overpowering desire to cooperate with John, to move forward in her relationship with him as he wished, whatever that meant, rose to take its place.

John broke into her thoughts. "What's wrong?"

"I don't like thinking of you in pain."

"I felt little after the first blows."

"Still."

They lay in darkness, neither one speaking until John braced himself on an elbow, leaned over Melissa, and stroked her cheek. The softest moonlight shone through the window. In its glow, Melissa saw the malevolence on John's face.

"You know, Melissa," he said in a silky voice. "I never suspected you'd betray me."

"I didn't betray you."

John's gleaming eyes chilled her. "Didn't you?"

The sudden shift in his mood unsettled her, but because she had to prove he could not intimidate her anymore, Melissa flung back his accusation.

"You're the one who forced me to be with him," she said with a boldness she did not feel.

"Irrelevant. Your role was to behave. Henry's job was to enforce it."

Melissa flipped over and folded the pillow around her head. "Stay mad. I'm going to sleep." But John's eyes burned into her brain, and Melissa stayed awake a long time.

Late one Monday afternoon, as Melissa stepped through the back door, the phone rang, and she hurried to answer it.

"Good. I caught you," John said. "I'm not coming home for dinner tonight."

"Why not?"

"Doctor's appointment. I'll eat on the way."

Except for fertility testing, John never went to the doctor. Alarmed, Melissa asked, "John, are you sick?"

"It's routine."

"Then take me with you. We could grab a bite together."

Silence.

"John, are you still there?"

He did not reply. His evasiveness irritated her.

"I thought we'd finished with secrets. Aren't we in this together?"

John paused a long time before speaking. "Be ready in half an hour."

Melissa, thoughtful, slowly hung up the phone. She hoped John wasn't ill. Reflecting back on the past months, she saw how the high stress surrounding his quick marriage, sterility, and subsequent tension with her, all the while maintaining an impossibly overloaded schedule that could break a weaker man, had affected him. He didn't sleep well at night, and, although John had always enjoyed coffee, he and his mug had become inseparable.

John's doctor practiced in Shelby, inside a quaint, remodeled, cottage-style house that, years before a Shelby's downtown existed, had once stood in the middle of a cornfield. At least, that's what John said as they walked across the street. The painted on the wooden sign by the front door read *Dr. Abner Rothgard*.

Melissa and John approached the front desk and waited for the receptionist to finish a phone call.

"John Simotes, you say?" She pulled out his chart and looked up at him. "We haven't seen you for some time."

What an odd statement, Melissa thought. John had turned human less than two years ago.

The receptionist attached several sheets of paper to a clipboard and handed it and a ballpoint pen to John. "Here. You'll need to update your information."

John sat on a chair and began filling out the forms. Melissa leaned near to watch him write, and John moved the clipboard away from her. "Do you mind?"

Melissa's cheeks grew warm. "Sorry."

To cover up her embarrassment, Melissa studied the magazine selection on the coffee table before her. She skipped over the parenting magazines and rejected *House Décor Now!* and *Fishing for Fun and Profit* before deciding on a worn women's magazine. The cover story featured a television actress and how she found fulfillment in her fourth husband. John completed his assignment and returned the clipboard to the receptionist.

Twenty minutes passed, and no one called for John. Melissa browsed over the pages, but John fidgeted with greater frequency and finally peered over Melissa's shoulder to see what she was reading.

On impulse, she closed the magazine and smiled at him. "Do you mind?"

He grinned back at her. "Touché."

The door to the office area opened, and a nurse in a starched white uniform stepped into the waiting room. "John Simotes."

John stood up. Melissa did not move.

"Coming?" he said.

"Sure!" She scrambled out of her seat and followed them, thrilled John had meant what he said, that secrets belonged in the past.

The woman led them to the first door and stopped in front of a scale. "Step up, please."

She slid the weights and jotted the result in the chart.

"First room on the right." Once she closed the door, the woman continued. "I'm Dottie Sherman, Dr. Rothgard's nurse. Have a seat on the table Mr. Simotes, and I'll check your vitals. Your daughter can sit here." She motioned toward a high backed chair near the desk."

Melissa concealed a smile, but John looked annoyed. "Wife."

"I beg your pardon?"

"I said, 'She is my wife.'"

Nurse Sherman looked confused. "Oh, I'm so sorry," she said, but she didn't sound sorry.

"It's quite all right," Melissa reassured her,

"No temperature." Nurse Sherman shook the mercury back into place. "Roll up your sleeve, Mr. Simotes, please."

With a sidelong glance at Melissa, John submitted his right arm to the cuff.

"Blood pressure's normal. How tall are you Mr. Simotes?"

"Six four."

The nurse opened a drawer, removed a faded, green-print cloth gown, and handed it to John. "Take off all your clothes, and put this on. Doctor will see you shortly." She closed the door.

John undid the remaining buttons of his shirt while Melissa watched him. "You're letting him see you without a shirt?"

"I have no choice."

"I thought nobody sees you without...."

John scowled at Melissa, but as he unbuckled his belt, the scowl faded. "You want to do this?"

"Oh, you're funny."

John slid off his pants and looked at the door. "I wonder how long before Dr...."

Melissa made a face at him. "Professor John Simotes, don't even go there."

"So you won't help with my gown?"

"You're capable."

John had just tied the strings when someone knocked on the door. Before John could reply, the door opened, and a short, stooped, man with heavy, thick-rimmed black glasses and artificially dark hair slicked to one side entered, skimming John's chart.

"Well, well, John, I thought you were ancient history. Been well?"

"Fine."

The doctor chuckled. "John, if you felt fine, I'd not be seeing you. Say 'Ah.'"

John obeyed that command and the others that followed. He coughed, breathed deeply, tracked the light the doctor waved above his head, and lay down on the table while the doctor fiddled under the gown.

"Are you sleeping at night?"

"Yes."

Liar, Melissa thought.

"Eating a normal diet?"

"Yes."

"Drinking plenty of water?"

"Yes."

"Defecating and urinating normally?"

"Yes."

"No sexual dysfunction?"

He looked at Melissa. "Any complaints?"

The doctor turned and noticed Melissa for the first time. "Who's she?"

John hesitated a long while before answering. "My host."

Melissa snapped to attention. John's *what?*

The doctor chuckled again. "And you're sleeping with her?"

"A happy host is a cooperative host."

"Every man has his method."

Fury burned inside Melissa. Why of all the...! Just who was this doctor anyway?

As if reading her mind, John said, "Melissa, this is Dr. Rothgard. He oversees my... treatment."

His host?

Dr. Rothgard snorted. "Treatment, my Aunt Betsy's backside. I can't oversee anything when you don't comply. Sit up."

His *host?*

With brisk steps, Dr. Rothgard crossed the room, dropped into his swivel desk chair, and wrote some notes in John's chart. His dusky fingertips caught Melissa's attention. She remembered from high school biology class that a blue color meant low oxygen, but the complexion of Dr. Rothgard's face appeared ruddy enough. How odd.

Dr. Rothgard turned and faced John once again. "Now for the truth. Any sensitivity to sunlight?"

"A little."

"Daytime sleepiness? Cravings for blood?"

"Occasionally."

"Hmm." He returned to John's chart. "How long since your transformation?"

"Nearly two years."

Dr. Rothgard rubbed his chin and stared hard at John. "We never initiated any maintenance therapy, did we?"

"No."

"Will you now give it a try?"

"Absolutely."

Dr. Rothgard turned back to the chart and made a few more notations. "You've waited a long time. At this point, I cannot guarantee its success." He jerked his head in Melissa's direction. "She's agreeable?"

"I guarantee it."

Melissa found her voice at last. "I'm not 'she.' I'm not a host. I'm Melissa, John's wife."

"Hmm." Dr. Rothgard opened a desk drawer and removed two small cardboard boxes. One contained sealed alcohol pads; the other held small plastic implements. He looked at Melissa. "Your finger."

Fuming at the doctor's condescending attitude, Melissa looked at John for his reaction, but he only provided a curt nod. Feeling outvoted and unsupported, she offered an index finger to Dr. Rothgard.

"Now pay attention. You're the dispenser."

He unwrapped the alcohol pad, wiped the tip of her finger, and then uncapped the piece of plastic to reveal a sharp needle. Melissa knew that needle. Her father, an insulin-dependent diabetic, had used similar ones to test his blood sugar. Melissa's heart pounded fast and hard. She hated needles.

"Hey, wait!" Melissa tried withdrawing.

With one rapid movement, Dr. Rothgard jabbed her finger. A bead of blood formed at the site where he pricked it. "John?"

Disgust passed over John's face. He remained seated.

"Now, now John don't be squeamish. It's necessary for survival."

John reluctantly slid off the table. He drew Melissa's finger into his mouth and sucked the oozing blood.

"Keep going," Dr. Rothgard said, studying his watch as he counted under his breath. "Okay, that's enough."

Melissa snatched away her finger. Dr. Rothgard closed the boxes and handed them to John.

"Consider that treatment number one. Since your symptoms are not severe, I recommend you repeat on a weekly basis, ten seconds at a time." He paused, looked from Melissa to John, and then smiled, a little sardonically it seemed to her. "The site where you obtain the blood is unimportant, as long as Marissa's the source, so make it as fun as you like."

Melissa glowered at him. "Melissa."

"If symptoms increase, call me. We can adjust the treatment."

Dr. Rothgard looked at Melissa, and his face grew stern.

"Now, listen carefully. If you see any behavior that concerns you, *call*. Don't trust John to do it. If his vampire state breaks through his human one, he will not have enough sense to obtain help." He gave Melissa a business card. "Use that number on the bottom, day or night, if you need me." He looked at John. "It's imperative you follow the schedule. You are not in any immediate danger, but that can change if you disregard my orders."

He shook John's hand, opened the door, paused, looked back with amusement at Melissa, and then left, chuckling and shaking his head.

Melissa controlled her temper until John checked out, and she'd shut the car door.

"Forget dinner!" she exploded. "Just...just take me home!"

John slowed for a red light. "Suit yourself."

How could he be so indifferent?

"You called me a host!"

John stared straight ahead. "I didn't invite you, remember? You asked to come, against my judgment."

"You should have told me!"

The light turned green. John gently accelerated. Melissa looked out the window and narrowed her eyes against the glowing orange ball sinking below the horizon. She knew her question would cause an argument, but she had to know.

"Tell me the truth, John, if you are capable of telling the truth. Do you love me?"

She sensed him hesitate.

"No."

"Then why did you marry me?"

"We made a bargain."

"Only until you became human." She turned to look at him.

"Who said that?"

"Well, I assumed…"

"You assume often, Melissa. How was I supposed to remain human?"

"You never said it would entail.…"

"I didn't know."

Melissa studied the floor mats and said nothing. Could she believe him? How could he not know? "You didn't tell me I had to marry you."

"I never said otherwise. You thoroughly enjoyed role-playing my wife."

She sighed. Would John chain her to a teen girl's fantasy? "And if I break the deal?"

"I'll kill you."

"What?" Stunned, Melissa again faced John. His hard features froze her heart. "I hate you," she said with a loathing she thought she'd never feel for him.

John's countenance remained unchanged. "A pity. I've grown rather fond of you."

A cocktail of emotions—terror, rage, hurt, longing—surged inside Melissa. "I...I...."

"And I'm thankful for all you've bestowed upon me. Truly."

Melissa folded her arms and scrunched into the seat. She would not cry in front of a man who had no regard for her. Instead, Melissa closed her eyes and concentrated on steadying her voice.

"That's just not good enough for me anymore," she said quietly.

John pulled into the driveway, lingering only until Melissa was safely inside the house before backing out into the street.

She did not even try sleeping that night. The bed she shared with John repelled and disgusted her. Instead, Melissa curled up in the stuffed chair by the window, pleaded her case to the golden sliver of moon dominating the jet sky, and brooded. She had asked, and John had told her. He did not love her. He had proposed marriage only to ensure access to her blood, to prevent a relapse into vampirism. Hadn't Henry warned her about making deals with John? Hadn't he explained how John now considered Melissa's blood his private possession? Why hadn't she listened to Henry when he insisted John did not love her and never would? Would John really kill her if she refused him? The thought frightened her, yet Melissa knew she could not, must not accommodate him, now that she knew how he really felt about her. She would not voluntarily give him her blood. If he wanted it, John must take it by force.

Melissa jerked awake. The bookcase clock read two o'clock. She heard the back door close. That's what had roused her from sleep. John had returned home.

He walked with quiet steps past the piano and toward the bedroom and then abruptly stopped. "Melissa?"

She did not answer. Why should she? Their farcical marriage had ended. Was it smarter to go home and attend Grover's Park Community College or move far away and get a job, any job? She had no life without John. She had no future. She had nothing.

John crossed the living room and knelt beside the chair. He lifted her hand and kissed it. She yanked it away. Undaunted, John rested his hand on her arm and asked, "Are you all right?"

Melissa's throat filled with bitterness. "Why should you care? You don't even love me."

"True, but I am grateful for your love. I need it to overcome this next stage."

The gall! She delivered her most withering look. "Why should I give it to you?"

John looked genuinely puzzled. "Why wouldn't you?"

"But you'd still rather have Bryony!"

"If I could, yes. But I can't."

Melissa's voice choked with misery and disappointment. "Why...her?"

John sighed in weariness. "Melissa, I have no explanation for it, except...."

Melissa glanced up at him. A wave of soft tenderness passed over John's face, but he looked away as he said, "I love her."

Anguish poured through Melissa like drenching, icy rain. This was *not* what she'd hoped to hear. Well, she'd demanded honesty from John. Now that she had it, she wasn't sure she wanted it.

"I'm second best? The consolation package?"

"You mustn't view it that way, Melissa."

She found a pattern on the chair to contemplate. Reds and blues crisscrossed with purples. Why did life have to be so complicated? Why couldn't John love her the way she wanted him to love her, the way she needed him to love her?

"So, you'll kill me?"

"You heard Dr. Rothgard. Without your blood, my dormant vampire traits will increase and overtake my humanity. At that point, since you refused me, I will kill you. I'll be unable to control it."

Melissa felt the edge she thought she had over John ebbing. How could he make such gross aberrations sound normal and logical? "Well, then, did you have to call me a host?"

John shrugged off the question. "Medical terminology."

Was he serious? One look at John, and Melissa could see he meant it. What else could she say? She returned to the comforting spot on the chair.

John took a deep breath. "A private student of mine called me tonight. She wants to discontinue her lessons because she is pregnant and can't afford them."

"So?"

"So, she doesn't want to keep the baby and offered it to us. Interested?"

Melissa turned disbelieving eyes toward John. "I thought you didn't want to raise another man's child!"

John met her gaze. "And I told you, I'm going forward. You're making concessions for me, and I'm grateful for them. I want to do the same for you."

Unconvinced, and in words laced with sarcasm, Melissa said, "You want to make another trade?"

Irritation crept into John's voice. "No, not a trade. Listen, Melissa, I've given it considerable thought. I've received another chance at life, and you're the only one who can maintain it for me. I won't waste this opportunity on selfish ambitions. I'm concentrating on what's important, becoming a good husband and raising a family."

"But...."

"And I want to do it with you."

Still suspicious, Melissa said, "What about music?"

"I'm not forsaking it. I'll continue to teach, compose, play, and occasionally perform."

"Fame and fortune?"

"The price is higher than I can afford to pay."

She contemplated this new John. "Will you be content with such an ordinary life?"

"I'll adjust."

Melissa fell silent, reflecting on John's words. She had erased all possibility of having children with him. Yet, it appeared John intended to live out his days with her. The marriage that, just minutes ago, appeared dead, now brightened with hope. John sincerely wanted a baby with her. Could she live with John knowing he did not love her, even if he clothed himself with the trappings of correct marital behavior? On the other hand, how dismal her life would be without John in it! She couldn't bear it. She had no immediate answer for him.

She sighed. "Can I think about it?"

"Sure." John rose, bent over the chair, and kissed Melissa with heavenly, almost believable ardor. He pulled back slightly, and said with a provocative smile, "Even better, how about if we sleep on it?"

They both forgot to set the alarm. On a normal day, John would have resented the intense pressure of being late for work, but today he displayed even humor.

"Have you given further thought to the baby?" John stood in front of the mirror and knotted his tie.

Melissa sat on the bed and put one foot into a pair of nylons. "How am I going to finish school and take care of a baby?"

"I told you. We'll raise it together."

Melissa said nothing as she maneuvered the other foot. She considered a conversation she'd had with Ann the other day. Ann, with great pride in her voice, mentioned how Jack had promised to share childcare. From what Melissa had seen of Jack during her last trip to Munsonville, he might change one diaper, if Ann helped.

John picked up his wallet. "I promise."

She involuntarily grimaced at his words. John noticed, sat on the bed next to her, and crossed his heart.

"I swear it," John said. "I will make this work, even if I must modify my work hours to suit your class schedule."

The depth of his candor finally dawned on her. "You *really* mean it?"

John glanced the clock. "If you're ready, I'll drive you to school. Tonight, let's go to Rudy's and celebrate our new life together."

What a wonderful evening! Melissa poked fun at John's well-done steak, and John mooed at the red slab on her plate. For a brief moment, Melissa wondered if John had ever brought Brenda Garboldi here and quickly dismissed the thought. The past is the past, she decided. If John can move ahead, so could she. On the way home, John treated them both to ice cream cones.

After turning into the driveway, John let Melissa out by the back door before parking the car into the garage. Feeling happier than she had in a long, long time, Melissa fumbled in her hand for the correct key. As she began to insert it, the door swung easily open. How odd. John must have forgotten to shut it all the way. She snapped on the kitchen light and gasped at the dining room view.

John's piano lay in shambles.

CHAPTER 15: A GIFT OF LIFE

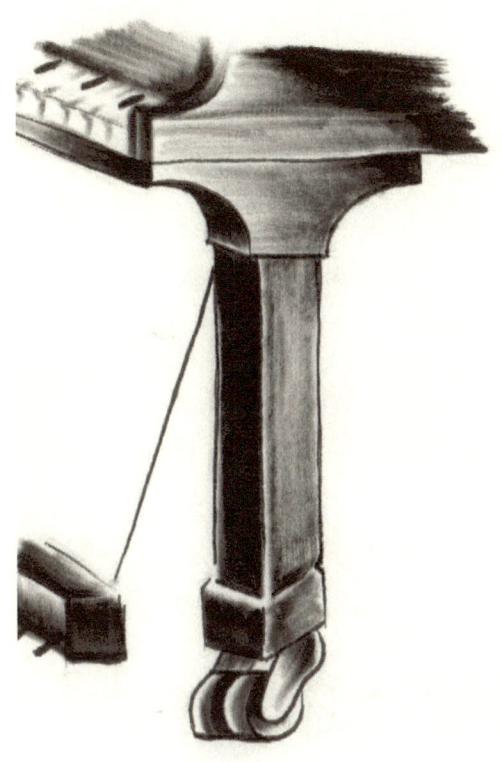

Melissa whirled around and tore out the door. John had already parked the car in the garage and was fast approaching the deck.

"John, someone broke into the house!"

Alarmed, John rushed up the steps and grabbed Melissa's shoulders. "Are you hurt?"

Quaking with anxiety, she could only shake her head.

He pushed past. Melissa closed her eyes and held her breath, poised for John's reaction to the destruction of his most prized possession. The cold air wrapped her like a vise; the night remained still and calm. She slowly exhaled. Streaming mist melted into nothing. The expected rage did not occur.

Bewildered, Melissa tiptoed into the kitchen and peeped into the dining room.

John stood near the wreckage and surveyed it with relative dispassion. Without looking up, he said, "Melissa, call the police. I'll check for other damage."

She heard John roaming about the other rooms as she dialed the telephone and reported the intrusion. Melissa returned to the dining room as John walked from the guest room, perplexed.

"Nothing else appears missing or broken," he said.

"I guess that's a blessing."

A shadow of annoyance passed over John's face. Melissa clapped a hand to her mouth and lightly bit her tongue. How could she have blurted out something so cruel?

Jenson police arrived in minutes. They searched the entire house and yard but found no evidence of intrusion and no other loss; nevertheless they took a report.

After they left, John, frowning, kicked through the piles of fragmented wood. "Look, Melissa, one leg is gone. See?"

She counted the columns as John pointed them out. One piano leg indeed was missing,

"That makes no sense. Who would break into our house, destroy your piano, and steal a leg?"

John retrieved the scattered sheet music, set the crumpled sheets on the buffet, and said, "I'll call the insurance company in the morning. Let's go to bed."

Still basking under the glow of the pleasant evening, for even the destruction of the piano could not spoil it for her, especially since the insurance company could so easily replace it, Melissa dawdled as she washed her face, brushed her teeth, and changed into bedclothes.

By the time Melissa had climbed into bed, John had fallen half-asleep. She crawled under the blankets and cuddled close, plastering his face with affectionate kisses.

John's eyes cracked open. He forced a drowsy smile. "The occasion?"

"I'm very proud of the way you handled tonight, with the piano and all."

"I told you. I'm trying."

John's voice slurred into a low snore. She snuggled into his arms, and he wound them around her. Happy that the better part of John had won out and pleased she'd mustered the good sense to wait for it, Melissa slipped into peaceful slumber, confident of a perfect future.

The following day, as Melissa exited her philosophy class, she bumped into John, who was waiting outside the door for her. Melissa's pulse instinctively sped up. John had never met her near a classroom.

She tiptoed to kiss him on the cheek, but John interrupted her. "Walk with me to the music room. My next students will arrive shortly."

Grasping her hand, John trotted ahead of her, talking at the same time. "I spoke with Debbie today, and she is most anxious to meet you."

"Debbie?" Melissa puffed.

"The pregnant student. I invited her to dinner for tomorrow night."

"So soon?"

"I want to secure the child."

"Don't we have time? How far along is she?"

"I don't know."

"You must have some idea!"

They had reached the sixth floor. An exasperated John dropped Melissa's hand.

"Melissa, you're talking to a man from an era when women hid pregnancies in flowing gowns and retreated at home until after the birth. One month, nine months; it's all the same to me." He gave her a quick, distracted kiss. "Shall I call her to confirm dinner?"

She wished she could conceive a reason to slow down the entire adoption process, if only to mentally catch up to John, but she couldn't think of one. So Melissa weakly said, "I'm not cooking."

"Big surprise." John turned into the music room.

The next evening, as Melissa spread garlic butter across sliced French bread, and John tossed the salad, she asked, "Are you going to tell me anything about her?"

"Such as?"

"Her name, for one."

"Debbie Polis."

"And?"

"And she's twenty-two, works as waitress in Shelby, and lives in a trailer with her artist boyfriend."

Melissa ripped off a sheet of aluminum foil and spread it on the table. Playing *Twenty Questions* regarding something as monumental as adopting their first baby irritated her. "Why does she take piano lessons?"

"Because she has always taken piano lessons, as she should. She's rather good."

She wrapped the last loaf of bread and slid them both into the oven. "Think she'll make something of her talent?"

"No. She's a waitress."

A knock at the front door, and John rushed to answer it. Melissa felt like screaming, "No! Slow down!" Instead, she tried looking agreeable since she couldn't feign excitement.

"Debbie," John said, "Meet my wife, Melissa."

Melissa wished she could dwell on those words, for just hearing John say them shot her to rapture, but he was waiting for her to greet Debbie, so Melissa forced herself to look at the woman standing beside him. Even if she wasn't pregnant, Debbie Polis, outdated feathered blonde hair falling softly over pudgy cheeks, still would be chubby. She stood uncertainly in the doorway, wringing her stumpy hands. Melissa had assumed all piano players had long fingers.

With a smile, Melissa said, "I'm happy to meet you, Debbie."

Inwardly, Melissa cringed at the prosaic greeting, but what else could she say? Certainly not, "Thanks for giving us your baby." She cleared her throat, feeling as nervous as Debbie appeared. "I hope you like spaghetti."

"I adore it."

During dinner, John and Debbie discussed every possible topic, from world peace to famine, except the one reason for which they had invited her to dinner, and Melissa grew restless and tired of hearing them talk nonsense. When would John introduce the pending adoption?

"More spaghetti?" he asked

"Thanks!" Debbie held out her plate.

"Have you seen the new restaurant, The Porter House, in Thornton? It's accepting applications."

"I thought she worked in Shelby," Melissa interjected.

"I do," Debbie said, turning wide eyes on her. "But I live in Thornton."

Enough!

.   "So, Debbie," Melissa said, passing her the garlic bread. To her annoyance, Debbie took two more slices. "When are you due?"

"I don't know," Debbie said around a mouthful of spaghetti.

Melissa glanced at John who grinned back at her, increasing Melissa's exasperation. How could John find this funny? This stupid woman was providing half their child's DNA.

"You don't know?"

"I can't afford doctors.'"

"Don't you have insurance?"

"There's no group plan for freelance abstract artists," Debbie took a large bite of garlic bread. "Or waitresses, either."

John reached for Debbie's hand. "Melissa and I will pay for your care. We plan to do everything to ensure a healthy baby and mother. We so appreciate your unselfishness."

Melissa's stomach turned at his flowery speech, but she managed to say, "Yes, Debbie, thank you for considering us to, you know...."

"I thought of you guys right away. Derek's not ready to be a father yet, and Professor Simotes seemed so upset about the miscarriage. It's the perfect solution. I just know you'll give her a good home."

Melissa glared at John, but he conveniently didn't notice. He was dishing out ice cream.

After Debbie left, and while they cleaned up the kitchen, John rambled about the new piano he had ordered. Melissa, still bristling about dinner conversation, only half-listened until she heard John say, "I'm glad Dr. Rothgard accepts prenatal patients, too."

Melissa jerked to attention. "Dr. Rothgard?"

"Of course."

She snapped a plastic lid on the leftover sauce. *"Dr. Rothgard?"*

"Did you think he performed only post-vampire care?"

"Oh, you're funny. No witch doctor is taking care of our baby. I'll call Ann in the morning and see who she uses."

"This isn't your decision. By the way, I told Mr. Schmidt you'd be quitting after finals."

"You, *what?*"

John rinsed the soap down the sink. "We don't need the money, but the baby will need his mother."

"So much for doing this together."

Melissa started to walk around John, but he blocked her way.

"We *are* doing this together. I'm cutting down my obligations, too. We agreed your education is a priority, and I won't allow a part time job to interfere with either school or raising our baby."

Touched beyond words at John's short speech, Melissa reached out for a hug. John turned away and said, "I'm not budging on Dr. Rothgard."

The sudden turnabout felt like a knife to her heart. She choked out, "I'm taking a shower and going to bed."

This time, John did not try to stop her.

She could not call Ann until after work the next day, but the second Melissa walked through the back door, she sped to the telephone and dialed it. Ann answered on the second ring.

"Melissa! How'd you know?"

"Know what?"

"That I had good news to share, you mind reader, you."

That's what I get for hanging out with vampires, Melissa thought. "What's the good news?"

"I felt the baby move today!"

"Wow!" Melissa momentarily forgot her reason for the phone call. Even if she adopted a dozen babies, she would never know this sensation. "What's it like?" Melissa asked, a little enviously.

"Like little butterflies soaring in my stomach."

Melissa closed her eyes and tried to imagine a zipping sensation in her mid-section, and she suddenly ached all over with the hollow emptiness of it. Was this how John felt? Would a miscarriage have been easier than a lifetime of barrenness? It wasn't fair. Even if she and John had fifty years of marriage, Bryony still owned two things Melissa would never possess: John's love and the exquisite joy of carrying his baby. Then Melissa remembered Henry's confession and his fear he might have fathered the baby that killed Bryony and stopped feeling envious of Bryony.

"Melissa, are you there?"

"Sorry. I was trying to picture it. Did Jack feel it?"

"I told him during the lunch hour, but he wasn't too interested. My mom said it's not a man thing."

"I'm sure he's excited, Ann. I've got news, too. John and I are adopting a baby."

"Adopting?" Ann's sounded skeptical instead of happy. "Why adopting?"

"We want to help an unwed mother who can't keep her baby."

"Oh."

Ann didn't believe her, Melissa could tell.

"Anyway, the mother hasn't had any prenatal care. Can you recommend a good doctor?"

"I'm using Dr. Rothgard in Shelby, if that helps."

Arggh!

"Um, I don't think he's taking any new patients. Can you suggest someone else?"

"I don't know anyone else. Dr. Rothgard has always been my doctor, and he'll be the baby's doctor, too, once it is born."

Melissa hadn't expected that blow. Where would she find someone to care for Debbie?

"Anyway, Jack wants to name the baby after him if it's a boy and me if it's a girl, but that's not very imaginative."

"I guess not." Maybe Dr. Anderson still practiced in Jenson. He had treated her anemia just fine. Maybe he could recommend a good doctor.

"I like 'Trenton' and 'Lauren.'"

"Those are nice...."

"Melissa, someone's knocking at the door. I've got to go!"

"Okay, later."

During dinner that evening, Melissa, still upset with John for again disregarding her feelings and opinions, kept her eyes on her plate and spoke little until John said, "The admission's secretary is pregnant. She gave me this."

Despite intentions of punishing John with her inattention, Melissa, curious, glanced up. John was reaching inside his shirt pocket; he handed Melissa a card: Dr. James Lofield. 231-9890. She flew out of her seat and hugged John so hard he nearly lost his balance.

"Thank you! Thank you! Thank you!"

John grinned and settled her on his lap, prepared to accept further expressions of Melissa's thankfulness. "Not bad for an ogre."

She planted tiny kisses on top of his head. "You're not an ogre."

"Remember that tomorrow. We begin our first at-home blood treatment."

Although not quite a week had passed since their visit with Dr. Rothgard, John had pronounced Saturday mornings for "blood-letting," since it was free of interference from work and school schedules. Melissa laughed as the appointed time approached, for John had cooked a large breakfast and then, after firmly refusing Melissa's help, washed and dried every dish. He even cleaned under the stove burners and wiped down the refrigerator shelves.

As John tied the half-full garbage bag, Melissa called his bluff. "Okay, quit procrastinating. I'm getting the supplies."

Melissa soon returned with the box from Dr. Rothgard. As she removed an alcohol wipe and lancet, John grazed the top of her hand with his fingertips. "Wait."

"You're acting like a baby," Melissa said, all the while savoring the lingering sensation of his touch.

She wiped her finger, took a deep breath, shut her eyes, and jabbed. She felt the prick, looked at John, and offered him its drop of blood. That wasn't so bad. Thank goodness for small needles. His face convulsed, and he looked away.

"Come on, John," she coaxed. "It's only a little bit of blood."

John dashed out of the room; the bathroom door slammed. With trembling fingers, Melissa dabbed away the already clotted blood. She despised a second needle stick, but concern for John subjugated her anxiety. What would happen to John if he couldn't stomach Dr. Rothgard's treatments?

Moments later, a ghostly pale John slunk back to his chair. Melissa tore off the wrapper from another wipe. Maybe levity would relax him.

"A fine vampire you'll make!"

"Just do it."

With a few false starts, and despite twitching lips, John swallowed the morsel, grimaced, leaned back slightly in the chair, and stared ahead.

Melissa watched him anxiously. "Are you okay?"

He set his jaw. His eyes blazed with fierce resolve. "I'm *not* going back, Melissa."

Once John had settled at the rental piano, and Melissa had cleaned up the scraps, she happily telephoned Debbie. As she delivered the news, Melissa noticed the music had abruptly stopped.

"Oh, thanks, Melissa! I'll call Dr. Lofield's office right away and make an appointment!"

Melissa hung up the phone. John stood in the doorway, thinking.

"I'm sorry," Melissa said. "Would you rather have told her?"

"It occurred to me that my parents should know about their first grandchild."

Dumbfounded, Melissa gaped at him before saying, "John! They're not your parents."

John picked up the receiver and dialed the telephone. "They don't know it."

"But how did you convince them...."

John was already talking to Carol, a signal John was closed to questions. Although Melissa spoke up more frequently, she saw no reason to needlessly anger John. Instead, Melissa picked up her library book and became so engrossed in its contents that a soft thud startled her. John had shut the piano lid.

"Didn't you want to call your parents, too?"

"What do you think?"

"Let's tell them in person, when we see them on Thanksgiving."

Melissa set the book on the end table, crossed the room, and sat by John. "I want to name the baby after my dad, if it's a boy."

A half-smile passed over John's lips and vanished. He lightly stroked her cheek. "The baby *is* a boy. And we're naming him 'John.'"

"How do you know it's a boy?"

"Strong hunch."

"Well, I think we should decide on a girl's name, just in case."

"Suit yourself."

"Debbie thinks she's carrying a girl."

"Debbie's an idiot."

John started to stand, when Melissa said, "How about Angela?"

"For what?" John paused and kissed her forehead.

"Our baby if she's a girl."

"Fine." John crossed the living room to the front door.

Melissa's heart sang with joy. "You don't care?" she called after him. "Really?"

"We're having a boy, Melissa."

Oh, how she would love to prove him wrong! Melissa smiled at John when he returned with the mail. "You just might be surprised, John."

John opened the first bill and did not respond. The phone rang. It was Debbie.

Her initial appointment with Dr. Lofield was for Monday evening. "Do you guys want to come with me?"

Although John declined, Melissa agreed to meet Debbie at the doctor's office. "Hold on, while I get something to write down directions."

"Oh, you won't need directions. He's in Jenson, about a block from the college."

Melissa jotted down the address, hung up the phone, and then scurried into the dining room to talk with John before he resumed playing. His refusal surprised her. She had assumed John and his controlling nature would wish to be present at Debbie's doctor's visits.

"Why don't you want to go?"

"Go where?" John opened the roll top and set the bills inside.

"To Dr. Lofield's?"

"Why on earth would I?"

"To support her."

"You can hold her hand." And John settled himself back at the piano.

"Don't you want to know how the baby is doing?"

The sound of piano music answered her. In resignation, Melissa left the room to pack. Her eyes landed on the box of John's medical supplies. They wouldn't leave Grover's Park until Saturday. She decided John's treatment could wait a day, until they returned home.

Thanksgiving morning dawned sunny but cold. The Simotes' departed Jenson at daybreak to avoid much of the holiday traffic and reached Grover's Park around noon. John spent the afternoon in the kitchen with Steve, preparing dinner.

Melissa waited until the traditional "What I am thankful for this year," stories circulated around the table before announcing hers and John's happy news. Her family received it with stunned silence.

Darlene spoke first. "How wonderful," she said, but her mother didn't sound as if she meant it. "Congratulations to you both. Brian, you're going to be an uncle."

Brian buttered his fourth roll. "Joy."

Steve stirred sugar into his coffee and forced a smile. "Have you discussed names for my first grandchild?"

Melissa waited for John to answer, but he said nothing, so she said, "We're at a bit of an impasse. I like Angela, but John doesn't think we're having a girl. I also want to name the baby after Daddy if it's a boy, but John wants to name it after himself."

"It figures," Brian mumbled to his plate.

Steve turned sharp eyes on him. "Did you say something?"

"Nope." Brian reached for the gravy.

"I have a suggestion," Darlene said. "Melissa, why don't you name the girl and let John name the boy? Winner takes all."

John set his fork on his plate and smiled approvingly at her. "Excellent idea."

"And Melissa, if you'd really like to honor your father, use 'Peter' for a middle name."

"Why should I name the baby after Grandpa?"

"Your father wanted that name for Brian."

"Then why didn't you use it?"

"Because I liked the name Brian, and he gave in."

Melissa beamed triumphantly at John, who accepted the plate of turkey from Steve. "I'm not your father, Melissa."

"No, but you're old enough to be," Brian muttered under his breath.

This time, Steve did not hear him, but Melissa did. She peeked under the table to check her aim and then kicked her brother in the shin.

Brian remained undaunted. "I'm going upstairs. Call me when everyone's done. I'll wash the dishes."

To Brian's chagrin, John insisted on helping. Brian sloshed the plates in the sink and sulked while John, exhibiting laudable patience, dried each piece of silverware and returned it to its rightful place in the drawer.

Melissa leaned on the counter and glowered at Brian. "Okay, what gives?"

Brian rinsed a glass and set it in the drain board to dry. "I don't know what you're talking about."

"Oh come on. Ever since you've met John you've been rude to him. Get off it already."

Brian dropped a serving dish into the sink. "You have a lot of nerve coming here and expecting everyone to rejoice over your baby after Mom just had a miscarriage."

Melissa's jaw dropped. "Mom had a what?"

"Are you deaf?"

She glanced at John, but he looked as baffled as she felt. "Why didn't anyone call and tell me?"

"Steve tried, but he could never reach you. But, oh, I forgot. You're not part of this family anymore, so why should you care?"

"Who says I'm not part of this family?"

Brian picked up the abandoned dish and scrubbed it. "You act that way. Maybe you should get your head out of John's rear once in awhile."\

His boldness shocked Melissa. She watched the serenity fade from John's face. His ability to humor Brian grew thin.

"Why of all the…" Melissa began.

"Melissa, how can you be so stupid? I can see straight through that 'I want to save the orphans of the world,' story. John got that girl pregnant and wants to keep the baby. It's that simple."

Incensed, John bent close to Brian's face, lowered his voice, and said with a leer, "You'd make a good cockroach, and I have a friend who can accomplish it."

The living room telephone rang. Melissa heard Steve's voice answer it.

"Brian! Phone call."

"Okay!"

Brian pulled the plug and water gurgled out of the sink. He yanked the towel away from John, dried his hands, and then draped the damp terrycloth over John's arm. "Better a cockroach than a rat." Brian left to answer the phone.

John threw the towel on the counter. "I swear, Melissa, if those blood treatments stop working, he's my first victim."

Melissa, hurt by Brian's comments, glared at John. "Oh, grow up! You're decades older than he is."

She stalked out of the room and trotted up the stairs to her mother's office. Once she stood before the door, Melissa hesitated. What would she say to her mother? She shot up a quick prayer for wisdom, took a deep breath, and then knocked on the door.

"Come in!"

Melissa slowly opened the door. Darlene sat at the typewriter reading over her notes.

"Mom," Melissa began. How could she ask, "Why didn't you tell me?" After all, she and John had kept their news a secret, too.

Darlene did not look up as she sifted through papers. "I didn't know until Steve took me to the emergency room."

"Mom, how could you not....?"

"Really, hon, I was thinking menopause."

Incredulous, Melissa just stared at her mother. Darlene swiveled the chair around to face Melissa. "Honest."

Worried and slightly guilty for her distance in her family's time of need, Melissa sat on the bed and studied her mother. "Are you okay?"

"Of course I am. Steve took it harder than I did. I raised my two, but this was his first. I doubt there'll be another."

"Mom...I...I don't know what to say."

"There's nothing to say. Actually, Melissa, I'm more concerned about you than me."

"About me?"

Darlene raised her chin and looked keenly at Melissa.

"Mom, it's not John's baby."

"Melissa, I wasn't born yester...."

"No, really. We saw a fertility doctor. John can't have children. He's really sensitive about it, too, so please don't mention it. He didn't appreciate Brian's smart remarks."

"I'll ask Steve to talk with him. He'll come around. It's just adolescent hormones."

Melissa spent a pleasant thirty minutes with her mother. Darlene now wrote a regular column for a national parenting magazine. This past semester, Melissa had earned such high grades in all her classes she anticipated making the dean's list. Her work ethic also pleased Mr. Schmidt, who was genuinely sorry to see her quit.

Darlene looked concerned. "How will you keep up that pace with a newborn?"

"Not to worry. John said he'll help."

Darlene suppressed an amused smile as she returned to her typewriter.

"Mom, he's saved up vacation time. He plans to stay home for a few weeks after the baby is born."

The lower level of the house had emptied by the time Melissa descended the stairs. She walked into the kitchen for a drink of water and saw two notes on the refrigerator.

One read, *Back in a couple of hours. Took John on a quick cleaning job. Love, Steve.* The second note, written in Brian's sprawling handwriting, simply said, *At Cindy's.*

Cindy?

Troubled at this new development, Melissa shut off the kitchen light and walked back upstairs to her old bedroom, the one Darlene had transformed into a guest room, the one Melissa shared this weekend with John. She felt torn between her now flourishing marriage and the family of her childhood. They had moved forward without her.

Melissa lay across the bed with the baby care book she had packed for down time, but after re-reading five times the paragraphs on umbilical cord care, Melissa realized she hadn't absorbed one word. She sighed, tossed the book on the night table, and decided a long bath would make her feel better. The scented water and dim candlelight unraveled the tangled thoughts in Melissa's mind and freed the best idea she'd had in a long time. She couldn't wait to tell John.

But John, already in bed, was facing the wall when Melissa re-entered her room and turned on the nightstand light. When had he and Steve come home? She noticed the wet hair that flopped across his shoulders. John must have taken a shower in the downstairs bathroom. Melissa climbed into bed and touched her husband on his back.

"John, are you asleep?"

No answer. Melissa poked his ribs. "John, are you…?"

John grunted.

"Let's modify my mother's idea."

Melissa heard no sound except for John's gentle breathing.

"If the baby's a boy, we can call him John-Peter. That way, I can honor my father, name the baby after you, and still give our child its own distinct name."

Confident John's silence translated into victory for Melissa, she burrowed into to her husband and draped on arm over his waist. "Besides, there could never be another you."

Melissa happily inched away as John rolled onto his back and looked directly at her. A half-grin spread across his face. He didn't appear quite so sleepy after all.

"Flattery gets you…." John leaned over Melissa and, with his free hand, switched off the light.

As soon as they entered the house from Thanksgiving in Grover's Park, Melissa said, "I'll get your stuff. It'll just take a few minutes."

"May I close the door first?"

"Take your time." Knowing thinly masked repulsion spurred the sarcasm in John's remark, Melissa couldn't help smiling a little as she walked to the bedroom to retrieve John's supplies.

John cringed at the blood Melissa offered him, but he also meekly accepted and retained it. "I'm glad this is only once a week," he said as he walked to the kitchen sink for a drink of water.

Melissa recalled how the taste of her blood on his lips once persuaded John to remain in her bedroom and let her watch him in action. "I can't believe you survived for so long on a blood-based diet."

He drained the full glass. "Drop the subject now, Melissa."

Debbie's appointment with Dr. Lofield went well, considering her overall lack of medical care. Her pregnancy had progressed farther than either she or Melissa had realized. Obviously, Debbie's weight had masked it. Debbie's baby was due the end of January.

Dr. Lofield said both mother and baby appeared healthy, but, because Debbie had sought no prenatal care, he insisted on weekly visits until she delivered. Debbie promised to comply, but Melissa didn't trust this scatterbrained girl and always accompanied her to the reception desk just to witness Debbie schedule the next appointment. On this particular day, Debbie looked forlorn and tired, so, on impulse, Melissa invited Debbie to her house for a cup of tea.

Debbie's face lit up at the prospect. "You sure I won't be bothering you and John?"

"Not at all. John has late classes tonight."

Debbie settled into the large, easy chair by the front window while Melissa prepared two cups of tea. When she returned, Debbie was leaning back in the chair with both hands on her swelling belly. "It's so cool, Melissa."

Melissa set the cups on the coffee table. "What is?"

"The baby. Wanna feel her?"

The question caught Melissa off guard. She had no desire to touch this woman, yet she longed to experience those same magic movements Ann had described. Squatting by the chair, Melissa rested the palm of her hand on Debbie's stomach and waited for a long time. Nothing happened, and Melissa's foot began to cramp.

"I think she went to sleep," Melissa said.

"No she didn't. Just wait. You'll see."

Melissa shuffled her feet and waited again. Nothing. She set her hand on another section of Debbie's belly. Still, nothing.

As Melissa retracted her hand, she felt the zip of a small fish. She paused, heart pounding for the elusive fluttering to repeat itself. Debbie laid her hand on top of Melissa's and inched it farther to the right.

A pause. A bump swelled into Melissa's hand; it rolled and slid away. She held her breath. Something flitted across her fingertips. Together, Melissa and Debbie fondled the baby is it stretched and rotated inside its mother.

Melissa, awed beyond tears, gazed up at Debbie who, eyes full, smiled down at her. What an amazing gift this woman was giving to her and John, a precious life for them to hold and love forever.

CHAPTER 16: BEGINNING AGAIN

"This Saturday," Melissa said on the way to Jenson College, "we need to do your blood treatment early. Laura's coming to stencil the baby's room."

John recoiled from the words "blood treatment" and tapped the turn signal.

Over the last few weeks, a near-normal routine had emerged in the Simotes' household, one that inspired Melissa with fresh confidence about her future with John. They now often shared a ride to and from school, discussing baby plans along the way, including medical updates on Debbie and adoption legalities.

"You don't mind, do you, John?"

"No."

"Can you make something really nice for dinner Saturday night? I haven't seen Laura in a long time and want to show you off a bit."

"Such as?"

"How about that veal dish you made at my mom's house?"

"I recall you didn't like it."

"No, it tasted good. I didn't care for the mushrooms, but I can scrape mine off."

John didn't answer, so Melissa wasn't sure if he had agreed to it or not. As she opened her mouth for clarification John announced, "By the way, Melissa, we're spending Christmas in Bradford Heights."

If John had dumped a bucket of cold water on her, Melissa wouldn't have felt more shocked. She assumed they'd spend Christmas with her family. Surely, now that Melissa knew the truth about John's identity and origins, he could release Marvin and Carol from whatever hypnotic suggestion kept them thinking they had a son.

"John, can't you stop playing this game with them?"

"Maybe I like the game." John pulled into the parking lot.

"Well, I don't see why you...."

John shut off the ignition reached for the door handle. "Maybe I like having parents." He looked back at her. "Quit presuming we'll celebrate every holiday in Grover's Park."

"But...."

"Think of your baby."

Melissa fell silent. She had never considered other options. Did that mean, as John insinuated, Melissa was acting selfish and childish? Really, why should she care if John had "adopted" a set of parents? Wasn't that similar to embracing Debbie's baby? Her heart softened at John's need for a present day mother and father.

"You're right," Melissa conceded. "We haven't seen them in months. Our baby is lucky to have two sets of grandparents."

Melissa called Darlene later that day and told her, as gently and diplomatically as possible, that she and John would be traveling to Bradford Heights for Christmas. Darlene took the news meekly but raised no objections.

On Friday afternoon, Melissa again accompanied Debbie to Dr. Lofield's office. She waited in the examining room while Debbie took a trip down the hall with a specimen cup. A few minutes later, Debbie returned and submitted to the scale and blood pressure cuff.

The nurse frowned as she wrote the numbers in Debbie's chart. Debbie sat on the exam table swinging her legs and flipping through a movie magazine, but Melissa's internal alarm sounded.

"Is something wrong?" Melissa asked.

"Miss Polis, the doctor will see you shortly." The nurse closed the chart and hung it outside the door.

Debbie noisily turned pages. Melissa listened to the ticking of the clock and brooded. After a very long time, the door opened, and Dr. Lofield entered the room. He did not greet them, as he was carefully reading Debbie's chart. Melissa didn't know doctors could look as he did, lean, blond, tanned, and muscular, as if he did nothing all day but work out in a gym and play volley ball on a beach.

"Well, Debbie," Dr. Lofield said at last, looking at her with an All-American, toothpaste commercial smile. "You obviously had a nice Thanksgiving dinner."

"Fine. Why?"

"You've gained five pounds."

He reached for the blood pressure cuff and repeated the reading. He listened to Debbie's heart and lungs. He raised the legs of Debbie's jeans, pulled down her socks, and pressed his fingers against her ankles. He stood slowly and said, "Lie down."

Dr. Lofield moved his hands around Debbie's belly to measure the height of her uterus. He rested the stethoscope near her navel and listened to the baby's heart rate. With a grave expression, he checked Debbie's blood pressure for a third time.

"Your blood pressure is slightly elevated." Dr. Lofield slid the stethoscope around his neck and hung up the cuff. "You have some ankle swelling, too."

"Is that bad?"

"Possibly. I anticipate some water retention in pregnancy, but when it's coupled with a rise in blood pressure, I take it seriously. I want you to eliminate all salt from your diet and rest as much as you can at home, on your left side preferably. I'll recheck you on Monday."

"I work tonight."

"No work until after the baby is born."

"I can't take off. They'll fire me, and I'm the breadwinner."

"Your job is to have a healthy baby. If quitting poses a financial hardship for you, call the office. My secretary knows places that will help you out for the next month. Contact me immediately if you experience any headaches, blurred vision, spots in front of your eyes, abdominal pain, or vomiting."

"Okay," Debbie said, but her eyes strayed to the magazine on her lap.

"Miss Polis, please pay attention. Do you understand what I'm telling you?"

Debbie closed the magazine. Looking up dazedly at Dr. Lofield, Debbie slowly nodded.

"I'll see you Monday," Dr. Lofield said, turning to leave.

On Saturday morning, as John prepared to leave for the grocery store, Melissa reminded him of his first obligation. He appeared annoyed, as if Melissa was hindering an important appointment, but she knew John was delaying the inevitable. John again gagged on the morsel, but otherwise accepted Melissa's blood without a whimper. Laura arrived an hour later. Melissa greeted her at the door with an enormous hug, which Laura returned with equal enthusiasm.

"Long time, old married lady."

Laura had cropped her hair short and close to her head. Focusing on art and spending time in the company of serious artists had wiped away her giddy flirtatiousness.

"Sorry I missed the wedding," Laura continued, "but I was preparing for a show."

"I can't wait for you to meet John."

Laura looked around. "Is he here?"

"No, he went shopping for dinner. He's a super cook."

They sat at the kitchen table and studied Laura's stencils. She had created a series of whimsical fairies in a variety of fantasy garden scenes, Tiny pixies toasted their toes before matchstick fires. Several water sprites hovered over a pond. Two delicately-drawn fairies flitted about primroses, while another group, wings spread and faces turned heavenward, danced with abandon. One male fairy in particular mesmerized Melissa. He reclined high up in a tree, curled his toes around a branch, pointed his thin face to the sky, and played a flute-like instrument. His long red hair entwined with the leafy boughs.

"Laura, these are gorgeous!"

"I'm painting them in bold and bright colors, not pastels. This way the baby, whether it's a boy or a girl, will like the pictures."

"Why fairies?"

"My mentor loves Celtic art, so it's influenced my work. Are you ready to start?"

Melissa marveled at how quickly Laura transferred her patterns onto the white walls. With poses and expressions so lifelike, the figures became enchanting company. Later that afternoon, John poked his head into the nursery, but the girls forbade his entrance.

"No peeking until tomorrow," Laura called from the crack in the door.

"See if you get dinner."

"See if I finish."

Melissa smiled from her cross-legged seat on the floor. Laura liked John, she could tell. For dinner, John did prepare the veal escalopes and accompanied it with nice wine, homemade rolls, and a colorful salad. For added bravado, he served the meal in a candlelit room.

Laura sucked in her breath when she walked into the kitchen. "Oooh, Melissa, you are so lucky! Does John cook like this all the time?"

"Pretty much." Melissa hoped she sounded off-hand and accustomed to nightly gourmet fare on her dinner table.

John and Laura's artistic elements bonded them; the conversation between them flowed as richly and quickly as the wine. John took an interest in Laura's art classes, especially once he learned she was studying at Artemis Rose Art College.

"You've heard of it?" Laura asked, holding out her glass.

John obligingly filled it. "I attended university with one of the instructors, a Colpa Ivanovich."

Colpa. Such an unusual name, yet to Melissa, it bore a wisp of familiarity. Why did she know it? Where had she heard it?

Laura dropped her fork on the floor. "That's my mentor!"

What was John pulling? They both knew, despite what John had led Katie's brothers to believe, he had never attended university. As John stood for a replacement fork, Melissa noticed his left hand. John had wound it with gauze.

"Oh, John, what happened?"

He handed Laura the fork and picked up his napkin as he sat down. "I cut it slicing the veal."

"Are you okay? Does it need stitches?"

"I'll live."

How could John be so offhand? "How deep did you....?"

"Laura, have you seen Colpa's series on The Tuatha de Da Naan?" John picked up his wine glass and took a sip.

Melissa inwardly sighed, and, feeling as if John had slapped her, meekly resumed her meal.

"Yes! I especially love her rendition of the three goddesses: Eriu, Banba, and Fodla."

After dinner, which John concluded with homemade ice cream, Laura insisted on helping with the dishes. John retreated to the dining room. As Laura washed, and Melissa dried, Laura swooned to the sounds John played.

"It's like heaven around here. I can see why you fell in love with him. Imagine, having your house always filled with music."

Thank goodness Laura hadn't noticed John's scornful treatment of his wife.

"It *is* lovely, and that's coming from a rental piano. Someone broke into our house and destroyed John's good one. We're still waiting for the insurance company to send us a check."

Laura started to rinse a plate but stopped, horrified. "Oh, gosh, Melissa weren't you scared?"

"A little, but we weren't home when it happened. It was odd, too, because the intruder didn't steal anything except a piano leg."

Laura ran the plate under the water. "That *is* odd. No idea who did it?"

A disgruntled student, perhaps? That wouldn't surprise Melissa, especially after the way John had been snapping at some of them following news of his sterility.

"None." Melissa quickly looked down and concentrated on carefully drying the plate.

"Has John picked out a new piano?"

"Of course. John always knows what he wants."

Melissa didn't broach the subject with John until they lay together in bed that night, although she'd been dying to ask him all evening. He was drifting into asleep before she finally worked up enough courage.

"John."

Silence, but his breathing quickened, so Melissa knew she'd awakened him. She also knew he felt less than elated about it.

"Why tell stories like that? You didn't go to university with Laura's teacher."

Nothing.

"Unless she's a vampire."

John's chuckled softly, but his eyes remained closed. "You're sure of it?"

"Um…" John's question took her aback. Melissa never felt sure of anything concerning him. "Well, did you go to the university?"

"No."

"Do you really know Laura's teacher?"

John opened his eyes and looked long and hard at Melissa. She didn't like the faint smirk playing on his lips. as he said, "Yes."

"Is she a vampire?"

248

"No."

"Never? I mean, she wasn't a vampire once and then became human again, like you."

"No."

"Then how do you....?"

"You don't want to know, Melissa."

"Yes, I do...."

Melissa stopped. Her cheeks burned, and she felt glad for the room's darkness so John couldn't see them. *John had slept with Laura's teacher!* He rolled away from her and then added, "You ask too many questions. That's why you get hurt."

Not until Laura folded tarps and packed up paints did she allow John to view the results of her weekend work. As John stepped into the room, his eyes quickly swept across the images; a barrage of undecipherable emotions passed over his face. Did he not like the pictures?

"Well?" Laura asked. "What do you think?"

John crossed the room. A winged creature with green translucent wings, bright green hair, and tiny black eyes resembling coal in a decidedly male face atop a slender, moth-like body, hovered over an insect-filled meadow. John peered closer at it and studied its detail.

"Quite good." John gestured toward the walls. "I'm impressed at what you accomplished in a weekend."

"I work fast.'

"Amazing." He nodded in approval, respect for Laura's work clearly showing on his face. "Perfect for my son."

"Daughter," Melissa corrected him.

For the next week, finals kept them both busy, which distracted Melissa from the disappointment at not returning to Grover's Park for Christmas. John axed the remains of Melissa's holiday spirit by vetoing her suggestion at setting up a Christmas tree, even a small tabletop one.

"I see no point," John had said, raising the piano lid.

"Christmas isn't Christmas without a tree."

"Melissa, you will have a tree, in Bradford Heights."

"I want a tree in our house, too."

"I don't like plastic trees, and we won't be here to care for a real one."

"But...."

A quick string of clamoring notes drowned out Melissa's objections. The phone rang. Feeling unsupported and thoroughly defeated, Melissa plodded from the room to answer it and picked up the receiver on the fourth ring.

"I'm kidnapping Ann on Saturday," Julie said. "Let's all have lunch together before you guys are tied down with babies. I'll treat."

"It sounds like fun," Melissa said, her voice toneless and flat. Feigning interested, she added, "No Katie?"

"Haven't you heard? She quit school and ran away with some old man."

"What?" Melissa forgot about Christmas trees and John's domineering and opinionated stance. "Who is he?"

"No clue. He's sixty-something and a vagabond that wanders all over the country in a motor home. Her parents are just livid. I'll pick you up after breakfast. We can walk around the mall until the restaurants open. Is that okay?"

"Sure!"

When Melissa awakened Saturday morning, John was gone. She quickly threw on her clothes and dashed to the kitchen where John, already dressed, sat at the kitchen table, drinking coffee and reading the newspaper. He looked very much like the John Simons Melissa had met her first morning inside Simons Mansion. John's supplies lay in perfect order on the table. A pleased smile spread across Melissa's face before she could stop it. John had finally accepted the terms of continued humanity.

"I'm glad you're so eager for a change," Melissa said, sitting down and reaching for a lancet.

John sipped his coffee. "I have no desire to advertise our macabre ritual to your friends. It's degrading enough to submit to it."

"It keeps you a man."

"A man?" John said with a short laugh and a snort. "No amount of your blood will compensate for...." He glanced up from the newspaper and glared at her. "Take care of it. Now."

"Of course. Right away."

As Melissa disposed of the scraps, she decided to call Debbie before her friends arrived. She had lost contact during finals but felt certain Debbie would have called her if need be.

"Everything's fine," Debbie said. "I'm still on bed rest, but the blood pressure's come down, some."

"I'm glad you're following Dr. Lofield's orders."

"It's hard, but I won't hurt my baby. The doc's got someone sending us food, and a local church paid this month's rent."

John's humor had improved by the time Julie and Ann called for Melissa. As Melissa followed them out the back door, John drew her close for a kiss. "We have plans this afternoon."

"What? Why didn't you say something?"

"I forgot."

"John!"

"No later than two." He touched his lips to hers.

Sharing the unexpected development with Julie and Ann embarrassed Melissa, but Julie seemed unaffected by it. "I'm having an early dinner with David anyway."

A new restaurant inside Jenson Mall offered a decent lunch menu at reasonable prices. They ordered hamburgers and gossiped about their lives.

"When are you due, Ann?" Julie asked.

The permanent wave in Ann's hair had half-grown out, a decided contrast to Julie's perfectly maintained page boy. Too bad Katie hadn't attended to Ann before she skipped town.

"January twenty-seven." With her straw, Ann stirred the lemon slice into her water. "But Dr. Rothgard thinks the baby will come sooner."

"You look great," Melissa said. Only Ann's belly was round; she had none of Debbie's swelling. "Pregnancy agrees with you."

"I feel fat," Ann said. "I've gained thirty pounds. I can't wait to have this baby and look normal again. How'd finals go?"

Julie shrugged her shoulders. "I probably made the dean's list again. How about you, Melissa?"

"I blew it. Too much on my mind, I guess." Melissa glanced sideways at Ann, who had once out-produced both Melissa and Julie in their studies with half the effort. "Are you and Jack ready for the baby?"

"I guess. Babies don't need much. I did wrap all my presents, just in case."

Julie leaned back and smiled. "You make me feel lazy. I'm going home for Christmas where my parents still take care of everything."

Ann turned toward Melissa. "Did Julie tell you about Katie?"

"Just the bare facts."

"No one knows any details. Katie just took off one night. Mrs. Miller found her note in the morning."

The time flew past and before Melissa knew it, the grandfather clock in the restaurant's lobby struck two. Sudden remembrance of John's admonition hit her like a sledgehammer. "Oh, gosh! I'm late."

"Take it easy, Melissa." Julie said in a soothing voice. "John's a reasonable man. He'll understand."

How odd that sounded from Julie's lips! Besides, John's final words reverberated in her uneasy mind, and Melissa closed her eyes to block them. "John" and "reasonable" were not synonymous terms.

Ann and Julie chattered together during the short, anxious trip from one end of town to the other. As Julie turned onto Melissa's street, Melissa noticed cars lining both sides of the road that had been quiet and empty when they had left just a few hours ago.

"Is someone having a Christmas party?" Julie said as she pulled into Melissa's driveway.

"Beats me."

"Will John mind if Ann and I stop in the bathroom before we head back to Munsonville, or is he in a hurry to take off?"

"I'm sure it's fine."

The almost eerie silence of her house disquieted Melissa. She expected to hear the piano strains of a musician impatient to leave. Where was he? Didn't he say they had plans? Bewildered, she stepped into the dining room.

"Surprise!"

People popped up everywhere: Mrs. Dalton, Mrs. Cooper, Jenny, Tracy, and quite a number of women Melissa had never met, whom John later said worked in the offices at Jenson College. Melissa stood gaping. John strolled into the kitchen and high-fived Julie.

Even more astonishing, Julie, of all people, beamed at him. "Did I do good?"

"You did great!"

Jack started pulling platters of sub sandwiches and cold salads from the refrigerator. Melissa stared at the piles of blue-wrapped presents stacked in one corner of the living room. A large white sheet cake sat on the buffet beside a miniature Christmas tree. Someone had decorated the tree with tiny gold balls and soft blue lights. Remnants of chips and dips filled the coffee table. Mrs. Dalton led the games: baby word scramble and baby-themed Bingo. Ann won an inflatable baby bottle, and Jenny received a package of candy pacifiers.

"This will be perfect for satisfying my sweet tooth when I'm studying." Jenny, looking very much like a baby herself in a black and violet peasant shirt with a Peter Pan collar, popped a pacifier into her mouth and pushed the rest of the package deep into her purse.

Melissa opened gift after gift. "Angela can wear a new outfit every day and not repeat herself once," Melissa marveled as she set another box aside.

"John-Peter, you mean." John stooped to retrieve scattered wrapping paper.

He saved the best present for last, an antique baby cradle from Carol Simotes. Melissa opened the envelope and read the scrawling penmanship inside the blank note card: *Someone built it for Marvin when he was a baby, and then John slept in it. Now it's my grandbaby's turn.*

Melissa traced the ornate rose carvings on the wood. She now owned a family heirloom she had no right to own. Something else about the afternoon bothered her, too, but for prudence's sake, Melissa waited until the last guest departed before approaching John.

"Thank you for a wonderful shower." Melissa stood on tiptoe to kiss him and mentally scanned a dozen tactful ways to ask.

John eased her away. "But?"

She couldn't avoid it. Feeling defensive, Melissa set her shoulders, raised her chin, and said, "Did you invite Debbie?"

With an impassive expression, John calmly replied, "Absolutely not."

"She's the baby's mother!"

"*You* are my son's mother. Debbie is merely the holding tank and quite an expensive one, too."

"That's heartless!"

John began stacking paper plates.

"'Heartless,'" John quietly said, "is your ungratefulness for an afternoon that required weeks of careful scheming."

The easy dismissal of Debbie troubled Melissa, almost as much as John's coldness in bed that night. Twice on Sunday, Melissa tried calling Debbie, but no one answered. So on Monday, and without telling John, Melissa drove into Shelby to give Debbie a Christmas present: the angel ornament adorning the top of the tiny tree from the baby shower.

"Merry Christmas," Melissa began when Debbie opened the door, then stopped, aghast at Debbie's puffy facial features, which had compressed her eyes into mere slits.

"What?" Debbie uneasily shifted from side to side. "Dr. Lofield said swelling is normal."

"Debbie, you're blown up like a beach ball. Does he know you're this bad?"

"Yes," Debbie hedged, but something in her tone suggested he did not.

Forgetting the secrecy of her trip, Melissa poured out her concerns to John while he graded exams. He did not comment or exhibit any concern. Afraid for Debbie's and the baby's safety, Melissa risked John's wrath and threw down her best card: "Was Bryony this swollen?"

John slowly looked up and regarded her with cold and distant eyes. Melissa steeled herself against his silent ire and repeated, "Was Bryony....?"

"Melissa." John didn't sound angry, only drained. "That happened a long time ago."

"So you don't remember?"

"Maybe she was, a little. Certainly nothing resembling your description. Perhaps Debbie should call Dr. Lofield."

"She says he already knows."

"Quite possibly, you're overreacting."

"What if I'm not?"

John stared evenly at her. "Do you want a second opinion from Dr. Rothgard?"

"No!"

Because of approaching inclement weather, John again allowed two days for the trip to Bradford Heights, and again John rose in the pre-dawn hours on Christmas Eve to complete the journey by early afternoon. As they left the motel room, the telephone rang. John set down the suitcases and hurried to answer it.

With real alarm in his voice, John said, "Thank you, Mom. I'll keep you and Dad posted." John hung up the phone, began dialing, and said, "Derek called my parents' house. Debbie had a seizure."

Melissa's legs shook, and she weakly sank onto the bed.

"Labor and delivery," John told the operator at Jenson Memorial Hospital.

Many years ago, a baby destined for greatness survived birth in a stable on this very night. Surely, that same God could protect her child. Please, please, please, Melissa silently begged, make Debbie and this baby be okay.

John hung up the phone and turned to her.

"The baby's fine." John said, "but Debbie is not. Derek said they're inducing labor as soon as they've stabilized her."

"John...."

"I want to go home. Do you mind?"

She sighed deeply, relieved John put their baby ahead of his own plans. "I was hoping you'd say that."

"It's not much of a Christmas for you."

"A healthy baby is the only present I want."

The overcast sky swelled with cold, damp air. Its first snowflakes fell as John merged onto the highway, and they continued falling fast and steady all through the congested morning traffic, slowing holiday travelers to a maddening crawl. Radio snow advisories, crackling with static, warned against travel. John didn't speak for most of the trip, but the troubled look on his face produced volumes.

They reached Jenson at two o'clock in the morning. John left the car at the emergency room's front doors and rushed inside with Melissa at his heels.

A security guard stopped her. "You can't leave that car here."

"But...."

"No 'buts.' Move it now, or I'll call the police."

John had vanished without her. Fuming at the guard's insensitivity and John's impatience, Melissa circled the parking lot seeking an empty space. Afterwards, she slipped and slid through the treacherous lot back to the emergency room. An anxious John met her at the front door.

"Debbie had a stroke. She's in surgery."

"Oh, no! What about the baby? Isn't it too little?"

"I don't know."

He took her hand and led her down the hall. Melissa obediently trotted beside him to the elevators. Inside, John pushed "five." As they moved upward, John said, "Dr. Lofield isn't performing the surgery. He's sick with the flu. They called Dr. Rothgard."

The elevator doors opened, and Melissa stepped out after John. Amazing, Melissa thought. Even fate bowed to John's wishes.

"You're sure he's the best?" Melissa asked doubtfully.

But John was talking to a nurse, who escorted them to a waiting area. Melissa tried losing herself in an old magazine, failed, and tried again. John paced, made frequent bathroom trips, and annoyed the nurses with constant requests for updates on the baby.

Once, he banged his fist on the wall and then covered that weakness by saying, "I need coffee. Melissa?"

She shook her head, settled back into the seat cushions, and prayed Dr. Rothgard's sterling reputation proved itself in the operating room. She doubted John could handle both infertility and a second dead baby. Melissa's body jerked, and she rubbed her fuzzy eyes to read the wall clock. Four o'clock. She had slept over an hour. Her gaze swept over the room. No John.

Melissa stood, stretched, and drifted to the water cooler. She brought the cup with her to the window. There she stood and noted the empty, white street. Nothing existed except cruel, tortuous wait. She crushed the waxed paper between her fingers, glad for something to destroy. A car horn beeped. Melissa sighed, turned away, and tossed the cup into the garbage can.

She jumped as the waiting room door swung open. John, masked and clad in a white gown, entered, tenderly nuzzling a bundle wrapped in an equally white blanket. The elastic string on a second mask dangled from his fingers.

"John!"

A wide grin spread across his face as he handed her the mask and pointed to the bathroom.

"The nurse said you'll find extra gowns in there." To the baby, John added, "John-Peter, it's time to meet your mother."

Melissa happily dashed away. She grabbed a gown, thoroughly scrubbed her hands, and hurried back to the waiting room.

John sat by the window, holding the baby close to his heart and murmuring to him. Melissa slid next to them, and John placed the infant in her arms. Awestruck and hushed, she beheld the little creature and cradled him close. Swirls of brown-red hair covered his entire scalp and overlapped his ears. His lips pursed full and pink. When he yawned and stretched, tiny arms emerged from his cocoon. Melissa thrust a finger into one palm, and the baby curled slight, slender fingers around it.

"Hello, John-Peter," she whispered.

At the sound of her voice, the baby opened his eyes and looked at her with liquid pools of brown, flecked with green.

John leaned his head against Melissa's and brushed the baby's cheek with an index finger. The reality of the moment hit Melissa.

"Oh John! He's really ours?"

"He's really ours."

Dr. Rothgard, still in green scrubs, his face lined with fatigue, stepped through the door and flopped onto a chair. In that moment, Dr. Rothgard, no longer merely a formidable vampire healer, rose to hero status in Melissa's mind, for he had brought John-Peter safely through a dangerous passage. Maybe, just maybe, he'd make a good baby doctor.

With a face and voice full of gratitude, Melissa exclaimed, "Dr. Rothgard, I can never thank you enough!"

With his head still resting against the chair back, Dr. Rothgard turned a weary face toward John and asked sternly, "Didn't you tell her?"

"It can wait."

Dr. Rothgard sat up straight. "John!"

Sudden terror wrapped Melissa into its wet blanket and chilled her bones. Slowly, she lifted her eyes to Dr. Rothgard.

"Know what? Is there something wrong with my baby?"

"Your baby's fine."

"Then...what?"

"I lost Debbie on the operating table."

CHAPTER 17: THE CHILD PRODIGY

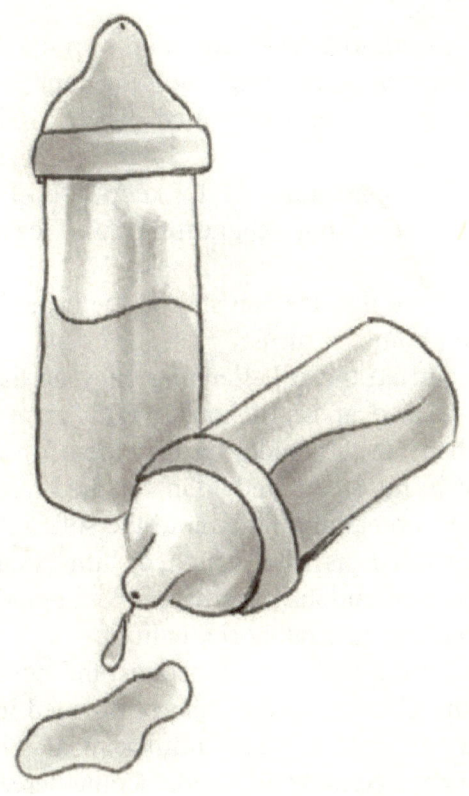

Although a month premature, John-Peter passed his first medical exams, and after less than a week in the hospital, Dr. Rothgard pronounced him healthy enough to go home.

"Keep him away from crowds for the first month," he said, "and bring him to my office in a week for another check-up."

Their first family ride home tinged bittersweet with the unexpected death of Debbie Polis hovering over Melissa's head. Why hadn't John-Peter's mother taken better care of herself? And why had Derek waited until Debbie seized before acting? Her swollen appearance magnified the urgency for medical help.

As if sensing Melissa's thoughts John said, "They're waking Debbie tomorrow night right here in Jenson. I think we should go."

Melissa almost cheered John's proposal. Despite the callous and condescending "holding tank," remarks, John's sense of decency had prevailed. Then Melissa recalled the final instructions.

"Dr. Rothgard told us to keep John-Peter away from crowds. You're not suggesting we leave him with a babysitter."

"Of course not. He can stay in the heated car. We'll enter the funeral home by turns."

John carried the still-sleeping baby up the back steps and into the hushed and still house. With great reverence, John laid the baby in the cradle by his side of the bed. John-Peter grimaced in his sleep, and John steadied him with one hand. John-Peter's breathing faded into the soft sighs of baby sleep. Melissa smiled as she watched him dream. Because of Debbie's tremendous sacrifice, Melissa's most sublime dreams had become euphoric reality.

Leaving the bedroom door ajar, the new parents walked back to the kitchen, where John rummaged in the refrigerator for the ingredients to make a quick meal. Then he faced her with outstretched arms and said, "Come here."

Melissa rushed to meet them and laid her head over John's heart. Its beating never failed to thrill her, a constant reminder that John still lived and shared that life with her. John wrapped one arm around her waist and stroked her hair with his other hand as he rested his chin on her head.

"Well, Melissa, we did it. We're a...."

A piercing cry interrupted John's sentence. John-Peter had awakened and demanded to be fed. Melissa giggled and grabbed a bottle from the electric warmer on the counter.

"While you're making dinner," Melissa said, "I'll tend to our son."

By the time Melissa had reached the bedroom, John-Peter's face was scrunched purple, and he was frantically waving his tiny, clenched fists. She set the bottle on the nightstand and lifted her small squirming son from his bed.

"It's all right, John-Peter," Melissa said in her most soothing tone.

The baby however, refused her comforting efforts. She tightened her grip on the writhing infant with one hand and reached for the bottle with the other one. John-Peter chomped down on the nipple, drained the milk in seconds, and howled for more. Melissa carried the crying baby into the kitchen.

"John, he still seems hungry."

He lowered the heat and covered the pot with a lid. "Give him another bottle. Dr. Rothgard said to feed him on demand."

"Isn't that too much formula at one time?"

John shrugged. "I don't know. Maybe he didn't receive enough in the hospital."

She had to do something. John-Peter was frantic. Melissa took a second bottle from the warmer and sat at the kitchen table to feed him. The baby accepted this feeding much slower than the last one and soon drifted to sleep. With a napkin, Melissa dabbed the dribbles from the corners of his mouth.

John pulled biscuits from the oven and then tossed the salad. "Dinner's ready. Shall I return him to the cradle?"

"I'll do it."

Gingerly, Melissa carried the sleeping baby back to the bedroom. This time, he did not stir when she set him down. She hoped John-Peter would stay asleep, at least until she and John finished dinner.

He lit a candle and opened a bottle of cabernet for the occasion. After Melissa settled in her chair, John raised his glass. "To the Simotes family!"

Melissa clinked hers against his. "Yes, oh, yes!"

They made it only halfway through dinner when John-Peter once again bellowed. Melissa started to rise, but John objected. "My turn. Sit and eat."

"He can't be hungry!"

"I doubt it. Quite possibly, he's lonely."

But the baby continued to wail though the closed bedroom door. Melissa helplessly picked at her creamed chicken.

John returned for a another bottle and said, "I'm baffled. It's as if he's starving. Call Dr. Rothgard."

He leaned against the counter and tilted the bottle to the baby's lips. John-Peter slurped its contents and resumed crying before Melissa had finished dialing. John held John-Peter near his shoulder and patted his back.

"Hold on," the receptionist said to Melissa. "He's just walking out the door."

Melissa cupped her hand over the receiver to drown the baby's cries. John gently jiggled the baby. Despite Melissa's frantic recounting, Dr. Rothgard seemed unconcerned with the baby's supposed crisis.

"Have you burped him? Sometimes babies confuse air in their stomachs with hunger."

"John did, but he's still acting hungry."

"For tonight, give him what he wants. Bring him to the office tomorrow. I'm sure there's a simple explanation for it."

Melissa hung up the phone and relayed the information to John. He reached for a bottle while Melissa prepared another batch of formula for the warmer.

"Well," she said, "I know parenting's a hard job, but I thought we'd have a day to get used to it."

After consuming his fourth bottle, John-Peter once again fell asleep. Melissa began rinsing the dishes, but John stopped her when he returned from the bedroom.

"I'll clean up," he said. "You take a shower while you have the chance."

John, too, made it to the shower before John-Peter woke again. Remembering Dr. Rothgard's advice, Melissa first burped the baby before giving him yet another bottle. John-Peter sucked it dry by the time an incredulous John had emerged from the bathroom.

"He can't be hungry!"

Melissa grinned. "I'm so glad you're taking the middle of the night feeding."

John frowned. "If this continues, neither of us will sleep."

Once Melissa settled John-Peter in his cradle, he showed no signs of disturbing his parents. Melissa gazed at her sleeping son as John turned back the bedcovers.

"John, he's so sweet. He looks like an angel."

He climbed into bed and patted the empty place beside him. Only with difficulty did Melissa resist the urge to continue gazing at the little, cherubic face. Nevertheless, John had one or two urges of his own, and he exploded when John-Peter interrupted with a shriek, and Melissa broke away to fetch him.

"Melissa, he's fine!"

"He's a new baby!"

Melissa flew out of bed and paced the floor with the still-screaming infant as John glared at her. "Maybe, he should just cry for awhile."

"I didn't know you believed in letting babies cry!" Melissa shouted over the din.

"I don't."

John-Peter chewed on his fists. Blinking back tears, Melissa left the room for a bottle. Why couldn't John understand she felt disappointed, too? She switched on the kitchen light, opened the warmer, and grabbed yet another bottle while John Peter bawled in her ear. Melissa started crying, too. As she sat on the chair to feed the baby, she felt John's hand lightly touch her shoulder.

"I'll take him," John said. "Go rest."

The bed's emptiness reminded her of last summer, when John, in his misery over his infertility, had forsaken it. She crawled under the rumpled sheets, jammed her pillow over head, and cried until she drifted to sleep. When she awakened, the luminous numbers in the lightening room read six o'clock. Melissa felt John's side of the bed. It was still empty. Deafening silence engulfed the house. Holding her breath, Melissa turned the door knob and eased open the door. She tiptoed into the living room, pausing at each creak of the floor. John, feet propped on the coffee table, head back, and baby on his chest, was lightly snoring. A pile of empty bottles lay on the floor next to the chair.

Melissa had no experience with newborns, but one thing she certainly knew. No baby should go through that much food. She couldn't wait for Dr. Rothgard to fix the problem.

But Dr. Rothgard gave them startling news. "John-Peter's lost weight."

"What!" John said. "That's impossible!"

"How much did you say he ate yesterday?"

"Over a hundred ounces, at least," Melissa said.

Dr. Rothgard scrawled something Melissa could not read, tore it from the pad, and gave it to Melissa. John, hands slightly shaking, began diapering the baby.

"Don't give him anymore formula than this...." Dr. Rothgard began.

"He'll just cry for more," Melissa said.

As if on cue, John-Peter screamed. John rummaged in the diaper bag for a bottle.

Let me finish. In between feedings, feed him some rice cereal if he seems hungry. Give him all the water he'll accept. Bring him back next week to check his weight, sooner if you're concerned."

He nodded his head in John's direction, but looked at Melissa. "How's your pigheaded husband doing?"

"Fine, I guess," Melissa said with a sidelong glance at John.

John-Peter announced the completion of his bottle with a large burp. John reached for the little coat he left on the baby scale, and John-Peter watched John as his father stuffed him in it.

"Is John consistent with the blood treatments?" Dr. Rothgard persisted. "Are they working?"

"I think so."

"Good. No backsliding?"

Melissa shook her head. As Dr. Rothgard moved to the door, Melissa remembered something she had meant to ask him.

"I do a question. When John went from vampire to a human again, did he lose any abilities in the process?"

"Like what abilities?"

John picked up the baby and gave her a warning look. Melissa refused to heed it, although she did pause before speaking. She wished for a more tactful way to pose the question. Finally, she bluntly asked, "Would the transformation cause infertility?"

Dr. Rothgard glanced at John, who scowled back at him and looked disgustedly away. After a prolonged clearing of his throat, Dr. Rothgard turned his full attention back to Melissa.

"The John of today is the same John of yesterday. If he's unable to produce a child now, it's unlikely he ever could. Remember," he sternly added with another ahem of his throat, "bring John-Peter back next week."

He picked up the chart and closed the door behind him. Melissa quickly reached for the diaper bag and sprinted for the door, but John, cradling the baby in a football hold by his side, grabbed Melissa's arm with his other hand.

She could not meet his eyes. "I'm sorry. I had to know. Didn't you?"

With a weary sigh, John let her go. "I already knew, Melissa," he quietly said.

The sun had set. Because of the lateness of the hour, and John-Peter's temperament, John swung through a fast food restaurant for hamburgers and fries, the first time, to Melissa's knowledge, he had ever done so. Then he stopped at a local convenience store for a box of rice cereal.

When they reached the tiny funeral home of Franklin and Mores, John offered to attend the visitation first and spare Melissa the emotional upset. "If it's that depressing in there, we'll go home. What's important is that someone represented our family."

He left the car running for the heat, John-Peter cooed once and then sunk further into sleep. Melissa watched the mourners enter and exit the building and hoped Dr. Rothgard's feeding advice worked. Wasn't he rumored to be the best?

John knocked on her window, and Melissa rolled it halfway down. "It's grim. Debbie looks terrible, and Derek's blubbering all over the place. I advise passing."

"No, I want to go."

She rolled up her window and waited for John to slide into his seat before she opened her car door. The chill of the night air caught her breath, and Melissa hugged her sides as she walked toward the funeral home doors.

No amount of forewarning from John could prepare Melissa for Debbie's still bloated body lying in the coffin. How unfair that she should leave the earth the second her newborn baby occupied it! Did her stupidity merit a death sentence? Melissa and John became parents because Debbie turned her relationship with a half-wit boyfriend into altruistic self-sacrifice. Why couldn't Debbie live to reap its rewards?

A short, slender man with long knotted brown hair stood at one end of the room, bawling and wiping his nose with the back of his flannel shirt. Melissa's heart reached out to him. He must have loved Debbie after all. Just the same, she shrank from his touch when he flung his arms around her neck and sobbed. Melissa struggled free from his steely grasp.

"I'm very sorry for your loss," she politely said.

Derek snuffled on her shoulder. "What'll I do without her?"

John did not share Melissa's sympathy for Derek. Perhaps he only felt irritated by John-Peter, who now roared with hunger.

"Derek should find a job and wash his own socks," John said.

Melissa reached for the diaper bag, but John tossed it into the backseat. "Don't bother. I gave him three more bottles while you were inside."

"But Dr. Rothgard said...."

"Dr. Rothgard isn't sitting out here with him. We'll make some cereal when we get home. And yes, I burped him."

New Year's Eve traffic jammed the roads; John-Peter's inconsolable crying jarred her nerves. Twice, John's eyes closed during the short trip home, and twice Melissa offered to take the wheel. John-Peter finally fell asleep when John turned onto their street. The baby did not wake up when John slid him out of the car seat nor after John lay him down in the cradle. John sat on the bed to remove his shoes and fell asleep, sitting straight up.

Melissa returned to the kitchen, reading the directions for the rice cereal. She wanted to be ready when John-Peter awakened. When she returned to the bedroom to ready for bed, John had passed out.

Because Melissa did not wish to disturb him, she snuggled into her chair with a novel. Soon, John-Peter's crying woke her. As Melissa rubbed her eyes, she saw John stumble from the bedroom carrying their wailing son. By the time Melissa reached the kitchen, John was sitting on a chair feeding John-Peter a bottle. Yawning, Melissa opened the box of rice cereal. After the baby ate half its contents, he finally dropped off to sleep.

Exhausted, Melissa's eyes fell on the stove clock. Midnight. John rose from the table with the baby, smiled, and kissed Melissa's forehead.

"Happy first anniversary, Melissa," he said.

At dawn, John-Peter drank three bottles of formula and polished off the rest of the cereal. John left the house to search for a store still open on a holiday. Two hours later, he returned with a case of formula and three more boxes of rice cereal. The cereal slowed John-Peter's appetite, as Dr. Rothgard promised it would, and improved his sleep and his disposition, but the baby did eat two boxes of it, as well as half the formula.

"We go back to Shelby in the morning," John said.

The next day, when Dottie Sherman laid John-Peter on the scale, she said, "He's lost another ounce."

Stunned, Melissa looked up at John and then back at Nurse Sherman. *"How?"*

"Aren't you feeding him?"

"Enough for ten babies," John retorted.

"Well, you can discuss that with the doctor."

Dottie set the chart on Dr. Rothgard's desk before she left the room. Melissa rested her chin in her hand and thought.

"John," she said, "are you sure Dr. Rothgard's competent?"

"John-Peter's voracious appetite is not Dr. Rothgard's fault. If anyone can discern the problem, Dr. Rothgard can."

Dr. Rothgard gave the baby a full exam while the baby intently studied his movements. The doctor shook his head, perplexed.

"Except for the weight issue, he seems perfectly healthy. John, perhaps you do need someone with more experience."

"Like who?"

"I'm thinking."

While the two men talked, Melissa noticed something about the baby. "John, can you stand near the window with him?"

John did as she requested. "Now sit back down." John did. Melissa looked hard at the baby. "Don't get mad, but would you stand straight under the light with him again?"

"Melissa, I'm tired. Do you mind explaining?"

"His skin looks green."

John's eyes grew large. *"What!"*

"Do you see, Dr. Rothgard? Not overtly green, just a tint."

Dr. Rothgard frowned. "Give me the baby, John."

He moved John-Peter in and out of the light and before returning the infant to John. John-Peter kept his eyes on the doctor.

"Doesn't he seem awfully observant for a little baby?" Melissa said.

Dr. Rothgard leaned against the door and closed his eyes, pondering this new development. After a long while, he opened them again and looked straight at Melissa.

"He's green, and I'm stumped. Let's start with some blood tests. In the meantime, buy some powdered formula and enrich those bottles. Feed the baby as often as he needs until we get his weight up and discover what's going on with him. As for the two of you, sleep in shifts if you have to, but sleep. What about work and school?"

"Melissa starts next week. I'm on vacation for the next two months."

"I'm sure we'll figure this out before then. In the meantime, keep him fed, and make sure you rest."

John-Peter fell asleep on the way back to Jenson from Shelby and, thankfully, did not wake up when they returned home. John starting dozing the second his head touched the pillow, but Melissa, tense with fear and worry for their newborn son, felt wide awake.

"John?"

"Hmmm....?"

"Do you think something's wrong with John-Peter?"

"Uh, uh." John's voice dwindled to the beginnings of a snore.

"Are you sure?"

John reached out a hand to stroke Melissa's and missed.

Melissa could not sleep. Each time her body relaxed, it sprang to life, ready to care for John-Peter should he awaken. But the baby continued to snooze, and Melissa finally drifted into heavy sleep.

She dreamed John-Peter slept in the nursery and woke crying for her. Melissa fumbled for the light switch but couldn't locate it in the thick, foggy mist. The baby's cries became insistent.

"Mama! Mama!"

"Hold on! I'm coming, John-Peter!"

Feeling her away along the walls, Melissa found her way to the baby's room. Her son stood in his cradle, swaying it to and fro. "Mama!"

As Melissa hoisted her son from his bed, he dug his claws into her shoulders and fastened his teeth onto the back of her neck. Melissa yelped and dropped John-Peter into the floor.

"Heyyyyyyyyyyy!" John-Peter screamed.

Melissa bolted upright. Sweat poured from her forehead. Both John's side of the bed and the cradle were vacant.

"John must have gotten up to feed him," Melissa mumbled as sleep once again overtook her.

CHAPTER 18: UNDER THE COVER OF NIGHT

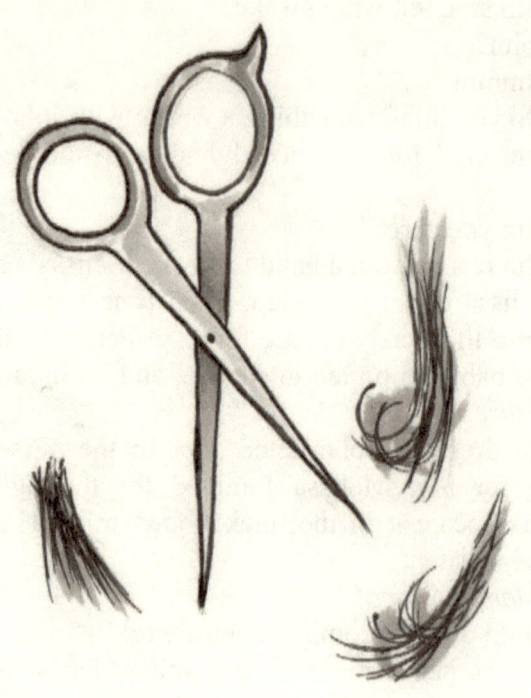

Dottie Sherman called the next day and reported normal test results for John-Peter's blood work. She then told Melissa to bring the baby back into Shelby for another weight check.

Melissa and John did so the very next day. John-Peter had nearly regained his birth weight.

"Keep up the good work," Dr. Rothgard said. "I'll see him in a month for his first shots."

"*Keep up the good work*," John repeated mockingly. "Do you have any idea what it costs to keep that baby fed?"

Soberly, they returned to the car. The victory felt hollow. John-Peter's insatiable appetite had sunk its teeth into the

Simotes' budget. He only lasted two hours between feedings, and even that took numerous bottles of formula, several boxes of cereal, and napping instead of sleeping at night to accomplish it.

Back at home, Melissa fed John-Peter while John cooked dinner, but they waited until the baby fell asleep before partaking of it. As they ate, John reviewed their situation. Jenson College allowed him six weeks of paid vacation leave, but because of John-Peter's situation, John had taken an additional two weeks of unpaid time. Originally, John had planned to keep the baby inside an unused classroom in the music department under the watch of a string of student babysitters; Melissa would complete her homework by day and care for John-Peter in the evening. John would utilize the later part of the day for correcting homework, preparing schoolwork, and teaching private students. However, neither one had bargained for the extra attention and expense their baby required. Unspoken doubts formed in Melissa's mind. What if John-Peter proved too much for a babysitter to handle? What if lack of sleep interfered with her concentration in school?

"Our grocery bill has risen by fifty percent, just to cover John-Peter's formula and cereal," John said. "What will happen as he grows?"

Melissa sighed as she sliced into a pork chop. "I wonder what makes him eat so much."

"And what will it cost us to find out?"

"We have insurance."

"Insurance doesn't cover everything. I'm cutting our budget."

The weekly cleaning lady would have to go as would the retired neighbor who shoveled the walks and mowed the grass.

"I'll ask Greg for more playing jobs," John said. "Even if he books me only...."

John-Peter's cries severed the air. Melissa dropped her fork and scurried to the bedroom. The baby nuzzled her neck and cooed as she paced the room. Eventually, the baby rested his cheek on Melissa's shoulder and watched her with wide eyes. After a long while, his eyelids drooped. Melissa held her breath, but the eyes popped open again each second she stopped. In desperation, Melissa added a little bounce to her walk. John-Peter remained alert. Melissa felt like crying.

"Oh why won't you go to sleep?" she said aloud.

John-Peter startled and then wailed. Melissa glanced at the clock. Only an hour had passed since the last feeding. The baby rooted along Melissa' neck, and she remembered her nightmare. She returned to the kitchen. John sat slumped in the chair, dinner untouched, sound asleep. When he heard Melissa, he jumped up and grabbed a bottle.

"I'll take him after I shower," he mumbled.

"Okay."

Melissa dropped onto the chair, pulled John-Peter away from her neck, and offered the bottle. A hot shower sounded good. One hour, three bottles, and a bowlful of cereal later, Melissa went searching for John to claim her shower. John had once again fallen asleep across the bed. One shoe dangled from his foot. She couldn't endure much more bone-crushing fatigue. Did all new parents have it this rough?

She laid John-Peter in his cradle, but the second his little body felt the mattress, the baby let out a loud wail.

"Shh," Melissa said as she rocked him.

"EEEEEEEEEEEEEEEEEEEEEE!" John-Peter screeched.

With a sidelong glance at her sleeping husband, Melissa removed John-Peter from his cradle and returned to the kitchen. The baby desperately gnawed her neck. Two hours and another large meal later, John-Peter slept at last. This time, when Melissa lay him in the cradle, he remained motionless. John, still dressed, had moved to his side of the bed. After first kicking off her shoes, Melissa joined him.

A tiny cry awakened her. Melissa sat up in the dark and peered into the thick mist. The cradle was empty. John slept undisturbed. Where had the baby gone? Clutching the furniture for guidance, Melissa followed the wailing as it grew loud and shrill.

The alarm clock!

Melissa groped through haze for the switch that would end the noise and return normalcy, just as it had years ago in her Bryony dreams. Her fingers closed around the clock and turned it off, but the jangling persisted.

What the....?

John-Peter flew out of the mist and onto her shoulder, sinking his gums into the back of her neck. Melissa jerked awake. The ringing continued. John had curled into a ball beside her. John-Peter lay on his back in the cradle, smacking his lips in sleep.

She hurried to the kitchen to answer the phone. The stove clock read two-thirty.

"Get John!" Carol gasped.

"Carol?" Melissa whispered back, trying to shake off sleep and straining to hear. Only Carols' racking sobs disturbed the house's unearthly silence.

Finally Carol blurted out, "Marvin's dead!"

Three days later, ignoring Dr. Rothgard's advice about crowds, the entire Simotes family traveled to Ohio for Marvin's wake and funeral. John received the news about Marvin's death without comment, but he appeared strangely preoccupied during the entire trip. During all services, John stood by Carol's side and greeted the mourners with the grace and gentleness befitting a good son. He ordered Carol into the break room when she seemed tired and brought her food and drink at the funeral lunch.

"How can I stay in that big house all by myself?" Carol sobbed, her head buried on John's shoulder.

"Sell it, and come live with us," John said.

Melissa blinked, and her mouth fell. John invited Carol to move in with them? Without even consulting his wife? That woman wasn't even his real mother!

Carol sniffed. "It's a good idea, but...."

"Decide soon," John said. "My offer won't wait."

Melissa controlled her temper just long enough for John to exit the parking lot. "Of all the inconsiderate...."

"Don't start on me, Melissa."

"You didn't even ask me!"

John's face hardened. "The conversation is closed."

How dare he! "We're not finished, John! We're...."

John-Peter began crying. Fuming, Melissa groped inside the diaper bag for a bottle. The baby fussed off and on, mostly on, during the entire two-day trip back to Jenson. The phone rang as John unlocked the door. He reached it on the third ring and handed the receiver for Melissa.

"It's for you," John said, "Jack Cooper."

Ann had a baby boy: Trenton Jack Cooper. Melissa grinned as she hung up the phone.

"I'll bet Jack's hopping mad about the name," Melissa said.

"As he should be. It's his first son, after all."

John carried the John-Peter into the bedroom to remove the crying infant's snowsuit. Melissa reached for a bottle.

One day, quite by mistake and to his great delight, John discovered John-Peter mellowed whenever John played piano.

"I don't believe it," Melissa said.

"Just wait until he starts crying." John's face glowed with exultation. "No more walking the floors."

John had no opportunity to demonstrate it. John-Peter's appetite accelerated that night. In addition to the formula, he devoured two extra boxes of cereal. When he finally fell asleep, neither Melissa nor John had the energy for anything more than a quick good-night kiss. Sometime during the night, the baby's piercing cries awakened her, but sleep shoved her back into dark unconsciousness, until hysterical wails again forced her awake. This time, early dawn dimly revealed the empty room. Melissa had just pushed away the blankets when John, face drawn, eyes barely open, but clutching a shrieking John-Peter, shuffled into the room. Melissa staggered out of bed for a bottle, wondering how long before Carol could move in. Clutching the baby to his chest, John adjusted the pillows to an upright position, leaned back, drew the blankets over him and the still screaming baby, and mumbled, "We'll wait here for you."

"Don't fall asleep with him in bed with you."

"I won't."

With the baby's cries echoing in her ears, Melissa sped to the kitchen, heated a bottle, and dashed to the bedroom. A yelling John-Peter squirmed against his sleeping father's grip.

Melissa snatched up the baby. "John! You promised not to fall asleep!"

John mumbled; a low snore escaped from his throat. Melissa didn't dare even sit on the bed with the baby. She curled in the living room's stuffed chair and drowsed as she fed John-Peter the first of his many bottles for the day.

At lunch, Tracy and Julie playfully nagged Melissa about holding out on the baby. It took all Melissa's strength to lift her ham sandwich.

"Dr. Rothgard told us to limit visitors," Melissa said, stifling a yawn, "because the baby's premature."

Jenny plopped in the seat next to Melissa, and her large silver hoop earrings swayed.

"How can you stand it?" Jenny asked, her fingers flaunting several new silver spoon rings as she peeled the wrapper off a straw. "Don't you want to show him off?"

"Well, sort of. Honestly, John and I feel so tired, we haven't considered it. We're just trying to cope."

"I hope he's friendlier than Ann's baby. All he does is sleep," Julie said. "Hey, did you hear Katie got married?"

Melissa nearly dropped her sandwich. "Married? Katie?"

"Yeah, she eloped with that old guy, the one who travels everywhere in that motor home."

The girls chatted about their new classes for a few minutes, until Tracy saw the clock and remembered she had to meet a professor about making up a quiz. Julie saw David across the room and decided to finish her salad at his table.

Only Jenny remained, and she stared coyly at Melissa. "Well, at least parenthood hasn't affected...well, you know...your love life."

"What are you talking about?" Melissa crumpled her napkin and tossed it on her plate.

Jenny giggled as she picked up her tray. "The back of your neck is full of hickeys."

Melissa cut her afternoon classes and sped home as fast as the speed limit allowed. Her dreams about John-Peter couldn't be dreams. Had the vampire part of John somehow spilled into his adopted son? As she stormed up the back steps, John flung open the screen door.

"I've called Dr. Rothgard," he said.

She pushed past him into the house. "John, we've got to talk."

"Didn't you hear me?"

Melissa shook her head, trying to clear her thoughts. "What!"

"I said, 'I called Dr. Rothgard.' John-Peter's cut his first tooth."

"His first tooth? John, he's barely a month old!"

"I know."

Dr. Rothgard weighed John-Peter, who had once again lost several ounces, and examined the infant's mouth, which now bragged four teeth, two on the bottom and two on top. Dr. Rothgard gave Melissa's neck the same care and listened to Melissa's account of her dreams, but he spoiled it by grinning at John, who did not return the smile.

"Don't say it," John warned him. "I didn't do it."

With a glance at the baby, Melissa anxiously blurted out, "Is John-Peter a vampire?"

Dr. Rothgard chuckled. "Place your hand over his chest. Feel his heart beat. Your baby is very much alive."

"Then has the anemia returned?" Melissa persisted. "What happens if I can't help John?"

Dr. Rothgard inspected her neck again and then peered sternly at her over his glasses, "How much blood are you letting John take?"

"Only what you prescribed." She looked at John for confirmation, but John was carefully studying Dr. Rothgard.

"Then I doubt it's anemia. Strange that I'm seeing bruises only on your neck. A blood test should give us the answer."

John impatiently cut in. "And the teeth?"

"I admit that's odd, but the weight loss concerns me more than the precocious development. I may consult a specialist."

As Dr. Rothgard left, Dottie Sherman entered to draw Melissa's blood. Melissa closed her eyes as she submitted to the dreaded needle. Holding a cotton ball to the wound, the nurse bent Melissa's arm at the elbow, and said, "Doctor says, 'Call tomorrow for the results.'"

For the second time that month, John stopped at a fast food restaurant. In silence, they ate hamburgers and fries as John drove from Shelby to Jenson. The unknown plagued Melissa's mind and heart.

She spoke only once. "What do you think?"

"I don't know," John curtly replied.

They made it as far as the college before John-Peter began to moan. By the time John had reached the house, the baby's fussiness had blossomed into a full-blown tantrum. The baby writhed and screamed as John unfastened the buckles of the car seat.

"Get his food ready, Melissa. I'll try settling him down."

Melissa flew up the steps and into the house, not bothering to remove her coat. She mixed a batch of cereal, removed a bottle from the warmer, and then took John-Peter from John's arms.

"Go ahead and shower," she said. "I'll keep him."

"Let me take him. I'll probably fall asleep again."

"I'll make sure you won't. Go."

John-Peter was working on his second bottle when Melissa heard the bathroom door close. Good. A shower might relax John. Half an hour later, John, hair wet and donned in shorts and T-shirt, returned to the kitchen. He frowned at the half dozen bottles lined up on the table, the empty bowl, and John-Peter dozing on Melissa's shoulder.

John eased the baby from Melissa's arms. "Your turn."

Melissa stumbled to the bedroom for a nightgown. How could one tiny baby drain two grown adults? The hot shower felt good everywhere except the back of her tender neck. Over the cascade, she heard John-Peter cries followed by the thunderous barrage of frenetic piano notes. She turned off the spray and listened. John-Peter had stopped crying.

Hastily grabbing her robe, Melissa flung open the door. John had moved the baby's cradle next to the piano; he manipulated the keys with gentle touches. Melissa inched closer and peered inside. John-Peter lay wide awake, still and listening hard. John caught Melissa's eye, and he smiled triumphantly. She sat beside him on the bench and let fatigue engulf her as the magical notes floated past her head. John, the baby, and the music wove together as one serene moment that Melissa wished would never end.

The front door handle jiggled, followed by a knock. John stopped playing. John-Peter began screaming. As John left to answer it, Melissa glided into his place and rocked the baby, but he only yelled louder. Melissa had just reached down to pick him up when she heard John's voice exclaim, "Mom!"

He deemed her a welcome third pair of hands to feed the baby, whose appetite grew as the night wore on. Carol moved both the baby and herself into the nursery. By morning, John-Peter had his molars, but Melissa's neck felt a little better. Carol reported that John-Peter, in-between meals, had thrashed so hard in the crib, he had nearly toppled it. The three of them ate a silent breakfast, punctuated by the sounds of John-Peter's screams, demanding release from the crib. Twice Melissa started to leave the room for him, and twice John ordered her to sit and eat the breakfast Carol had made.

"I can't eat," Melissa protested. "His crying makes my stomach hurt."

John stuffed the last bite of black toast in his mouth. "I'll get him."

After he left the room Carol said, "Where does your baby get his moods? John was always so sweet-tempered. I sure hope that doctor has some insight."

"Me, too," Melissa said, biting into a strip of equally black bacon while trying to ignore her son's shrieks of displeasure. Sweet-tempered? Way to go, John, she thought. Must be nice to program your own childhood memories.

"He is adorable though. He so looks like John at that age."

Melissa scowled and gingerly tasted the cold, rubbery eggs.

"I'm amazed John got involved in baby care. Marvin couldn't be bothered. You're very fortunate, Melissa."

"I know," Melissa said with a sigh, giving up.

Melissa couldn't wait until classes ended to call Dr. Rothgard, but her blood tests showed no abnormalities. Dr.

Rothgard did, however, want to her come immediately to his office to pick up vitamins for John-Peter.

"I've specially formulated them to meet your baby's needs," Dr. Rothgard said. "How do your bruises look?"

"John said this morning they're fading." Melissa gingerly felt the back of her neck. "Will John-Peter be okay?"

"I think so, although his case is unusual. Give the vitamins a week, and then let's recheck his weight."

John made the trip to Shelby for the vitamins, while Melissa vainly tried catching up on homework. Melissa had expected a battle, but John-Peter dutifully swallowed the capsule.

Later that evening, as Carol inspected the reddish wisps past the baby's ears, she announced, "He's young, but I do think John-Peter's ready for his first hair cut. Melissa, do you have a blunt pair of scissors I could use?"

Melissa did. She walked to her bedroom and returned to the nursery with a pair she kept in her top dresser drawer. Carol snipped the little bits of hair around the baby's as well as the straggly pieces that hung past his neck.

"There," Carol handed the scissors to Melissa and cuddling the infant close to her face. "Grandma's made you nice and sweet."

Very early the next morning, Carol barged into their room and shouted, "Go look at your baby!"

A dazed John shook his head and ran his fingers through his hair, but he stumbled after Carol. He returned a moment later, visibly shaken. Fully awake, Melissa realized she and John had slept uninterrupted the entire night.

"John," Melissa nearly whispered it. "What's wrong?"

Did she really want to hear the answer?

"Melissa, John-Peter's hair not only grew back, it's well past his shoulders."

CHAPTER 19: THINGS ARE NOT WHAT THEY SEEMED

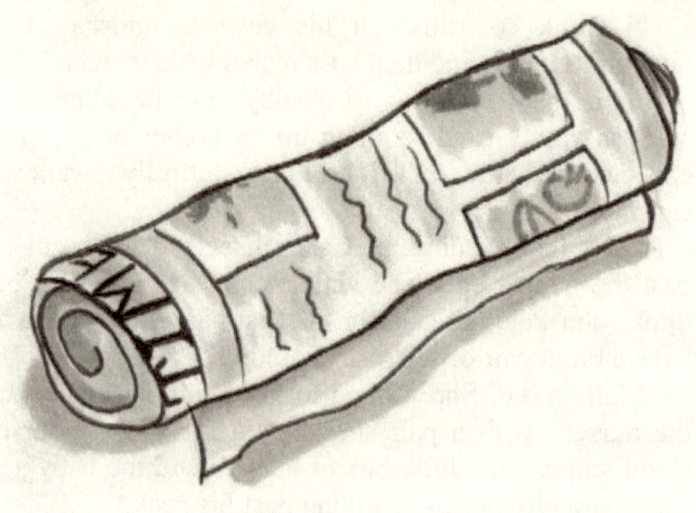

Within seconds, John was on the phone with Dr. Rothgard's answering service, demanding an immediate callback. John-Peter, on cue, started crying. Melissa, uneasy and disquieted about this new development, brought him to the kitchen table.

Carol's eyes opened wide at the sight of John-Peter ravenously slurping down his breakfast.

"You do know that's the tenth bottle he's had this morning!" Carol exclaimed.

Melissa shrugged and continued feeding the baby. What could she say?

Thus ignored, Carol, clad in a frayed pink robe and matching scuffs, her hair uncombed, resumed bustling about the kitchen, cracking eggs and frying bacon. She reached for a loaf of bread and put four slices in the toaster just as John-

Peter announced the end of his meal with a loud burp. Melissa rose and moved John-Peter from the crook of her arm to her shoulder and rubbed his back. The phone rang, and John stopped pacing to answer it.

"We'll be there." John hung up and tapped Melissa's shoulder. "Ten o'clock. This time, we're not leaving his office without an explanation. A real one."

He paused to stroke John-Peter's head, frowned at the fiery strands sweeping his small son's shoulders, and then sauntered out of the kitchen. Melissa had general science at ten; perhaps Jenny could take notes for her?

"John's getting dressed now?" Carol removed dripping crumbling bacon slices to a paper-towel lined plate. "Breakfast is nearly ready."

"I'll tell him," Melissa said, satisfied John-Peter had no lingering burps waiting expulsion. "I'm going to change the baby."

"What about the food?"

"We'll be right back."

Cradling the baby with one arm, Melissa knocked on the bedroom door, called out, "Your mom says breakfast is almost ready," before proceeding to the nursery. She lay John-Peter in his crib and reached up to the shelf for a diaper. The baby moved his hands before his eyes and examined their creases. Melissa unsnapped his sleeper and eased out tiny arms and legs.

"How's my little baby?" Melissa cooed, hoping chattering might dispel her growing anxiety.

In response, John-Peter happily kicked unencumbered legs across the sheets. Melissa opened the middle dresser drawer and scanned the shirts.

"Blue or green today, baby?" She reached for a dark blue shirt embellished with a bright orange carrot.

"Green," John-Peter said.

Melissa stopped, hand dangling. Cold prickles crept up her spine. Taking a deep breath, Melissa slowly turned. John-Peter had brought his left foot to his mouth and was chewing on his toes. Had the baby really talked, or had she imagined it?

John-Peter removed his foot and looked straight at her. "Green," he repeated.

Melissa flew from the room and banged on the bedroom door. "John! Open up! John!"

John flung open the door. He was fully dressed, except for his shoes. "What, now?"

"He talked."

"Who talked?"

"John-Peter."

The color drained from John's face. "The baby *talked?*"

Melissa nodded and tugged at John's hand, but he resisted.

"And he said what?"

"Green."

"Green?"

"I was looking in his drawer for a shirt and pretending to talk to him. I asked if he wanted blue or green and he said, 'Green.'"

John rushed into the nursery with Melissa behind him. John-Peter was kneeling on hands and knees and rocking back and forth. His hair now hung halfway down his back. John curled his fingers around a thick, tangled lock and frowned.

"Isn't he too young to be moving like that?" Melissa said.

"Yes."

The baby squirmed and fussed in his car seat for the entire ride to Shelby, while Melissa tried amusing him with every baby game her inexperienced brain could muster. She played *Pat a Cake* and *Pease Porridge Pot* and sang several rounds of *Farmer in the Dell* and *London Bridge* until John-Peter's restlessness and mild protests escalated into outright screaming. Melissa reached behind the seat and patted his leg, hoping to soothe him, but John-Peter pinched her hand.

"Out!" he demanded.

John tightened his grip on the steering wheel. "Dr. Rothgard had better be in a conversational mood."

If he wasn't, Dottie Sherman had probably convinced him otherwise. At John's insistence, Nurse Sherman had immediately ushered the Simotes into an examining room, all the while instructing them to remove the baby's clothes and place him on the scale.

The second the silver tray made contact with John-Peter's little back, he arched away. "No! Cold!"

Nurse Sherman, pen poised over the chart, dropped both, yelped, and fled from the room. John positioned John-Peter on the scale, held the thrashing boy with a hand, and narrowed his eyes. "*Don't* move."

The baby opened his mouth to scream, looked up at John, and shut it again, although he continued to writhe beneath his father's firm grasp.

"What does he weigh, Melissa?"

"Eleven pounds, eight ounces."

John handed the baby to Melissa and stooped to retrieve the scattered chart and pen. John-Peter, back in safe territory, threw back his head and howled his disapproval. John had just finished recording John-Peter's weight when Dr. Rothgard zoomed into the room and slammed the door behind him.

"What is going on?" Dr. Rothgard shouted over the baby's yells.

John crossed his arms, glowered, and deliberately dropped his voice. "You tell us."

Dr. Rothgard yanked John-Peter from Melissa's arms and roughly set him on the examining table. The harshness of the act momentarily jolted John-Peter into bewildered silence. Nevertheless, John-Peter's sullenness quickly returned as Dr. Rothgard listened to his heart and lungs, and he jerked away his face when the doctor tried looking in his ears.

"Stop!" John-Peter yelled.

"John, hold him still."

When Dr. Rothgard finished the exam, he flung himself into the desk chair, banging it against wall, and scribbled furiously on a piece of paper. Melissa watched the doctor with one eye as she tried to dress the non-compliant John-Peter.

"Quit moving!" Melissa snapped, patience gone.

"Hungry!"

John fished in the diaper bag for a bottle and held it near the baby's mouth. John-Peter snapped his jaws over the nipple and nearly bit his father's hand. Dr. Rothgard handed the sheet of paper to John and then sat back, mopping his face with his handkerchief.

"Well, good news," Dr. Rothgard said, trying to smile and miserably failing. "John-Peter's finally gained weight."

"Unsatisfactory," John said. "Try again."

"I've also called Thornton Medical Center and told them these tests are a priority. Get them done today and return to my office tonight."

"More!"

Melissa jumped at John-Peter's shriek. John propped another bottle, which John-Peter attacked as if he hadn't eaten in a week.

"Dr. Rothgard," Melissa asked, trying to steady her quavering voice. "What's wrong with our son?"

"Accelerated development for one, but I want to rule out a few conditions."

John seemed far from appeased. "Such as?"

"Chemical imbalances, brain tumors, things like that."

Panic and fear rose inside Melissa's throat. "John!"

John's eyes gripped Dr. Rothgard. "What are the odds?"

"Slim to none." Dr. Rothgard met John's gaze with a severe look of his own. "But he does have a sketchy medical history. I did warn you about taking a chance."

"Chance?" Melissa said, looking from Dr. Rothgard to John and back again. "Chance on what?"

"If John-Peter was your biological child, then we'd know more about his genes and certain familial traits. Without that information, there's more guesswork involved."

"But we do know his background," Melissa began, but John quickly interrupted with, "No thanks for your overcharged, useless opinion."

"John," Dr. Rothgard began.

"We'll return tonight. You better have answers."

At the hospital, technicians drew multiple vials of the baby's blood and scanned his little body from head to toe. Each time, John insisted on accompanying John-Peter to his various tests, and each time medical professionals barred his admittance.

"We do our job better without overbearing parents breathing down our necks," one nurse sneered before she whisked the baby from sight.

John, bristling at yet another foiled attempt, stomped around the waiting room. Melissa leaned back in the chair and closed her eyes. Perhaps John might have gotten his way if he hadn't been so autocratic and insulting to the hospital's staff.

"I'll have their jobs before the day's end."

"I don't like this either, but we have to assume they know what they're doing."

"They better."

Neither one felt like eating lunch. They spent the afternoon moving John-Peter from department to department and up and down multiple floors. In between, John paced, and Melissa fretted.

"John, what will we do if something's really wrong with him?"

"I don't know, Melissa."

Their tension had mounted to near frenzy by the time they returned to Dr. Rothgard's office. John-Peter broadcasted their arrival by screaming with hunger, although he had just completed a bottle half an hour ago. Heart chaotically pounding, Melissa, perched on a chair to feed the baby and listen to what Dr. Rothgard, who was simultaneously reading through multiple reports, had to say.

"First," Dr. Rothgard said, "the good news. I've reviewed your son's tests and every one appears normal."

Melissa looked at John to gauge his reaction, but John, steadily watching Dr. Rothgard, only said, "Which means what?"

"Which means one of two things. You can either pursue further, experimental testing to determine the source of your son's precocious behavior, which we will probably never discover, or take him home and love him the way he is." Dr. Rothgard looked away and studied an abstract painting on the wall. "I recommend the latter."

John-Peter sighed, stretched, and burrowed deeper into Melissa's arms as she fed him another bottle.

"But," Melissa said, "we don't understand the way he is."

Dr. Rothgard turned toward her and laughed weakly. "Your view is shared by many parents, even those who produce babies that follow the textbook rules." He now looked sternly at John. "I won't tell you what to do, but I will say this. The more you poke and prod that child, the more you risk putting his differences in the limelight. Only you can decide what's more important: the pursuit of finding out what makes him tick or raising him as normally as possible."

He was holding something back; Melissa felt certain of it. One glimpse at her husband, and she could tell Dr. Rothgard's answer did not satisfy John any more than it convinced Melissa.

"I told you before...."

"And I told you, John, to consider carefully the decisions you make because you will live with the consequences. On the plus side, you have an extremely intelligent, healthy son. That's not even close to the same answer I gave another couple earlier this morning. They would be overjoyed to trade places with you."

"Since when," John said evenly, "does genius percipience tarnish an infant's skin green?"

With a trembling hand, Dr. Rothgard reached for a pencil, but he accidentally knocked it onto the floor, where it rolled under the desk. When he finally faced John, his face appeared visibly shaken.

"John, I don't know. However, most people won't notice a faint tint underneath his skin. It's imperceptible in normal lighting.

Suddenly, the years of parenting this child loomed long, winding, and perilous. Uncertain, Melissa hugged her sleeping son closer to her. "So what do we do now?"

Dr. Rothgard rose to leave. "Childproof your home because John-Peter will soon be into everything. Oh, yes, and keep up those vitamins. Now that he's finally gaining weight, the boy's extreme hunger should level out."

John looked ready to explode. "And tell the rest of the world what?"

Dr Rothgard tried to smile but managed only a pained grimace. "The same thing every parent since the beginning of the time believes. That your child is a genius. In your case, it will be the truth." He picked up the baby's chart and stalked from the room.

John said nothing all the way home. John-Peter, to Melissa's amazement, continued to sleep. Maybe the tests tired him out. He did not even stir when Melissa set him down in the crib.

As she shut the bedroom door, John met her in the hall. "Get in the shower. We're going to Rudy's."

Melissa's heart skipped a beat at the news. How long since she'd been alone, really alone, with John? "What about John-Peter? Won't he...."

"John-Peter is staying with my mother."

"She's fine with it?"

"I haven't told her yet."

Carol wasn't "fine with it," but John hustled Melissa out the back door anyway, pushing the door closed in Carol's face and shutting out her loud objections. John moved Melissa down the stairs and into the car.

"Do you think this is a good idea?" Melissa worried as John backed into the street for the return trip to Shelby. "Your mother doesn't seem happy with us."

"She'll live."

So many cars packed Rudy's parking lot that Melissa doubted they'd obtain a table, but she soon learned John had made reservations. So he had planned this! Warmth filled Melissa from head to toe that, in the midst of their chaotic lives, John had arranged a night of their own. As the waiter directed them to their table, John lagged behind Melissa.

"You go," John said. "I'm making a phone call."

John soon returned and ordered prime rib for them both, which revived fond memories of that first date and restored hope inside Melissa that she and John could work out their problems.

As the evening progressed, Melissa couldn't decide which relaxed John more, the wine or the temporary suspension of intense childcare duties. Either way, he appeared to be enjoying himself.

Melissa speared the last piece of meat on her fork and offered it to John. "Bite?"

"I'll stick to the jerky on my plate, thank you."

"I think it's funny you don't like the taste of rare beef."

"It's bad enough that I'll swallow your blood tomorrow."

"You're not used to it?"

"I'll never be used to it."

The waiter approached the table. "Dessert?"

"Coffee for me," John said.

"Ma'am?"

"Coffee for her, too."

The waiter hurried away.

"John, it'll take me forever to get to sleep. I never drink coffee."

He merely shrugged, tossed his napkin on the table, and leaned back. "I'm in no hurry. Are you?"

Images of John-Peter screeching in a frantic Carol's ear flooded Melissa's mind, but she brushed them away. It felt so nice to sit here with John, just the two of them. As they talked, she and John avoided the subject of John-Peter. John had finally received a check from the insurance company. His piano would arrive in time for Easter, when he would host its maiden concert for Melissa's family, whom he had invited to spend the holiday in Jenson, as a surprise for Melissa.

"Since John-Peter's issues aren't vanishing soon, it's about time they met the newest family member," John said, accepting a refill.

A quick mental image of Melissa's Grover's Park home flashed through her mind and vanished. How long ago living there now seemed! Melissa started to praise John for having taken the initiative, but he had already changed the subject.

"This fall, Jenson College is initiating an accelerated program, available only for certain majors," John said. "English, with an education concentration, is one of them. If you schedule a full set of classes this summer and stagger them in the fall, you could student teach in the spring and graduate next year."

The news stunned Melissa. "But how can I with....?"

"Of course, it will mean a heavy workload for you and additional sacrifices for me. However, I believe we face more challenges with John-Peter. You can't risk losing that degree. I want you to pursue this program."

"When do I have to let the school know?"

"Monday. Openings are limited."

The waiter approached the table with the check. "I'll take that, sir, when you're ready."

John reached for his wallet. "I'm ready."

Melissa smiled bleakly through the disappointment that was rapidly replacing the evening's enchantment. How unfair the wonderful date had already ended!. Some of the tension returned to John's face as he paid the bill. With an almost furtive look around him, John clasped Melissa's hand and conducted her to the car. His actions unnerved her; remaining happiness ebbed. Had she done something to make him angry? The night had been perfect; she didn't want to ruin it, so Melissa was afraid to even speak, until John missed his turn to Jenson.

"John," Melissa touched his sleeve. "You went the wrong way."

"No, I didn't."

"That's not the way home."

"I'm not taking you home, Melissa."

"Wait a minute, you can't...."

John swung the car onto the shoulder and screeched to a halt. Despite the speeding traffic shaking the car, he slid close to Melissa, pushed her against the door, and kissed her hard. His hands moved over her face, through her hair, and down. Too soon, John broke away, and, with the fingers of one hand still twisted in her hair and the other firmly holding her neck, he said in a low, dark voice, "You listen to me."

Melissa, feeling like a trapped rabbit, yet wishing John would kiss her again, could only stare up at him.

"It's been many weeks," John said. "We are not going home tonight."

"But what about John-Peter or your mother?"

How could Melissa object when he looked at her like that? She noted the moon beyond John's window, closed her eyes, and made a silent wish that John would say those three magic words to her tonight. He did not say them, not there, nor in the hotel room he had reserved for them. But John kept Melissa so delightfully occupied until dawn that she forgot, for the time being, her hoped-for moment did not occur. Melissa awakened late afternoon feeling more refreshed than she had in weeks.

A livid Carol Simotes greeted Melissa and John when they walked through the back door Saturday evening.

"Don't ever pull a stunt like that again!" Carol shouted.

Melissa turned on John. "You didn't tell her?"

John strolled to the living room and began flipping through the mail. "Of course I told her. Remember, I left to make a phone call?"

Carol marched over to John, stood on tiptoe, and put her face close to his. "I had no choice but to stay with the baby! Your father and I would never have…."

The ire plainly showed on John's face as he lifted only his eyes, but his voice emerged easy and cool.

"You're residing here for free," he said. "If you don't like it, leave."

Her mother-in-law couldn't leave them!

Carol gasped but quickly recovered. "I'll be gone within the week. Don't worry about me!" She stomped out of the room, turned, and flung back, "And for heaven's sake, give that baby a bath. He smells!"

Gone? How would they survive without Carol? John had to return to work in a week, and Melissa, already shuffling through foggy days of physical exhaustion, mental fatigue, and worry for her small son, hadn't the strength or courage to combine school with caring for her the ever-changing and constantly broadening needs of John-Peter. Even now, she heard him banging the crib off the nursery walls. Perhaps, John, annoyed at Carol's outburst, would see the foolishness of his reckless remarks and change his mind.

John tossed down the mail. "My mother is right," he said, and relief shook Melissa from head to toe. "John-Peter needs a real bath." And he headed for the nursery. Melissa, reeling from this fresh disappointment, assembled her school books and trudged to the kitchen to call Jenny.

The baby tolerated baths even less than hunger. He screamed as if his father was stabbing him. Over the shrieking, Melissa quickly jotted some information, noted the assignment, and apologized to Jenny, even as she hung up the phone. She ran to the bathroom and found Carol had beaten her to the door. John was wrapping John-Peter in a towel.

"Lots of new babies don't like baths," Carol no longer seemed angry. Maybe she didn't really intend to leave. "He'll come around."

John's baby grand piano arrived at the end of the week, just after he had driven Carol and her suitcases to the bus station. Melissa objected to the callous disposal of the woman John claimed as his mother, but John acted dispassionately casual about it. By contrast, John ordered the movers to handle his piano with the care befitting fine China and monitored each step until the prize sat safely in place. John's eyes gleamed as he caressed its keys.

John-Peter crawled under the piano and clamped his teeth onto a pedal. "Play!"

John merely laughed as he crouched down, pulled out his son, and bore him aloft to the kitchen. "Tonight, after dinner."

John-Peter studied his father with round, solemn eyes. Melissa couldn't believe how fast the baby had developed in just the past week. Although not quite four months old, John-Peter now owned a full set of teeth, a vast one-word vocabulary, and the ability to scoot around either on his knees or his haunches. He displayed a marked preference for certain colors--browns, reds, greens, oranges and yellows—and refused clothing of any other hue. John-Peter's cherished opinions extended to his food choices, too, for Dr. Rothgard had instructed Melissa to start feeding John-Peter solid food. Although Melissa had tried complying with the feeding chart Dottie Sherman had given her, John-Peter eschewed meat of any kind and craved fruits and vegetables. John experimented making ice cream from soy milk just for John-Peter. A nonchalant Dr. Rothgard merely upped the baby's vitamin dosage and told Melissa to feed the baby anything he desired.

After dinner, as promised, John played to a captive audience of two; the official debut must wait for Melissa's family to arrive.

Father and son were still sitting at the grand instrument when a weary Melissa finally went to bed, soaring away to dreamland on the music John's skilled fingers continued playing. A loud thump, followed by John-Peter's screams, suddenly awakened her. She could scarcely discern the sleeping form of John in the pitch black room. Melissa snapped on the light and flew out of bed.

"What the hell?" John mumbled.

"It's the baby!"

Melissa bolted to the nursery, but John-Peter's crib was empty. His wailing came from the kitchen. John reached the room first and snapped on the light. What a sight!

John-Peter sat cross-legged on the floor, rubbing his head and crying, great tears splashing down his cheeks. Surrounding him were empty cereal boxes and banana peels. Every cabinet door stood wide open. Dented cans lay on the counters. The contents of a ripped macaroni box had spilled into the sink.

Melissa, teetering with sleep and shock, gingerly knelt on the floor and put her arms around her baby. "John-Peter," she said in a comforting tone.

"Hungry!" John-Peter moaned.

"John-Peter no longer sleeps unattended," John quietly pronounced.

"How will you arrange that?"

She'd never get proper rest if they moved John-Peter back to their bedroom.

"I'll explain it in the morning. Go to bed."

Melissa hesitated, glancing down at the mess on the floor.

"I'll take care of it, Melissa."

"But...."

John picked up his son and pointed to the door. "Out."

He spent the night on John-Peter's floor, lying flush against the door so the baby could not escape. Lethargy plainly showed on John's face, proof John-Peter was beating him down, too, although John emphatically denied it.

Then the mail arrived.

"John, what's wrong?" Melissa said as she set John-Peter on the floor.

She didn't like the distressed look on John's face. The baby scampered away in the direction of the piano.

"Music, Father!"

"After dinner." John set the mail on top of the desk. "Nothing's wrong."

The troubled look lingered on John's face during dinner, a silent affair interspersed with John-Peter's comments. They began when John-Peter refused the stir-fry, even after John removed the beef strips from it.

The baby had pinched a broccoli floret between his fingers and drew it to his lips, then cried out, "Icky!"

He pushed the vegetable pieces on the floor.

"John-Peter!" Melissa shouted.

Melissa picked them up and threw them away. John rose from the table and turned on the wok.

"John, you're not making him something special!"

"It will only take a minute."

"No meat!" John-Peter screeched.

"No meat, John-Peter," his father said as he scraped the remaining vegetables from the bowl into the hot oil.

Soon, John set another full plate on the table. The baby quickly gobbled it down and bellowed, "More food!"

"Say, 'Please,' John-Peter," Melissa said irritably.

"Please!"

John repeated the process, and John-Peter rapidly shoved carrots, broccoli, and mushrooms into his mouth. As he ate a third helping, John wearily rose and began stacking the dishes.

"John, I'll get those tonight."

"It's no problem."

"But I'm in the mood for music," Melissa lied, afraid of John's ashen complexion.

John-Peter shoved a fistful of the remaining vegetables into his mouth and tugged at his seat straps, excited at the prospect of a song. "Down, Mother, down!"

Two days later, Steve entered the house with a suitcase under each arm and gripping two more. Brian followed, his hands also full. Darlene held a box. John escorted them into the guest room and then slipped away to the nursery.

In amazement, Melissa watched the little parade. "How much stuff did you bring? You're only staying overnight."

Brian pushed past Melissa with his bundles. "Overnight! Mom's living here until the middle of May!"

"She is? Why?"

Glancing to see if anyone might hear him, Brian lowered his voice. "Because your husband's too incompetent to take care of his own baby."

He dropped the bags on the floor and slunk out of the room before Melissa could retort. Just wait, Brian, she thought, suppressing a giggle, until you meet your nephew. That ought to bring you down a notch.

Darlene, as if she overheard, called back, "John told me your son is a handful and asked if I could help out for a few weeks. That's the best part about writing. It's very portable."

Melissa proceeded to give the grand tour of the house, minus the nursery where John was prepping his young son to meet his real extended family. Back in the main area, Darlene admired the polished wood of John's piano. With a friendly wink, Steve asked Melissa if she needed more bookshelves. Brian picked up the television guide and settled into the couch to flip through it.

Darlene turned away from the piano and looked toward the back bedrooms. "Where's the baby, Melissa? Is he sleeping?"

"No, John's changing his diaper. John-Peter doesn't take naps."

"He doesn't? He's so young."

"Well," Melissa hedged. "He's a bit unusual."

At that moment, John-Peter poked his head around the corner of the living room. Darlene beamed. "There he is! Aw, he's so cute."

John-Peter looked uncertainly at her. "Grandma?"

The color drained from Darlene's face, and she dropped onto the piano bench. Steve stared at the baby, mouth slightly hanging open. Brian, surprised, but curious, leaned forward for a closer look. Melissa hurried to fetch John-Peter.

"Yes, that's Grandma," Melissa said, carrying him over to the guests and hoping she sounded offhand. "Come meet everybody: Grandma, Grandpa, and Uncle Brian."

The baby grinned and waved. "Hello, everyone! I'm John-Peter, and I'm a musician!"

John entered the room, saw Darlene's distress, and headed for the kitchen. He returned seconds later, carrying a glass of water, which Darlene accepted with shaking hands and a thankful glance.

"You see why I had difficulty explaining this to you," John said.

Darlene took a sip and nodded through quivering lips.

Steve remained rooted to the floor, the look on his face clearly revealing he wasn't trusting his senses to process the scene before him, although his color had returned.

Brian, however, approached Melissa with outstretched arms and said, "Come to Uncle Brian."

John-Peter eagerly leaned forward, and Melissa let him go. Brian studied the baby's green-flecked brown eyes and scraggly, abundant red hair, while John-Peter gazed at Brian with bemused toleration.

"What a neat baby," Brian, all vestiges of cockiness gone, looked in wonderment at Melissa. "You're really lucky."

"Lucky" wasn't exactly the word Melissa would have chosen, but Brian wouldn't be staying long enough to find that out for himself. So Melissa only gently said, "Thank you."

"I really like his eyes, Liss. They're so full of wisdom."

Steve insisted on treating everyone to dinner at Berkley's. Although they, except John who stayed at home on the premise needing to prepare for his return to work, ordered the signature hamburgers and French fries, John-Peter nibbled a roll and gobbled a platter of spinach. Brian fed the baby the tomato slice from his own plate.

"I'm surprised he ate it," Melissa sipped her iced tea. "John-Peter won't eat anything that's been in the vicinity of meat."

"I figured that when he ordered the salad." Brian grinned mischievously and added, "Did you see the look on that waitress' face when he talked?"

Steve watched John-Peter cram Brian's pickle into his mouth. "What does his doctor say?"

"He ordered a bunch of tests and said he's fine," Melissa said.

"I...I can't get over it," Steve said. "Look at all those teeth, and...that hair!"

Melissa hoped no one noticed John-Peter's green skin. "I know. John cuts it every night, but it always grows back.

After they returned from dinner, John, although restless and distracted, entertained Melissa's family with the best of his pieces, originals as well as several classical compositions. John closed the lid after a number by Brahms, much to the chagrin of his infant son.

"Father, you didn't play...." John-Peter began.

"Bid good-night to everyone," John lifted the boy from the bench and set him on the floor.

But John-Peter scrambled away to the nursery. "No! You're contemptible!"

He slammed the door and thumped loudly on the bedroom walls. Melissa started to rise, but Brian moved faster than she did.

"Let me get him, Liss," Brian pleaded. "Please!"

Melissa glanced at John, who nodded his permission. Brian started to make a face at the exchange but then stopped, apparently thinking better of it, and slipped into the nursery. Half an hour passed before Brian returned, holding John-Peter in his arms.

"He's okay," Brian said, and John-Peter nodded in agreement. "He just wants to play something for everybody."

Later, when reflecting back on that moment, Melissa knew that if John had remained in the room, John-Peter's show would not have occurred. But John had left to answer the phone, and Melissa had not seen it coming.

Brian set the baby on the piano bench and raised the lid for him. John-Peter shoved his hand away, shrieking "No! Let me!"

With an amused half-smile at Melissa, Brian took several steps back, but John-Peter watched him with suspicious eyes until Brian walked into the living room and sat on the couch next to Steve. John-Peter stretched his fingers, and with the greatest solemnity, began playing the first notes of *Bryony*.

Something twisted hard inside Melissa, and she cried out against the painful betrayal. Steve's jaw opened and stayed that way. Darlene brought her hand up to her forehead and hung her head, thinking. "I've heard that song, but I can't think where."

John rushed into the room, swooped up John-Peter, and threw down the lid. The baby howled at this thwarting of his shining moment as John carried him out. A BAM of the nursery door, and John-Peter's cries faded into the awkward silence ruling the living room. Darlene and Steve exchanged confused glances.

"Hey!" Brian started to rise from the couch, but Steve set his hand on Brian's shoulder and lowered him. Brian instead glared at Melissa. "What's the problem with your husband? Can't he share the stage?"

"Brian," Darlene gently said. "It's not your house." She looked expectantly at Steve.

"Well...." Steve ran a hand through his hair and shifted position. "The boy certainly knows his mind."

It took every ounce of control for Melissa to wait until she and John had climbed into bed to settle her mind. One look at John, and Melissa knew she'd better hurry. John wasn't in the mood for conversation.

"John..." she began.

He silenced her with a kiss. She tried to pull away, but John doggedly persisted until Melissa relaxed and wrapped her arms around him. He moved lower. Maybe she could coax some answers from him before her body overruled any objections.

"Why did you tell my mother we only needed temporary help? John-Peter's issues won't be fixed in a couple of weeks."

John kept going.

With a single, fluid motion, Melissa broke free. "Talk to me!"

John froze for an eternity. Slowly, he raised menacing eyes. Melissa's resolve instantly vanished, and she nervously smoothed her hair away from her face.

"Aren't you teaching summer school?" she weakly asked.

He stared at her with a mixture of incredulity and vexation and then slid back to his place on the bed.

"I arranged my schedule to begin later in the day, after you come home from school."

Melissa didn't like the dark look of determination on John's face. He was up to something; she just knew it. "I don't see how that will fix anything."

"One of us will be with him."

"But at night?"

"I'll bolt and padlock his door."

In a flash, Melissa sat upright. "You'll do *what?*"

"Go to sleep, Melissa."

John leaned over her and switched off the light. Melissa lay awake, silently ranting for a long time.

John-Peter received an eclectic first Easter basket: a variety of colorful fresh fruits and vegetables from his parents, a plush green rabbit from his uncle, and one large, chocolate bunny from his grandparents, which John-Peter gave to Brian. The uncle could not coax his small nephew into a tiny bite, not even from one of the ears.

"Gack!" John-Peter gagged audibly and jerked away his face.

After a simple Easter breakfast prepared by Brian, Steve and John banished everyone from the kitchen to begin cooking Easter dinner. So Melissa and Darlene accompanied Brian and John-Peter to the neighborhood park and gossiped while Brian pushed the baby on a swing.

Melissa explained to her mother about the accelerated program she would begin that summer at Jenson College and

John's work schedule adjustment. As Darlene listened to her daughter's convoluted plans, a wistful expression crept over her face.

"Hon," she gently said, "Don't you ever wish you waited to tackle adulthood?"

In that moment, Melissa clearly saw the wall between her life and the one she had left behind. She could never convey to her mother just what marriage to John meant. How could she reveal the bargain she'd made with John several years ago in Munsonville? What would her family say if they knew John had drunk her blood in her bedroom and that she still shared her blood with him for his own survival?

"Of course not." Melissa shielded her eyes and watched Brian swinging with John-Peter on his lap. The baby clung to the chains, but he gazed upward at the trees while Brian gently moved the swing back and forth. "I love John, and I love my son. I wouldn't change my life for anything. Everyone goes through tough times."

Darlene smiled in reluctant resignation. "Well, he's a beautiful baby, Melissa, and I should know. I had two."

True to form, Steve and John prepared a veritable feast of food, more than anyone could consume in three sittings. By mid-afternoon, Steve and Brian had packed Darlene's car, ready to return to Grover's Park.

"Call me when you want to come home," Steve said.

He kissed Darlene good-bye, then turned to Melissa, hugged her hard, and said, "Holler if you need anything. You've filled your plate to heaping."

Melissa, crushed under Steve's embrace, could only manage a strangled, "Thanks, Steve."

Only with the greatest disinclination did Brian relinquish John-Peter to the floor. "Bye," he said. "See you in a couple of weeks."

"Bon voyage," John-Peter said, as he darted to the piano.

The pleasant atmosphere lasted less than twenty-four hours, just long enough for John bring the mail inside the house and open it.

"Damn!"

"What?"

"More medical bills." John slapped the invoices onto the heaping stack on his desk.

"What about our health insurance?" Melissa asked anxiously.

"Health insurance won't cover Debbie's prenatal care, John-Peter's delivery, and my...treatments."

John looked so grim, Melissa thought a distraction might help. "Mom and I are heating up leftovers. Can you play for us while we do so?"

"No. I must leave."

John had not returned by the time Melissa had readied for bed. Darlene was settled in the nursery rocking chair with a book, planning to stay awake with John-Peter all night, if necessary. Neither one had mentioned John's disappearance. Sometime in the night, Melissa waked to John's kisses. Dazed and half-asleep, she valiantly struggled, and failed, to return them with the same frenzy in which he delivered them. John's ferocity frightened and exhilarated her; more than once, a pair of fangs burrowed into her neck. Paralyzed in the shadowy twilight of lucid dreaming and full alertness, Melissa could only surrender to an engulfing, indestructible force that plunged her below the surface of her will and interminably ravaged any portion of her soul she had not yet relinquished to him.

As Melissa stirred from oblivion to full consciousness, her sight fell upon her husband who, sleepy and wan in the morning sunshine, hardly appeared beastly. Melissa, under the guise of brushing back her hair, ran her palm lightly over her neck. No wounds. Had last night really occurred? She started to sit up, but John set his hand over her chest and pushed her back.

"I've accepted a second job," John said.

By the resolute expression on John's face, Melissa knew this would not be good. "What kind of second job?" she warily asked.

"Delivering newspapers in the middle of the night."

"John, how can you....?"

"I need to pay the medical bills."

"Can't we make payments?"

John leaned very close and stressed each word in a low even voice. "My salary won't cover post-vampire care."

She recoiled at this rebuff and asked in a small voice, "Who's going to stay with John-Peter while I sleep?"

"That's the best part," John said, good humor returning as he rose from the bed. "I can take him with me."

With Darlene there to help, John spent most of the day at Jenson College. He arrived home, quiet, but refreshed, in time for dinner. Later that night, when Melissa emerged from the bathroom after taking a shower, father and son sat poised on the piano bench, waiting for her.

"Play!" John-Peter bounced in eagerness.

And John played, piece after piece, until the walls rippled with music. After two hours, Melissa's head was nodding on her chest, although John showed no signs of slowing. A solitary note and an abrupt stop of the music jerked Melissa awake.

"Go to bed, Melissa," John said, "before you fall onto the floor."

"What about you?" Melissa's voice slurred as unbidden sleep overcame her.

"I'll stop when John-Peter gets tired."

Melissa looked dubious. John-Peter, face still aglow with excitement, appeared nowhere ready for slumber.

"All right, John."

She shuffled to the bedroom. Her head fell onto her pillow, and she groped for the blanket as the music wafted through the cracks in the door. Melissa woke inside Simons Mansion as the first rays of dawn pierced the darkness of her room. The sounds of John's piano floated up the stairs toward her. Why, John certainly was playing early. Melissa decided to surprise him.

Now fully dressed, Melissa poised with one foot at the landing, ready to descend the staircase, wavering. John hated when anyone disturbed him at the piano. Would her presence fill him with joy or anger? She remembered the long performance John executed for her that evening, with John-Peter, their very own son, sitting by his side. All doubts vanished as Melissa took the stairs by twos, just as Bryony did when no one, especially John, was looking.

Yet as Melissa reached the door of the music room, John began playing *Bryony*. Hopes again crushed, Melissa's hand hung suspended above the door knob. She could never compete against Bryony. Worse, John would resent her intrusion upon his private moment, maybe even hate her for it. Even now, Melissa felt John's fury oozing through the door like the mist now curling about Melissa's feet.

Melissa blinked and sat up. No moonlight, and no mist, filtered into the inky dark bedroom. But something else did. Every note of *Bryony* resounded as clear as the finest tones of a crystal bell. Did John play it assuming that Melissa, sound asleep, would never hear and know? She squinted at the alarm clock. Nearly two o'clock in the morning. Hadn't John promised to quit when John-Peter went to bed?

Fully alert, temper rising, Melissa slid out of bed and opened the bedroom door, prepared to deliver the verbal assault she felt John deserved. In the unlit dining room, Melissa saw the little body of John-Peter kneeling at the piano playing *Bryony*. John was nowhere to be seen.

CHAPTER 20: UNRAVELING THE PAST

John flew out of the bathroom, grabbed her shoulders, and swung her around.

"Stop!" he hissed, and Melissa smelled toothpaste. "You're scaring the baby."

Her screams instantly dropped to strangled, anguished whimpers. A wailing John-Peter, still sat on the bench, his fingers hanging from his open mouth. Big tears splashed onto his cheeks; drool dripped from chin. His eyes looked wild with fright. Guilt doused Melissa's hysteria, and she quickly scooped John-Peter in her arms.

"It's all right, baby," Melissa cooed, stroking John-Peter's hair and rubbing his soft back.

John-Peter hiccupped, sniffed, and laid his head on Melissa's shoulder. Righteous anger rose afresh. She knew John could never forget Bryony, but this....

Melissa glared over her son at John. "How could you do it!"

"Do, what?"

"You taught him to play her song!"

Annoyance flickered over John's face, and Melissa swore she saw him roll his eyes.

"I most certainly did not," John said, but he avoided Melissa's accusing gaze by gathering his notes and closing the piano lid. "He just...picked it up." Then John's countenance softened, and he veered his gaze to one side. "Melissa, turn."

His concern disconcerted her even as it compelled her to obey him. With gentle fingers, John lifted strands of hair from her neck and said, "The bruises have returned."

"What!"

He pulled her nightgown away from her shoulders. "They're halfway down your back."

"Dr. Rothgard said I was fine!"

"Dr. Rothgard's apparently mistaken."

"Don't you like him?"

"I do, but I don't like those bruises."

"I'll call him in the morning. You're due for a check-up anyway." Melissa considered something else. "John, please don't mention this to my mother. I don't want to face questions I can't answer."

As she dropped back off to sleep, Melissa suddenly realized that her mother had slept through the entire commotion. Maybe, Melissa fuzzily thought as drowsiness overcame her, they hadn't sounded as loud as she had thought.

They saw him the next afternoon. Dr. Rothgard greeted them with unusual friendliness. He even chucked John-Peter under his chin, which the baby rewarded by banging his rattle on Dr. Rothgard's nose. That action did not perturb him the least bit.

"Cut the ceremony." John said, and his eyes were mean. "Stop the bruising."

"John, what the devil are you talking....?"

"The bruises on my neck," Melissa said.

A tinge of fear leaped into Dr. Rothgard's eyes, but it vanished as quickly as it came. "They're...back?"

John took a step forward, and Dr. Rothgard chuckled.

"Settle down, John, and don't be hasty. Society frowns on Old World vampire tactics. Melissa, let me examine you."

She pulled her hair away from her neck. Dr. Rothgard moved her head from side to side and looked up at John, perplexed.

"John, these are faded. I see no fresh bruises."

Why would Dr. Rothgard lie? Certainly, John could decipher the difference between a fresh bruise and an old one. Confused, Melissa looked up at her husband. "John?"

He ignored her. "For the money I pay you, we deserve better care. Rerun her blood work."

"John!" Melissa said, shocked. "I think you're out of line."

"You always do."

Melissa turned back to Dr. Rothgard. "I'm really sorry John's acting like this. We're just on edge with everything going on...." Her voiced trailed away when she realized Dr. Rothgard hadn't heard. Instead, he rubbed his chin and studied John in a most pensive manner.

"John, you win. I'll redo Melissa's blood work, and I'll draw it myself." Dr. Rothgard opened a drawer and removed several tubes. "But you're next."

"Good," John unbuttoned his sleeve. "Find the problem this time."

"Melissa, make a fist."

She complied, peeping at Dr. Rothgard's face as he swabbed her arm. Melissa almost laughed aloud at his amused expression. Dr. Rothgard wasn't mad. He was humoring John.

"A pinch."

Melissa winced as the needle pricked her skin. She watched Dr. Rothgard fill several vials with her blood. He untied the tourniquet and raised her arm, setting a cotton ball over the tiny wound and taping a bandage over it. He repeated the process with John. Next, Dr. Rothgard examined John from top to bottom.

"You health appears perfect." Dr. Rothgard slid the stethoscope off his neck. "How are the blood treatments working for you?"

"Fine."

"Any symptoms?"

"No."

"Any concerns?"

"Have I called your office?"

"Hmm. I'm wasting my time talking with you." Dr. Rothgard opened the middle drawer, removed a sheet of paper, and handed it to Melissa.

"Contact me immediately if John exhibits these symptoms or if any aspect of his behavior concerns you. My number is at the bottom."

Dr. Rothgard patted John-Peter's head but nodded at Melissa. "Keep up the good work," he said, then exited the room.

Melissa scanned through the list. Daytime drowsiness. Craving for rare or raw meat. Decreased urination or sex drive. Extreme mood swings or aggression.

John snatched the paper, wadded it into a tight ball, and tossed it into the garbage can. "I'm fine. When that changes, I'll let you know."

Melissa retrieved it and tucked it into her jacket pocket. "Dr. Rothgard gave this to me, not to you. Don't you remember what he said months ago? If the vampirism returns, you won't have the sense to call him."

"Yes, I would. I'm not going back."

She patted the paper through her coat. "Then you shouldn't care if I hang onto this." Melissa started to slide John-Peter into his sweatshirt, but he fought her attempts to clothe him in it.

"Hungry, Mother!"

John picked up the baby and the jacket. "Let's go. He can eat in the car."

The next few months passed in a blur, especially since they no longer had Darlene to help them. Melissa had little contact with John that summer and during the fall semester. Because John kept John-Peter up by night with him, the baby had no trouble sleeping during the day while Melissa attended school. When she returned home in the late afternoon, John, in shirt and tie, picked up his briefcase, lightly kissed her good-bye, and strode out the door. Melissa spent quiet, albeit entertaining, evenings with her son. Although not quite a year old, John-Peter spoke in complete sentences and played several piano compositions with ease. Melissa did not know when John-Peter practiced, but she suspected it happened during school hours when John oversaw her son's care. She wondered if they rehearsed songs from the past; she wondered if either of them played *Bryony.*

John-Peter's red hair grew long and tangled; he had no fondness for baths or combs. Only when John-Peter pushed the limits of hygienic decency, did John assume his rightful magisterial role and bullied the boy into the bathtub. Yet, just as often as not, John let the matter slide rather than fight, a stance that surprised Melissa, long accustomed to John's controlling nature.

The only quirk of the son that irritated and frustrated his father was the continual misplacement of footwear. The baby simply refused to keep shoes on his feet, preferring to toddle on his natural soles, which conflicted with trips to the grocery store and the running of errands. John-Peter's shoe budget began rivaling his food budget.

"How can one baby misplace so many shoes?" John said one night as he crawled around the living room floor and peeked under the furniture.

Melissa's head popped up from behind the couch. "Maybe you should leave John-Peter here. You can't take him into the distribution center without shoes."

"Tonight, and only tonight, he'll wear several pairs of socks."

The next afternoon, John purchased two more pairs of shoes, one to remain in his car and the second to reside on the top shelf of his closet until an occasion arose that required

John-Peter to be shod. That very night, the baby threw the shoes out the opposite car window as John heaved the first newspaper out his. John's retribution was quick and fierce. No piano time for a week. The consequence worked. Although John-Peter continued walking about the house barefoot, he never again lost another pair of shoes.

Her lack of closeness with John, however, dismayed and disheartened Melissa. She missed John terribly and seriously considered easing away from her degree just to regain their lost time as a couple. To compound Melissa's misery, John didn't seem at all affected by their increasing distance from each other.

"I miss you in bed with me," Melissa told John one night as he readied to leave. "Even just sleeping. Don't you?"

John glanced down at her with a mixture of incredulity and disgust. "How can you ask? I, too, detest it, but, for the present time, I see no other alternative."

His callousness cut deeply, and Melissa's eyes filled with tears. John noticed, and his eyes narrowed but then just as suddenly, his expression mellowed. He drew Melissa close to him.

"Don't be discouraged, Melissa," John said in a kinder tone. "This is your last full school semester. Remember, you begin your internship after Christmas."

Nevertheless, John momentarily abandoned his lofty commitment to Melissa's education when she shared with him the location of her student teaching.

"*Munsonville!* Why?"

"John, how can you ask 'why'? You know why!"

"Because of your feelings for Henry? You're married to me, remember?"

"I don't have feelings like that for him. We became friends and he inspired me."

"Did you kiss him?"

Melissa said nothing. John, of all people, should know a kiss from anyone except Bryony meant nothing to Henry.

"Henry didn't befriend women, Melissa."

"You're wrong! Besides, why should you care who's important to me? You're still in love with Bryony."

Melissa dealt a low blow, and she knew it. Without another word, John reached for his briefcase and sped out the back door, slamming it behind him.

Because the newspaper route required a seven-day a week commitment, Melissa and John stayed in Jenson for Thanksgiving, John-Peter's first birthday, and Christmas; Darlene, Steve, and Brian traveled to Jenson to celebrate those special occasions with them. In January, a family check-up with Dr. Rothgard brought welcomed good news. Despite placing on the low end of the growth charts, John-Peter was now definitely thriving. John's blood treatments were pronounced successful. Melissa's bruises had become ancient history. But January also brought sadness. Melissa was leaving Jenson.

To help save money, Ann had suggested Melissa stay with her and Jack during the week and return home only on the weekends. Melissa felt torn. She despised the chasm between her and John; she feared leaving town would widen it. Furthermore, she dreaded prolonged separation from John-Peter. And yet, Melissa yearned to escape, for loneliness plagued her when John was most near. He had not touched her in many, many months, not since beginning that detestable newspaper route.

So, taking a deep breath and fearing his worse reaction, Melissa had told him, but John only said, "And my blood treatments?"

"I'll be home every weekend to give them to you."

"Then I agree with Ann. Since you're quite attached to Munsonville, you should go."

Panic seized Melissa. She was losing John, and he didn't care. "Who will keep John-Peter while you teach at night?"

"That's my problem."

Since John would not budge, Melissa, with a heart full of unsaid words and uncried tears, packed her suitcases for Munsonville. Even John-Peter did not appear sad at her departure. Didn't she mean anything to them at all?

John's good-bye kiss was casual, and he held John-Peter when he delivered it. The baby flung his arms around Melissa neck and planted a huge, wet kiss on her lips. "I shall see you Saturday, Mother."

She had trapped herself in a misery of her own making, for, deep inside, Melissa knew she could never make John love her; moreover, she now knew it had been foolish to try. Melissa student taught under this blanket of despair and allowed this last of her school years to waft away like mist before her eyes. As if in a dream, Melissa stood in the familiar classroom and taught the same English lessons Harold Masters had once taught her. She stared in disbelief at the youthful, trusting faces gazing back at her and realized that, just a few short years ago, she was one of those kids.

At night, Melissa sought asylum in Ann and Jack's spare bedroom, blocking out their frequent arguments while Melissa planned the next day's lessons. They fought over money; they fought over Jack's drinking; they fought over the state of Ann's poor housekeeping; they fought over Trenton; they fought over Sue's Diner; and they fought over the second baby Ann was now expecting.

On Friday afternoons, Melissa couldn't hurry home fast enough, but, on Sunday evenings, Melissa just as eagerly hurried back to Munsonville, away from the man who grew farther apart from her every week. She had still not returned to the Simons estate; she brooded over why she avoided it. Under the guise of classroom research, Melissa often passed hours at Munsonville Public Library where she gazed at the oil painting of John Simons and dwelled on her girlish fantasies. Her wishes of a life with John had come true, and yet, at the same time, they had eluded her. Why wouldn't the magic return?

One warm spring afternoon, Melissa did it. Perhaps the tender greenery sprouting up from the ground beckoned her, or perhaps the warm wisps of wind stirring the air also stirred inside Melissa her buried feelings for the past. Either way, when the final school bell for the day had rung, Melissa headed for the road leading to the former Simons estate. As she turned onto that familiar drive, she glanced backward at the entrance to the woods. Of course, she saw no mist. Why should she? The vampire had defected to Jenson.

As she neared the top of the hill, Melissa half fancied Simons Mansion before her, but when she reached it, she saw only saw mothers pushing squealing tots on swings and older children chasing each other in a swift game of tag. She meandered along the drive, past the back of the estate until she reached the old servant's cottage. A fence and a *No Trespassing* sign prevented admittance, but Melissa tugged the gate anyway. In the distance, a man looked up from his gardening work, waved, and dashed to meet her.

"I'm sorry, miss, but no one is allowed back here," the man huffed and puffed.

"How come?"

"It's a maintenance office, miss. We store all of our equipment and supplies here. You're welcome to wander about the rest of the park."

Melissa thanked him and left. She desperately missed John and longed for the upcoming weekend, yet once back in Jenson, Melissa could not bridge the gulf. What had happened to John and her?

She stayed in Munsonville through the eighth grade and high school graduation ceremonies, returning to Jenson only one day before her own graduation at Jenson College. This time, leaving Munsonville did not sadden Melissa; she would return in the fall to begin her permanent teaching position. Melissa delayed sharing those plans with John. Somehow, their future together had disintegrated. Besides, she had an entire summer to enlighten him. In the meantime, perhaps they could rebuild their lives.

Melissa accepted her diploma in the same haze as she accepted joyous embraces and congratulations. Her mother cried with joy and pride; Steve looked as if he might do the same. Even Brian hugged her. Looking up, Melissa saw, in the distance, her husband and son. Breaking free from the group, Melissa hurried to meet her other family. John-Peter noticed her first and waved.

"Mother!" John Peter escaped from John's grasp and rushed toward Melissa. He was waving a piece of paper. "I drew this for you!"

Melissa scooped the boy in her arms and look at his masterpiece: a childish likeness of her face surrounded by an abstract blend of earthen colors.

Anxiety marked his face as John-Peter searched her eyes. "Do you like it?"

She smiled and kissed him. "I love it."

John-Peter squirmed in her arms. "There's Uncle Brian! Down, Mother!"

Melissa set the boy on the ground, and he ran toward Brian. John edged closer to her, and she let him. He kept one hand behind his back while he caressed her with the other.

As he drew away, Melissa saw John's eyes shine with pride and another emotion that she could not read.

"Congratulations, Melissa," he said in a low, gruff voice.

With a flourish, John removed his hand from behind his back and offered Melissa his gift.

It was a bouquet of one dozen purple roses.

CHAPTER 21: ENTER THE JESTER

At dusk the following evening, as Melissa carried the kitchen garbage bag to the cans behind the garage, a large German shepherd bounded into the yard and knocked her down.

"Prince!" a voice from next door called out.

With a groan, Melissa gingerly rolled onto her side and slowly sat up. A slender young woman, long sleek hair flying behind her, dashed into the yard toward the dog. The shepherd recognized her and sped away.

"And don't leave again, ya hear?"

After spinning around three times, the dog dropped to the ground and panted.

The woman shook light brown hair out of her face. She seemed barely older than Melissa.

"Sorry," the woman said. "He never strays. Excitement of the move, I guess."

"Um...."

"I'm Penny Blake, and that there is my dog, Prince. My husband Mark is around here someplace. We have a boy, Andy, who will start school in the fall. You got any kids?"

"Yes, but he's still a baby." Melissa eased herself to a standing position. She'd sure feel sore tomorrow. "I'm Melissa Simotes. My husband, John, is a music professor at Jenson College."

"Nice! Well, gotta to go. Lots of unpacking. Good meetin' you, Melissa."

By the time Melissa returned inside, John had finished the dishes and was wiping the counters with a rag. John-Peter sat at the kitchen table with a large sheet of paper spread before him. With meticulous care, the baby dripped dots of green watercolors in groups of triple spirals.

"I just met the new neighbors." Melissa stretched a fresh bag around the lip of the can.

"New neighbors?"

"They have a little boy and a dog."

He wrung the dishrag into the sink. "John-Peter and I are leaving for the grocery store. Care to accompany us?"

"Sure!"

The phone rang just as they prepared to go. John held out the receiver. "It's for you." He removed John-Peter from Melissa's arms as she reached for the phone.

"Who is it?" Melissa mouthed, but John had already turned away, so Melissa, wondering, timidly asked, "Hello?"

"Hi, Melissa! It's Katie!"

"Katie?"

The other girl giggled. "Did Julie tell you I got married?"

"She did."

"Well, my husband's working on this project so we're living in Munsonville for awhile. Can you have dinner with us tomorrow night? Please?"

"I don't know. I'm just walking out the door. May I call you back?"

"Sure!"

Melissa jotted Katie's number, hung up, and then recapped the conversation, including the dinner invitation.

"What do you think, John? Should we go?"

"If you wish. Summer school doesn't begin for a week."

"Oh, thank you!" She lightly kissed his cheek and then grinned mischievously. "I hear her husband's really old."

John held open the door for her. "That, Melissa, depends on your perspective."

As John methodically weaved through Keppler Brothers' produce section, John-Peter, sitting tall and erect in the grocery's cart's baby seat and childishly swinging his legs, assumed control of the shopping list with the authority of a general leading his army.

"Apples, Father."

John inspected the fruit one by one before placing six into a plastic bag. "Next?"

"Spinach."

He selected a bunch, but John-Peter cried out, "No! Rotten!"

John separated the leaves and peered inside. "Where?"

The baby snatched the bundle from his father, inverted it, and spread apart the stems. "Here. See?"

"I do." John held up his next selection for John-Peter's approval. "And this one?"

"Perfect-o!" John-Peter wrinkled his forehead and pointed to the list. "Pronounce this word, Father."

John leaned over the cart. "Kohlrabi."

"Definition?"

"A vegetable related to cabbage."

Melissa marveled at their interaction. "He's amazing!"

"I merely taught him a few useful words. Since he reads music, why not?"

Back at home, John and John-Peter put the groceries away while Melissa returned Katie's phone call. Melissa marveled at the major changes in their lives since Ann's wedding last year. Katie even had a baby girl.

"I can't wait for you to see Karla; she's the cutest little thing, lots of black curls, just like her daddy. I'll bet John-Peter's really cute, too."

From the playful, frolicsome piano music filling the kitchen, Melissa knew it was John-Peter playing, not John.

"That's putting it mildly." Melissa then stuck a finger in one ear and pulled the cord to the basement landing. "Where are you staying, Katie?"

"Believe it or not, my parents are letting us keep the motor home in the back yard."

"You're kidding!"

"Nope. They seemed pretty upset about it at first, but they changed their minds when they saw how happy I am."

"Are you happy?"

"Of course, silly. I can't wait for you guys to meet my husband. I'm sure he will have lots in common with John. Cornell's a professor, too."

"He is?" Melissa wondered if Julie had not given her prejudiced information about Katie's situation. "What kind of professor?"

"He's a professor of the esoteric."

"The what!"

"The esoteric. You know, the occult."

"I know what esoteric means," Melissa said, losing patience with her old friend. "Katie, you can't be serious."

Katie giggled. "I sure am. Not only is he smart, he's very compassionate, which is why we travel around the country. That's all Cornell does is help people, kind of like an old-fashioned medicine man. He goes from place to place teaching people about the mystical world they can't see and fixing their problems."

This last statement did it for Melissa. "He solves their problems? For free?"

"Big problems, little problems; it doesn't matter to Cornell. He just likes doing good for people. Sometimes all a person needs is a charm to get that job promotion, but other times the problem is more serious, like when an evil spirit haunts a house. Cornell will go in there and get rid of it."

316

"He gets rid of the house?" Melissa couldn't take much more of Katie.

"Not the house, silly. Anyway, I'll see you tomorrow night. Cornell says I'm a great cook, but that's a given when you're on the road all the time."

Before John departed for the route that night, he woke Melissa, the first time in many, many months he had done so, but Melissa almost wished he'd passed. John's performance lacked the passion of the past; his mind and heart seemed far away.

After he and John-Peter left the house, Melissa lay brooding far into the night, mentally reviewing her short relationship with the living John and hunting for the cause of his changed heart. Even their lack of conflict bothered Melissa. How did a person address spousal complacency?

The deafening silence between her and John during their drive to Munsonville the next evening might have made a depressing trip had not John-Peter broken it by crooning loudly in an operatic voice.

Melissa held her hands to her ears. "What is he singing?"

"Gilbert and Sullivan. We watched a documentary last week, and he's become obsessed with them."

"So much for the theory that television rots the mind."

As they neared the Miller house at the top of Blue Gill Road, Melissa noticed the formidable presence of the large motor home parked in the back yard. John turned into the driveway and pulled close to the other vehicle.

Melissa groaned at the sight of it. "Can we go home?"

Amateurish paintings of astrologic symbols, hexagrams, and magic wands covered the motor home's white exterior. A sign painted across one side read: *The Thaumaturgical World of Professor Cornell Dyer: Amulets, Fortune-Telling (with and without cards), Ghost-Hunting, Horoscopes, Numerology, Palm-Reading, Potions, Séances, Spells, and Vampire-Slaying.*

John nudged Melissa and grinned. "What! No window washing?"

"Please, let's just leave."

"And miss a delightful evening?" John turned off the ignition and glanced at the back seat. The baby lifted one sneakered foot for his father's approval.

"The sign says he kills vampires," Melissa persisted. "It's not safe."

John opened his door, John-Peter's cue for unbuckling his car seat and scrambling out of the car. "I'll take my chances."

"Aren't you scared?"

"Terrified. But we vampires like to live dangerously. It's in our blood."

Melissa held her head and groaned again. "John, that's so old."

"Look again, Melissa. So am I."

Katie must have heard their arrival for she flung open the vehicle's main door before Melissa knocked.

"Melissa!" She threw her arms around her friend's neck. "Cornell, they're here!"

Except for the blush on her cheek and the deep glow in her cornflower eyes, Katie hadn't changed. She still had her baby fat, and she still combed her hair to one side and held it in place with a shiny gold metal barrette. In a huge display of exuberant affection, Katie wrapped her arms around the three of them in a single embrace. John-Peter brushed his hair out of his eyes and stared at Katie as if she were mad.

"Oh, Melissa, your little boy's so cute! Johnny, Al says not to be a stranger."

"Tell Al that works two ways."

"Cornell, these are my friends, Melissa and Johnny Simotes and their son, John-Peter."

The tall and bulky Cornell Dyer, dressed in bleached and faded jeans taut at the seams, a T-shirt tightly stretched over his barreled chest, and blazer patched in colorful squares of polyester, reminded Melissa of a giant Panda, albeit one with a mop of thick, curly black hair and a small-squared off mustache, as he lumbered to the front door to greet them. The soft hand that shook hers in a hearty greeting resembled a large marshmallow; the lips that kissed her cheek felt like a wet sponge. Melissa glanced up at John. Did he also feel repulsed?

But John stood in the doorway of the living room, with John-Peter's arm looped around his leg, intently surveying its cramped contents. Every wall held either shelves of books relating to the supernatural or chained, bolted, and padlocked cabinets. Was that supposed to impress people? How could Katie fall for this nut? Cornell looked as phony as they came. Melissa again tried catching John's eye.

Katie held her hand up to her face, leaned close to Melissa's ear, and spoke in the type of hushed voice one generally reserved for religious ceremonies.

"You might think Cornell's overly cautious with the locks," Katie whispered, "but he keeps all of his paraphernalia in there. Some of the ingredients for potions and things are really hard to come by. You can't be too careful in this business."

If ever an alarm clock needed to whisk me back to reality, Melissa thought. Aloud she said, "I'd hate to run out of eye of newt at a pivotal moment."

Her friend's face lit up. "Oh, good, Melissa, you *do* understand." In the distance, Melissa heard a baby's cry. "I'll be right back. I've got to get Karla."

John slowly moved about the room and then stopped abruptly, pulled a book from the shelf, and held it up for Cornell to see.

"How did you obtain this?"

Cornell smiled. "Ah, a good friend gave it to me for my last birthday. You must be a clever man if you know that tome."

"No copies exist."

"Well, as you can see for yourself, that is not entirely true."

John turned back to the book and shook his head. "Amazing."

"What book is it, John?" Melissa said.

"The Alchemy of Sir Wallace P. Erkart."

"I'm sorry?"

"It's an ancient, but completely mythical, collection of incantations and metaphysical methodologies."

Book in hand, John absently sank into a chair. John-Peter crawled onto his lap and read along with his father. With unusual reverence, John carefully turned the book's brittle pages.

"Through the ages, many workers of the dark arts referred to this book, but no one has ever produced one," John murmured.

Cornell, looking pleased, approached John with a decanter. "Some wine, my friend?"

John nodded, but he remained bent over the book. Cornell poured the crimson beverage and then raised his glass. "A toast! To old friends and new!"

Still reading, John returned the gesture. Cornell clinked his against John's and, to Melissa's surprise, John glanced up at him and warmly smiled.

Katie returned with the baby, extraordinarily striking with Katie's little face, pug nose, big blue eyes, Cornell's dark curls, and black lashes fringing her eyebrows when she opened her eyes.

"She's really friendly. Do you want to hold her, Melissa? I've got to check dinner."

Melissa accepted the baby from Katie and settled in the rocking chair. Karla gazed openly at Melissa with those lovely eyes. What a sweet baby! Before long and still clutching a potholder, Katie leaned in the doorway and announced, "Dinner's ready, guys."

Cornell removed the tome from John's hands. Reluctantly, John let it go.

"Come, let us dine," Cornell said. "The book will be here when we return."

Katie hadn't exaggerated about her cooking. Even John pronounced the meal "excellent."

"Where did you learn to cook so well?" he said, accepting a second helping of Chicken Primavera from Cornell.

She blushed at John's compliment. "From cookbooks. I read a lot when we're traveling. Cornell's not a picky eater so that gives me plenty of room to experiment."

Cornell patted his hefty stomach. "You see what comes of indulging my wife."

After dinner, Cornell and John retreated to the living room with John-Peter prancing at his father's heels. Katie left to lay the sleeping baby down in her crib. In Katie's absence, Melissa rinsed and stacked the dirty dishes.

"Melissa, that's not necessary," Katie protested when she returned.

"Are you kidding? It's almost like a treat. John washes the dishes at home."

"Well, okay. You can dry."

Katie talked so fast and so long about Cornell and his work that she had washed half the dishes before she paused long enough for Melissa to interject, "How did you meet him, Katie?"

"At a séance. A friend of mine from beauty school hosted one of Cornell's specials. It really was love at first sight. We just couldn't stand to be apart from each other, but he had appointments to keep. So what choice did I have but to run away with him?"

"I hope you'll be that understanding of Karla when she does the same thing someday."

Katie disregarded that remark. "My parents were bent out of shape about it for awhile, but what could I do? Fight fate? Anyone can see Cornell and I belong together."

Melissa bit her tongue and changed the subject. "Cornell doesn't look sixty."

Her friend gave a little gasp and dropped the plastic cup she was washing. "Sixty! Who told you Cornell was sixty?"

"I don't remember," Melissa lied.

"The idea! Cornell's only fifty-one."

They stayed at the kitchen table talking about Melissa's student teaching and the possibility of Katie finishing beauty school if she and Cornell remained in Munsonville for a few months.

"How long do you usually stay in one place?"

"It depends what someone needs from Cornell. He's doing research right now, so we're stuck until he's done."

"Research on what?"

The grandfather clock in the next room struck midnight. The route!

"Hold on, Katie. I need to talk to John."

She walked into the living room where Cornell and John conversed in low tones. John-Peter leaned against his father's chest, sound asleep. John's head lay on the back of the chair, but his arms clasped his son.

"Excuse me."

Both men turned at the sound of Melissa's voice.

"I hate to interrupt, but John works tonight."

John's eyes flew to the clock; immediately he was on his feet. With a slight grimace, John-Peter cracked opened his eyes and then returned to dreamland. Cornell rose and offered John his hand.

"Thank you, Mr. Simotes, for the pleasure of your company this evening. Perhaps we can do it again?"

"Absolutely."

Melissa and Katie said quick good-byes as John hurried out to the car.

"Let's get together soon," Katie said.

"Sure," Melissa agreed without enthusiasm.

The combination of the dull evening and quiet ride home lulled Melissa to sleep. She didn't realize John had pulled into the driveway until he jiggled her shoulder. She awoke with a start.

"I'll wait here until you're safely in the house."

"You're not coming in?"

"No."

Melissa hesitated before reaching for the handle, but John made no move to kiss her. Sighing, Melissa opened the car door and put one foot on the ground.

Clang!

John's door flew opened, and he leaped from the car, taking big steps toward the back of the garage. At the same time, Penny Blake dashed across her lawn toward their house. An unearthly screaming wail pierced the night.

"Hey, you monster!" Melissa heard Penny shout. "Let go of my dog!"

"Mother!" John-Peter was instantly wide awake and excited. "She saw a monster!"

"John-Peter, be quiet." Melissa strained to hear more, but her ears met only with silence.

An eternity passed before John emerged from behind the garage, and Penny led away Prince. The dog jerked at his chain and snarled at John. Melissa huddled inside the car until John returned. She hadn't realized the dog was vicious. She wished the Blakes had never moved to Jenson. What would she do as John-Peter grew older and clamored to play outside?

John opened the car door. "It's fine, now Melissa. Hurry up and get inside. I'm late."

Melissa quickly exited the vehicle and scurried up the stairs. By the time she had closed the back door, John's headlights were passing the kitchen window. With the terror of the dog's antics waning, drowsiness hit Melissa full force. She fell asleep the moment her head met the pillow.

A light flashed in her eyes. John had turned on the nightstand lamp. He sat on the bed and began removing his shoes. Melissa propped herself on an elbow and watched him.

"Hi," she whispered.

"Hi." John slid off a sock.

"I'm glad you had fun at Katie's tonight."

John's tired face remained solemn. "I'm glad you suggested it. Cornell Dyer is quite the revolutionary."

The mention of Cornell Dyer irritated Melissa. "How can you talk all night to a man who sells rabbits feet for a living?"

The sober look continued on John's face as he removed his belt and slid his pants to the floor. "That book...."

"Oh come on, John! The book's a fake."

"You're wrong. That book, and plenty of his other material, too, is genuine and accurate. I believe Cornell."

"I'm going back to sleep." Melissa switched off the light and flopped onto her pillow. John stretched out next to her in the dark.

"Melissa, you would not believe the voluminous amounts of research this man has singlehandedly accomplished and documented. He's filled shelves with the details of his experiments. They're referenced and cross-referenced, graphed and charted. I couldn't read it all if I spent every night there. The man's a pioneer into another realm."

"He's a glorified birthday party magician. Can't we forget about Cornell tonight and concentrate on other things?"

Melissa snuggled into John, but he rolled away from her, drawing the covers around his shoulders. She sighed in disbelief. "Come *on*, John...."

"I cannot fathom your cavalier attitude toward the supernatural. Have you forgotten what you married?"

"John...."

"How, perhaps, would your mother react to my blood treatments?"

An awful thought came to Melissa's mind. "You didn't tell Cornell Dyer!"

John rolled away and folded his pillow over his head. "I'm done talking, Melissa."

He slept until late that afternoon and then cooked a hasty dinner. After John had cleaned the kitchen, he gathered John-Peter into his arms and announced his intention to spend the remainder of the evening in Munsonville. Melissa made a face and looked back down at her book.

"Coming?" John asked scornfully.

"I don't think so." Melisa replied in a similar tone.

"Suit yourself." John slammed out of the house..

Having spent all day at home with the baby, Melissa did not relish a quiet evening at home without John. The silent piano and empty bench intensified her desolation. With a full and heavy heart, Melissa realized how accustomed she had become to John's nightly practices when he wasn't teaching. During those months she lived in Munsonvile, the only sound in the evenings was that of the junior Coopers screeching at each other.

Melissa finished that book and then scanned the bookshelves, seeking a childhood novel to soothe her, but the familiar balm failed to perform its duty. She spent the remainder of the evening wrapped under a blanket in her favorite chair, watching the children across the street playing hopscotch and hide and seek until dusk fell and mothers opened front doors, calling them home for baths.

She woke when John kissed her forehead from his return from the route and then stumbled into the bedroom after him. Hopefully, a second night in the presence of Cornell Dyer had satisfied John's desire for more.

Unfortunately, every day that week mimicked the one before it. John now rose late and cooked a quick supper before he and John-Peter departed for Munsonville. On Friday evening, John again invited Melissa to accompany him.

"I don't know," Melissa said as she tied the garbage. "Can't you just stay home tonight?"

"Except for work, I faithfully cared for my son while you finished school, remember? It's only for this week. Summer classes begin Monday."

"I know."

"So why are you acting so selfish?"

Hot tears stung Melissa's eyes. Selfish! Why didn't he want to be with her?

Melissa grabbed the garbage, pushed past John, and stomped out the back door. She marched all the way to the garbage can until her foot slid out from under her. She hit the ground hard, still clutching the bag.

She tried to stand, but her ankle hurt. Had she sprained it? Broken it? Bracing herself against the garage, Melissa painfully rose to her feet and looked around for the cause of her spill. The partial head of a squirrel stared up at her. She clapped a hand to her mouth and chocked back vomit. The back door banged, and Melissa heard footsteps. She removed her hand and yelled, "John!"

He reached her in seconds and followed her gaze. "That damn, mangy dog!"

John tossed the bag into the can and went for a shovel. Melissa closed her eyes while John scooped the squirrel into the trash.

"I'll talk to the Blakes tomorrow," John said, "and you no longer take out the garbage."

He offered his arm to Melissa to help her up, and she accepted it, feeling as if she had reconnected with the John in her Bryony dreams, save for the white tails. Reveling under his protection and care, Melissa limped into the house where John prepared an ice pack for her.

The next day, Melissa and John-Peter ate breakfast at Berkley's with Jenny before she went home to Oklahoma for the summer. Because Melissa had not visited with Jenny for a long time, they lingered into early afternoon over food and conversation while John-Peter colored on placemats.

A livid John met her at the back door. "Where have you been?"

"With Jenny. Didn't you read my note?"

John pointed to the kitchen table. His blood supplies sat out in perfect order.

Melissa slapped a hand to her forehead. "Oh, shoot! I forgot."

"You forgot?"

"I'm really sorry. I'm doing it now."

Melissa hurriedly plopped John-Peter on the living room floor and hobbled back to the kitchen. John scowled as she unwrapped the alcohol wipe and drummed his fingers on the tabletop while Melissa fumbled for a lancet.

That did it for Melissa. "How about a little appreciation?"

"On the contrary," and John's voice was low and menacing, "you owe me."

"Owe you?" Melissa's skin prickled, and she shivered with foreboding. "What do you mean, 'Owe you?'"

"You betrayed me."

"I did not. I saved Henry's life."

Melissa pricked her finger and offered it to John. He roughly pushed her hand away. With an infuriated sigh, Melissa grabbed another needle and said, "Stop acting like a baby. You need my blood to survive,"

"The blood you gave me for the high privilege of portraying my wife."

Something was very wrong, and it disquieted her with a queasy uneasiness. Her hand shook as she brought it down, and she rammed the needle into the side of her finger. In frustration, she slapped the lancet onto the table.

"Henry said that's how your mind worked. I traded you samples, not every drop in my body."

"I should have killed you."

"You tried! You sent me upstairs to die in a fire you set!"

That was a gamble. Melissa had no proof that John had set the fire.

"You brazenly showed up uninvited."

"I didn't," Melissa gouged a third finger and offered it to John. "Kellen stuck me there."

John sprang to his feet. "Kellen, too?"

"What do you mean, 'Kellen, too?' I'd never give Kellen my blood. I despise Kellen!"

John took two steps, and his fingers plunged into her shoulder. "Talk to me."

"Ow!" Melissa struggled to free John's grasp. "There's nothing to tell."

His other hand lightly encircled her throat, and he brought his face very close. The leer on his face paled to the malevolence flashing in his blue eyes and straining his low voice. "Talk...to...me."

"Kellen jerked me around some stupid time warp," Melissa pulled hard, but John's hand was relentless, "and talked about how he became a vampire."

"And?"

"And he told me how good your blood tasted, that you were done with me, and that I had beaten you at your own game."

"And?"

"And that I would make a fitting assistant to him."

Insistent fingers sank deeper. "You refused."

"John, of course I did. I love you!"

Why did John look like that? Melissa shrank back, but John shook her shoulder. *"And?"*

"And Kellen said he was sending me back to the fate I deserved. The next thing I knew, I was standing in the library at Simons Mansion."

"So Kellen helped you escape the fire."

"I didn't escape. Bryony pushed me out the window."

The hand around her neck tightened; his voice became a strangled whisper. "Liar! All the years I...." He paused, swallowed hard, and looked away. "I'd know if she was there."

"I'm not lying!" Melissa choked out. "She did help me!"

John shoved Melissa back; she grabbed the table, and then John overthrew the table. John-Peter screamed. John wavered, flung open the back door, and disappeared.

Crying, moaning, and shaking, Melissa staggered to the living room and scooped up the baby. She stroked his matted hair, all the while murmuring, "There, there," but the rent in her heart ached worse than the prints from the hand of her husband. Even as a vampire, John had never struck her.

With the uppermost tip of his finger, John-Peter traced his mother's purple blotches and then howled louder. That sound returned Melissa to reality. She had to be strong now, for all three of them.

Still clutching her son, Melissa tripped over John's blood supplies and groped for the phone. She did not have to find the number. She had memorized it long ago, just in case.

"Answering service."

"May I please leave a message for Dr. Rothgard? There's a problem with my husband."

CHAPTER 22: FALLING APART

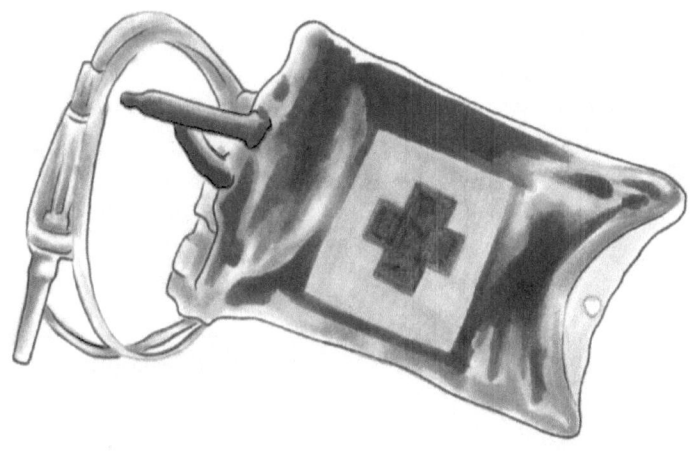

The phone rang, and Melissa braced a hand on the wall as she stepped over the kitchen table to answer it. "Hello?"

"How long ago did he leave?"

"Maybe ten or fifteen minutes ago."

"I'll be there in an hour. If he returns before I get there, don't let him in the house."

The dial tone hummed in her ear. Please, oh please, Dr. Rothgard, Melissa silently begged, please keep John from becoming a vampire.

Thank goodness John had not broken the table, but with her sprained ankle, Melissa would need Dr. Rothgard's help to set it upright. After first imprisoning John-Peter in his room, she hobbled around the kitchen, retrieving the scattered supplies for John's blood treatments and laying them on the counter.

In the background, John-Peter kicked at his door.

"Knock it off," Melissa shouted.

"Let me out!" the little voice loudly demanded over his kicks.

"No!"

Over John-Peter's intensified efforts, Melissa heard a knock at the front door.

"You have to wait," she called over her shoulder as she hurried to answer it.

"Father won't like that!" a faint voice retorted.

Melissa opened the door and Dr. Rothgard, carrying a large sack, pushed past her and onward to the kitchen. By the time she had joined him, he had turned the table on its legs and drawn up two chairs.

"Sit down. How much room do you have in your freezer?"

"Lots. John wanted to go grocery shopping today but didn't."

Dr. Rothgard opened the freezer door and stacked one frozen plastic bag after another inside it. He reserved two bags, placed them inside the sink, and ran cool water over them.

"What's inside them?" Melissa said.

"Blood."

From the medical bag, Dr. Rothgard had removed a box of gloves, a bottle, some needles, several tubes and rubber stoppers, a tourniquet, alcohol wipes, gauze, tape, and a box that said "biohazard."

"Where is your bathroom?"

Melissa pointed toward the sound of John-Peter's banging. "The middle door."

He grabbed the bottle and left the room. She heard the sound of running water over the din of John-Peter's angry feet. She opened her eyes when the chair next to her scraped on the floor. Dr. Rothgard was stretching a pair of gloves over his hands.

"Make a fist," he said.

He was filling the fifth vial when John's car pulled into the driveway. Dr Rothgard removed the gloves and tossed them into the garbage.

"Well," Dr. Rothgard said. "It didn't take long for John to get his fix, did it?"

John walked through the back door carrying a large brown paper grocery sack in each arm. If he seemed surprised to see Dr. Rothgard, he didn't show it. John merely leaned against the door to close it.

"I figured she'd call you," he said.

Dr. Rothgard regarded John equally as calmly. "That was your job."

"Stuff your vampire regeneration theories. We had an argument, and I left to cool down. Period."

"Melissa, where are your glasses?"

"Upper cabinet, left side of the sink."

More distant banging. *"Father!"*

John listened and then advanced toward Melissa. "You locked John-Peter in his bedroom?"

"Only until I cleaned...."

"How dare you?"

"Stop!"

John froze at the doctor's command. Dr. Rothgard finished pouring a bag of the thawed blood into the glass and said, "Get over here and drink this."

To Melissa's amazement, John snatched the glass from Dr. Rothgard's hands and drained its contents in one gulp. Dr. Rothgard opened another and before he could pour it, John grabbed it and quenched it straight from the bag. He didn't cringe; he didn't shudder. Where was the revulsion of John's earlier blood treatments?

"Satisfied?" John asked with a sneer in his voice.

Dr. Rothgard frowned. "Not yet. Lie down for an hour before I examine you. I want to ensure the treatment took."

"After I get my son."

John sauntered toward the nursery. Melissa heard John-Peter's exultant cries of "Father!" followed by John's low tones before the door closed.

Dr. Rothgard picked up the bag. "I'm putting this in my car. I'll be back in a minute."

"Wait, Dr. Rothgard."

He paused in the doorway and looked at Melissa. She took a deep breath before she continued. "Whose blood was that?"

"Yours."

"Mine? But... how? I never gave you that much blood."

Dr. Rothgard looked uncomfortable, but he said, "I created a synthetic version when I ran tests on you. I was hoping we'd never need it."

"So all that blood in the freezer is....?"

"Yours. For emergencies."

"And the blood you took today?"

"The foundational ingredients to make more, just in case."

The deception bothered her, yet she also appreciated Dr. Rothgard's rapid response to John's plight. While she contemplated this twist in John's and hers saga, Dr. Rothgard returned with a second medical bag, and John-Peter took a seat at the piano. Dr. Rothgard stretched out on the couch and set his bag on the floor beside him.

"Wake me in an hour, would you, Melissa? Had a rough night last night."

"No problem."

Dr. Rothgard closed his eyes. Quickly, he reopened them. "What the dickens is that child playing?"

"Chopin's piano concerto number one," John-Peter said, without missing a note.

Dr. Rothgard once again shut his eyes. "Remarkable."

The hour passed without incident. Melissa grabbed a book, burrowed into her favorite chair, and forced herself to concentrate on the plot over the doctor's snorting and snoring, John-Peter's practicing, and the knowledge that John reposed in the bedroom in a partial vampire state. She glanced at the clock. In ten more minutes she would wake Dr. Rothgard. But at the appointed time, the doctor grunted in his sleep, jerked, and sat up with a start.

"What time is it?" Dr. Rothgard demanded.

"Five o'clock."

"I'm going to check John."

Dr. Rothgard picked up his bag and walked to the bedroom. He rapped on the door and did not wait for an answer before he entered it, closing the door behind him. Melissa stretched her arms and returned to her book.

Fifteen minutes later, the doctor emerged. "When does John leave for work?"

"I'm not sure. It varies. I think about eleven or twelve."

"Let him rest until then, if he wishes. I think the crisis has passed. That's the good news. The bad news is that John now needs daily blood treatments, with an extra full glass of blood once a week. That should prevent further incidents."

Melissa involuntarily shuddered.

"I'm sorry, Melissa, but if you're still motivated to keep him human...."

"Of course I am!" Melissa insisted, more determined than ever to help John.

"How are you doing on supplies, alcohol wipes and the like?"

"I probably have enough for a week."

"Wait."

Dr. Rothgard opened his bag and pulled out a small square of paper, which he handed to Melissa.

"This will save you a trip into Shelby. Take this to Jenson Drugs and give it to the pharmacist. He'll know to bill me."

"Thanks!"

"And call me when you run low on blood."

"I will."

Dr. Rothgard looked across the room at John-Peter, still huddled over the piano keys. "Keep up the good work, young shaver. You'll give Beethoven a run for his money yet."

Melissa and John-Peter ate a quiet supper that night, hot dogs and canned baked beans, with John-Peter eating only the beans. After dinner, she gave John-Peter his vitamins, a ritual that accompanied every meal. How would they have coped without Dr. Rothgard?

John-Peter must have sensed trouble because he even allowed Melissa to sponge bathe him that night, although she did not quite dare to wash his hair. While her son napped, she debated the merits of crawling into bed next to John or staying awake until he and the baby left for the route. She fell asleep trying to decide. When she woke, dawn had just begun lightening the living room. In a sleepy haze, Melissa set the crumpled paperback on the end table and stumbled into the empty bedroom. She awakened the second time to bright morning sun and the comforting sensation of John's arm wrapped around her waist as he slept. John-Peter, also asleep, curled in a ball at the foot of their bed. Warm and content, Melissa laid her hand on John's as she drifted back to sleep.

Melissa expected some initial resistance from John to his new schedule of blood treatments, but he adjusted to them with surprising ease. For the next several weeks, no husband or father could outshine John in effort or accomplishment, and Melissa joyfully basked in her new life.

Instead of sleeping far into the day, John was now sitting at the piano everyday well before noon. Melissa amused herself by luxuriating in the childhood pleasure of reading until her eyes prickled. What a delicious vacation between the intense college studies and a fulltime teaching career. Melissa decided to savor it for as long as she could stretch it.

Once John awakened, the toddling figure of John-Peter never strayed far from him. Today, perched on a stool at the kitchen counter, John-Peter observed the dinner preparations, handing his father various ingredients as John called for them and combining items in a bowl when John requested it.

Melissa, who was reading the afternoon newspaper at the kitchen table while they were cooking, knew John-Peter longed to chop vegetables, too, but John had issued a moratorium on knives until John-Peter passed his second birthday and first demonstrated supervised competency of their use.

Which meant John-Peter, cheek propped by one hand, consoled himself with offering plenty of unsolicited advice as John prepared dinner.

"More sage, Father."

"There's plenty."

"You put in more last time."

"Slide the cutting board here."

"Mother doesn't like mushrooms."

"I know, John-Peter."

"And you don't like garlic?"

"Correct."

"You can add extra onions, though."

"I planned for it."

"Cut them really small or they stick to the roof of my mouth."

"Very well."

Silence except for the sound of sizzling vegetables. The fragrance of olive oil filled the air. A headline caught Melissa's attention: *Where oh where has my little dog gone?*

In the past three days, nine Jenson families have reported the disappearance of their pets. In all cases, the animals had been outside, but either leashed or safely confined in a fenced yard.

When the owners went to retrieve them, the animals had simply disappeared. None of the neighbors of the lost pets noted any suspicious activity near the homes where the animals vanished.

Melissa looked up. "John, listen to this." She read him the full story.

"That damn dog," John said and covered the pan with a lid.

Melissa folded the newspaper. "How can you be sure it's Prince?"

"He ran out of our yard one night with a kitten in his mouth. Smart, the way he's eluded even the police."

She cocked her head in surprise. John had never shared that with her. "You've called the police?"

"Absolutely. The safety of my family is at risk."

After dinner, John permitted John-Peter to slosh in the water under the guise of cleaning a dish or two, the only time John-Peter appeared to really enjoy getting wet. The baby still hated bath time.

"Look, Father, I'm a tsunami!"

John-Peter slammed his little fists into the water, spraying water out of the sink and onto the tile behind, the cabinets above, and the floor below.

"Correction," John said as he wiped his own face on a towel and lifted John-Peter off the chair. "You're finished."

Father and son retreated to the dining room where they commenced practice sessions at the piano, which, on nights John did not teach, continued long after Melissa had gone to bed. That suited Melissa just fine, because if the pair still concluded each mini concert with *Bryony,* Melissa did not wish to know it.

Weekends, though, broke the routine. John took them to the zoo, the beach, or an art museum. The only unpleasant moment on any of these family field trips occurred at the arboretum where John-Peter argued with their tour guide over the magical uses of bryony

"Some people call it the mandrake," the guide said.

"They're wrong," John-Peter said.

The guide peered down at the small boy in John's arms. "I beg your pardon?"

"Unscrupulous merchants eager to derive a quick profit would often sell bryony to gullible patrons," John-Peter looked up at his father. "Isn't that what you said?"

John shifted uneasily under Melissa's suspicious gaze. "Yes, that's what I said."

Because John had tried so hard to be good, because he had not embarked on one trip to Munsonville since summer school began, and because he had made dinner plans at Rudy's for his birthday, Melissa decided she could return the favor and invited the Dyers to dinner for an additional birthday celebration. While John cooked Hungarian beef for dinner, Melissa occupied her son in the living room where he read to her from a book of Grimm's fairy tales.

"Mother, why does the giant fish keep granting the fisherman's wife's every request?"

"I guess because it wants her to learn a lesson."

"I wish I was a powerful fish. I'd rule the sea and strike terror into anyone who dared approach me."

Before Melissa could answer him, a rumble outside the house caused John-Peter to toss the book onto the floor and to stand on Melissa's lap for a peek outside.

"They're here! I'm telling Father."

John-Peter leaped to the floor and raced to the kitchen to announce the good news. Melissa pulled the curtain aside. The giant recreational vehicle spanned the entire front yard and part of the driveway. She turned away before she noted the rest: *The Thaumaturgical World of Professor Cornell Dyer*. What would the neighbors think?

Melissa held open the door for Katie, who was cuddling the sleeping Karla in her arms. Cornell plodded up the front steps behind her, carrying a folding crib.

"Hey, Melissa, where can Cornell set this thing up?" Katie whispered.

"In the guest bedroom," Melissa said, keeping her voice soft.

Cornell joined John in the kitchen while Melissa toured Katie through the house. Katie declared John-Peter's room her favorite.

"I love all these fairies on the walls," an enchanted Katie said as she moved about the room examining each one. "Did you hire a professional?"

"No, a friend of mine from Grover's Park painted them for us as her baby present."

"I wish I had her talent. Look how lifelike they are! You can close your eyes and picture yourself in each scene. I'd love to meet a real fairy."

Since Katie was so affirming of Laura's work, Melissa decided to humor her. "Has Cornell ever seen a real fairy?"

Before Katie could open her mouth to reply, John-Peter pattered into the room. "Father says dinner is ready."

Melissa breathed a sigh of relief. She really hadn't wanted to hear Katie rattle paragraphs about the glorious exploits of the fraudulent soothsayer. Cornell, however, did not require Katie's public relations skills to promote his image. He monopolized the entire dinner conversation with anecdotes about haunted houses and the inherent danger involved when one hunted and manipulated the unseen spirit world.

"Do you hunt at night?" John-Peter said, sucking a spoonful of red sauce.

"Most of the time, yes," Cornell said with a wide smile.

John-Peter puffed out his chest. "Father hunts at night, too."

John flicked John-Peter's forearm, and the boy looked at him, aghast.

"Cornell," John said. "More wine?"

Cornell raised his glass as John reached for the bottle. "Gladly, my friend."

Melissa almost dropped the bowl of egg noodles she passed to Katie. What did John-Peter mean by saying that his father hunts at night, too?

After dinner, which included the last of the ice cream, John and John-Peter entertained their little audience with a variety of classical piano music, from the rollicking Hungarian dances of Brahms to the poignant sonatas of Schubert. At the completion of several, new original pieces, John announced John-Peter would conclude that night's concert with a selection he diligently practiced for several weeks: *Apres Midi d'un Faune,* by Debussy.

John-Peter, Melissa keenly noted, did not object to the omission of *Bryony*. Could it be that John had eliminated the song after all, and the little boy no longer remembered it?

Both Cornell and Katie gave John-Peter his first standing ovation.

"Ooh, I love that piece," Katie cooed. "It sounds just like fairy music."

"Bravo!" Cornell shouted. He whistled through his fingers. "Perhaps someday I will hear you play at Carnegie Hall."

Melissa watched John-Peter exchange a knowing glance with his father, and she bristled at the secret communication between them. Just how much did John-Peter know about John? *Father hunts at night, too.* Perhaps she needed a nice long talk with her son. Unfortunately, tonight was not the night. The Dyers stayed until John left for the route.

"Have a safe ride home," Melissa said from the confines of Katie's exuberant hug.

"Oh, don't worry about us," Katie said. "Cornell's an excellent driver."

"Au revoir!" John-Peter called from his father's arms as he waved his hand in a farewell gesture.

As tired as she was, Melissa could not fall asleep. Impressions of the past and present possessed her mind, more real than any specters Cornell Dyer claimed to have witnessed: A creature in the woods of her dreams, dressed in a suit, running on all fours, his golden mane streaming behind him. John's enthusiastic acceptance of Dr. Rothgard's glass of blood. John-Peter's childish declaration, "Father hunts at night, too."

The up and down movements of the mattress beneath Melissa's back jolted her awake. John-Peter bounced on the bed with all his might. When he saw Melissa crack open an eye, he began to sing, "Happy Birthday to you! Happy Birthday to you! Happy Birthday, dear Father! Happy...."

In seconds, John was awake. As he carried John-Peter to his crib, John said, "I told you to go to sleep."

"If you get up now, you'll have a longer birthday."

"I like short birthdays and plenty of rest."

John closed the bedroom door. In the dark, John slid under the covers and snuggled close to Melissa, nuzzling her neck. Instantly, she felt fully alert. John spent such a long time kissing and fondling her that the pink rays of dawn streaked across the quilt and the walls before he made any further move. Then, without warning, John's body sagged and he rolled away from her.

"Forget it," he mumbled.

What happened? Had she done something wrong? Was something bothering him?

Melissa touched his shoulder. "John?"

"We're losing the battle, Melissa," came the muffled reply.

Whatever was troubling John had disappeared by the time he and John-Peter woke for the day. They planned a mini birthday celebration for just the three of them, before Carol Simotes arrived for the weekend to babysit John-Peter. Melissa had picked up a cake from Berkley's, and John-Peter played *Happy Birthday* on the piano.

"Please, Father, may I light all thirty-two candles?" John-Peter squirmed with excitement at the prospect.

"I don't think so," Melissa said.

John struck a match.

"My hand won't get tired from lighting that many," John-Peter insisted.

John tried smothering a grin and failed. "Well, they might," he said, glancing at Melissa with playful mischief in his eyes, "if we light an accurate amount."

On the way to Shelby, Melissa wondered if someone hadn't flipped a switch inside John. Without warning, his mood darkened. John scowled as he drove and, despite her numerous attempts at light conversation, refused to speak to Melissa. The second the waiter seated them at the table, John left.

"Be right back," he muttered.

But John did not come right back. An hour passed and still no John. Melissa reluctantly submitted her order to the waiter. He had just delivered her salad when John staggered into the room, stumbled into the table, and toppled into the chair. Do not, Melissa ordered to herself, let him get to you.

To the waiter Melissa said, "Could you please bring my husband a menu?"

John waved away the request. "No need. I want a steak. Rare."

The waiter scribbled the order on his pad of paper. "Soup or salad?"

"Whatever."

"Baked potato?"

"Sure."

The waiter hurried to the kitchen with the order. Melissa picked at her salad and stared at John, who mocked the frightened concern on her face.

"What's your problem, Mrs. Simotes?"

"You ordered a rare steak."

"So?"

"So, you don't like rare steaks. John, what's wrong?"

"Here we go again! Must I explain my every move? It's a damn steak!"

"John, please lower your voice. Everyone's watching."

He leaped up, jerking the table and sloshing Melissa's water onto the linen cloth. Really afraid now, Melissa watched John remove his keys and hurl them into her salad. The force sent the plate sliding into her lap.

"Keep your pristine meal. I'll find my way home."

Bitter tears stung Melissa's eyes at this unexpected ending to John's birthday. What went wrong? John was cooperating with his blood treatments, so vampirism couldn't be the cause. She remembered John-Peter and the candles. Maybe, John disliked reminders of his true age. Inside, Melissa panicked. What had she done to upset him?

Melissa motioned for the waiter and canceled John's order. The waiter noticed the ruined salad and hastened to bring her another one. Melissa choked down the food, alone, trying hard not to cry and failing. The waiter refused the offered tip.

"Keep it," he said. "The evening should not be totally unpleasant for you."

Melissa drove a miserable ride home, compounded by her clumsiness at driving stick shift. She turned on the radio for company, but, again, it seemed every station played only love songs with piano music for background. In anguish, Melissa snapped it off.

No light shone from inside the house when Melissa pulled into the driveway. As she passed the side window, she saw the flickering colors of the television set and the back of Carol's head from where she sat on the couch. Melissa crossed her fingers, hoping John-Peter had donned his best behavior that evening.

As she locked the car door, Melissa heard a scuffle from behind the garage. She paused, key in hand and waited, heart thumping, to hear it again. This time, the sound of a thud greeted her ears.

"Who's there?" she called in a shaky voice.

Silence. On tottering legs, Melissa walked toward the back of the garage.

BANG!

Prince hurled himself at the garbage can, knocking its lid to the ground.

"Hey!" Melissa yelled.

Her voice startled the dog in mid-jump. He bumped into the can on the way back to the ground, tipping the can onto its side and spilling its contents all over the grass.

"Stupid dog!" Melissa yelled as the dog raced away from her yard.

She steered herself for the unpleasant task of picking up the mess. With squeamish hands, Melissa hoisted one torn bag into the garbage can and then gingerly reached for the second one. She dropped it in horror when she saw the maggots. Wrinkling her nose at the noxious smell, Melissa peered closely at the decaying slush on the ground. She'd found the missing neighborhood pets.

CHAPTER 23: NO HOLDS BARRED

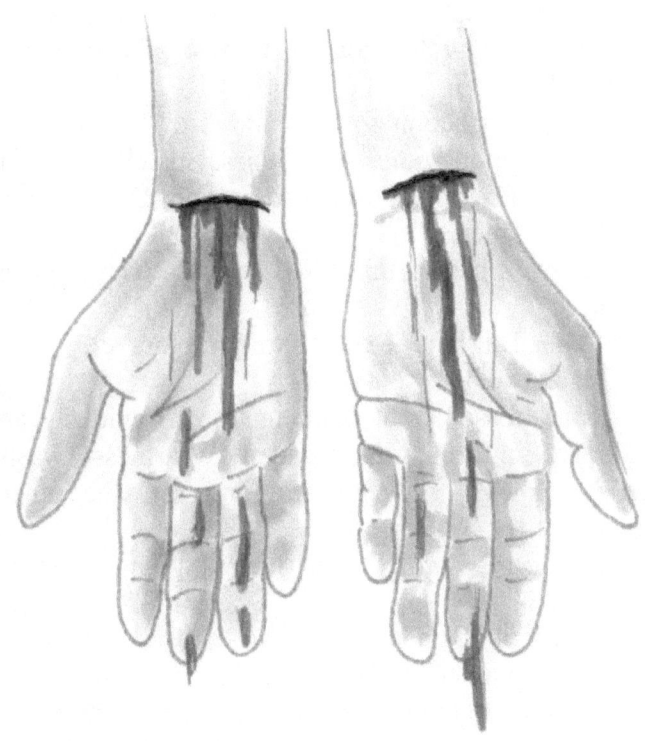

"Dr. Rothgard's answering service."

"This is Melissa Simotes," Melissa panted as she attempted to catch her breath, for she had run all the way into the house. "Please have Dr. Rothgard call me as quickly as possible."

"What's the problem, Mrs. Simotes?"

"My husband, John Simotes, is sick."

"And his symptoms?"

Could she trust the voice on the other end of the receiver? Should she tell the entire truth? Just how much did Dr. Rothgard's staff know about his practice anyway?

"He's, um, not eating right."

Carol walked into the kitchen as Melissa hung up the phone. "Melissa, what's wrong? Where's John?"

"I don't know."

Anxiety crept into Carol's voice. "What do you mean, 'You don't know?' I thought the two of you went to dinner together."

"We did, but John got mad and left."

The telephone rang, and Melissa snatched it off the hook. The male voice on the other end was not Dr. Rothgard's.

"Is John there?"

Melissa's heart sank. "No, he isn't. May I please take a message?"

"Yeah. Tell him he can't avoid me forever."

Click. The line went dead.

Arms crossed, foot tapping, Carol obviously anticipated additional information. Sudden weariness washed over Melissa. She looked at Carol and saw the other woman looked tired, too.

"I'm sorry, Carol. I don't have any answers for you. I...I wish I did."

Carol looked unconvinced, so Melissa smiled in her most reassuring manner. "John's probably tense over something at work." Then, to emphasize her stance, Melissa hugged Carol. "And thank you so much for watching John-Peter tonight. I know he can be a handful."

Her mother-in-law's face brightened. "Oh, Melissa, I forgot to tell you. He's potty-trained!"

"In one night?"

"I know he's young, but I was changing his diaper and thought, 'Why not at least introduce him to the concept?' He caught right on and refused another diaper."

Melissa thought about the other mothers at the park and nearly laughed out loud. Those women engaged in a running contest about whose child teethed first, walked first, and spoke first. The competition would soon die if Melissa ever decided to enter it.

"Where's John-Peter now?"

"In his room, reading."

Melissa walked to the nursery and tapped on the door. Her son lay on the floor, turning the pages of a large book.

"John-Peter, Grandma's going back to her motel. Come say 'good-bye' to her."

"Righto!"

John-Peter stood, stretched, and then trotted to the front door where Carol stood waiting for him. She picked him up and kissed his forehead.

"Be a good boy for your father on the route," Carol said. "He's not having an easy night."

The baby patted her cheek. "Not to worry, Grandma. Father's only grouchy when he's hungry."

"Maybe he should bring a snack with him." Carol looked expectantly at Melissa, and she squirmed under the older woman's gaze. John would scorn any lunch Melissa packed.

"No need," John-Peter said. "He always stops when we're out."

The phone rang as Carol walked out the door, and Melissa rushed to answer it.

"Melissa, what's the emergency?" Dr. Rothgard said.

She craned her head around the corner, but John-Peter was sitting in front of the television. Nevertheless, Melissa lowered her voice.

"I think John is killing and eating animals."

"What makes you think so?"

She told him about the vanishing pets, the mess she found inside the garbage can, Prince's behavior, John's insistence that he alone take out the garbage, and John-Peter's references to his father's hunting behaviors.

"Besides, he seems to be getting worse. We went to our favorite restaurant tonight for his birthday, but he created a scene and stormed out after he ordered a rare steak. John hates undercooked meat."

"Has he consumed any additional blood from the freezer?"

"I don't know. I'll check. Hang on."

Melissa set the receiver on the table and examined the freezer's contents. Three, maybe four, extra packets appeared to be missing. However, Melissa noticed something equally as bad as John's extra consumption of blood, but she could not dwell on it now. She reported the information to Dr. Rothgard.

"Where is John now?"

"I don't know. But he does have to leave for the route soon."

"When does he wake up for the day?"

"About noon."

"Hmm. I'll stop at your house tomorrow after work. About seven o'clock. Don't tell him."

"Thank you so much, Dr. Rothgard!"

"I'm here to help. Remember that."

After Melissa hung up the phone, she joined John-Peter on the couch. "What are you watching?"

"Life of Mozart."

"What station is carrying these documentaries?"

"Father said it's a student-operated station from the college. Its reception only travels a few blocks."

"Mind if I keep you company until your father comes home?"

John-Peter's face shone, and he snuggled into Melissa. The documentary fascinated John-Peter, but Melissa found it dry and amateurish. Her eyelids grew heavy. John-Peter shook her shoulder hard.

"Mother, wake up!"

Instantly, Melissa sat up straight. "What's wrong?"

By the light of the television, Melissa saw the somber expression on the little boy's face.

"Father's not home. We're late for the route."

She rubbed her eyes, trying to focus. "What time is it?"

"Two o'clock."

Two o'clock! Where had John gone? Melissa stalled, trying to think. "Maybe he went to the distribution center without you."

"No, Mother."

"Well, if he was running late...."

"He wouldn't go without me."

The finality in John-Peter's voice disturbed her. What made her son so certain John would be back for him?

"What happens if your father doesn't show up? Do they dock his pay?"

"They fire him."

Melissa shook her head in confusion. "Well then, whom do I call to say he's sick?"

"He's not sick, Mother."

What could she do? Melissa hated to see John lose the job since they still needed the money, but she didn't even know the location of the warehouse where John picked up his newspapers. She regarded John-Peter, who continued to stare at her with subdued, serious eyes while toying with an idea.

"John-Peter, do you know where your father works?"

"Of course. It's on the other side of Jenson."

"Okay, let's go."

A big smile unfolded on John-Peter's face. "Yippee! Mother's coming on the paper route!"

He slid off the couch and dashed into his bedroom, while Melissa eased the cramps from her arms and yawned. She had just located her car keys on the kitchen counter when John-Peter appeared at the back door, shoes on feet, jacket in hand, ready to go.

"Don't worry, Mother. It's easy."

With blissful confidence, John-Peter rattled the directions to Melissa as she drove through the quiet streets of downtown Jenson. Fifteen minutes later, John-Peter pointed toward a large building.

Lights blazed from the inside, a service door opened wide, and swarms of people milled about the parking lot, pushing shopping carts full of plastic-wrapped newspapers.

"Go around the back and park by Uncle Ed. That's what Father always does."

"Uncle Ed?"

"That's Father's boss."

Melissa steered the car into the alley that ran adjacent to the warehouse. No sooner had she turned off the ignition than John-Peter leaped from the car.

"John-Peter!"

The little boy tore into the building and disappeared amongst the throngs. Melissa followed him as fast as her feet could take her. She looked left and right but could not locate him. Where had he gone?

Finally she saw him, sitting on a workstation in the middle of the warehouse, near the left wall. John-Peter sorted piles of newspapers into various stacks. As she walked in his direction to join him, Melissa saw a pot-bellied, bespectacled, gray-haired man wearing blue jeans and a white and red-striped shirt. He was pushing a pallet jack full of newspapers toward the table where John-Peter sat.

Ed Calkins! The Steward of Tara!

Her son looked up from the stack of newspapers he was counting and waved to the man.

"Hi, Uncle Ed! I only need eight 'Thornton Times' today. We had a stop."

Ed paused and bent to count eight newspapers from a bundle before placing them on the table near John-Peter and asking, "How many 'Detroit Daily News?'"

"Sixty-three."

Walking around to the other side of the pallet, Ed lifted a bundle of newspapers and set it on the floor by the work station. Next, he cut the plastic strap from a second bundle and began silently counting.

"They're in bundles of fifty today, John-Peter," Ed handed the little boy the loose papers.

John-Peter recounted them and offered one back. "You gave me fourteen."

"I gave you an extra one, just in case. Your father was short one yesterday."

"Aye, aye, Captain."

John-Peter crawled to the other side of the station for a sleeve of blue bags, which he hung on a hook screwed into the plywood divider. He then pushed a stack of newspapers near the bags and proceeded to, one by one, fold the papers, slide them into a bag, and toss them into a nearby grocery cart.

Ed pulled the pallet to the next work station. "Where's your father tonight?" he called over his shoulder.

"Not here yet, but my mother is helping."

The man stopped, turned, and noticed Melissa. "You have quite a boy here."

"Thanks."

Ed continued down the aisle. Didn't he remember her?

"Mr. Calkins!"

He stopped again and faced her, one hand still grasping the handle of the jack. "Excuse me?"

Melissa hurried to reach him. "Don't you remember me?" The look on Ed's face showed he clearly did not, so Melissa tried again. "You offered me a job once."

Ed smiled a bland, polite smile. "In the newspaper business, you see a lot of people come and go."

"Hey, Ed!" a tall, thin man in army fatigues called from three work stations away. "My bundle's three papers short."

"Be right there!"

Ed and the pallet jack moved down the aisle. Melissa picked up the paperwork that lay on the table.

"How many different publications do you and your father deliver?"

John-Peter continued to bag. "Between five and seven, depending on the day."

"Well, I'm glad that *some* newspapers don't force its carriers to run around in the middle of the night."

Teenage boys and girls delivered the afternoon *Jenson Reporter,* or the "Jenson Joke" as John called it, from their bicycles to the porches of the town's neighborhoods. The small newspaper could not compete with the larger ones, and Melissa assumed its days were numbered, even with its low subscription price, the only reason John let her keep it in the first place. It cost him less than two dollars a month.

John burst onto the scene. He shoved a stack of newspapers to the other side of the table and then snapped its strap, which he tossed into an overflowing garbage can. The strap floated lazily to the floor. He coolly and silently counted the newspapers in that bundle.

"What are you doing here?" John said in his frostiest voice, not bothering to look at her.

"Saving your job," Melissa said in a voice she hoped sounded equally as nasty.

"Your help is unwanted."

"Tell me that tomorrow when you're due for a blood treatment."

"Hosts abound."

"Not with my blood."

What was John trying to prove by starting an argument?

"Well, anyway, you're late," Melissa said. "You can yell at me later. Right now, let's get these papers bagged so you guys can leave."

John-Peter beamed at the notion of working with both parents. "You may roll next to me, Mother."

John carried a stack of newspapers to Melissa and hung a sleeve of bags on the hook next to her. "I'm taking you home before I start throwing."

"That's fine."

As he rolled, John's mood continued to mellow so that by the time John began loading newspapers into his car, he was nearly genial. John-Peter scrambled into his car seat and buckled the straps. As Melissa walked behind the car to the passenger side, she sensed John's presence behind her. She slowed her pace and felt an arm go around her waist.

"Hey," John said in her ear as he pulled her close to him. He turned her around to face him, put a hand on each cheek, and lifted her face to look at her. "I'm sorry. My actions tonight were inexcusable."

Melissa softened under his touch. She had not expected it. Keep it light, she told herself. Don't anger him.

"It's okay," Melissa said. "Let's just forget it."

John kept one hand on her cheek and with the other one he swept the hair off her forehead and there dropped a tiny kiss.

"Thank you for your help tonight, Melissa," he said in a low voice.

She wrapped her arms around him and laid her head on his chest. He'd been so distant, and she'd been so afraid. Was it wrong to hope? What if his vampire nature won? What if she lost him forever?

"Father! Let's go!"

Slowly, reluctantly, Melissa slid free from John's grasp. "You don't have to take me home first, if you don't have time." She crossed her fingers, praying John would relent and take her on the route. She couldn't bear to part with him tonight, not after he'd held her so close.

"No," John said. "You need sleep."

In less than ten minutes, John had pulled into the driveway and dropped Melissa by the back door. Darkness still prevailed, but the sky had lightened. Would John get into trouble for being late? Deep sleep consumed her the second her head hit the pillow; she did not waken until shortly before noon. John never stirred until mid-afternoon.

The telephone call that filled her with dread never came until John was cooking dinner. Melissa recognized the man's voice as the one who had asked for John the previous night.

"Hold on. I'll get him." Melissa held out the phone to John. "It's for you."

From the moment John said, "Hello," a voice on the other end began ranting. John hung up the phone.

"Who was that?" Melissa said.

"It's Derek. He wants visitation with John-Peter."

"You're kidding! Why now?"

"He's claiming we used deceptive practices to adopt John-Peter. If we don't acquiesce to his demands, he'll sue us."

"You're not caving into him, are you?"

"Absolutely not! Worms have no rights as far as I'm concerned."

"What if he gets a lawyer?"

"He won't. Derek's a demented fool."

A banging interrupted the conversation. Before Melissa could leave the kitchen to answer it, John-Peter skipped into the room. "Mother, there's a man at the front door."

"I've told you not to talk to strangers!"

"I didn't. I peeked through the window."

The thumping grew louder. Melissa swung open the door as the large, burly man again raised a meaty fist.

Melissa glared at him. "May I help you?"

"Get your husband out here now!"

A stout, red-faced little boy stood next to him. He stuck out his tongue at John-Peter.

"John! I think you'd better come over here."

Melissa had no intention of inviting the unpleasant duo inside her home. The man began taking one step into the house, saw Melissa's angry face, and changed his mind.

John-Peter turned around and leered at the man. "Father's coming! Father's coming!"

Recognition flickered over the other boy's face when John walked into the room. The man's florid complexion grew dark crimson when he saw John.

"Name's Mark Blake. I live next door. My dog's dead, and my kid Andy saw you kill it."

John-Peter's eyes flashed with fury. "That's a lie! My father wouldn't hurt your decrepit beast!"

He tightened his fists and advanced toward the smirking Andy, but John's arm barred any further movement. John-Peter consoled himself by raising his fists and shooting his opponent his most threatening expression. John said nothing, which enraged Mark Blake.

"See here, Simotes, do I need to get the police?"

"Call the police." John calmly shut the door.

As they sat down to dinner, Melissa again heard a knock on the door; she also saw the shadows of revolving red lights. John left the room to talk to the police. Melissa studied the blue floral pattern on her plate and tried not to think.

"Father worked really hard to prepare a good dinner."

Melissa sighed. "I know John-Peter."

"He wouldn't want us to eat it cold."

"We're waiting for him anyway."

John returned to his place within a few minutes, unfolded his napkin, and helped himself to the platter of country fried steak. He then piled a mound of string beans on John-Peter's plate next to the baked potato. As he lifted his fork to his mouth, John noticed Melissa staring at him. "What?"

"John, what happened?"

"Nothing happened."

"You're not worried about that Blake guy?"

"I was at work last night, and I can prove it."

"You didn't....?"

John glanced at John-Peter, and Melissa fell silent. The boy busied himself with the string beans. One at a time, he pinched them between his forefinger and his thumb, leaned back his head, and dropped them down his throat.

His actions unnerved Melissa. "Stop that right now!"

John-Peter ignored her and opened his mouth wider for another green bean.

"John, make him stop. He'll choke."

"John-Peter, mind your manners at the dinner table."

"They're snakes," the boy said as he picked up another one and gave it the same treatment. He smacked his lips and turned cunning eyes at Melissa. "You want me to eat meat. Well, snakes are meat. Right, Father?"

John's voice grew stern. "Behave, or you'll get down."

"John, why have you stopped....?" Melissa allowed her voice to trail away. The question was leading to an answer she didn't want to hear.

John leaned slightly forward and studied her with the fixation of a cat monitoring a mouse. "Stopped what?"

Melissa swallowed hard, remembered the freezer full of blood and only blood, and looked away. "Why have you stopped making ice cream?"

John laughed softly and reached over the table to lightly stroke her cheek. Heart overflowing with love at his mere touch, Melissa turned to face him, and her breath froze in her throat. The malignant expression on John's face chilled her.

"Oh that," John said casually, as he rose. "I've lost my taste for it."

In silence, John washed the dishes while Melissa swept the floor. John-Peter was drying the forks when Melissa heard a rattle. Dr. Rothgard opened the door and strolled inside.

John did not look happy, nor did he appear surprised. "Your house calls have become an annoying habit."

"So has your misbehavior. Sit down."

John gave Melissa a strange look. "Did you invite him?"

"No, she did not." Dr. Rothgard set his bag on the kitchen table and jerked his head in the direction of John-Peter. "Get the boy out of the room."

John-Peter tossed the towel on the counter and jumped off the chair. "I heard; I heard," he said in a voice mimicking Dr. Rothgard's.

Still, John-Peter glanced behind his shoulder as he plodded from the kitchen. A moment passed, and Melissa heard John-Peter's door close. She walked to his room and opened it again to be sure. John-Peter was sitting on the floor with a bag of blocks scattered around him.

"I'm really in here," John-Peter said.

Melissa chuckled. "Just checking."

When she returned to the kitchen, several vials of blood lay on the table. Dr. Rothgard, his face troubled, was peering into John's eyes with the aid of a little flashlight.

"All right, John, what's the largest animal dinner you've consumed? Other than the dog?"

John glanced sideways at Melissa and said nothing.

"Speak up, John, I haven't got all night. Do you think she's clueless?"

"Five raccoons." John shifted under Dr. Rothgard's steady gaze. "And a half."

Horrified, Melissa could only dumbly repeat, "And a half?"

John's eyes narrowed. "Next time, shall I store leftovers in the refrigerator?"

"Stop it, both of you!" Dr. Rothgard looked at Melissa. "You're through with school, right?"

"I graduated at the beginning of the month."

"Are you working yet?"

This time, Melissa squirmed under John's watchful eye. "Um, not yet," she hedged, unwilling to mention Munsonville.

"Until I can adjust John's blood treatments to stop his illicit activities, he needs constant supervision," Dr. Rothgard said.

"So that means I have to....?"

"Accompany him on the route? Yes."

Dr. Rothgard opened the freezer and began removing bags of blood and thawing them in the sink. Melissa searched John's face, still disbelieving that he had lied to her and looking for his reassurance. John returned the gaze, with a smirk and eyes of stone.

"John, that blood is in there for you to drink. No need to hoard it; making more is easy to do. Perhaps if you have a glass or two before the route, you'll find your taste for animal blood decreases, and your overall mood improves. So, what do you say, Melissa?"

Dr. Rothgard's idea did not enthuse her. Up at night, sleep by day? Ugghh! She couldn't, however, let John know that. So Melissa lifted her chin, smiled, and said, "Sure, why not?"

What an ironic turn of events. This time, instead of arranging the chaperone, John was receiving one.

The entire Simotes family never rose until early afternoon. Cooking dinner became a family affair, although often a hurried one, because several nights of the week John had to rush to the college for summer evening classes. During his absence, Melissa and John-Peter amused themselves in a variety of ways. They walked around the neighborhood, sometimes stopping at the nearby park, where the two would share a swing and giggle until their sides ached. Mostly, they remained at home. To Melissa's dismay, John-Peter's inflatable pool sat unused because of his aversion to water. Melissa had many happy childhood memories of splashing in a wading pool with Brian, but no coaxing would induce the boy to dip a toe. Nevertheless, Melissa could and did indulge his fondness for creative materials. Together they finger painted and watercolor painted or sat on the concrete driveway and drew chalk landscapes.

When the sun dipped at the edge of the sky, they ran around the yard and caught lightening bugs. Melissa showed John-Peter how to punch holes in the metal lid of a peanut butter jar to catch and observe the insects before setting them free. The tiny, glowing creatures fascinated him.

"Look, Mother," he said, tilting the jar to see the underside of one such bug. "It's like having my very own star!"

When darkness settled for the evening, Melissa curled in her chair while John-Peter practiced the piano. One night he hit an impasse and pleaded with Melissa for permission to call the music room.

"You can't!" Melissa stretched her legs and adjusted the tiny pillow behind her head. "Your father is busy teaching."

"I won't keep him long. Besides, I'm a student, too."

"Not a paying student."

A few seconds later, John-Peter stood by Melissa's chair. "Your hand, Mother."

Melissa held it out, and John-Peter dropped a quarter into it. "Now may I call the music room?"

She grinned and ruffled his snarled hair. "Leave your father alone."

About ten o'clock, Melissa and John-Peter ate lunch. John came home by eleven, drank several glasses of blood, and the three of them piled into his car in order to arrive at the distribution center before midnight. That's because the first truck of newspapers, if on time, arrived thirty minutes after they did, so John wanted time to review any customer starts and stops for that day. John-Peter counted the advertisement inserts that went into each publication, and Melissa hung different color bags on each hook.

Although Melissa required a couple of nights to learn the proper newspaper-folding techniques, the airless building motivated her progress in both skill and speed. She hated working inside the warehouse, but once she left it behind her, and John turned onto the road that took them from Jenson, the reward portion of the job began. Melissa found an especial thrill in slinging an object from a moving vehicle.

John split a country route with Ed Calkins; together they delivered everything on the outskirts of Jenson all the way past Thornton. On occasion, John delivered Ed's part, if the carrier that drove into Munsonville didn't arrive for work that night, and Ed had to cover it.

"Newspaper carriers are an interesting breed," John said. "Some deliver the same route for years while others work for a few days and never return."

Despite their differences, newspaper carriers had one common characteristic: the ability to sleep anywhere, anytime. John laughed at Melissa's expression the first time she saw rows of work stations housing snoring drivers.

"If a truck is late, you might as well sleep," John said. "Late trucks mean late routes and less sleep. Carriers often pull off the road for fifteen minute naps."

Melissa didn't like the idea of John-Peter sitting in a car while John slept. "Have you ever done it?"

"Never. I feel my best at night."

Ed Calkins pushed the pallet to John's station. "Well, John-Peter, how many 'Thornton Times' today?"

"Nine, Uncle Ed. The guy past the gas station restarted."

Ed grabbed a handful of newspapers, counted nine, and set them on the workstation. The headline caught Melissa's attention.

Thornton man commits suicide.

A landlord coming to collect his rent found the body of Derek Wilder, 25, of Thornton, on the floor of his trailer. Both wrists had been slit.

One neighbor said that the man had been fighting depression since the death of his wife eighteen months ago. Funeral arrangements are pending.

"John!"

"What?" John scribbled something on his route book and did not look up.

Melissa, remembering John-Peter, handed John the newspaper. "Look."

With a grim expression, John read the few lines that story contained. He returned the newspaper to her without a word.

"John, do you think if we had..." Melissa glanced at John-Peter, who hummed under his breath as he bagged newspapers and tossed them into a cart. She lowered her voice. "You know, if we had allowed Derek...."

He shrugged. "It's proof we made the right decision. The man was unstable and unfit to care for children."

"You're not sorry he's dead?"

"I'm relieved he's gone from our lives."

An appalling thought struck Melissa. What if Derek hadn't killed himself? What if John....?

"Double bag!" Ed called.

John-Peter sighed. "Now he tells us." He leaned over the carts, scooped an armful of newspapers, and began tossing them onto the table.

"What are you doing?" Melissa asked in surprise.

"We have to flip the newspapers over and put a second bag on them," John-Peter said. "It's either raining or going to rain."

"I'll help you."

By the time Melissa and John pushed their grocery carts to the service door to load, with John-Peter lounging like royalty on John's stack of newspapers, the rain was pouring down in stinging sheets. Thunder shook the skies, and each bolt of lightning lit the night with the brightness of the noon sun.

Melissa looked outside and felt trepidation rise within her. "We're not really delivering in that, are we John?"

He grinned at her timidity. "We are."

"But...."

"If you think this is bad, wait until we roll down the windows to throw."

She shuddered at the prospect.

Whoever called rain cozy had never driven down a dark country road in a blinding thunderstorm. The rain pelted the roof and beat on the glass harder and faster than John's windshield wipers could remove it.

"John, maybe you should pull over."

"Why?"

"There's no visibility."

"I can see just fine, Melissa...damn it!"

"What?"

"I missed my turn. I have a new start down that road."

Twenty-minutes passed, and John still had not located the address. In frustration, he pulled onto the shoulder and reached for his route book from above his visor. Melissa squinted into the darkness. Another car lay several yards beyond them, only this one had fallen halfway into the ditch.

"John," Melissa said, "I think that car ran off the road."

He did not look up. "I saw. It's Ed's car."

"Don't you care?"

"He's probably sleeping."

John's blatant lack of concern aroused Melissa's suspicions. Something felt terribly wrong. With trembling fingers, Melissa quietly undid her seat belt and set one hand on the door handle.

"Then," she said, "I'm asking him about the address."

John started to object, but Melissa flew out of the car, sank into mud, and slipped and slid on the swampy ground. The rain lashed through her jacket, drenched her skin, and rattled Ed Calkins' car. As Melissa reached the front passenger window, she saw Ed's head against the seat rest. His eyes were closed. She knocked. Ed did not move. She banged. Still nothing except the insistent deluge of rain. How hard could a man sleep, even a newspaper carrier?

In desperation, Melissa beat on the glass with both fists. When Ed again did not respond, she tugged the handle, and the door flew open. She slid into the front seat and slammed the door.

"Hey, Ed?"

Ed gasped, opened his mouth, and blood poured forth. That's when Melissa noticed the dark stain spreading across his shirt.

"Oh, God, Ed! I'm going for help!"

A shaky hand clawed Melissa's jacket. In fright, she pried it away. With the other hand, Ed dropped a plastic leprechaun.

"For the boy," he croaked.

This was no time to argue. Melissa snatched up the toy and flung open the door. "Hold on, Ed, you hear? I'm getting help!"

Melissa skidded across the mud back to John's vehicle and hurled herself back inside, spraying water across the dashboard.

"John!"

John-Peter touched Melissa's shoulder with a squeamish hand and grimaced. "Mother, how wet you are!"

"John!" Melissa panted. "It's Ed! He's hurt!"

She had never seen John move so fast. In an instant, he was at Ed's car. She strained her eyes to see through the downpour, but to no avail. John-Peter crawled into the front seat beside Melissa and gazed at her with wide eyes.

"Is Uncle Ed badly injured?" John-Peter asked.

Melissa's voice caught in her throat. "I'm afraid so, baby."

"Don't worry, Mother. Father can help him. He can fix anything."

Oh, the naïveté of children! She bit her lip, trying to see through the onslaught. "I certainly hope so."

"What's that in your hand?"

Melissa had forgotten the leprechaun. She loosened her grip, and a macabre face leered up at her. Its tiny black eyes glinted under a pair of bushy red eyebrows. A thatch of wild red hair slid out from under its tall green hat. In the center of its belly, a series of numbers in the billions spiraled downward. John-Peter studied the strange piece and then looked up in astonishment.

"Mother, why do you have my leprechaun?"

John knocked on the passenger window, and Melissa opened it a crack. Water poured into the car.

"I'm driving him home!" John shouted over the rain's clamor. "Can you keep pace if I drive slowly?"

"Shouldn't he go to the hospital?"

"*Melissa*! Can you follow me?"

"Yes!"

John dashed back to Ed's car. For the next half hour, Melissa crept behind John down the forsaken road until they came to a small subdivision. John made a series of turns before pulling into the driveway of a sprawling ranch home. Melissa watched John help Ed from the car to the side door of the house where they both disappeared. In a moment, John was running full speed back to the car. He squeezed buckets of water from his dripping hair, heedless of the already soaked seat cushions.

As he backed out of the driveway, John blew the air from his lungs and said in an offhand way, "Well, John-Peter, we're really late now."

By the time John started tossing newspapers, the rain had slowed to a drizzle. Melissa fell asleep after the third throw. She awoke in her own driveway where the sun made feeble attempts to push through the overcast sky. The rain had stopped.

John laughed softly and stroked her cheek. "Some route partner you are!"

The sight of John brought back memories of last night. Now, in the daylight, the incident with Ed Calkins felt like a fading illusion. Tired and hungry, the three of them stumbled into the house and consumed a hasty breakfast. John promised to compensate everyone at dinner that night.

"Vegetable stir-fry?" John-Peter asked in a sleepy, but hopeful, voice.

"I can manage that."

Not until she lay beside John did memories of last night's monsoon plague her. A series of images rolled in her mind, like the frames of an old black and white silent movie. The driving rain. Ed in distress. The wicked leprechaun. She had to know.

"John?"

"Hmm?"

"What happened to Ed?"

A pause. "Nothing. He became sick on the route, and I took him home."

"But he was bleeding!"

"Melissa, you dreamed it."

Had she?

"But...but isn't he the Steward of Tara?"

"He is." John rolled onto his side. "Now."

"I don't get it."

His arm jerked. John was drifting to sleep.

"John, did you do something to him...?"

"Go to sleep, Mel..." His voice slurred into slumber.

"No!" She sat up in bed and roughly shook John's shoulder. "Did you make him a vampire?"

Her answer was John's easy breathing. In desperation, Melissa pummeled his back and screamed, "You turned him into a monster!"

Instead of becoming angry, John merely rolled over, drew Melissa into his arms, and stroked her hair. Her hysterics turned into frightened wails as she fully realized just how Ed Calkins had realized his immortality. Hadn't Henry once implied, at the Simons Mansion garden party, when he insisted Melissa was playing croquet in her bedroom, that Melissa' travel into the nineteenth century was really a vampire's hypnotic trance? Time was no longer linear but a twisted, convoluted circle of confusion. To her astonishment, John let her cry, and gradually, Melissa's sobbing turned into anguished whimpering.

"How could you?" Melissa whispered. "Oh, John, how could you?"

"Melissa, he would have died."

"He did die!"

"But it's a happy death. He's as ruthless as he always deluded himself to be."

Melissa bolted up right. "Promise me you won't do it again!"

"Melissa, I can't...."

"Promise it! No, swear it John! You can take all the blood you need from me, once a day, ten times a day, if that's what it takes to keep you human. But no more animals, no more ruining innocent lives, no more turning people into vampires, no more...."

She thought about Derek, but fresh, feverish tears stopped up her flow of words. John once again pushed her head onto his chest.

"All right, Melissa," John said in a weary voice, "I promise. No blood except yours. Unless...."

John's arm relaxed, and Melissa felt its grip on her loosen.

"Unless what?"

"Unless nothing. Let's get some sleep. I can't think anymore."

Ed Calkins was absent from newspapers that night and the next night and the next night. Melissa saw him on the fourth night, pushing a pallet full of newspapers, looking the same as he always had. Maybe his absence *had* been due to illness. Maybe Melissa had dreamt the chest wound. Ed couldn't be a vampire, could he?

As Ed counted out newspapers, John-Peter tried talking with him, but Ed rudely interrupted him. "Excuse me, but I have ruthless business at the next table."

Ed approached the next carrier. "Would you care to sign my petition? You see, my birthday falls between Lincoln's birthday and Valentine's Day, so I believe it should be a national holiday, complete with a parade."

Crestfallen, John-Peter folded another newspaper and reflectively bagged it. "Mother, does Uncle Ed seem different to you?"

"In what way, dear?

"I...I don't know. Just...different."

"Well, he was sick."

John-Peter remained unconvinced. "Maybe that's it."

Because John had forty new starts that day, the Simotes' finished the route past deadline for the second time in a week. Dazedly, Melissa awakened to the late afternoon sun streaming through the windows.

Thump!

The paper boy had just thrown the *Jenson Reporter* onto her front porch. Oh, wow, it was late! If John didn't hurry, he'd be tardy for class.

"John," Melissa nudged him.

"Five more minutes," he mumbled.

"All right."

At least, Melissa had time to peek at the headlines while John drowsed. John-Peter was already awake and sitting in Melissa's favorite chair, munching an apple and flipping through the pages of a large book. Melissa kissed the top of John-Peter's head and unfolded the paper.

Across the front page were the words: *"Vampire" kills woman suffering from dementia.*

Jenson Nursing Home staff found the body of 93 year old Agnes Scofield in her bed. She had been completely drained of blood. Scofield, a resident of the nursing home since 1973....

No! Nooo! Nooooooo!

Slowly, deliberately, Melissa crumpled the newspaper. Despite her most heartfelt pleadings, *John had lied!* The bathroom door creaked. She wavered with indecision. It was now or never.

Heart thudding, Melissa scooped up John-Peter. On impulse, as she flew passed the hall, she kicked the bathroom door fully open and flung the newspaper at him.

"What the sh...Melissa!"

She raced into the kitchen, grabbed her keys and purse, and dashed out the door. Precariously clutching the baby on her hip, Melissa leaped over the stairs two at a time and sped to her car. She yanked open the door and threw John-Peter into his car seat.

"Hurry up, and buckle in!"

Squealing the tires, she had almost backed into the street before John appeared on the front porch.

"Melissa! Stop!"

Shaking with rage and horror, Melissa leaned her head out the window. "Kiss my ass!"

CHAPTER 24: BACK TO THE WOMB

Melissa had left the house with no clear idea where she was headed, but, as she drove, she found herself veering straight for the interstate. She looped the cloverleaf that took her out of Jenson and toward Illinois.

She made good time, too, until she neared Detroit's rush hour. When traffic slowed to a crawl, she peered in the rear view mirror at John-Peter, dozing in his car seat. He might as well sleep. They would be in the car for several more hours. Once the vehicles moved unencumbered, Melissa heeded Carol's warning about John-Peter's new toilet habits and exited the highway for a rest area. After she parked, Melissa moved John-Peter's car seat to the front passenger seat. She needed his company and hoped she could entertain a precocious eighteen-month-old. She needn't have worried. John-Peter amused them both.

He flipped through the radio station, identifying various classical piano pieces for Melissa while he hummed along with their melodies. If he happened upon a rock station, he clutched his throat with mock, retching noises.

"Some people do call that music," Melissa said.

John-Peter made a sour face. "Like who?"

"Like your mother."

"Father allows this?"

"Your father isn't the last word on everything, John-Peter."

"He should be," John-Peter said as he spun the dial. "He's really smart."

They drove several miles in silence. The wind from the partially cracked window whipped John-Peter's hair around his face. Melissa had long ago abandoned all notions of keeping it trimmed since it grew back almost as soon as she cut it. On the rare occasions John took the scissors to the mop, John-Peter submitted with the meekness Melissa wished he also displayed for bathtubs. Suddenly, Melissa had an idea. As she contemplated John-Peter's waving arms while he played conductor, she decided this might be a good opportunity to drill him.

"So, John-Peter, do you know where we're going?"

He stretched to his full height to see out the front window and twisted his neck to check the back window. He leaned to forward and peered through the side window.

"John-Peter, what are you doing?"

"Locating landmarks."

"And?"

"Shh. I'm reading signs."

Melissa smothered a grin. No wonder the boy accompanied John on his route. He'd be indispensible to Melissa if she lost her way. John-Peter folded his arms in victory, a gloating smile on his face. "Chicago!"

"Close. Grover's Park. We're going to visit Grandma and Grandpa."

"And Uncle Brian, too?"

"Uncle Brian, too."

John-Peter wriggled with excitement, and then his face fell. "Will we be home in time for the route?"

"No, honey, we're staying for a few days."

Looking troubled, the boy looked up at her. "What about Father?"

"He'll be fine."

"But we're a team!"

Here was Melissa's chance. "How so?"

"We split the work fifty-fifty. Father said that's the fairest way."

"Do you divide everything?"

"Yes, everything."

"Even the hunting?"

John-Peter made a face. "Remember? I don't eat meat."

"What kind of meat does your father eat?"

"He said not to tell you because you wouldn't understand."

How dare John manipulate their son!

"Well, he's wrong," Melissa said, trying to speak calmly. "I do understand. What kind of meat does your father eat?"

John-Peter traced the curve of the car seat. "Oh, I don't really pay attention because *I don't like meat.*" He looked up at her. "Mother, if this is so important to you, why don't you ask Father?"

"Because he's not here."

"Oh." As he considered Melissa's last comment, his face brightened. "Now it's my turn. Why do you have my leprechaun?"

Melissa gripped the steering wheel and kept her eyes on the road while trying to maintain nonchalance. John-Peter interpreted her interrogation as a question and answer game. If she humored him, she might learn more. "What leprechaun?"

"The one from Uncle Ed."

"Uncle Ed gave you a leprechaun?"

"Yes. He said it would bring me good luck."

"That hideous thing?"

"Beauty is in the eye of the beholder."

Melissa choked down a laugh. What a queer answer from a toddler! "If he gave it to you, why don't you have it? Did you lose it?"

"No, he took it back to make adjustments."

"What kind of adjustments?"

"I don't know. May I have it now?"

"When we get to Grandma and Grandpa's."

The answer seemed to satisfy John-Peter. He leaned over the edge of his car seat, close to the door panel, fumbled, and then triumphantly pulled up the large, hardbound book he had been reading when Melissa snatched him away. John-Peter set the book on his lap, turned its pages, and studied the pictures.

"What are you looking at, honey?"

"'The Myths of the Irish.' Uncle Ed gave it to me." He held up a picture for Melissa to see. "If you think my leprechaun is ugly, observe this!"

A quick glance revealed a sneering leprechaun perched inside a pot of gold. The picture bothered Melissa, but it delighted John-Peter. "Isn't he great?"

"I prefer happy leprechauns."

"Then you're ignorant about leprechauns."

"That's not true," Melissa said in a lofty voice. "They came from a race of warriors."

John-Peter's eyes grew round. "Who told you that, Mother?"

"Someone I knew from a long time ago."

His spontaneous laughter rang through the car. "Oh, Mother, you're so young! How can you know someone from a long time ago?"

"Well, I know I'm hungry. Shall we have dinner?"

"Yes!"

A few miles back, Melissa had passed a sign advertising a family-style restaurant in a small town called Baxterville and hoped it featured a salad bar. She guided the car down the ramp and stopped at the traffic light at the bottom of the hill.

"I see the restaurant, Mother!"

"Where are your shoes?"

"I don't know."

After they parked, John-Peter crawled on the floor of the car, peeking under seats for one shoe, then two. Five more minutes passed while John-Peter demonstrated how he could undo the knots and retie the shoes once he slid them onto his feet. As they walked into the restaurant, the boy slipped one grimy little hand into her larger one and squeezed.

"I love you, Mother," he said in a sweet, baby voice.

She returned the squeeze. "I love you, too."

The dinner hour had ended; few people occupied the dining room. A salad bar graced the center of the room. Melissa felt like cheering, although she still had to wash John-Peter's hands, filthy from crawling on the car's floor.

John-Peter screamed when his hands touched the water as if Melissa had run them under acid. An elderly woman stood next to Melissa and applied lipstick, although Melissa saw her cast disapproving looks at John-Peter from the corner of her eye.

"Stop it!" Melissa hissed in his ear. John-Peter's wails subsided to whimpers.

The salad bar offered so many varieties of food that Melissa ordered only the salad bar, too. John-Peter heaped his plate with carrots, broccoli, cauliflower, radishes, green peppers, purple onions, mushrooms, cucumbers, and tomatoes. With a spoon, he dug a well in the center and filled it with, three-bean salad, garbanzo beans, and sunflower seeds. Melissa had to admit the colorful array of food looked mighty appetizing.

"What's that you're eating, Mother?"

"Beef barley soup."

"Barley's all right, but beef is icky." He glided to the floor.

"Where are you going?"

"Crackers."

"Oh my God, it can't be! Melissa?"

Melissa turned at the familiar voice. Before her stood Jill Eaten looking as perky as when Melissa last saw her, despite her tailored three-piece beige suit. Melissa motioned for a seat, but Jill declined.

"I'm late for a meeting. I just wanted to say, Hi.' Do you live around here?"

"No, we're still in Jenson. I'm on the way to visit my parents."

"Well, I wasn't sure after what happened with John. Gotta run. Nice seeing you."

"Wait, Jill!" Melissa jumped up, and Jill paused. Had Melissa heard her ex-roommate correctly? "Is something wrong with my husband?"

Now it was Jill's turn to look astonished. "Melissa, you do know John got fired."

"Fired?"

"For his misbehavior."

Melissa reeled as if Jill had dropped a bucket of ice onto her head.

"Apparently he hadn't learned his lesson after losing half a semester without pay last January. Well, you can't teach an old dog...." Jill glanced at her watch. "I'm really sorry, Melissa, but I *have* to go."

Three miles down the road, John-Peter's head bobbed onto his chest. *Fired?* Melissa scanned the radio stations until she found something metal and loud, but her heart continued to beat raucously in her ears. *Fired?* John-Peter did not stir, so Melissa cranked up the volume. *Fired?* Their financial plight made sense to her now. How long since Jenson College had let him go? If John wasn't teaching at night, what was he doing? Killing neighborhood pets and old women in nursing homes?

Not until ten o'clock did Melissa turn down the street of her parents' house. For the first time, she felt the weight of her retreat, along with a twinge of regret for not calling ahead first. She pulled into the driveway behind Steve's work van and sat there for many minutes, dredging up the courage to face the consequences of her decision. Finally, Melissa took a deep breath.

"Well, here goes," she said aloud.

Leaving her sleeping son in his car seat, Melissa trudged to the front door. As she raised her hand to knock, her courage momentarily faltered. What would she tell her parents? Brushing aside her misgivings, Melissa knocked as hard as she could. She heard a scuffle; the porch light shone in her eyes; and the front door opened.

Steve stood in the doorway gaping at her. "Melissa! What in heaven's name...."

"I've come home."

"Well, of all the...." He stepped onto the porch, and tightly hugged her. "Are you okay?"

How could she possibly answer that question? Melissa might be retreating to her parents' house, but she could never make them understand the true reason behind her escape.

"Can we talk about it later?" Melissa said, voice breaking. "I've had a rough day."

"Of course. Come inside."

Steve held open the screen door for her, but Melissa hesitated.

"Wait. John-Peter's sleeping in the car."

Steve guided her inside. "I'll get John-Peter. Try not to give your mother a heart attack."

"Where is she?"

"Almost ready for bed."

Weariness engulfed Melissa the second she entered the house. She sank into the couch, reveling in its plush softness and the quiet cool of the air-conditioned room.

Steve carried John-Peter, still asleep, up the stairs. Melissa heard a door creak open. "Oh, gosh, Steve....!"

"Shh. Don't wake him. I'm putting him in the guest room. Melissa's downstairs."

Darlene descended the stairs, looking at Melissa with questioning eyes. "Melissa?"

"Oh, Mommy!"

In seconds, Darlene was sitting on the couch, and Melissa was curling into her embrace, crying, crying, crying. Her mother stroked her hair and rubbed her back and said, "There, there," over and over again until Melissa felt nothing bad could happen with Darlene this close.

As Melissa's storm subsided, she saw her mother shoot a look of concern toward the other end of the room. Melissa turned her head. Steve was leaning against the living room wall, a grieved expression on his face.

Melissa looked from one to the other. "May I stay here tonight?"

"You may stay as long as you need to stay," Steve said. "This is still your home."

"I suppose you're wondering why we're here."

Darlene glanced up at Steve and then gave Melissa a feeble smile. "That can wait for the morning. Get some sleep tonight. We can talk later. All right?"

Melissa nodded and hugged her mother. "Thanks, Mom."

She hugged Steve on her way up the stairs. "Thanks, Steve, for everything. I really mean it."

He grinned and patted her back. "That's what fathers are for."

Melissa pondered those words as she cleaned up for bed. She thought of the fathers she'd known in her life: Frank, Steve, and even Fr. Alexis who listened to her ramblings about vampires. Mostly, Melissa thought about John, someone who wanted to be a father so badly he did what he'd vowed never to do. He adopted another man's son, the son of a man he could never respect.

She pattered on soft carpet to the guest room. The last time she'd occupied it, John had been with her, and John-Peter lived only as a vague concept in their minds. In this very room, she and John had bantered about baby names before John made wonderful love to her. Would anything ever be the same between them?

Melissa slid beneath the cool sheets near the relaxed body of her sleeping son who reposed on his back, arms and legs flung out like a starfish. She closed her eyes and prayed sleep would be swift, but images of John crowded any rest that might have come, and those images were not pleasant.

She envisioned John attacking and killing Prince as he pawed through their garbage can. She pictured John sneaking into the trailer, slitting poor Derek's wrists, and drinking his blood. She saw him crushing the life's breath from an elderly woman before feasting on *her* blood. Anguish welled within her as she wondered how much of his returning vampire life John had shared with his son. She hoped the damage to John-Peter could be reversed. She hoped the baby would be too small to remember. She hoped reconciliation with John was possible. John-Peter would miss his father.

Melissa woke to sunshine. She automatically groped John's side of the bed, but John wasn't there. Her eyes flew open, and she recognized her bedroom. John-Peter had already vacated the room.

She quickly dressed and then descended the stairs to join her family. Melissa discerned the distant roar of a lawn mower somewhere outside. Darlene sat at the kitchen table, talking with Brian and drinking a cup of coffee. Brian stood at the stove, scrambling eggs.

"Morning, Liss," Brian said as if an unnatural situation did not exist. "Hungry?"

"Sure!" Melissa sat next to Darlene. "Do you still make great toast?"

"Of course."

With pride, Brian transported the modest feast to his sister. "Crusts off, two sides buttered," he said.

"Smells great, Brian!"

After Brian joined them, Melissa asked, "What are your plans for today?"

"Well, Steve and I have an office building to clean. We probably won't be done until early afternoon. Then tonight, I'm taking Cindy to a movie, if Steve will give us a ride."

Melissa choked on her eggs. Brian...dating! When had this occurred? She looked closely at his face while he ate. For that matter, when had be begun shaving?

Steve walked through the back door with John-Peter at his heels.

"He's a handy little guy to have around," Steve said. "He picked up all the sticks in the yard before I cut the grass, and then he helped me weed the garden. I've never seen such a discriminating eye in a child."

John-Peter echoed Steve's sentiments. "I know my plants, and they know me."

"That is an understatement," Melissa said. "Please pass the salt, Brian."

Steve poured himself a mug of coffee, just as the phone rang.

"Sit," Darlene said, standing up. "You've been working all morning."

Brian set his fork on his plate. "Steve, will you give Cindy and me a ride to the movies?"

Darlene returned to the kitchen. "Melissa, it's for you."

Melissa's heart pounded. Was it John? Then why hadn't Darlene said so? Maybe her mother wanted to surprise her. Maybe John's vampire self had threatened her.

She walked to the phone table in the hall with as much casualness as she could muster, picked up the receiver, and said, "Hello?"

"Dr. Rothgard here. I called the house with John's test results, and he gave me this number. What's going on?"

So John knew she had come here! Why hadn't he called, even to speak with his son?

"Everything's fine," Melissa lied. "I'm just spending a couple of weeks with my parents."

"Why didn't John didn't come with you?" Dr. Rothgard sounded surprised.

"He couldn't take the time off work."

"What about the blood treatments?"

Melissa's voice was bitter. "I guess he's not getting any. Besides, I don't think they're working anymore."

"Well," Dr. Rothgard said, his voice gruff, "that's the reason for my telephone call. I've reviewed John's blood work and that, coupled with his recent physical exam, leads me to agree with you. I think he's fighting a losing battle."

Oh, how terrible those words sounded from Dr. Rothgard. So, it was official. Melissa's head spun; her eyes burned; her reason for living crumbled. Until now, the shadowy fear of John's vampire retransformation lurked only in the recesses of her fearful imagination. Dr. Rothgard's brief statement breathed life into her delusions. Why did he have to call and spoil this beautiful morning?

She blinked hard and took a deep breath. "So what comes next?"

"Stall for time, if you'd like to keep your husband. I'm restocking your freezer. The more of your blood John consumes, the more human traits he will retain, at least temporarily. However, his humanness will not last forever."

"How long?"

"Hard to say. Most of my patients do not revert, but then most of my patients are so motivated to remain human they follow my orders, and, as a result, lead long vigorous lives."

Melissa squeezed her eyes against hot tears. Her persistent efforts had been in vain. She and John had no future together.

"However, that requires a connection to the host, something John refused to do, at least in the beginning. But that's John's pattern. He stubbornly tackles issues his own way and waits too long to ask for help. By then, it's too late."

John's pattern? Melissa pondered that statement, puzzled. Just how long had Dr. Rothgard known John?

"Damn it, Melissa, you'd think John would've learned his lesson after that fool Bryga convinced him that her so-called midwifery skills were adequate to deliver Bryony's baby. John stupidly dismissed all the servants. He never sent Henry for me until Bryony was hemorrhaging!"

CHAPTER 25: SURRENDERING TO FATE

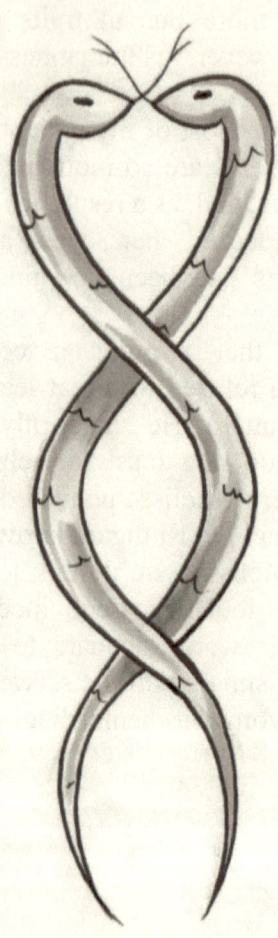

The family honeymoon lasted only until Saturday night.

On the first day Melissa spent in Grover's Park, Darlene took her and John-Peter clothes shopping since they had left Jenson without packing a suitcase. John-Peter's rigid choice of colors amused Darlene.

"Isn't he too young to be so opinionated?" Melissa said as Darlene paid for the clothes.

"Not really. That's why toddlers love to say, 'No.'"

All week Melissa helped Darlene around the house and accompanied Steve on several evening cleaning jobs. Brian played Steve's assistant by day and John-Peter's nanny on those nights Melissa helped Steve.

Brian spent all day Saturday at Cindy's house because the next day, she planned to celebrate the Fourth of July at his house. Steve grilled chicken for dinner so Melissa offered to clean the entire kitchen by herself. When she had dried the last dish, she hung the towel to dry and joined her parents in the living room. That's when the trouble started.

Steve was sitting in the chair by the lamp reading the newspaper. John-Peter was perched on his lap and reading, too. As the boy braced his head on Steve's chest, Melissa' saw her step-father wrinkle his nose and move John-Peter's head away from him.

"Melissa, don't you ever bathe that child?"

"John does, sometimes, because John-Peter fights me. He doesn't like getting wet."

"Sometimes?"

"Well, he feels it's important for John-Peter to be himself, to express his own opinions."

Steve's eyes narrowed. "That's well and good when we're talking about the boy's intellectual development, and if you two want to raise a filthy child, that's your business. However, John isn't the boss in my house."

He set down the newspaper, stood up with John-Peter, and said, "I'm taking my grandson to the bathroom and introducing him to the joys of soap and shampoo. And he can dislike it all he wants."

At the words "soap and shampoo" John-Peter's eyes opened wide with fright. By the time Steve reached the second floor, John-Peter's frantic shrieks were filling the entire house. Melissa had no idea how long the phone had rung by the time she heard it. She scrambled to her feet and sped to the phone, grabbing the receiver in mid-ring.

"Hello?"

"Melissa?"

"Dr. Rothgard?"

"Yes. I packed your freezer full of blood. John won't squeeze so much as an ice cream bar in there. He's set for awhile, so don't rush home. Enjoy your visit with your family."

"Dr. Rothgard, I can never thank you enough!"

"Call if I can assist further."

Melissa thought of something. "Oh, wait, I do have one question."

"Yes?"

She glanced in the living room at Darlene, who was flipping through a magazine. Melissa cupped the receiver and edged closer to the kitchen.

"When John becomes a vampire again," she whispered, "is it possible for us to start over?"

"You mean as host and parasite?"

Melissa cringed at those words. "Yes."

"Anything's possible. But I must caution you. Because your blood failed, John might need a new host to come back."

"But my blood didn't fail! John did become a man again. You said the failure was John's fault, because he didn't maintain it."

"True, but because of it, as a vampire, John might develop immunity to your blood."

Melissa said nothing and gazed into space.

"The blood doesn't have to come from a woman," Dr. Rothgard quickly added. "Maybe yours would work, maybe it wouldn't. It's just something you should keep in mind."

"Okay."

"Now will you do me a favor?"

"Anything!"

"Do not repeat my idle words from the other night. I wasn't thinking clearly when I spoke them. Chalk them up to the ramblings of a doctor frustrated by the irrational behavior of a pigheaded patient."

"So they're not true?"

"Melissa, I have to go. I'm being paged."

The dial tone beep beep beeped in Melissa's ear. Deep in thought, she returned to the living room. Darlene placed her magazine on the end table and looked hard at Melissa.

"Melissa, it's time we talked."

"You know, Mom, I'm really not in the mood for conversation."

Darlene raised her voice. "I don't care if you are or not. A week ago, you show up late at night and give us no explanation for it. Twice, by my count, a doctor calls the house. I want to know what's going on."

With a sigh, Melissa dropped onto the couch. "I'm not sure I even know."

"Then let's start at the beginning. Why did you leave home?"

She hesitated, considering her words before she uttered them. Melissa did not wish to mention John's termination from Jenson College until she could confirm it. The insinuation had, after all, come from Jill.

"Because, I think," Melissa said slowly as she assembled her answer, "John is doing some things that are not good."

"Like what things?"

"I don't know."

"Then what makes you think John's in trouble? Is he sick?"

"I think so."

"Melissa, you're going to have to level with me if you expect Steve and me to help you and John-Peter."

Jumping to her feet, Melissa threw up her arms in exasperation. "What do you want me to say? I don't have any answers. The doctor who called is John's doctor. He doesn't like the look of some tests, and John's behavior is erratic. I couldn't take it anymore, so I left."

Darlene contemplated Melissa's outburst and then looked at her with a softened expression. "Well, I guess that's the fall-out from being so close to your father."

Indignation filled Melissa. "What does Daddy have to do with this?"

"Nothing, except you did what many girls do. You married your father."

"That's insulting comparing John to Daddy."

"You are quite wrong, and I knew it the minute I laid eyes on John. You find him attractive because he's artistic and accomplished, the same traits your father had, yet you also butt heads with John when you can no longer tolerate his pride."

"Lots of people are talented, but they don't let it go to their heads. John has the largest ego of anyone I've ever met."

Darlene's voice was quiet. "With, perhaps, the exception of your father."

"I can't believe you're talking about him that way!"

"Melissa, how can you be so blind? Men like your father and John don't become full of pride because they are successful. They succeed because of their pride. It consumes them and drives them forward, compelling them almost beyond their control to perfect their work, to reach that impossible mark they've set. And when they do attain it, because attain it they must, are they satisfied? Are they happy? No, they focus on those who might compete against them and set higher goals."

"Daddy was nothing like that!"

"Oh, wasn't he? You have no idea what it took to salvage your father's self-esteem when his body fell apart. He functioned as a father to you and Brian because I made it possible for him to do it. It would have been much easier to do everything myself."

"I never saw you complain or fight with Daddy."

"We never let you see it. Put your husband in your father's shoes. How do you think John would feel if he lost his health, his virility, his eyesight, his legs, his kidney function, and, on top of it all, his ability to play the piano?"

"John would die first." Melissa's words resounded in her head. She remembered John's declaration at their first blood treatment: *I'm not going back.* But Dr. Rothgard said John, indeed, was returning to vampirism. Would John really choose to die and leave his family behind? "Daddy wanted to live."

"He wanted to raise you two, but I also think he would have preferred death to broken health. Melissa, you may not like the decisions John is making, and no one says you must. But he's going to do what he thinks is right for him, and you can't change that. You can only choose to make this a miserable journey or a peaceful one."

"I don't see how," Melissa said with bitterness. "John only thinks of himself."

"Just walk with him, Melissa. You don't have to agree with him."

"John doesn't care if I support him or not."

"I think you're wrong."

"Mom, he doesn't love me!"

Darlene walked to the couch and sat down by Melissa. "Why do you say that?"

"Because he's never said it."

"Melissa, many men...."

"He was married to someone else before me."

Darlene heaved a large sigh. "Oh, I see. Divorce?"

"No, she died. He's never gotten over her. I just thought...."

Her mother smiled. "You just thought he would one day fall in love with you."

Melissa nodded. "Boy, was I wrong!"

"Honey, do you remember a conversation we had a long time ago about love? You asked me if I loved Steve the same way as I loved your father."

"I remember."

Darlene closed her eyes and smiled. "Oh, Melissa, there was no one like your father, tall and handsome with the bluest eyes. He'd been all over the world, twice, never intending to marry. In all the years we were together, I don't think a day passed where I didn't thank my lucky stars for the good fortune of marrying him."

"That's how I feel about John. Don't you love Steve the same way?"

"With Steve, it's, well, different. I don't adore Steve; we're friends. I cared for your father, and Steve looks after me. It's not that I don't love Steve because I do, but I love him differently."

"So which is better?"

"That's just it. Neither one is better. They are what they are. Melissa, I'm sure John cares for you. He may not feel the exact same emotions he felt toward his first wife. He may not love your in the way you wished he would love you. That doesn't mean he feels nothing."

The sound of Steve's voice startled them both. "Well, meet the new and improved John-Peter."

Melissa turned around to see Steve holding her pajama-clad son, damp hair clinging to his face and fabric. The baby's face was red from screaming. When he saw Melissa, John-Peter sniffed and buried his head into Steve's shoulder.

"I'm impressed," Melissa said.

Steve grinned. "I made a deal with him. He submits to a nightly bath, and he can run around here barefoot all he likes."

That night, a whispering voice roused her. Mist swirled inside and outside of her Munsonville bedroom windows, but the hazy moonlight illuminated the shadowy figure of John Simons sitting beside her on the bed. John had removed his waistcoat and was now unbuttoning his shirt. He reached into his pocket and extracted, not the musical watch that played *Bryony*, but the pocket knife with which her had slashed the rope tethering the boat the night he first made love to her. With slow, careful movements, John opened the knife and passed it back and forth before Melissa's face. The moonlight glinted and flashed in her eyes. Her gaze followed the blade as John pulled the knife to his chest. With one swift motion, John sliced a deep, dark gash, and then slid his hand around Melissa's neck, entwining his fingers through her hair, drawing her to his wound, and pressing her lips against it. Melissa recoiled from the metallic, sticky liquid, but John pushed her harder. She held out until her lungs nearly burst and then with a half-gasp, half-moan, she surrendered. To her surprise, his taste did not repel her. It was, as Kellen had once remarked, delectable, mellow, yet full-bodied. Melissa helplessly clutched John and thirstily swallowed the blood trickling into her mouth.

The vision changed. Melissa was sitting on the bench beside John in the music room, puzzled by what had just transpired. She placed a hand on John's thin arm, aghast at the bagginess of his sleeve.

"Why did you offer me your blood?"

John raised his head to look at Melissa. His eyes sank into a thin and sallow face. The once abundant hair hung in sparse, limp strands over his shoulders and down his back. He grabbed her cheeks with bony and gnarled fingers and locked glaring eyes at her.

"I'm protecting my investment," John snarled.

Fourth of July dawned brassy, sticky, and hot. Darlene suggested setting out the sprinklers for John-Peter, but Melissa informed her she would be wasting her time.

"Give him plenty of fruit juice popsicles, and he'll be fine," Melissa said.

Cindy arrived at the house soon after breakfast. The heat didn't seem to affect her. She wore white and pink shorts with a pink-flowered shirt; her curly blonde hair was pulled away from her thin face with a pink bow. Her appearance reminded Melissa of strawberry ice cream.

Brian even remembered his manners. "Cindy, this is my sister, Melissa Simotes. Melissa, this is Cindy Parker."

"Hi Cindy. Brian's said lots of nice things about you."

She smiled a bright, sweet smile. "Thanks, Melissa." Her voice had a musical quiver to it. Melissa could see why Brian liked her.

Not once all day did Cindy move from his side. She partnered with him when they challenged Darlene and Steve to badminton and held the tongs while Brian and Steve grilled the ribs.

Both Shelly and Laura had come home for the summer, and Darlene surprised Melissa by inviting them to dinner. Unlike Melissa, they were following a traditional class schedule and had one more year to complete before their graduation.

The second the girls laid eyes on John-Peter, he charmed them with his appearance, mannerisms, and speech. Glad for the receptive audience, John-Peter even asked them if they preferred Bach to Beethoven.

"Oh what a doll," Shelly said. "He's like a little leprechaun."

Sharp chills cut through Melissa's body, despite the heat. She didn't find Shelly's comment cute, and she did not know why.

Laura knelt beside John-Peter and hugged his little body. "Do you like the paintings I made for your bedroom?"

John-Peter's countenance sobered. "Are you the fairy lady?"

"Why, yes, I am!"

"Who modeled for you?"

Laura gazed at his earnest, little face. "No one modeled for me. All the figures came from my imagination."

John-Peter placed one finger against his cheek, tilted his head, and gazed up at her with cunning eyes as he reflected on her answer. "Are you sure?"

Darlene walked outside with a pitcher of iced tea and a stack of glasses. "Anyone thirsty?"

Shelly and Laura left soon after dinner. Near dusk, everyone else piled into the cleaning van for the high school parking lot, which had a clear view of the fireworks. Everyone else, that is, except Melissa. She didn't want to miss John if he called. Hovering around her was last night's dream, loneliness for the John of her Bryony dreams, and terror of, once and for all, losing her only reason for being: John. She did not know what to do.

Melissa never knew when sleep relieved her despair, but sometime in the middle of the night, John-Peter's crying awakened her.

"Shh, baby," Melissa said, holding him close and stroking his little head. "Did you have a bad dream?"

"Yes!" came the mournful reply.

"Mother's here. The bad dream's all gone."

"No it isn't!" John-Peter wailed. "I can still see it!"

"What do you see?"

"Father! His eyes are gone and snakes are crawling from the holes."

"John-Peter...."

"When opened his mouth to talk, worms slank out and his chin fell off."

John-Peter clung to Melissa and trembled. Had he somehow sensed his father's struggle to retain human form? She rubbed his back. "Father's okay, John-Peter. It was only a bad dream."

"He's dead!"

"No, he isn't." Melissa tried making her voice sound soothing.

"I want to go home!"

He expressed her exact sentiments. Melissa longed for home and longed for John. She couldn't bear to be without him, but neither could she stand to be with him in his present state.

"We will go home," Melissa said, kissing her son's wet cheek. "I promise."

"Tomorrow?"

"Well, I don't know...."

"Please!"

Memories flooded her mind and touched her heart: John cradling John-Peter the night he was born, John sleeping in Melissa's chair with dozens of bottles scattered on the living room carpet, John teaching John-Peter how to play the piano, John cooking and washing dishes with his little son by his side, and John throwing newspapers instead of pursuing a musical career because he and John-Peter were a team. She hugged her baby hard. He had not mentioned John one time since they had arrived in Grover's Park. She had not known he missed John this much.

Melissa relented. "All right. We leave tomorrow."

John-Peter grinned through his tears. "May I have my leprechaun now?"

Darlene received the news of Melissa and John-Peter's departure without comment, except to express confidence the situation would work itself out. Steve filled Melissa's car with gas and gave her fifty dollars, just in case. Brian kept his hands inside his pockets and said nothing.

"Now remember," Steve said to Melissa as he hugged her good-bye. "Don't let worries build up. We're just a phone call away."

"Thanks, Steve," Melissa said, grateful for an understanding family. "I'll remember. I promise."

Darlene wrapped loving arms around Melissa. "Don't forget what I said," her mother whispered into her ear.

"I won't," Melissa whispered back.

With indignation plainly showing on his childish face, John-Peter stood in the driveway with his hands on his hips. and demanded, "Why all the secrets?"

Brian lifted John-Peter over his shoulders. "Because you're a kid, and adults don't tell kids anything."

"Uncle Brian?"

"Yes," Brian said as he set John-Peter in his car seat.

"Will you visit me before you go back to school? You may share my room."

"We'll see."

John-Peter's face fell. "That's what big people say when they don't mean it."

"I'm very busy, John-Peter, with work and all. But I'll try."

"You really mean it?"

"Buckle in."

"Okay," John-Peter adjusted his straps and then fished inside his pocket. "Do you want to see my leprechaun?"

Brian was already walking toward the house. Melissa caught his arm. "Are you really coming to Jenson?"

Her brother looked past her to see if John-Peter heard. "Not while that creepy husband of yours lives there."

"You stayed last Easter."

"That was then. This is now. If you can't tolerate Mr. John Simotes, why should I?" Brian shook Melissa's hand from his arm and traipsed into the house.

The atmosphere became cooler, less humid, the further north Melissa drove. She sent Steve silent thanks for the extra money. His generosity more than covered lunch and the large

386

cup of coffee sitting in her cup holder. By mid-afternoon, the sun glowed only warm enough to cause John-Peter to nod off when Melissa exited at Thornton. He was still sleeping when Melissa pulled into the driveway. She decided to leave him in his car seat for the few minutes it would take her to check on his father. If John did not appear stable, she would leave.

As she climbed the back stairs, Melissa saw the wide-open door, a sure sign John was at home. She stepped inside the kitchen. John was leaning against the kitchen counter, picking at a plate of noodles with an indifferent expression, an expression that did not change when he saw Melissa.

"I'm home," Melissa simply said.

"Obviously."

"That's all you're going to say?"

"I didn't kill them, Melissa."

"Why couldn't you tell me that?"

"You should have known."

Darlene could have saved her breath. Her motherly advice proved worthless. Melissa stood in stunned shock at John's callous attitude. Her absence had meant nothing to him.

"I thought you might have missed me."

"I did."

"Why didn't you call?"

"I couldn't."

"Pride?" Melissa said with scorn.

John did not answer her. He rinsed his plate and set it in the sink.

"Then what?"

He folded his arms across his chest. "I'm sick."

"You look perfectly healthy to me."

As soon as the words left Melissa's mouth, she noticed the dark circles underneath John's eyes, waxy sunken cheeks, deep lines around his mouth, and sallow skin. In a flash, she recalled dreaming of a skeletal John sitting at the piano inside Simons Mansion. Had John sent a warning through her sleep? Her mind scanned Dr. Rothgard's list of symptoms, and she fired off a series of questions.

"Have you been eating?"

"Somewhat."

"Drinking?"

"Gallons."

"Water?"

Silence.

Melissa lowered her head. He'd been drinking blood, of course, but her mind refused to accept it. She raised her eyes to look at him.

"Sleeping?"

"Daytime napping."

"Urinating?"

John shrugged. "Maybe a week or two ago."

Fingers of fear snaked up Melissa's back. The end was really coming, and she didn't know how to stop it. Maybe, despite John's hypothesis that Melissa's blood possessed healing balm, it had never been in her power to permanently bring him back to life.

"*Maybe* a week or two ago? You don't know?"

"I didn't chart it."

His coldness hit her hard. Why had she come home? John didn't need her!

"Fine!" Melissa spun on her heel to leave, but John tugged her sleeve and held her back.

"You tell me," he said, gently. "You're the one that threw the newspaper."

Melissa's eyes opened wide. "That long ago?"

John nodded.

She marched to the freezer. It contained only two packages of blood. How long ago since Dr. Rothgard called her and said he'd restocked it? Two nights? Three?

Melissa choked back mounting fear. "Where's all my blood?"

"I drank it."

No! It couldn't be true!

She shook her head and waved her hands, hoping to banish John's hurtful words, but Melissa started crying anyway. John wrapped his arms around her and pulled her close. When was the last time he had held her? When was the last time she had let him?

388

Melissa laid her head on his chest, but now it hurt too much to cry. John rested his chin on her head and said nothing. He still felt so strong, so solid. She couldn't let anything bad happen to him, even if she had to lose gallons of her blood.

John drew her away and tipped up her face to look at her. Whenever John did that, he melted her heart. Now, Melissa only felt dread. He studied her face for a long time without speaking.

"It's over," he said in an even, low voice.

Melissa started to pull away, but John held her fast and said, "I'm dining with Cornell Dyer tonight. Care to join us?"

She eyed him with suspicion. "Dinner with Cornell? Why?"

"To review my options."

CHAPTER 26: OF GARLIC WREATHS AND HOLY WATER

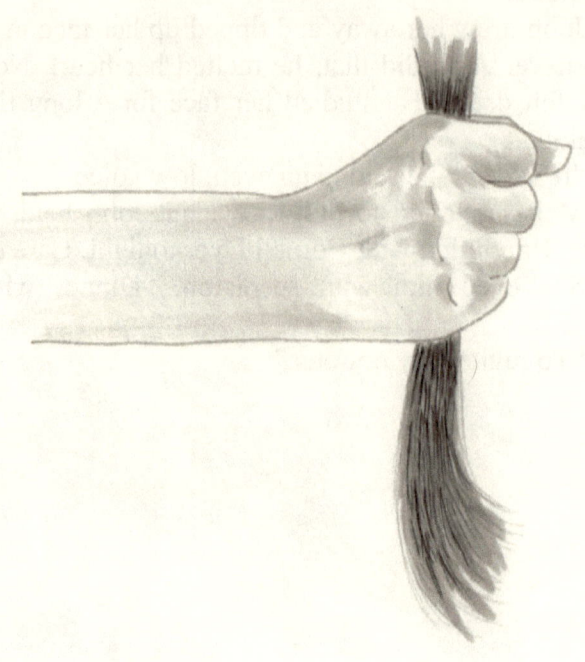

"Tonight?" Melissa couldn't believe that, on her first night in Jenson, John wanted to eat with Cornell Dyer! Her eyes noticed the wall clock. John should be walking out the door to class. Maybe John really *had* lost his job. "But...I just got here."

"So stay home."

How could he say that so easily? Why hadn't he missed her as much as she missed him? Why had she allowed her mother to raise her hopes? Except for blood, John had no use for her.

"What about John-Peter?"

"Ask Katie to watch him."

Why did John flip every conversation to his advantage? "Katie's coming, too?"

"She will if you ask."

"But not to dinner?"

"No."

"I don't understand. Why do you want me to go if Katie...."

"Melissa, will you meet with us or not?"

Suppressing a sigh, Melissa picked up the phone and began dialing. That's when she remembered John-Peter still napping in the car seat.

"John, will you get him? I didn't intend to leave him that long."

"Of course."

Katie answered on the fourth ring.

"Did you have a nice time at your mom's? John mentioned you took a mini vacation."

"It was okay. Listen, Katie, John and Cornell are having dinner tonight, and John wants me to go with them. Could you watch John-Peter at my house for a couple of hours?"

"Sure!"

Melissa hesitated, scanning the back door to make sure John wasn't near. "You don't mind?"

"Mind? Why should I?"

"Because you're not invited."

"Oh, Melissa, you silly, this is business. I don't interfere in Cornell's work. It's too important. If watching John-Peter helps you guys out, I'm happy to do it."

Melissa decided to go all the way. "Do you have any idea why Cornell wants to talk with John?"

"No. Should I?"

John's footsteps sounded on the deck stairs. "Katie, I've got to go. I'll see you soon."

She hung up the phone and rushed to open the door for John, who was nestling the cheek of the sleeping bundle in his arms.

"His schedule's messed up," Melissa said, feeling defensive and hoping John-Peter would be alert for tonight.

"It doesn't matter. I quit the route," John tossed out as he walked to John-Peter's bedroom.

Quit the route? What if the college really did fire John? Another, more awful thought came to mind. How had John known Melissa had been thinking about the route? He hadn't read her mind, had he?

"I'm going to shower," Melissa called through the closed nursery door.

As she stepped out of the bathroom, she saw Katie carrying a large cooler to the kitchen.

"Produce from Ma's garden," Katie said with a happy smile. "John-Peter won't go hungry tonight."

"Where's John?"

"With Cornell."

Disappointment welled up inside Melissa. She had assumed John would want to ride with her. She glanced out the front window. The large vehicle sat in front of the house.

"You drove the RV here yourself?"

"Sure did. It's easy once you're used to it."

"I'm impressed," Melissa said, and that part was true. "I could never do it. Where did you drop off Cornell?"

"A little cafe just outside Jenson. It's brand new. Cornell said John wanted privacy."

For once, Melissa felt thankful for John's covert ways. She'd rather be found dead than caught in the presence of someone like Cornell Dyer. Melissa noted Katie's directions, and away she went. Gray's Cafe, a slate building just before the strip mall, featured a rustic wood interior and dim lighting, the perfect place, Melissa thought, for a vampire to meet a so-called slayer. John and Cornell sat in the back, engaged in what appeared to be rather serious conversation. Binders and brochures were scattered over the table.

"I ordered for you," John said indifferently, his only acknowledgment of her presence. He nodded at Cornell. "Continue."

After an uncertain glance at Melissa, Cornell opened the first page of a binder and slid the book close to John.

"Well, as I said, you may choose from several packages. Of course, the traditional and perhaps most successful means of preventing your vampire return is to drive a stake through your heart. We do have to accomplish it before the third day after your death, the time you are most likely to rise as one of the undead, or it might not work. I then decapitate you with a silver blade and stuff your head with fresh garlic. It is, of course, the most expensive, because of the risk involved."

"Risk?"

"Well, to me. I have to break into the funeral parlor, unless you use one of my partner facilities, and then perform the deed before the burial. Or I sneak into the cemetery after dawn and dig up your coffin. You can only imagine the consequences to me if someone detects me, or, even worse, should I fail."

John nodded.

"For an extra fee, which provides superior protection, I can, after the decapitation, remove your heart and your intestines and then chop your body into four parts, one limb per quarter."

"Cremation?"

"Yep, if you want it. I could either scatter the ashes to the four corners of the earth or bury you in four different locations, which is tricky to do in modern times. Now John, if you haven't already picked a grave site, another possibility is to bury you under running water. The ancients were fond of that method, although I daresay, with twentieth century regulations, it still might be more feasible to first cremate you."

"I meant cremation alone."

"Well, John, cremation only is indeed an option, but I must apply the proper methodology. Consecrated wine and holy water can incinerate your corpse to a crisp. However, I don't often recommend just cremation because of the extra step involved for me."

"Which is?"

"I gotta feed the ashes to a wolf."

Disgusted, Melissa dropped her fork on her plate and glared at Cornell. He noticed and, with haste, flipped through the pages. He smiled at her and looked back at John.

"Ah, here's one the missus might like. We stuff your coffin with any combination of three known materials that will trap you there: wild roses, salt, or poppy seeds. Then we wait until after you are buried and pound iron stakes and silver nails through your coffin into the ground. There is absolutely no desecration of your grave, and the iron stakes will not be visible. The downfall? It's not as foolproof as a wooden stake straight through the heart. However, we can add an extra measure of protection by pouring holy water through the holes."

John reached for another binder and opened it. "And this?"

"My priciest and riskiest option. I own a couple of silver bullets reputed to have been blessed by a fourteenth century priest. Although they come with a certificate of authenticity, you are taking a chance with them. Plus, silver bullets only work after you return as a vampire."

John reviewed the photos with interest. "Delivery?"

"I fire them through your head."

Melissa's patience broke. "Honestly, I can't believe you're so cavalier about ending John's life. This is my husband and my son's father. You talk about vampire slaying as if it was the next big, marketing trend. My husband is not your stepping-stone to fame and fortune."

Cornell looked from Melissa to John with a puzzled expression. "Is something wrong? Shall I not continue?"

Melissa appealed to the man at the other end of the table, the man becoming more distance from her with each passing minute. "John, please! He's a charlatan."

John set aside Cornell's book and coldly said, "You forgot something, Melissa."

"You weren't this extreme with Henry, and he didn't come back!"

"This is not your funeral." He leaned slightly forward. *"Yet."*

Melissa pushed away her chair from the table. "I need air."

Losing John hurt enough, but Cornell Dyer's capitalization on her agony was more than she could bear.

How long Melissa frantically paced outside the restaurant she did not know, but at some point the front door opened, and Cornell stepped outside. He lit a cigarette and leaned against the building.

"Nice evening," he said around the butt.

"Bug off."

Cornell blew out smoke. "You don't like me, Melissa."

"Wow! You really do have a crystal ball."

"Well, lots of people don't like me. They think I'm a kook until they need my help to bend the laws of nature in their favor or to save them from an enemy they cannot perceive."

"And then you take their money."

Cornell inhaled deeply into his lungs before he spoke again. "Life. What an transient entity. We imagine we can create it. We can take it away from someone if we choose. Yet there are individuals who become stuck in that strange land between life and death, where their ability to either live or die becomes complicated."

His words stirred up an ashen wasteland of disoriented, groping shades eternally seeking, and forever missing, the elusive thread of life. Melissa saw John among them, and her heart broke with loneliness for him.

"And yet, I firmly believe each vampire owns the right on whether or not to continue existing. Not everyone wants that sort of immortality. It's my job to oblige their requests for relief."

He puffed a cloud from his mouth while carefully observing Melissa. Oh, why wouldn't he go away and leave her alone?

"No wonder people think you're crazy! Listen to you, talking about vampires! You offer nothing but cheap scams to part innocent people from their money."

Cornell crushed the cigarette under his foot. "If you really love him, Melissa, you'll let him go."

"I've had enough of your crap. Tell John I went home."

Melissa drove away seething over the insufferable Cornell Dyer. However did Katie put up with him? She'd take John and his blood treatments a million times over Cornell's underhanded self-glorification.

Katie hailed Melissa's return with a sunny, "Back so soon?"

"They didn't need me anymore, so I left."

"Good decision. Let the men talk, I say. I made some tea. Want some?"

"Sure." Melissa settled at the kitchen table. It seemed so normal, this sipping of tea and the trickling of warm amber, not blood, down her throat. "Where's John-Peter?"

"Still sleeping. I didn't know what time he woke up for newspapers. Karla's down, too, so I've had a nice, quiet evening."

"Katie," Melissa uncertain as the best way to proceed. She couldn't understand Katie's rapturous attachment to the man. "Where did you meet Cornell?"

"When I was attending Molly Blake's, one of my instructors invited us to a séance at her house. I'd never gone to a séance. I'd only played with that spirit board at your house, remember?

Melissa nodded her head and took another sip of tea.

"Anyway, before her uncle had died, he had promised to leave his money to her because she had taken care of him for so long. But when the will was read, my teacher got nothing. So she hired Cornell to contact her uncle and find out why he lied to her."

"And did he?" Melissa asked.

"What, lie to her?"

"No, did Cornell talk to her uncle?"

"Yes. He'd written a second will that left everything to her."

Katie's statement astounded Melissa. Could Cornell really be legitimate? Surely, Cornell could not have known the location of a second will.

"And the uncle told Cornell where she could find it?"

"No, the uncle stopped talking to Cornell at that point," Katie said, "but I'm sure she found it."

Melissa inwardly groaned. She couldn't believe this obvious phony had duped Katie, who lit up like a firefly at every mention of Cornell's name.

"Oh, Melissa, you should have seen Cornell in action during that séance. So authoritative with the spirits. So commanding of the situation. Of course, I just had to meet him."

"Of course," Melissa said with a short, rueful laugh.

"He was talking to some of the guests while eating cake. I understood why everyone wanted to be near him, so I patiently waited my turn. He was speaking to the last person when he looked up, and, Melissa, you won't believe this, he saw me. Cornell Dyer noticed me."

Melissa absently swirled the remaining tea in her cup. She felt like throwing up.

"I told him what a wonderfully awesome job he had done that night, and he thanked me. Then he cut another piece and offered me a slice, too. I didn't really want any cake because of my diet but then decided the cake must taste very good because I'd seen Cornell eat three pieces. I couldn't be rude and refuse it!"

Was Katie serious?

"I see your point," Melissa agreed, hoping Katie did not detect the sarcasm in her voice.

"Anyway, we chit chatted for a while, and then Cornell asked if I'd like to see his office. That's the RV. Well, you can imagine how honored I felt to enter the mysterious chambers of the great Professor Cornell Dyer!"

"Wow."

"Without divulging any of Cornell's secrets, I can only tell you he shared things with me that night he said he never shared with anyone else. And when he kissed me...oh, Melissa, the difference between the kiss of a boy and a grown man!"

Melissa thought of Jason Frye and said nothing.

"Now you're probably thinking, 'Well, Katie's young. She only wanted Cornell for his body.' But Melissa, I grew a lifetime that night with Cornell, and it's what a man's got upstairs that counts. Cornell has a brilliant mind."

A tiny laugh escaped Melissa's lips, and she put her head into her hands to hide it. What had happened to Katie?

"When morning came, I'd made up my mind. Why should I spend a lifetime cutting hair when I could help Cornell on his benevolent mission?"

Melissa raised her head and stared disbelieving at Katie.

"And your parents were okay with this?"

"Well, not at first, but you know parents. They're fine with Cornell now."

John-Peter stumbled into the kitchen, rubbing his eyes, droopy from sleep, but when he saw Katie, his face brightened, and he leaped into her lap. "Did you come from Munsonville just to visit us?"

Katie ruffled his hair. "Cornell had a meeting with your daddy. Are you hungry? There's a surprise in the cooler for you."

John-Peter slid down to check. In the distance, Karla began crying, and Katie left to comfort her. John-Peter, still squatting on the floor, scooped up a handful of raspberries.

The back door opened, and John and Cornell entered, just as Katie returned to the kitchen with Karla, contentedly cooing around her bottle. Cornell held out his hand, and Katie blissfully ran up and kissed it.

"We're staying in Jenson tonight," Cornell said. "John gave me directions to a campground."

Katie turned to Melissa. "See? It's just as I told you. Life with Cornell is such an adventure. I never know from day to day where his work will take us."

As long as Cornell's work took him far from Melissa's house, Melissa didn't care where Cornell went. But she didn't feel comfortable telling it to Katie. Instead, she hugged her friend good-bye.

"Thanks for keeping John-Peter for me."

"Anytime, Melissa, anytime."

Melissa accompanied the Dyers to the front door, the only way she could ensure they wouldn't prolong their stay. After Katie stepped onto the porch, Cornell grabbed Melissa's hand, slapped one business card into it, and said, "Call me at this number tomorrow morning when John wakes up."

She tried to return the card, but Cornell closed her fist around it and gave her an enigmatic smile. Melissa snatched her hand away.

"Cornell Dyer, it'll be a cold day in hell when I call you."

"That's "Professor" to you."

Before Melissa could think up a fitting retort, Cornell added, "Oh, and you'd better dig out your parka, Melissa, because you'll call me all right."

Melissa slammed the door after him, marched to the kitchen, and tossed Cornell's card into the kitchen trash. John had just started to play when Melissa returned to the dining room. John-Peter watched him with a puzzled air.

"Father, is there time? Don't we have to leave for the route?"

"No." John sat the little boy beside him on the bench. "Tonight we shall play as long as we like."

John-Peter's face shone, but Melissa could not, would not rise to his excitement. Even after Melissa closed the bedroom door, the doleful strains ran through her mind even as sleep numbed it. Sometime in the night, Melissa awakened to the jostle of the mattress as John climbed into bed. She closed her eyes, squeezing them against betrayal as John moved close.

"Melissa," he whispered, "Are you asleep?"

She did not roll toward him.

"Yes," she said through gritted teeth.

John lay silent for a long time. Melissa only felt his warm breath caressing the back of her neck. She tried not to pay attention to him, but how could she not? Melissa was losing him, and he didn't even care. John still did not touch her, but he remained so close, Melissa heard him swallow.

"I'm scared," John said. "Will you hold me?"

CHAPTER 27: THE GREAT FAST

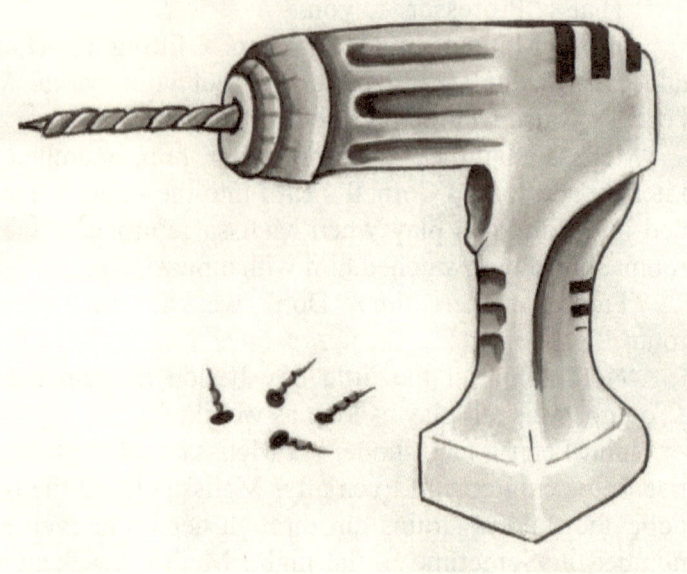

The bedroom door burst open, and John, eyes wild and hair disheveled, stumbled into the room. One pant leg flapped open; red streaks smeared his shirt. He grabbed his pillow and the blanket and then dashed out the door.

"John!"

Melissa flew out of bed after him. She heard the pounding of his feet as he dashed down the basement stairs, and she headed after him. As she reached the bottom, she heard a closet door slam followed by the sound of a light "click." She ran to the door and grabbed the door knob. It spun freely in her hands. Melissa banged on the door.

"John, open up!"

Silence.

She beat with her fists. "John! John!"

"Mother!"

John-Peter was calling from the top of the stairs. He mustn't come down, he mustn't! Melissa sped back up the stairs and wrapped her arms around the little boy who regarded her with grave eyes.

"Your father's not feeling well," Melissa said, trying to sound soothing and calm. "I'm calling Dr. Rothgard."

"Shouldn't Father be in bed?"

"Well, yes. That's why I'm calling Dr. Rothgard. He'll make him do it."

John-Peter pattered to the refrigerator and opened it.

"May I have the watermelon from Katie?"

"Sure, go ahead." Melissa was already dialing the telephone and only absently noting John-Peter climbing onto the counter for a plate.

"Dr. Rothgard's answering service."

"Would you please leave a message for Dr. Rothgard? My husband is sick."

"I'm sorry, but he's out of the country until the end of the week."

"What?"

"He's instructing all emergency patients to go directly to Jenson Memorial Hospital. Otherwise, call back during regular business hours and...."

Melissa slammed down the phone. Now what?

"Want a piece of watermelon, Mother?"

John-Peter was clutching a chunk of the fruit in his outstretched hand. Streams of sticky juice trickled down his arm. Melissa pulled the kitchen towel from the rack, wet one end, and wiped the mess from his skin.

"That's okay, John-Peter," Melissa said, trying to control her trembling voice. "I'm not very hungry right now."

John-Peter popped the watermelon into his mouth and grabbed another piece. "When is Dr. Rothgard coming, Mother?"

Melissa fought back panic as she began pacing back and forth across the kitchen floor. "He's not. He's gone until the end of the week."

"Then who will help Father?"

"I don't know!"

John-Peter picked up his plate, tilted it to his mouth, slurped the remaining juice, and then said, "Maybe you should call Cornell Dyer."

Oh, how she despised the sound of that man's name!

"John-Peter, please be quiet."

"Father says Cornell is a genius."

"I'm trying to think."

"I know, that's why...."

"Your father is sick, remember?"

"But, Mother...."

"Mind your own business!"

John-Peter's face crumpled. He slid from his chair and dashed from the room. Melissa's heart broke at the sight, but she felt too angry to go after him. Hating herself for doing it, Melissa frantically pawed through the kitchen garbage can.

Cornell answered on the first ring. "Ah, Melissa, I've anticipated your call. John is home?"

"He's barricaded himself in a basement closet."

"Be right there."

Melissa hung up the phone, already regretting making that call. She trudged to John-Peter's bedroom and peeped inside. John-Peter lay on the floor, hands clasped behind his neck, staring at the ceiling.

"John-Peter?"

He didn't move.

"I've called Cornell. And I'm sorry I snapped at you. I'm upset about your father."

John-Peter turned toward Melissa. "If anyone can help, Cornell can."

She pushed open the door and sat next to him. "Why do you say that?"

"Because that's what Cornell does, remember, Mother? He helps people. Besides, Father trusts him."

He pointed to a fairy, filmy and corn-flower blue, hovering like a bumblebee over the outstretched white flower. Above it, a cloud of even tinier creatures flew from amongst the petals and dispersed into the background.

"Who is that, Mother?"

"In the painting?"

John-Peter nodded.

"That's a fairy, dear."

"I know that," John-Peter said with impatience. "I mean, what's the fairy's name?"

"You can name it whatever you wish. It's your room."

His eyes gazed around his walls. "I want to visit those places."

Melissa smiled. She remembered feeling the same way about the Cinderella pictures hanging on *her* bedroom wall when she was a little girl.

"You can go anytime you like," Melissa said, "Just use your imagination."

She reclined on the floor next to John-Peter. Together, they spun tales of a mystical, magical fairyland over which she and John-Peter ruled. The story so engrossed them that they both jumped at the sudden pounding.

"It's Cornell!" John-Peter ran from the room.

"Hold on! Don't answer it."

But John-Peter had the back door wide open by the time Melissa reached the kitchen, and Cornell was dragging a large trunk inside. From the window, Melissa saw the large motor home occupying their driveway.

Melissa's mouth dropped. "What are you doing with that?"

Cornell only said, "John-Peter, would you show me the way?"

"Noted and affirmed."

Katie, with Karla on her hip, stepped through the doorway. "Here, Melissa, would you please hold her? I've got to get something for Cornell."

"Katie, I can't...."

But Katie thrust the baby at Melissa anyway and ran outside. Cornell was now thump-thumping the trunk down the steps. Katie soon returned, lugging several large beams of wood.

Melissa blocked Katie's entrance. "Hold on! What's Cornell doing with those?

"How should I know?" Katie breathed hard from the effort. "Are you going to let me through or not?"

Before Melissa could answer her, two meaty hands clasped Melissa's shoulders and pulled her aside. Cornell lifted the beams from Katie and proceeded to the basement.

Katie, looking offended, only said, "What's gotten into you, Melissa? You're acting pretty, darn strange."

Stupefied at Katie's audacity, Melissa held out Karla and said, "Here. Take your own baby."

"I can't. I'm helping Cornell."

Katie once again disappeared into the back yard, but she soon returned, this time, struggling to bring a large piece of sheet metal into the house, just as Cornell appeared at the top of the stairs to retrieve it.

"What are you doing?" Melissa exploded, pushing Karla back to Katie. "You're supposed to be helping John!"

"I am."

Whistling a tuneless song, Cornell proceeded down the stairs, with Melissa directly behind him. When he reached John's hideout, Cornell braced the sheet metal against the wall, next to the beams, and said, "Maybe you should go upstairs while I work."

"Get him out now!"

"That's not what John wants."

"I don't care! Break down this door!"

"Nope." He squatted down and opened his tool chest.

Melissa grabbed his arm. "You're not barricading him in there!"

"My contract is with John.

"Leave now, or I'll call the police."

"Call. They'll have a few questions for John about last night anyway."

"Last night? What happened last night?"

The whirring of the drill answered her. In frustration, Melissa stomped upstairs. Katie was sitting at the kitchen table coloring with John-Peter.

"It's fine, Melissa," Katie peered into the crayon box. "Cornell knows what he's doing."

"   John will starve!"

"I think that's the point."

John-Peter carefully traced a tree with green crayon and asked, "Cornell is starving Father?" with the same tone as he might have asked what John was cooking for dinner.

Katie smiled benevolently at him. "Remember? It's to help your father give up hunting."

"Oh, good." John-Peter shaded a leaf. "I always felt sorry for the poor animals he ate."

Melissa's mind whirled at this surreal turn of events. *John had allowed his baby son to witness....*

"Mother, have you ever heard a rabbit scream in pain and fight?"

Betrayal, outrage, and the terrifying reality of what John had become crashed down on her. Melissa ran to the bathroom, hoping she'd make it in time, hoping she would never stop throwing up, knowing she could never vomit away the disgusting, scary truth. Over and over her stomach heaved, long after she'd emptied it.

Energy spent, stomach cramping, throat burning, Melissa leaned her head against the cool bathroom tile and remembered the last time she felt this way, several years ago at the Crossroads Tap, when John led her out the door and onto the grass. How she had feared losing John to her literature teacher; how small that fear now seemed; and how much easier to lure John away from another woman than from the abode of the undead. If John reverted to his old ways, could she make him human again? Would he still desire it?

Trembling from exertion and fright, Melissa braced her hands on the stool and slowly, unsteadily, stood. She ran cold water in the sink and splashed some over her face, not caring that it dripped onto her neck, unmarred still from the marks of John's fangs. Straightening, Melissa caught her reflection in the mirror, surprised at the youthful face returning that gaze. She didn't look nearly as old and ghastly as she felt.

She opened the bathroom door in time to see Cornell strut through the dining room and into the living room. He plopped onto the couch, turned on the television, and braced his feet against the coffee table. Melissa angrily strode across the room and shoved his feet onto the floor. Cornell yawned, but did not otherwise react, except to pick up the television guide. and ask, "What's good this time of day?"

Melissa snatched it from his hand and threw it onto the table. "Forget about TV. What happens now?"

"We wait."

"Wait for what?"

Katie interrupted the impending argument. "Melissa, I'm taking Karla and John-Peter to the park. Come with us?"

"No!"

"Then nap while I go with them. It's going to be a long night. You should rest."

Katie gave Melissa a gentle nudge toward the bedroom. Melissa angrily shook away her shoulder. Katie shrugged and led the children out the back door. Cornell had stretched his legs across the coffee table and was already watching television. Furious and frustrated at her diminishing control, Melissa retreated to the bedroom. If anything, sleep offered a brief escape where fear for John and bitter anger toward the Dyers could not touch her. Yet, when Melissa finally sank into restless slumber, impressions of John from his Victorian past and leisure suit present jumbled together in her head along with piano music, blood, and the oppressive mist that spiraled tightly around her.

"John!" she cried aloud.

The abrupt return to consciousness sent her heart racing. Someone was knocking.

"Melissa?" Katie pushed the door open. "Are you all right?"

She struggled to free herself from the tangled bedclothes, while Katie patiently watched.

"Dinner's almost ready. Come eat with us."

Even with the curtains still closed, Melissa could feel warm sunshine pouring into her bedroom. "So early?"

"Cornell wants the kids and me safely inside in the motor home before dusk. He said it's up to you whether or not you want to stay in the house."

Since when did Cornell make those decisions? Melissa more than had her fill of his smugness, but she would not force his eviction, not yet, on the outside chance his unorthodox methods might help John. For some unfathomable reason, John esteemed this man's opinion and so-called skill. Cornell had better live up to it.

"Sure," Melissa said tunelessly, as she finally broke free of the sheets.

Katie's stroganoff tasted delicious, but how could Melissa enjoy it with John trapped in the basement, and Cornell shoveling down serving after serving faster than he could possibly taste it? In imitation, John-Peter smacked his lips at every bite of the vegetable casserole Katie had thoughtfully prepared for him, but Melissa hadn't the energy to correct him.

After dinner, Katie whipped through the dinner dishes with astonishing speed, and John-Peter impressed her with his drying skills by keeping up with her. Restless, Melissa swept the floor, and, for the first time since she'd found the cache of animals behind the garage, took out the garbage. Although still light outside, the sun had begun its usual dip toward the horizon line. Melissa trudged the bag to the back of the garage, lifted the lid of the can, and dropped the bag inside it. It hit the bottom with an accusing thunk. Its emptiness reinforced the fact John had eaten very little conventional food while Melissa stayed in Grover's Park.

She replaced the liner inside the kitchen can the exact moment John-Peter jumped from his chair. "I'll get my pajamas," he said to Katie as he tore to his room.

Melissa trailed behind him. John-Peter curled his toes around the edge of the open, bottom drawer to peek into an upper one. She seized him under his arms and set him on the floor.

"And what do you think you're doing?"

"Getting pajamas."

She selected the top pair and handed them to John-Peter. He shook his head. "No, I want the turtle ones Grandma bought me."

"Honey, they're in the laundry."

His lower lip protruded in a pout, reminding Melissa that, despite his accelerated intelligence, John-Peter was still a baby.

"Wear the orange ones tonight."

"Why didn't you wash the green ones?"

"Because I'm helping Cornell care for your father."

The answer seemed to satisfy John-Peter. He snatched the pajamas from Melissa's hands and started for the door. He paused, one hand on the knob, and turned to look at her.

"Will Cornell really make Father well again?"

"Yes, I believe he will," Melissa said with a confidence she did not feel.

"Can't I say good-night to Father?"

"He's sleeping already. Maybe tomorrow."

"Okay."

He zipped into the living room, and Melissa heard him announce to Katie, "I'm ready to go camping!"

Melissa walked them to the back door.

"That's a wonderful idea, telling John-Peter he's going camping in the motor home, even if it is just parked in front of our house."

Katie smiled down at John-Peter and then back at Melissa. "It'll help distract him, for tonight, anyway."

John-Peter tugged at Melissa's hand. "Kiss me good-night, Mother."

She bent to return the kiss and ruffle his hair. Suddenly overcome with intense love for this child she shared with John, Melissa pulled him tight and whispered, "Be good for Katie. I'll see you in the morning."

"We're sleeping in a tent."

"Not a real tent," Katie hastily added. "I'm just throwing a blanket over a table, but it will be tent enough for us."

As she closed the back door behind the little party, Melissa heard footsteps on the basement stairs. John? But no, it was only Cornell, clumping through the house into the living room where he returned to slouching on her couch.

"Won't be long now," Cornell said.

Little by little, the sunny sky transformed into brilliant colors and faded into darkness. Melissa huddled in her chair, pretending to read while Cornell guffawed at God only knew what. Gradually, his head bobbed onto his chest, and an occasional snuffle escaped his lips. From the amount of food he had consumed, Cornell should have slipped into a coma.

The first sound was a definitive, distant "thud," almost as if someone bounced something against a wall.

Cornell's eyes jerked open. "It has begun."

A second thud followed the first. Soon came frantic clattering, fierce walloping, and rapid banging as John's unearthly bellowing filled the house.

"Oh, Cornell, he's trying to get out!"

"Yes."

"Can't you let him go?"

"I've built a secure enclosure."

"It's cruel!"

"It's for the best, Melissa."

The entire house shook with John's pounding and shrill, diabolical shrieking. Melissa covered her ears with her hands, but she could not obliterate the deafening clamor.

"Cornell, the neighbors will hear!"

"The basement should contain the noise."

"Are you sure?"

"Well, that's why I also casted a spell. Let's hope it works."

John's raging continued throughout the night. At dawn, he produced a few half-hearted sputterings. An uneasy silence signaled the end of the nightmare. Melissa's head pounded, and her body shook from the terrifying noise. A weary Cornell trudged to the basement with Melissa flying after him.

"Are you letting him out?"

"Not hardly."

"I'm coming with you."

"Not recommended."

"I don't care!"

Cornell descended the stairs with weary halting steps. Melissa pushed past him, ran to the reinforced fortress, and cried out," John!"

A feeble voice answered, "Where's Cornell?"

Melissa's heart sank. "He's right here, John."

Cornell thumped on the door. "John!"

"What's she doing here?"

Cornell shot Melissa an "I told you so" look and rubbed his hands over his face in frustration. "Dishonoring your request."

Melissa heard a scuffle behind the door. "Melissa, do me a favor."

She leaned her cheek against the door. "I'm here, John. I'll do anything you want. What's the favor?"

"Stay out of the basement."

The phone upstairs rang. Melissa wavered, uncertain what to do. She could not and would not stay out of the basement. John might trust Cornell to keep his best interests at heart, but Melissa did not. Maybe Dr. Rothgard was calling. She ran upstairs and caught the phone on the fifth ring.

"Hi, Melissa," Katie said. "I didn't wake you, did I?"

"No, I'm up." Fresh disappointment washed over Melissa as she glanced at the stairs.

"I fed John-Peter his breakfast, and I'll keep the kids amused out here most of the day. I figure that way you can get some sleep. Rough night last night, huh?"

"That's an understatement."

"Well, tell Cornell I love him when you see him. I know he's busy, and I've got to get back to the kids. John-Peter and I are playing pirate ship, and he's a much better pirate than I am. I've already had to walk the plank twice."

Melissa and Cornell spent the day in the living room not talking to one another as they intermittently dozed. In the early afternoon, Katie brought the children into the house with her so she could begin dinner. Again, as soon as they had tidied the kitchen, Katie hustled them back into the motor home.

John's raging began again at sundown. Each blow against the door and each wailing howl cut through her with slicing pain. Melissa withstood it as long as she could before she made up her mind. What was it Henry once told her? John acknowledged only one opinion, his. But John had married her. Shouldn't that mean something? At John's insistence, they had been joined and fused. They drank from a common cup and owned the locks from each other's hair. Melissa no longer cared what John thought. His opinion was no longer the only one that mattered.

At daybreak, Cornell immediately rose and headed downstairs. Melissa wasted no time. She sped on tiptoes to the kitchen and picked up the phone.

"Operator?" Melissa said in a hushed voice. "My husband is very sick. I need an ambulance immediately."

"What is your address?"

Melissa provided the operator with the necessary information. Too late, Cornell disconnected the call with a frantic, *"What are you doing?"*

"What any reasonable person does in a medical emergency. I sent for help."

"Do you comprehend what you just did?"

"No, and please don't threaten me by saying the police want John. I think the police will be more interested in what you're doing to him, so you'd better get John up here before the paramedics arrive."

Cornell's shoulders sagged in defeat, but he obediently descended the stairs. "I pity your ignorance."

"And I despise your pompous 'holier than thou' attitude."

The grinding whirr of a chair saw filled the house, and Melissa smiled grimly at the noise, since it was bringing John, and real assistance for him, close at last. Soon, Cornell was half-walking, half-dragging John up the stairs. Melissa's hand flew up to her mouth, and she stifled a crying scream. She had not anticipated John's battered appearance.

His hands and face were bruised and lacerated; his clothes hung ragged and torn. One eye had swelled shut; the other looked red and glassy. Blood foamed at his mouth and caked his damp and matted hair.

Cornell guided John to the couch, and Melissa crouched on the floor beside her husband. "John, you're going to the hospital. Everything will be fine now, I promise."

John groaned. His head rolled and fell against the back of the couch. "Don't do it," he ordered, but the faint and raspy voice lacked authority.

"No more quackery. Real doctors will treat you now."

"No."

The appearance of the ambulance sent Katie bounding into the house, Karla on her hip and John-Peter treading on her toes. "Is everything all right...oh, my God!"

She spun on her feet and hurried John-Peter back outside. As they left, Melissa heard John-Peter ask, "Will I see Father today?"

Three paramedics filed into the living room, the youngest gasping when he saw John's appearance. Melissa took a deep breath and squarely faced the posse.

"My husband recently lost his job, and he's not handling it well. Look at what he's done to himself. He needs professional help."

Two paramedics headed for the door. "We're getting a stretcher," one said to Melissa.

John glared at the remaining paramedic and hissed. "I'm not going."

The youngest paramedic looked at Melissa, shuffled his feet, and cleared his throat before he said. "Mrs. Simotes, we're sorry, but unless your husband...."

Melissa interrupted him. "But he does want to go." She sat on the couch. "John, if you won't do this for yourself, and if you won't do it for me, then do it for John-Peter. You're his father. Look how much he loves you. Don't give up without a fight."

"Haven't you heard a word I've....?"

She took his mutilated hands into her gentle ones. "At least go with some dignity, like the man I've loved all these years, and not as some rabid animal. Give John-Peter a good, final memory of you."

The other two paramedics returned. "Unfortunately, Mr. Simotes, since you've injured yourself, we're required by law...."

John's one open eye gazed at Melissa with a terrible anger. The he looked away, disgusted. "You got your way, Melissa."

Melissa shot a look of triumph at Cornell Dyer. "Can you and Katie keep John-Peter for awhile?"

Cornell gave her a strange look. "Sure, Melissa. I'm not going anywhere."

She dashed out the kitchen door and backed her car near the edge of the driveway, waiting for the paramedics to load John into the ambulance, but they had placed the gurney on the sidewalk and had not moved it further. Melissa tapped her fingers on the steering wheel, impatience growing by the second. What took them so long?

One of the paramedics approached Melissa's car. "He won't let us move him until he talks to you."

Melissa slammed her car into park and sped toward the stretcher where John lay. She bent down and started to lovingly say, "John," when he grabbed her hair at the scalp and yanked her close.

"Ouch!" His unexpected strength shocked her.

"Melissa," John said in a hoarse voice, barely louder than a hiss. A savage eye gripped hers. "Stop hindering my orders to Cornell."

"John, please don't do this!"

"After I die, he'll...."

"No!" Melissa's eyes filled with tears, more at John's words and his insistence on leaving her than any physical pain he was inflicting. "You can't make me obey you, John. You'll be dead."

She couldn't bear the hatred on John's face. Why wouldn't he listen?

"Listen, John, we'll start over. We remade you into a man once. We can do it again. Oh John, please don't give up. Please say you'll try. Please don't leave me, John. I can't do this without you!"

John let her hair drop. Melissa breathed out with relief. Finally, he understood. Everything would be all right. If the doctors couldn't save him, then she, Melissa, would do it.

Only she did not like his cagey expression or the wily smile playing about his lips.

"Come closer," John said.

Melissa did, and an iron vise grabbed her throat.

"That was no dream at your mother's house. You now share my curse."

"But...." Melissa began until John's fingers choked off her words.

"If you allow me to return again from the grave, I swear I will take you back down with me."

CHAPTER 28: STRONG-ARMED

Melissa flew through the hospital's main doors and straight to the woman at the front desk, crying, "My husband came here by ambulance. Where is he?"

"What is his name?"

"John Simotes."

The woman shuffled through paperwork and then said, "You can't go back there yet. They're still stabilizing him. Have a seat in the waiting room. Someone from registration will call you in a few minutes."

Melissa bristled at the woman's unfeeling attitude, but before she mustered a retort, a uniformed young man approached her. "Ma'am, your keys, please."

She whirled to face him. "I beg your pardon?"

He held out his hand. "I'm from the hospital's new valet service. I'm here to park your car."

"Oh!" Flustered, Melissa unzipped her purse and dug through its contents. She produced the keys with a flourish. "Here you go."

"Just the car key, ma'am."

The ring defied all efforts of her trembling fingers to remove the key, and Melissa grew more desperate by the second. Why couldn't she see John? Finally, the valet himself took the jangling mess, selected the appropriate key, and dropped the others back into her palm.

"Melissa Simotes."

She startled at the sound of her name. An older, immaculately coiffured brunette stood in the waiting room, scanning the area. Melissa hurried to meet her.

"I'm Melissa Simotes."

"This way, please."

Melissa followed the woman to the fourth cubicle at the far part of the waiting room.

"You may have a seat." The woman pointed to a pair of chairs near the desk.

Melissa sat, glad for the opportunity to relieve her wobbling legs and collect her thoughts. The woman rolled a form into the typewriter on her desk. Melissa read the plastic sign: Lynette Campbell.

"Your husband's name is John Simotes?"

"Yes."

"Date of birth?"

"June nineteenth."

The woman paused in expectation. When Melissa did not answer, she asked, somewhat irritably, "And the year?"

Melissa said nothing. Lynette turned and looked at her.

"I...." Melissa began. She couldn't tell this woman in what year John had *really* been born, but would it affect his medical treatment? "I'm not sure."

Lynette stared at Melissa in surprise. "You don't know it?"

Melissa shook her head.

"Well, then, do you know his age?"

"His exact age?"

"Mrs. Simotes...."

"Thirty-two," Melissa started and then realized John's age had not changed the entire time she known him. "I...I think."

"Place of employment?"

Melissa hesitated and then answered, "Jenson College."

"Occupation?"

"Music...professor."

"And your home address?"

Melissa recited her address and phone number, as well as the address of the school and the phone number to the main office and the music room. She glanced at the clock. Precious minutes ticked away. What was happening with John?

"Religious preference?"

"None."

"Do you have your insurance card?"

Groping on the floor for her purse which somehow landed under her chair, Melissa again unzipped her purse, rummaged for her wallet, and produced the desired piece of cardboard. Lynette took it from her hand and typed the information. Melissa fidgeted on the edge of her chair and twisted her wedding ring, the only connection, except John-Peter, she still had with John. Why did this take so long?

Lynette slid the card across her desk to Melissa. The typewriter keys clattered a few more times before Lynette pulled the paper from the roller and set it on her desk. She picked up a pen, drew a large "X" in two places, and pushed both pen and paper to Melissa's side of the desk.

"This form allows him to receive treatment here," Lynette said. "Sign and date it then write his name where it says, "patient," and state below that you are John's wife."

The pen refused to obey her fingers. Increasing her grip, Melissa scrawled the requested information on the

417

appropriate lines. The illegible script looked foreign to her. She hoped Lynette could read it.

"Can I see my husband now?"

"Sit here one minute. I'll check."

Lynette vanished on the other side of the door behind her desk. That one minute turned into five and then ten. Twenty-two minutes passed by Melissa's count until Lynette Campbell's reappearance.

"Come with me, Mrs. Simotes."

Lynette led the way through that same door from which she just came and down a long hallway into a small office.

"Wait here, please," Lynette said, "The doctor will see you shortly."

"No!"

The force of her words astonished Melissa more than they seemed to astonish Lynette. Her face remained passive as she said, "Mrs. Simotes, I'm sorry, but these are the doctor's orders."

"Where's my husband? Why can't I see him?"

"The doctor will explain everything when he arrives." Lynette shut the door after her.

Melissa sat and watched the wall clock tick away the time until she could no longer bear the interminable waiting. She paced around the floor, feeling like a caged animal. An hour passed, then two. Where was that doctor?

She opened the door and ventured into the deserted hallway. Not a soul was in sight. Melissa held her head high, threw back her shoulders, and headed straight for the emergency room. A set of double doors opened, and a volunteer walked through them.

"Excuse me, sir," Melissa said. "I've taken a wrong turn. Can you show me the way to my husband's room?"

"Who's your husband, miss?"

"John Simotes."

The man frowned. "I don't know that name, but I can find out for you."

He pushed a large wall button, and the doors once again swung back. Melissa wove through the crowds of bustling hospital staff, keeping her guardian angel in her sight. He marched to the nurse's station where several telephones were ringing.

"This woman is looking for her husband," he said and then disappeared toward the exit.

The nurse did not look up as she reached for a receiver. "Name?"

"John Simotes," Melissa quickly said.

"Hold on." The nurse answered the phone.

With the woman occupied, Melissa inched from the desk and sauntered among the curtained rooms, peeking around the enclosures, hoping to catch a glimpse of John. She started to enter the sixth room when she heard, "Hey, you can't go in there!"

The nurse had left the desk and now trotting in her direction.

"I'm looking for my husband," Melissa said, defensively.

"Wait right there. I'm getting his doctor."

She soon returned with Dr. Lofield, smiling his amiable, plastic, television-style smile. Melissa had not seen him since she had accompanied Debbie on a prenatal visit. What did he want? Had he learned about John and came to express his concern?

"Mrs. Simotes," Dr. Lofield said. "We really need to talk."

Now Melissa understood.

"You're his doctor? But, I thought you only took care of pregnant women."

"Actually, no. I'm an internist with a sub-specialty in obstetrics. I took Debbie's case as a favor to a colleague, especially considering her medical condition. Dr. Rothgard is not available, so I've been assigned to John's case."

"What's going on with John? Why can't I see him?"

"Come with me. I'll even bring you a cup of coffee."

"Tea."

He guided Melissa out of the emergency room and back to the office where she had sat most of the morning.

"But...."

"I'll be right back. I promise."

Still suspicious, Melissa stood in the doorway and watched him walk down the hall into another room. Within seconds, he returned, carrying two paper cups. He handed her one of them, and she sipped it. It was lukewarm and weak, but it was definitely tea.

"See? What did I tell you? Now come and sit down."

Dr. Lofield shut the office door behind him. Melissa collapsed into a chair against the wall. Finally someone friendly wanted to help her. Dr. Lofield sat next to her and sipped his coffee. His helpful attitude relaxed Melissa.

"When can I see John?"

"I needed some emergency paperwork in place first."

Something in the tone of his voice made her feel wary. "What sort of emergency paperwork?"

"You know, Mrs. Simotes, I've waited a long time to put my name on the medical map, and your husband will help me do it. You see, I'm actually trained in several subspecialties, although, mark my words, I am no Dr. Rothgard."

"I don't know what you are talking about."

"Ohhh, I think you do. This morning, your husband arrives at the emergency room exhibiting some very interesting symptoms. He's obviously been beaten to a pulp, and he's malnourished and dehydrated to the point that he's producing very little body fluids. That would kill most men, but instead he continues breathing; his heart is pumping strongly, and his brain is alive and well. Now, Mrs. Simotes, what would you make of that?"

Melissa stared at her cup.

"And all this," Dr. Lofield said, "comes from a man who already carries some very dark secrets."

Startled, Melissa returned his gaze. "What are you saying?"

Dr. Lofield replied with a warm, saccharine smile that unsettled Melissa.

"I'm wondering," Dr. Lofield said, "just how the adoptive parents of Debbie Polis' baby wound up with a boy when Debbie gave birth to a girl."

What?

Melissa shook so hard, her tea sloshed over the rim, but she didn't care. How would Dr. Lofield know if Debbie had a boy or girl? He wasn't even there.

"Someone's given you the wrong information." Melissa tried keeping her voice steady and confident. "We adopted a baby boy from Debbie."

That candied smile grew into a sinister grin.

"Mrs. Simotes, I have her amniocentesis to prove it, the very amniocentesis I ordered five days before Debbie died. You see, Melissa, when Debbie's condition worsened, I checked the baby's lungs for maturity and scheduled her for surgery. She should have entered the hospital the next morning. You *did* know Debbie had mild kidney damage due to her poorly controlled diabetes?"

"I want to see my husband," Melissa repeated, but her words lacked the necessary thrust needed to force this monster to back down. If Debbie had been carrying a girl, then...impossible! Dr. Rothgard certainly would have known if he'd delivered a boy or a girl.

Dr. Lofield, undeniably enjoying her discomfort, continued. "So, I went to bed that night, right after the ten o'clock news, the same as usual, and woke up five days later. My staff claimed I called in sick with flu. I never had the flu, and I never made any such telephone call."

Why was he lying to her?

"Maybe you were so sick that you don't remember it," Melissa said, but she doubted her words even as they left her mouth.

"When I tried to pull Debbie's hospital records, I found no evidence of the surgery I scheduled for her. In fact, there is no evidence Debbie Polis was ever a patient at this hospital. Fortunately, I made copies of every record I had on Debbie and locked them in a safe place. Because after Debbie told me your husband had been badgering her to switch her care to Dr. Rothgard, I smelled foul play."

No! It couldn't be true, Melissa thought, yet her heart rapidly sank. She closed her eyes against further information, but Dr. Lofield kept talking.

"Rumors abound of Dr. Rothgard and his brand of alternative medicine, or should we say 'experimental medicine,' although his record is as clean as a whistle."

He paused. Melissa, alarmed, opened her eyes. The smile had vanished from Dr. Lofield's face. "What I wouldn't give for a tour of that man's basement."

Melissa felt sick to the core. Her hopes that medical science might save John began to dwindle. "What about my husband?"

"I plan to conduct every possible test until I arrive at the cause of his incredible condition."

"You can't do that! I'm his wife! I won't let you!"

"But, I," Dr. Lofield said, drawing out the moment, the artificial smile returning to his lips at Melissa's reaction. "I have a court order."

Melissa stood up. "I'll fight it."

"Then you won't see your husband."

She took a deep breath, thinking fast. *Cornell Dyer.* As much as she hated to do it, she had to talk to Cornell. She had no one else who understood John's vampirism. She hoped Cornell was still at her house; she hoped he'd answer her phone. In the meantime, Melissa decided to play along with Dr. Lofield.

"So if I concede," Melissa said, "I'm able to see John."

Still smiling, Dr. Lofield stood. "Bingo!"

"May I see him now?"

"Why not?"

He walked to the desk and dialed the telephone. "Norma, I have Melissa Simotes in the first office in the west wing. Will you please send someone to accompany her to the intensive care unit?"

Dr. Lofield hung up the phone and shot one last triumphant smile at Melissa. "See how well things work when you cooperate?"

He extended his hand to her, which Melissa ignored. "Let's keep in contact, Mrs. Simotes. If you need any updates, stop at the nurse's station, and someone can page me. Have a wonderful day."

"Drop dead."

Dr. Lofield raised one eyebrow in surprise at her outburst, but he never stopped smiling. A teenage girl in a pink and white striped uniform met Melissa at the door almost as soon as Dr. Lofield left it.

"Hi, I'm Mindy. I'm taking you to the fourth floor."

Mindy pressed the "up" button on the elevator. They rode the elevator in silence. Once they arrived, Mindy guided her to the nurse's station and said, "This is John Simotes' wife. Dr. Lofield sent her up."

The nurse kept her eyes on her paperwork and pointed to the room adjacent to the desk. Without bothering to thank her guide, Melissa fairly ran to the room. Through the partly open door, Melisa saw tubes, machines, and a sleeping, battered John.

"Excuse me, ma'am."

Melissa whirled at the sound. A short, balding man wearing a clerical collar had spoken to her. She almost cried aloud. She couldn't tolerate one more person keeping her from John. This man's countenance, at least, seemed genuinely kind.

"I don't wish to intrude, but I'd like to give you my card." She wavered at the request, not wishing to be rude.

"I understand it's a difficult time. Call if you have need of my services."

"Thanks."

Melissa hurried into the room, tossed the card onto the bedside table, and moved close to John. How he had changed in just a few hours! The white sheets magnified John's frailness; his gaunt frame disappeared into the hospital gown; his peaked face and nearly bald head, both splotched with darkened areas, sank far into the pillow. The room's only sound was the steady "beep, beep, beep," of the machines and John's labored breathing.

What had she done?

Melissa had assumed doctors would have bandaged him up, forced food and liquids into him, and sent him home, ready to resume care with Dr. Rothgard. The sight of the withered figure disintegrated any vestiges of hope John might recover. Maybe John had been right. This could be the end...for now.

"He can't stay dead," Melissa murmured. "He just can't. I don't care what John thinks. We're supposed to have a future together. We have a son to raise."

At the mention of "son," Dr. Lofield's words, *I'm wondering how the adoptive parents of Debbie Polis' baby wound up with a boy when Debbie gave birth to a girl,* reverberated in Melissa's head.

John turned his head and opened an accusing eye. He was lying in this hospital bed because she, Melissa, had foiled his decision. She could not bear to see him looking at her in that manner.

"Oh, John," she cried, tears streaming down her face. "I am *so* sorry. I was only trying to help you. You have to believe me!"

"What does it matter?" John's voice sounded faraway. "They won't fix it."

"Maybe they can make you comfortable."

"Don't waste your worry on it."

"John, how can you say such a....?"

"Worry instead about what will happen to you if the scientists get to me before Cornell does. Because if they do, you will soon see me again in the worst way."

John's voice faded into unconsciousness. Melissa watched him for awhile, and then she picked up the telephone and dialed her house. She let the phone ring twenty times before she hung up. She thought hard, trying to remember Cornell's number, and dialed again. This time, she heard a click after the third ring and the sound of Cornell's voice: "You have reached The Thaumaturgical World of Professor Cornell Dyer. We offer amulets, fortune-telling--with and without cards--ghost-hunting, horoscopes, numerology, palm-reading, potions, séances, spells, and vampire-slaying. The professor is busy saving the world right now, so please leave your name, number, and a detailed message after the beep. He will return your call as soon as possible."

So much for helping people in need!

Disgusted, Melissa slammed the phone into the receiver. John grunted. Melissa held her breath and silently berated her foolish lack of consideration. John, however, had slipped back into sleep. Melissa slumped in the chair nearest the window. The memory of her conversation with Dr. Lofield drowned out the medical equipment. *I plan to conduct every possible test...I have a court order.* Who knew the entire truth? Did John, and would he ever be well enough to reveal it with her? Did Dr. Rothgard, and would he be honest enough to share it? How much had John divulged to Cornell? John-Peter said John trusted Cornell. And if John-Peter wasn't Debbie and Derek's baby, then....?

Melissa remained in John's room all that day and into the next one, too. Kind cafeteria workers sent Melissa trays of food, reminding her of the early days at Jenson College. How long ago they now seemed! She dozed intermittently in the chair. John was in and out of the room, undergoing Dr. Lofield's promised tests and procedures. Every couple of hours, Melissa telephoned both her home number and the telephone number that belonged to Cornell Dyer. Each time, Melissa either listened to the insistent ringing of the phone or the recorded message: "You have reached The Thaumaturgical World of Professor Cornell Dyer...."

At one point, a policeman paid a visit and inquired about John's beaten appearance. Melissa accompanied him to a lounge and answered his questions, insisting John himself inflicted the wounds. Melissa had the sneaking feeling he did not believe her. When she returned to John's room, Melissa called Carol Simotes, also to no avail.

The following day brought more of the same. Melissa stiff, cramped, and exhausted from sleeping in a chair, tried again to contact Cornell. Surely Katie, who was caring for John-Peter, would answer the phone! John left for more tests and returned looking ghastly and asking for water, the first time he had requested anything since Melissa had been there. Glad to do something constructive for him, Melissa ripped the paper wrap from a straw, set it into the plastic cup, and placed it near his lips.

A knock, and someone opened the door a crack. The head of the priest who spoke yesterday to Melissa poked into the room. He regarded John with a quizzical look.

Melissa heaved an exasperated sigh at his presence. "You again!" She turned toward John. "John, I am so sorry. I didn't send for him, I...."

The priest looked at John, confused. "Beg pardon, Mr. Simotes, but if this is a bad time...."

John's short, rueful laugh ended in a bark and a painful fit of coughing. He waved the water away and said, "All time is bad for me. Come in."

With a sidelong glance at Melissa, the priest walked into the room and shut the door. "I wanted to be certain you hadn't changed your mind."

Melissa felt any lingering energy drain from her as she set the glass on the nightstand and sank into a chair. "John, you sent for him?"

"I did. Do you have a problem with it?"

"No, I...well, I'm just surprised, that's all."

As she adjusted to this unexpected development, John observed her with annoyance.

"Do you mind?" he said in a cold voice.

"What?" Melissa said, still in shock. "No, of course not."

She reached for her purse, kissed John on the forehead, and walked toward the door.

"Oh and Melissa...."

She turned around. "Yes, John?"

"Go have dinner. This will take awhile."

Melissa plodded to the elevator, incredulous that John had actually contacted a priest and forlorn that he had banished her from the room. She pressed the "down" button. Her life with John had consisted of one mystery after another. Why did she expect his death to be any different?

The elevator door opened, and Melissa bumped into her mother and Steve.

"Mom!"

"My God, Melissa!" Darlene smothered Melissa with kisses. "What's going on? It's all over the news!"

Steve held up a hand.

"Darlene," he said. "Why don't we sit in the cafeteria? I'm sure Melissa's famished."

"Steve, I have the right to know...."

"At least, allow her something to eat before starting the third degree."

Soon, they were riding down the elevator to the hospital's lower level. Melissa sagged onto Steve's shoulder, and he put a comforting arm around her.

As they moved through the food line, Melissa reviewed her story, the same story she told every health professional and the police. John had lost his job. John had become depressed. John had barricaded himself in the basement, and, she, Melissa, had called his friend Cornell to get him out of there and to persuade him to get the help he needed.

"The doctors have no idea what's wrong with him?" Darlene said.

"Not yet. They're running tests."

Steve stirred sugar into his coffee. "How can we help you?"

"I don't see where it's possible."

"We could take John-Peter to Grover's Park."

Keep John-Peter? *Unthinkable!*

"I know you'd rather he stayed here," Steve said, "but it might be good to remove him from the spotlight."

No! What if John asked for him?

"Besides, I know he's a handful. It's nice of Katie and Cornell to step in, but we're his grandparents. We want to help. It's our place to help."

"I know, but...." Melissa hadn't known John's mysterious condition had leaked to the media, but she was fairly certain what rat had done it. "Well, may I at least think about it?"

"Of course you may. We're not here to pester you. We only want to support you."

They said their good-byes at the cafeteria door because the hospital permitted no one, except Melissa, into the intensive care unit. Darlene, still looking worried, scribbled the number to Jenson's bed and breakfast on a piece of paper and handed it to Melissa.

"Keep us posted, okay, hon?"

"Will do," Melissa said, flinching as her mother's desperately tight embrace crushed her ribs.

Although John appeared to be sleeping, he must have heard Melissa enter the room because he opened his eyes, albeit with difficulty, and hoarsely spoke through parched and cracked lips.

"Are you sorry I wrote that false letter asking you to come to Jenson?"

So John had sent it, as Melissa had always suspected, although she never could muster the courage to ask him.

"And the scholarship?" Melissa said. "You arranged that, too?"

John nodded, weakly, haltingly, still watching her from dark and hollow eyes.

Why had John chosen deception over the truth? Surely, he knew how much Melissa had always longed for him. He needed only to have asked. Besides, because of Melissa, John had lived as a human once again. He had worked as a highly accomplished and respected music teacher. He had become a husband again. He had known, for the first time in nearly a century of existence, the sweet joys of fatherhood. And Melissa herself had experienced, if only for a few, short years, the fulfillment of her heart's greatest desire: an intimate life with John. For her, that alone was worth every drop of blood in her body.

In the end, what could she say? "No, I'm glad you sent it."

John closed his eyes. "Good."

CHAPTER 29: A FAIRY TALE ENDING

Before her mother and Steve returned to Grover's Park with John-Peter, they accompanied Melissa to Franklin & Mores funeral home on the outskirts of Jenson to make arrangements for John, as per Dr. Lofield's suggestion earlier that morning.

"I only hope," Dr. Lofield had told her, "that your husband will live long enough for me to uncover his secrets."

Melissa just glared at him.

"You're sure you won't help me on this one? It might go easier for you in the long run."

Melissa had pushed past him to the door. "I think you're a miserable excuse for a doctor."

Compared to the throngs outside Jenson Memorial Hospital, Melissa's street appeared desolate and forlorn. Why hadn't the media representatives camped outside her house, too? Melissa saw a single vehicle: Cornell's motor home. Steve nudged Darlene with his elbow.

"It belongs to Katie's husband," Melissa said. "He's a bit...different."

"Mother!"

John-Peter flew out the back door and flung his arms around her knees. Melissa lifted him into the air for enthusiastic hugs and kisses.

"Are you having fun with the Dyers?"

He pouted. "Katie is fun, but Cornell won't let me play the piano."

"He *won't?*"

Just as suddenly, John-Peter leaped from her arms and ran back into the house. "Katie! Mother's home!"

Katie was drying dishes. From the doorway, Karla crawled out from under John's piano. Why, of all the nerve! Just wait until she caught up with Cornell. She'd....

"Melissa," Darlene said, "if you don't mind, I'll start packing clothes for John-Peter. Do you have a suitcase?"

"Yes," Melissa said between gritted teeth. "It's in the spare bedroom closet."

"I'll get it," Steve said, heading in that direction with John-Peter.

"Why do you need a suitcase, Grandpa?"

"Because you're visiting us for a couple of days."

"Is Mother coming, too? What about Father? Is he better now?"

Steve had walked into the spare bedroom, so Melissa did not hear his answer. In the kitchen, Melissa scanned the long list of messages from students and staff at Jenson College as well as Melissa's friends and Carol Simotes.

"She and a friend had driven down to Florida, but as soon as she saw John on the news, she decided to pack up and return home," Katie said. "Carol wanted to take the first flight out of there, but her friend felt too nervous to make the trip all by herself. They should arrive in town first thing in the morning."

Would John even last that long? Carol might not mean anything to John, but he was the world to Carol.

"Don't worry about calling any of them back right away," Katie said. "I've given everyone updates, and they've all sent their best wishes for John's recovery."

"Where's Cornell?"

"He's working in the motor home, catching up on research and scheduling appointments."

Melissa suddenly recalled Cornell's comment about "casting spells" during John's first night in cellar custody. Was that why her street looked so empty?

"Katie," Melissa began in a hushed voice, so her family would not hear, "do you know if Cornell....?"

"I think we've got everything, Melissa. We're ready to go when you are."

Melissa turned at the sound of her mother's voice. Steve stood beside Darlene and held John-Peter. Strangely quiet, the baby looked at Melissa with doleful, disbelieving eyes. Even if Dr. Lofield would permit John-Peter to see his father, Melissa could not expose her son, and his green skin, to the media hounds swarming the hospital.

The phone rang, and Katie answered it.

"You'd better take this one, Melissa. It's some business." Melissa accepted the receiver. "Hello?"

"Mrs. Simotes, this is Dave at Archer's Repair Shop in Shelby. Your music box is ready, anytime you'd like to pick it up."

"My *what?*" Melissa said, her voice quavering.

"Your music box. Your husband dropped it off last month and said to call you when I'd fixed it. It's working, good as new."

Melissa cupped trembling hands over the phone. "Mom, it's a repair shop in Shelby. John had taken my music box there. I know it's out of the way, but that was Grandma's and...."

Steve cut her sentence short. "We'll pick it up. What's the bill?"

"I don't know." Melissa removed her hand from the phone. "Mr. Archer, what do I owe you?"

"No charge. Your husband paid the bill in advance."

Dazed, Melissa hung up the phone.

Steve shifted John-Peter's weight. "Ready, Melissa?"

She hedged. "You go ahead. I need one more thing."

"We'll wait for you in the car," Darlene said, picking up John-Peter's suitcase and heading for the door.

Heart pounding, Melissa crept down the stairs, afraid of what she might see, but curious to view the remnants of the prison John had prepared for his final human days. When she reached the bottom stair, she gaped in surprise.

The basement appeared intact, as if John had never barricaded himself in it. In wonder, she walked to the closet. Except for a few holes in the door and its frame, one would never guess anyone had tampered with it. Cornell had done a good job cleaning up after John's ferocious struggle with his two natures. Head down, shoulders sagging, spirits sorrowing, Melissa trudged up the stairs and out to the waiting car.

She said good-bye to her family in the hospital parking lot, near the cafeteria doors, to avoid the crowds. That's when John-Peter, quiet and subdued for the short ride there, realized the truth of the Grover's Park trip.

"No!" John-Peter screamed, clawing at Melissa's shirt and hair as she attempted to leave. "Don't go!"

"Baby," Melissa said, trying to disengage herself. "Father is very sick, and he needs me."

"Take me, too!"

"I can't. The hospital won't let me."

"I miss him!"

Steve pried the boy's fingers from Melissa, and she dashed away, fingers in her ears, but she still heard John-Peter's heartbreaking shrieks. Impulsively, she spun around and blew a kiss in the direction the car had gone.

"I love you, baby," Melissa called under her breath, forcing back tears,

As she rode up the elevator to the fourth floor, Melissa didn't even try calming her thudding heart. Her entire life was unraveling at the seams, and she couldn't stop it. She was passing a lounge on the way to John's room when she heard someone say, "Dr. Rothgard!"

Melissa retraced her steps and craned her neck around the doorway. Except for one heavy-set, balding man snoring in a chair, the room appeared empty. The voice had come from the television set.

Cameras surrounded Dr. Rothgard as he trotted from an airplane into the direction of the airport. Newscasters thrust microphones into his face.

"Dr. Rothgard, what's the latest report on John Simotes?"

"Dr. Rothgard, is it true you plan to sue Dr. Lofield for overstepping the bounds of his authority?"

"Dr. Rothgard, are you really into human experimentation?"

The doctor hastened from view. A reporter came onscreen and said, "We now take you live to Jenson Memorial Hospital."

The picture flashed to the hospital grounds, near the main entrance. A second reporter smiled and said, "We have here today Dr. James Lofield, the attending physician for John Simotes, the Jenson College music professor who...."

Melissa scurried away from the lounge. God, she thought, if you exist, please prepare a special hell for egomaniacs like Dr. Lofield. She entered John's room just as a nurse was removing a blood pressure cuff from his arm. Every tube and machine had vanished.

"Where's all the equipment?" Melissa said.

"We disconnected them," the nurse said, checking John's pulse, "per Dr. Rothgard's orders."

"He's back on the case? What happened to Dr. Lofield?"

"Mrs. Simotes, talk to Dr. Rothgard. He'll be here soon."
Melissa couldn't control her rising excitement. Dr. Rothgard was on his way. John would soon be healed!

"What's his blood pressure?" Melissa asked.

The nurse hesitated and turned to leave. Irked, Melissa repeated a little more loudly, "What's his blood pressure?"

Another horrible, frightening pause. The nurse squarely faced Melissa.

"He doesn't have a blood pressure," he nurse said, "or a pulse. His heart stopped beating this morning. Didn't anyone call you?"

"But...." Melissa watched the bedclothes heave up and down. "He's...breathing...."

"Again, Mrs. Simotes, you really need to speak with Dr. Rothgard."

Melissa slumped in a chair to wait for Dr. Rothgard. All that day, John slept a restless sleep. His limbs jerked; his eyes blinked open and closed. He muttered unintelligible phrases through lips swollen twice their normal size. The nurse periodically returned to again check his remaining vital signs.

"Why do that anymore?" Melissa said toward evening.

The nurse removed the thermometer. "Dr. Rothgard wants it continued until he gives orders to stop."

Melissa sighed and glanced at the deep fissures in John's dry lips. "Could you please bring some ice chips?"

"Mrs. Simotes, he's refused all hydration."

"Well, maybe he'll accept ice," Melissa said, irritably. "Is there any harm in trying?"

"Not at all."

John did not fight the ice chips, but Melissa doubted he'd even noticed them. She burrowed into the chair and watched him sleep, ignoring her own aching muscles that screamed for rest.

At dusk, John's telephone rang. It was Steve.

"Melissa, we're back in Grover's Park, and John-Peter is doing fine. Your mother is fixing him dinner right now."

"Okay, thanks."

"However, there is someone here who wants to talk with you."

She heard muffled voices in the background, and then Brian's voice said, "Hey, Melissa."

"Hey."

"How's John?"

"The same."

Silence.

"Listen, Melissa, it's true I don't like John, but I never wanted it to end like...."

"I know."

"I'm sorry you're going through it."

"Me, too."

Melissa melted yet another batch of ice chips against the chafed lips that once kissed her with passion and tenderness. She knew her actions were pointless, and yet it gave her something constructive to do for John. How could she spend the remaining decades of her life never again knowing his kisses or feeling his arms around her? As if he'd read her thoughts, John opened his eyes, mumbled unintelligible sounds, and closed them again. Melissa, listless and drained, returned to her chair, where, hand in hand with John, she walked the grounds of Simons Mansion while John pointed out the different gardens and orchards. A thundering of hoof beats, and Melissa turned away from the waiting carriage to John, but John had gone, and in his place stood Henry in his midnight blue suit, looking as shrunken as the last night Melissa had last seen him inside the library at Simons Mansion. Henry's eyes gleamed from sunken sockets, and his mocking grin spread across his emaciated face. He extended an atrophied hand, and, with a start, Melissa sat up, blinked hard, and looked across the room. At that moment, John's eyes popped open. Wild and glassy, they darted this way and that, and he writhed uncontrollably. Melissa lightly touched him on the arm, hoping to calm him, but John picked and clawed at the sheets, while muttering one word over and over again.

Bryony.

The nurse, who must have heard the shout, injected something into John's arm, and he soon faded back into sleep. Restless and despondent, Melissa wandered to the lounge, plopped into a chair near the window, and recalled one very special night she had shared with John in this hospital, the Christmas morning John-Peter was born.

Instantly, Dr. Lofield's words flashed in her mind as if on a screen: *I'm wondering how the adoptive parents of Debbie Polis' baby wound up with a boy when Debbie gave birth to a girl.*

In anguish, Melissa closed her eyes. This time, she was losing John for good. She could feel it.

How easy it was years ago to be with him! A crank of the music box, a drifting into sleep, and Melissa began a glorious day as Bryony inside Simons Mansion. Her mind to wandered to her first encounter with John Simons, long before she made that provocative bargain with him in her bedroom, when she and Shelly had researched his biography at the Grover's Park library, after Darlene had announced they were moving to Munsonville. Yet, not until Melissa had written a research paper on Bryony had she cared about the John and Bryony Simons love story. Even then, Bryony's romantic good fortune excited Melissa more than John Simons the man had. When had she fallen in love with John?

Was it the first time he waltzed with her at that initial ball, or when he kissed her later that night, after she panicked at the sight of the gruesome vampire players in her dreams? She closed her eyes and recalled the warmth of his hands through his white dancing gloves, the piano music that filled Simons Mansion, the applause that rang through Carnegie Hall. Was it when she had persuaded John to let her watch him drink her blood so she could feel close to him, the same blood that returned his humanity, allowing him to become a man who could make real love to her? Who would have guessed John would abandon a promising music career in the twentieth century to crawl around the living room floor to find a tiny shoe so he could throw newspapers with his son, because they were partners?

Dr. Rothgard dropped into the chair next to Melissa. "The end, I think, is near."

Melissa nodded, her throat tight against rushing thoughts, half-formed words, and dying dreams. Dr. Rothgard had tried his best to help John. What more could Melissa say? She had already thanked him.

The doctor clenched and unclenched his hands. He cleared his throat. "He didn't hurt anyone, Melissa. That's one reason why John initiated the termination process. He wanted to leave before it happened."

Melissa stared, unseeing, ahead and said tonelessly, "John killed Derek."

"He did not."

The confident assurance in Dr. Rothgard's voice...*how did he know?* In surprise, Melissa glanced at him. Could Dr. Rothgard hold the answers to the mysteries surrounding these last few weeks?

"And the woman in the nursing home?"

"Melissa, I haven't a clue. Do you think John is the only vampire in town?"

Melissa sighed, looked away, and closed her eyes. She didn't know what to think anymore. "So why did Dr. Lofield leave the case?"

"He capitulated once he realized he had no evidence against John."

She turned back at him, astonished. "But Dr. Lofield said he had copies of records that could incriminate John!"

Dr. Rothgard, stretched his legs and contemplated his shoes.

"Then he should be more careful whom he hires to manage his office. I am telling you, Dr. Lofield has no record of Debbie. None."

His underhanded implication should have devastated Melissa, but she felt too drained to care. So Dr. Rothgard knew more than he would divulge, did he? How far could she push him for answers?

"Did Debbie really have a girl?"

His face twitched, but Dr. Rothgard only said, "I delivered a boy."

"You're sure?"

He said nothing, so Melissa tried a different approach. "Were you a vampire when you treated Bryony?"

Dr. Rothgard leaned his head against the cushion and stared at the ceiling.

"No, but I knew vampires existed. Their limbo between the complimentary poles of death and life intrigued me. I understood how one could bring a vampire to the death side of the equation, but what of the other side? Since a vampire hadn't fully died, could one bring such a creature back to complete life? I did not advertise my investigations; interested parties always found me. After John's death, he approached me and demanded to know how far I had developed my theories. I shared with him my research into the subject, but I made it clear I'd amassed only theories, not test subjects. But thanks to John, that soon changed."

"Because John offered himself to you?"

A page for Dr. Rothgard boomed through the loudspeaker. He rose to leave. "You should get back to John's room."

"I will."

Walking to the door, Dr. Rothgard said, "I know you wish things had turned out differently between you and John, but there's nothing you can do to change that now."

"Dr. Rothgard," Melissa called out in anguish and despair. "I love him!"

The doctor stopped, one hand on the doorknob. He did not look back at her.

"You know, Melissa, most vampires don't marry their victims. Think about it."

Melissa refused to think about it. John never returned her love, and, in this moment, she did not care if he ever would, if only he would not leave her. Dwell in this world without John in it? Unthinkable! She'd never survive. She turned reluctant steps back to John's room, knowing every step that brought her closer to him also hastened the moment of their final good-bye.

She once again settled into her chair, but the ticking of the clock inside John's room strained Melissa's nerves to the point of fire. As evening dissolved into the morning's wee hours, John's noisy breathing doused the clock's irritating racket. Melissa jerked awake and glanced at the time: two in the morning. When had she fallen asleep? What had caused her to awaken? Had John said something to her?

"John?"

From under heavy lids, John rolled unsteady, filmy eyes at her.

"Melissa." his voice rasped.

In seconds, Melissa was crouching by his side. "Shhh. Don't try to talk."

"Listen...to...me."

John's lungs wheezed and squealed as he struggled to speak.

"John-Peter...." he began.

"He's okay, John."

"....is not our son."

"Yes, he is John." Melissa soothingly stroked the remaining limp strands of her husband's hair.

"Damn it!"

Melissa jumped and dropped her hand. John's chest heaved. His eyes burned. His throat rattled.

"He's...a...changeling."

"A what?" Melissa's eyes searched his face. "John?

John stared at Melissa and through her. He was gone.

CHAPTER 30: LAST RITES

In the hour before daybreak, Melissa pulled into the driveway of the bungalow she had once shared with John. As she did, the high state of alertness, Melissa's constant companion these last few days, instantly forsake her. Her head buzzed; her muscles burned; her eyes prickled from days of napping.

She felt tempted to pass out in the car, but the real fear that a reporter might discover her abode, despite any incantations Cornell might have muttered in her direction, convinced Melissa otherwise. She crept from her sanctuary and dragged her weary body to the back steps, the very steps John had once carried her up, and into the house. Only the hum of the refrigerator broke the house's stillness. Its freezer still held two packs of Melissa's blood, nourishment John no longer required. She averted her eyes from John's piano on her way to the bedroom. Melissa flung back the covers, which released John's scent from his side of the bed. After folding a pillow around her head to block it, Melissa sank into blessed darkness.

A piercing sound split the air. Melissa cautiously opened her eyes. Beyond the pounding in her head, the clanging reduced to normal limits; it was the telephone. She rolled over, but the bells pealed through the house and into her brain. Vexed beyond endurance, Melissa kicked away the tangle of the bed sheets and groped her way to the kitchen.

"Hello?" she mumbled into the receiver.

"Melissa?" Carol said. "Did I wake you?"

Really? Just how long had the phone rung, fifty, sixty times?

"No," Melissa forced up through her tight throat.

"I hate to bother you, but...." Carol's voice trailed away. "May I come over? I just got into town. I stopped first at the hospital, and they told me about John."

Carol cried softly into the telephone. Would Melissa be forever saddled to this ridiculous woman simply because John hypnotically inserted false memories into the Simotes' minds?

"Sure, come on over."

She hung up the phone and stumbled around the kitchen, squinting against the bright morning light, preparing a pot of coffee. Growing up, Melissa often wondered why Darlene needed caffeine to begin her day. Had her mother experienced this same anguishing haze when Daddy had died?

Melissa had downed the first mug and was pouring a second when she heard a knock on the door. She opened it and beheld Carol Simotes, hair disheveled, eyes red and swollen, and a drawn face marred with mascara-streaked tears.

"Oh, Melissa, I can't stand it!"

As she held open the screen door for Carol, sudden revelation hit Melissa. Why, she and Carol held more in common than she could ever disclose. The woman who stood before her believed she was John's mother because John led her to believe it. Melissa and Bryony shared common memories because John allowed Melissa to experience them. Was either hallucination less deceptive than the other? She fell into the outstretched arms of her mother-in-law and cried with her. Long before they separated, Melissa knew she would invite Carol to spend a few days with her, and, by the look on Carol's face when Melissa asked her, Carol expected the invitation. Melissa wished she had asked John how and why he had picked the Simotes' to be his parents, but that decision of John's would forever remain a mystery. When Carol returned to her car for the suitcase, Melissa sped to the freezer and dumped the last two bags of blood into the garbage can behind the garage. Melissa hoped no animal would treat itself to a late night feast. The phone rang as Melissa entered the house.

"This is Kevin Mores from Franklin and Mores Funeral Home in Jenson. We won't be handling your husband's burial. Another funeral home has already claimed his body."

"What!"

"Yes, ma'am. Mr. Simotes made prior arrangements with Happy Hunting Grounds, the new funeral home in Thornton."

"Happy Hunting Grounds?"

Why, when Melissa had tried so hard to retain John's pride and dignity, had he chosen a facility with such a facetious name?

"Yes, ma'am, that's correct."

"Um, do you have the number?"

Melissa wrote the information and repeated it twice to Kevin Mores. Her mind just would not accept this last stunt from John. Carol stepped into the kitchen as Melissa, dazed, hung up the phone.

"Apparently John will be buried from Happy Hunting Grounds in Thornton."

"Melissa, you can't be serious!"

"John did it," Melissa said. "If you don't mind, I'd rather deal with it later."

They spent a limp day before the television set; for dinner, they ordered pizza, something John never would have done. The silent piano stood lonely in its abandonment; its stilled notes screamed for attention from a master it would never again know.

"I wish John-Peter could play for us,' Carol absently said.

The phone rang again. Too beaten down to feel like moving and too forlorn to speak, Melissa nevertheless obediently plodded to the kitchen and answered it on the twelfth ring.

"Hello," she said listlessly.

"We heard about John on the news," Darlene said. "Are you all right, hon?"

"Fine."

"We're leaving early in the morning."

"Okay."

"If it helps, I do know how you feel."

"I know."

"John-Peter wants to talk to you. Are you up for it?"

"Sure."

A swishing noise ensued as her mother handed John-Peter the phone.

"Mother?" cried the excited voice on the other end.

"Hi, baby."

"Is Father really in heaven? Grandpa says he is."

What did one tell a toddler when his father died? Was it better to offer soothing platitudes, or was stark reality more honest?

"Yes, he's in heaven now, John-Peter."

"Grandma says I'm coming home tomorrow. I can't wait. I miss you!"

How easily children accept and move on! Melissa reeled at her son's effortless optimism; she staggered under the force of her own crushed and shattered rainbow. The expiration of John's last breath extinguished any hope of future happiness. She had pleaded for absolution, but a long, hollow life had responded. The symbolic alarm clock jarred her senses and jangled her thoughts. She no longer dwelled in a fairyland of fulfilled Bryony dreams, but a solitary wasteland where even memories of John would fade into a past that was no longer Melissa's to clasp.

"I miss you, too, honey," Melissa choked back. "Be good for Grandma and Grandpa. I'll see you in the morning."

"Okay. Bye."

He smacked a loud kiss into the phone, and Melissa fell backward against the wall. She was done.

"Carol," Melissa managed to blurt out as she trudged back to the bedroom. "I'm going to lie down." She shut the door and immediately toppled into bed. She hoped sleep arrived soon. She hoped never to awaken.

But with that sleep came mist. It encircled Melissa's head as she walked through the graveyard that night, searching amongst the headstones for the one marked John Simotes. Melissa knew John would soon rise from the ground and demand the return of Melissa's blood, to reclaim his place among the human race.

The mist pressed around her and thickened into a suffocating blanket. Melissa halted her steps, unsure of John's final resting place in the ghostly fog. The ground heaved. A hand shot up and pulled her down.

"John!"

The earth rumbled and crumpled. Millions of hands clawed to the surface. The foundation collapsed; Melissa plunged into the caverns. Dirt filled her mouth and plugged her throat. Her pounding heart burst her ears. She woke clutching her pillow, sweat drenching her clothes. The pounding continued. Someone was banging on the front door. She lay back down, shoved the pillow over her head, and willed the intruder to leave. What if it was some ambitious reporter hoping for a slick statement, or worse, some whacko seeking who knew what from her?

The telephone rang. She'd let Carol answer it. Thirty, forty times and then it ceased. Someone tapped on her bedroom window.

"Melissa," the muffled voice called through the glass, and Melissa groaned. "Open up. It's me, Cornell."

The terror of her nightmare diminishing, Melissa now trembling more from exhaustion and fury that this pseudo witch doctor had the audacity to disturb her in the throes of misery, staggered to the window, opened it an inch, and said through gritted teeth, "Get out, or I'll call the police."

Cornell blinked in surprise and leaned his elbows on the ledge. "You're not going like that?"

"What?" Had Melissa heard correctly? "I'm not going anywhere!"

"Didn't John tell you?

John? Now Cornell had her attention.

"What was John supposed to tell me?"

"Ah, no you don't." A victorious smirk stretched across Cornell's face. "Being late means unpleasant repercussions. See you out front in five minutes!"

Melissa grabbed the window sash, but Cornell slunk away before Melissa could slam it on his obnoxious, stubby fingers. She glanced at John's alarm clock: almost midnight. Damn Cornell!

She dressed in haste, wondering if Carol was still awake. But no light came from the living room. Melissa paused by the spare bedroom door, eased it open a crack, and heard her mother-in-law's steady breathing. She tiptoed out the front door and quietly closed it behind her. John's car was parked outside the house with its engine running. Melissa slid inside, glared at Cornell, and said, "You better have a good explanation for this."

Cornell pulled away from the curb. "I already gave you one."

"You haven't given me a thing. Where are we going?"

"Thornton."

"In the middle of the night? Let me out!"

"Don't you want to see John? He said you like to watch."

His statement took her breath away. "We're really going to see John?"

"Yup."

"Is he okay?"

"You be the judge of it."

"John asked for me?"

"Sort of."

Further attempts to engage Cornell in conversation were futile. Melissa peered into undecipherable blackness and unsuccessfully willed her thudding, excited heart to calm down. Cornell was bringing her to John. Melissa repeated the wonderful words over and over until they became a mantra of promised joy. She should have known. Why hadn't she believed? Melissa finally comprehended the meaning of her recent nightmare. Death failed to retain John in the past. Why should it now wield any power?

Moments later, Cornell was shaking her shoulder and saying, "Melissa, wake up. We're here."

Melissa lifted her throbbing head off the window and tried assessing her location. Peering through the night, she recognized Dr. Jorgenson's fertility clinic. Across the street sat the funeral home, construction completed. A large neon sign displayed the red blinking words *Happy Hunting Grounds.* She ignored the ostentatious greeting, for her heart had caught in her throat and stayed in rapturous anticipation. John lay inside, ready to meet her.

Cornell parked in back and strode to the funeral home's exit. He carried an all-too-familiar black metal box. Melissa scurried after him.

"Why do you need a tool chest?"

Cornell did not answer. Instead, he inserted a key into the lock, swung open the door, and pressed several buttons to his left, disabling the security alarm. He turned on no lights but walked with sure, confident steps down the hall and into the last room on the right, with Melissa traipsing behind him.

"Well," he said. "Here we are."

As Melissa's eyes adjusted to the darkness, she discerned the outline of a coffin at the opposite side of the room. John?

"Cornell...."

But Cornell continued to the front of the room. He stopped when he reached the coffin and set his tool chest on the floor. He did not make any further move. Melissa hurried to join him.

"What do we do now?" she whispered.

"Wait."

Melissa glanced down at the form of her husband. He wore the same black tie and tails in which he had performed at the college's Victorian Nights fundraiser, just a few short years ago. Why hadn't John informed her of his final arrangements? The rigid lines on his face and the squarely set jaw disturbed her. Even in death and with the cosmetic provision of modern funeral homes, John lacked serenity.

They stood motionless, not speaking. From time to time, Cornell gazed around the room, but, otherwise, he remained at attention, as if he guarded the coffin. Melissa blinked; she rubbed her eyes. Had her tired mind tricked her? She could have sworn John's right index finger had twitched.

"Hey, Cornell...."

Cornell was kneeling by his tool chest. He removed a single piece of wood, sharpened to a point, and picked up a large mallet.

"Cornell?"

He swiftly positioned the stake over John's heart and swung. John's eyes flew open.

"Stop!" Melissa screamed.

She bit Cornell's arm, but the mallet struck. John roared. Melissa punched Cornell; Melissa kicked Cornell, but he delivered blow after driving blow, until he leveled the stake with John's chest. Dropping the mallet to the floor, Cornell shoved Melissa aside, wiped his sleeve across his dripping forehead, and shouted, "Now you know why John didn't tell you!"

Melissa sank to the floor, covered her face, and plunged her fingers in her ears. She cried, and she screamed, but her cries and screams could not drown the sound of Cornell sawing through John's neck bones. She caught a whiff of garlic. *God, how she hated Cornell Dyer!* He had tricked her into witnessing his despicable act. She hoped he fried. A large, gentle hand touched her shoulder, but Melissa slapped it away from her.

"Come and see, Melissa," Cornell said in a soft voice. "Look how peaceful he is."

Something in Cornell's tone demanded her obedience. He offered Melissa his hand, and, wondering, she accepted it. Cornell pulled her up and led her to the coffin.

"It's all right now, Melissa."

Only the lingering scent of garlic hinted at Cornell's actions. Melissa's sorrow melted at the sight of John's slackened features, eyes hinting at sweet repose, lips softened in contentment, and hands in unburdened submission and acceptance. Could that placid figure really be John? Never had she seen him so calm, so relaxed, so open. Briefly, her happiness for John displaced her grief at losing him.

As Cornell bent to pack his tools, Melissa remembered what she had wanted to ask him. If anyone could define an unfamiliar term from a former vampire, it would be this vampire slayer.

"Cornell," Melissa said, "what's a changeling?"

A beam of light swept over the room, and a German accent called out, "What's going on in here?"

Melissa froze. The words had come from a voice she never again had hoped to hear.

Cornell peered across the room. His eyes widened with recognition, and his features relaxed as he breathed a sigh of relief. The man walking toward them had black hair and a black goatee. Every article of clothing, from his suit coat to shoe tops, was also black.

"Oh, it's you Mr. Wechsler," he said. "You had me going there a minute."

Alarmed, Melissa grabbed Cornell's sleeve. "Wechsler? As in Kellen Wechsler?"

"It's okay, Melissa," Cornell said, still mellow, even as he shook his arm from her grasp. "Mr. Wechsler owns this chain of funeral homes. He hired me to wipe out hidden vampire populations."

A dim light lifted the room's darkness. Kellen advanced into the room with unhurried steps, never once removing his black eyes from Cornell's face. He didn't appear to notice Melissa.

"Is he dead?" Kellen said.

"Yes, sir," Cornell said. "One more vampire extinguished, just as I promised you."

Kellen flew to the coffin and then spun around to face Cornell. His black eyes snapped with rage.

"You fool!" he hissed.

Melissa glanced at the door and then back at Kellen, Vampires possessed tremendous speed. She could never outrun him.

"You...disobeyed...my...orders!"

Cornell stepped back before speaking. "Mr. Wechsler, when you did not appear, I had no choice...."

"Silence!"

Immediately, a mischievous grin appeared on Kellen's face, and he began tap dancing before them. Bewildered, Melissa could only helplessly watch. Kellen pirouetted and sang in a sing-song voice:

To entertain the man of fame,
Kellen wants to play a game!

He danced, circling Cornell, pausing at his face. With a leer, Kellen sang:

To entertain the man of fame,
Kellen wants to play a game!

To entertain the man of fame,

Kellen leaped backward, forward and then backward and forward again. He waved his hands around Cornell's face.

Kellen wants to play a game!

Cornell's eyes irresistibly followed, up, down, and around again. Kellen snapped his fingers once; Cornell froze. With a wide flourish, Kellen reached inside the tool box, withdrew the silver blade that had decapitated John, and plunged it deep within Cornell's chest.

"No!" Melissa shouted.

Cornell dropped with a thud, crimson rapidly soaking his shirt. Melissa turned to flee, but Kellen tripped her and laughed gleefully while she crawled to the other side of the room and huddled in a corner, fully expecting a similar fate.

As Kellen turned toward Melissa, the sneer vanished and Kellen fell screaming to his knees. Melissa shrank into the wall. Inch by inch, Kellen crept closer. He sniffed her shoe, much as Scooter once sniffed the bushes behind the servant's quarters at the Simons estate. Kellen moved to her ankle and then her knee, inhaling deep breaths and letting them out again.

"It can't be!" he cried. *"It just can't be!"*

Kellen snuffled all the way up Melissa until he reached her scalp. He even took a whiff of her hair at the nape of her neck. An ear-splitting shriek pierced the room's quiet. Kellen howled. He wept. He frothed. He tore his hair.

"Arghhhhh!"

Kellen threw himself full length onto his stomach, pounding the floor with his fists and kicking his legs back and forth. He looked so like John-Peter at bath time that a giggle escaped from Melissa's lips. Enraged, Kellen lunged at Melissa and seized her neck with both hands.

"What have you done?" Kellen screamed.

One by one, he tightened his fingers. Melissa squeezed her eyes shut and prepared her to accept death at the hands of John's enemy.

Without warning, Kellen released her and dropped next to her. First he chuckled, and then he laughed maniacal guffaws. Stupefied, Melissa could only watch and gawk.

"The joke's on me after all," Kellen said, wiping his eyes with the back of his hand. "To think John took such measures."

"What are you talking about?"

"Surely, Melissa, you must know!"

Impatience at Kellen's riddles replaced Melissa's fear of him. "Know what?"

"That I won't hurt you. John's blood flows right through your veins!"

So that's what Kellen had smelled on her! Now she knew why John said she shared his curse! John's failure to return as a vampire freed Melissa from the damnation of becoming one, but the blood of John Simons the man ran in her body and straight through her heart, blood that was mellow, yet full-bodied, with no lingering aftertaste.

In that dream at her mother's house in Grover's Park, John had told Melissa he was protecting his investment. She hadn't known John intended to safeguard her from Kellen! Didn't that mean John really did care about her? John's former manager would not think twice about hurting Melissa, unless he had a reason to spare her, and that would be feasting eternally on the blood John had denied him for nearly a century. Melissa knew any speculation about why John hid that information from her was useless. John always managed his affairs in his own way, in his own time, for his own reasons. Why would death change the way he operated? What an odd, comforting feeling to know John's blood mingled with hers, that she would carry a part of him inside her until the day she died. In death, John became closer to Melissa than he had ever chosen to do in life.

With a sweet smile of victory and satisfaction, Melissa wrapped her arms around herself and happily leaned back. The smile vanished when she saw Kellen's demeanor transform from bitter defeat to high optimism.

"A pity," Kellen said, delighting in drawing out his words, "that the same protection does not apply to the boy. The father should also have supplied his son with a little bedtime snack."

Terror and panic quickly replaced Melissa's triumph. "You wouldn't dare hurt John-Peter!"

"Well, that all depends."

"Depends on what?"

"Why on you, of course," Kellen said in voice so smooth Melissa might have called it kind if she had not known him better. "I think, Melissa, the time has come for you to make another bargain."

EPILOGUE

Seventeen year old John-Peter Simotes lay in his bed, the effects of last night's dream lingering inside his mind.

He heard a faint knocking on the upstairs bathroom door and his mother's voice announcing to his stepfather that breakfast was served. John-Peter heard the rattle of the doorknob and the squeak of the door as it opened.

The boy stretched and rolled onto his side, dragging the comforter over his head. He was in no hurry to get up. Rising from the warm enclosure of his bed meant enduring his stepfather's caustic remarks about long hair and the bacon and eggs John-Peter would refuse to eat. It also meant John-Peter would have to wipe the sink's surface so he could set his toothbrush down with no fear of it attracting his stepfather's stray black hairs.

Thinking about his stepfather irritated him, no big surprise since most things irritated him. Instead, John-Peter pondered the strange dream he had last night, the dream that began right after he heard the click inside his head.

In his dream, John-Peter was walking through a dense forest. He feared neither the blackness of the woods at midnight nor any possibility of becoming lost. His steps were firm; he had no doubt of his destination or the direction needed to attain it. After a time, the dense forest thinned out, and light emerged among the branches. A campfire crackled from the nearby clearing. He had arrived.

Ducking behind a wide tree for cover and then peering around its trunk, John-Peter saw a little, wizened man sitting on a thick stump. He clenched a stout pipe in his teeth and balanced a log between his short, stubby legs. With a long-handled knife, the troll worked a series of carvings into the wood and then set down the knife. He rubbed his hands up and down the slashed wood, twisting and squeezing it. John-Peter heard a pop, and the man lifted the wood to his ear and listened.

Chuckling in glee, the man hammered the log into the ground, leaving half of it exposed. He waved his arms and uttered a string of nonsense. An arm sprouted from one side, followed by another. Next came a neck and, finally, a head full of thick, red hair.

The head rotated on the stick until it leered at John-Peter. The boy screamed. He knew those eyes. He knew that face. They were his.

John-Peter sighed and kicked back the covers. No chance for falling back to sleep. He groped under the pillow for his leprechaun. Good. Still there. He slid off the bed and padded on bare feet to the closet. He slowly opened the door and studied its mirror. This time, only *his* reflection greeted him.

He squatted down, reached far back into the closet, and pressed hard. A board flew up, and the boy lifted out his a brittle, yellowed newspaper. He sat cross-legged and carefully unfolded it.

Commercial psychic desecrates the body, kills self.

Thornton: The body of nationally esteemed occultist Cornell Dyer was found dead early this morning at Happy Hunting Grounds funeral home.

The franchise's owner, Kellen Wechsler, discovered the body when he arrived for work. He found Dyer lying beside the coffin of John Simotes, the Jenson College music professor who died July 11 from a baffling and as yet undiagnosed illness.

The deaths are under investigation, but it appears Dyer first drove a stake through Simotes' heart and then decapitated the remains and stuffed Simotes' head with garlic before stabbing himself.

The family has canceled visitation for Simotes. Burial will be private.

John-Peter contemplated the blurry photo of his father. Try as he might, neither the picture nor the story jogged any buried memory of John Simotes. The only father John-Peter had ever known was his stepfather.

"Are you awake?" his mother called up the stairs. "Breakfast has been waiting for ten minutes!"

John-Peter scooted to the door, rose to his haunches to grasp the doorknob, and turned it just far enough to slightly open the door. If he didn't answer, his mother might come upstairs.

"Be right down!"

John-Peter refolded the newspaper and returned it to its hiding spot. An urgent need to urinate overcame any reluctance to encounter his stepfather, and he quickly dressed. Before he left the room, John-Peter slid the curtains on their rods and flooded the room with morning sunshine.

Denise M. Baran-Unland is a freelance writer, creative writing teacher, and founding member of the writer's group, WriteOn Joliet. She has six homeschooled children, three step-children, six god-children, nine grandchildren, and several cats that behave like children. Visit her at www.bryonyseries.com and www.denisembaranunland.com

Matt Coundiff is a freelance illustrator and artist at A Thin Line Tattoo in Plainfield. Matt enjoys drawing tribal images and designs with hidden letters, but he'll tackle any art-related project. His favorite mediums are colored pencil and marker, although he has experimented with watercolors and acrylics. Matt is married to a beautiful woman; they have two awesome children. Contact Matt at matt.coundiff@gmail.com.

"IF YOU ENJOYED *VISAGE*, CHECK OUT THE FIRST BOOK IN THE BRYONYSERIES."

Bryony

Denise M. Baran-Unland

Denise M. Baran-Unland

Illustrated by Kathleen R Van Pelt

"What shall I do first?" Melissa whispered.

John reached out his hands. "Touch me," he said in a low, smooth voice.

She hesitated. Even in the dim light, Melissa saw how thin and pale they were. Her insides recoiled at the thought of touching a corpse. Then Melissa remembered how much she wanted to be Bryony. This was nothing new; John had already siphoned blood from her. Could it harm her to continue for a little longer?

"I'm not afraid," she told herself, but she did not believe it. "I am not afraid. I am not afraid."

After her father's sudden death, seventeen-year-old Melissa Marchellis moves onto the former estate of nineteenth century composer and pianist John Simons, where a mysterious mist stalks her, ghostly piano music invades her bedroom, and lovely visions of John Simons' young wife Bryony, who died in childbirth, fill her dreams.

So, when John proposes a trade, a trip to the past as Bryony in exchange for her blood, Melissa happily agrees. She soon seesaws between a life of school, slumber parties, and cute boys to dancing at balls, attending formal dinner parties, and hosting garden fetes.

But fantasy and reality blur when her eccentric, middle-aged English teacher penetrates her dreams as Melissa's dashing vampire chaperone; her brother Brian adopts a peculiar stray cat after a friend disappears in a midnight exploration of the dilapidated mansion; and another girl with a similar vampire pact is gruesomely murdered.

Caught between the danger of her agreement and her escalating infatuation with John Simons, Melissa contends with other vampires and their agendas, while struggling with her feelings for an undead musician.

www.bryonyseries.com
www.bryonyseries.blogspot.com
www.facebook.com/BryonySeries

Cover Design by
CAL Graphics, Inc.
www.calgraphicsinc.com

"This is BY FAR AND AWAY the BEST VAMPIRE book I have read since *Interview with a Vampire*. Unland has captured the unforgiving beastly charm and aristocratic rogue in John Simons and company. I literally read this book over three days and was clamoring 'MORE!'when it ended. I am delighted there are three more installments coming! A vampire-lover must and no sex, disturbing violence, or vulgarity. A piece of classic literature from the twenty-first century."

~Tommy Connolly, Chicago actor

"I enjoyed *Bryony* immensely. The mixture of the past and present was fascinating. Another of my favorite things about this novel was its sheer originality. Many vampire stories have the same tired feel to them, but John was a completely unique character with an entirely individual method of 'enchanting' both Melissa and Bryony. John was wonderful, and I immediately fell in love with him. The only thing that would have been better was if I could hear him play!"

~Casey Rae Garcia, former Paperchase Supervisor, Borders Books Music & Cafe, Oak Brook, Illinois

"I really enjoyed *Bryony* because it wasn't like any other vampire book I'd ever read. I can't wait to introduce this novel to my "Teaching English as a Foreign Language" students. This book is awesome because it provides a true, stark look into the world of vampires while providing lush imagery of the romantic, Victorian era then coming back around to real life in nineteen seventies America. There is so much teaching material I could use in this book, from the radical glimpses into history to the inspiring lines of poetry. I know my students will enjoy this novel as much as I did!"

~Andrea Hinz, English as a foreign language teacher, Germany.

"Unland performs brilliantly in *Bryony*, successfully combining multiple views of modern perceptions of vampires. She retains the monstrous horror of the creatures of the night, not needing to display scenes of intense violence and gore, as well as presenting their seductive and sensual side without illustrating acts of unnecessary sexuality. At the same time, she weaves a tale of a girl on he cusp of womanhood attempting to decipher what her true perceptions and emotions are complicated by what may or may not be illusions granted to her by a vampire who shows a unique interest in her. It is definitely a fascinating read that I was unable to put down and has me eagerly waiting for what will be revealed in the upcoming additions to the Bryony series."

~Dragon Alexander, Producer and Director for Blackwood X Productions LLC and sixteen-year member of the International Vampire LARP, One World By Night.

TO BOOK DENISE FOR AN EVENT OR SPEAKING:

Denise M. Baran-Unland is available to speak to people of all ages about her writings, (including the BryonySeries), the creative writing process, and her self-publishing experiences.

Contact her through www.bryonyseries.com or www.denisembaranunland.com.

"I definitely recommend the author Denise Baran-Unland to visit classrooms. As the author of the new series that begins with the *Bryony* novel, Mrs. Baran-Unland visited my English classes and discussed the writing process (including all the editing and revising), how dreams can come true for anyone, and how her life experiences have shaped the successful person she has become. I was extremely delighted to see her interact with my Freshmen English students and keep their attention while discussing writing as well as her new series of books. I look forward to inviting her into my classroom in the near future for more conversations with the students."

~Maggie Maslowski
English
Freshmen Academy
Joliet West High School

"Kudos to Denise Baran-Unland for sharing her writing and publishing journey. The members of our writers' group found her presentation both informative and inspiring. For all writers, the great dilemma is "It's done. Now what?" Denise takes you to the "now what" with practical advice based on her experience and research. Our members heard a seasoned traveler tell them that it is possible to get off the paper and to navigate the world of publishing."

~Mary Ellen Michna, co-founder with Colette Wisneski, of Word Weavers writer's group.